William Richard Wood Stephens

The Life and Letters of Walter Farquhar Hook

William Richard Wood Stephens

The Life and Letters of Walter Farquhar Hook

ISBN/EAN: 9783337020019

Printed in Europe, USA, Canada, Australia, Japan

Cover: Foto ©Raphael Reischuk / pixelio.de

More available books at **www.hansebooks.com**

THE

LIFE AND LETTERS

OF

WALTER FARQUHAR HOOK

D.D. F.R.S.

BY

HIS SON-IN-LAW

W. R. W. STEPHENS

PREBENDARY OF CHICHESTER AND RECTOR OF WOOLBEDING
AUTHOR OF 'LIFE OF S. JOHN CHRYSOSTOM' 'CHRISTIANITY AND ISLAM' ETC.

IN TWO VOLUMES

VOL. I.

THIRD EDITION

LONDON

RICHARD BENTLEY & SON, NEW BURLINGTON STREET

𝔓𝔲𝔟𝔩𝔦𝔰𝔥𝔢𝔯𝔰 𝔦𝔫 𝔒𝔯𝔡𝔦𝔫𝔞𝔯𝔶 𝔱𝔬 𝔥𝔢𝔯 𝔐𝔞𝔧𝔢𝔰𝔱𝔶 𝔱𝔥𝔢 𝔔𝔲𝔢𝔢𝔫

1879

PREFACE.

ONE of the earliest recollections of my childhood is concerned with the subject of this Memoir. When I was about five years old, I accompanied my father and mother to London, on a visit to my uncle, then Mr. William Page Wood. As we were going up-stairs on our arrival, my eye was caught by an oil-portrait of a man with red hair and a large mouth, which hung over the door of the drawing-room, and I exclaimed, ' I don't think he's a pretty man.' The justice of the criticism was not denied. My mother allowed that he was not 'pretty,' but in-formed me that he was very good, and, moreover, that he was my uncle's greatest friend. And from that time forward I became very curious about 'the good man,' as I was taught to call him.

That portrait on the staircase was one of the things I looked forward to seeing on our annual visits to London. I looked at it with increasing interest year by year, as I gradually heard and better understood who the subject of the portrait was ; how he was Vicar of a very large and very smoky town, far away in the north ; how he had built a great church there, what thousands of people flocked to it, what beautiful music was sung there, what eloquent sermons he preached, and how deeply he was beloved by the people; and then, again, how full of mirth he was, what funny letters he wrote, and what droll things he said and did. And on further acquaintance with the portrait, I could see there was a sparkle in the eyes, and a bright honest smile playing about the whole countenance, which largely compensated for the plainness of the features; and I almost felt remorse for having ever ventured to say that the person depicted was not a 'pretty man.'

The interest which I thus learned to take from childhood in the life of the Vicar of Leeds must be offered as my principal apology for attempting to tell the story of that life. During my boyhood, indeed, and early youth, when he was in the plenitude of his strength and full tide of his work, I very rarely saw him, but I constantly heard about him; and when in his old age I became connected with him through my marriage, and resided near him, he often talked to me like a veteran soldier of his old campaigns, and thus filled up and coloured for me in a great measure that picture of his life which the descriptions of others had already drawn in outline. It may seem to be a disadvantage, on the one hand, that a biographer should not personally have witnessed the work of his subject, but on the other, he may be able to write the history of past conflicts and controversies more dispassionately and calmly than one who has lived in the midst of them and has actually taken part in them. At the same time, no one can be more deeply sensible than I am how exceedingly difficult it is to put together a faithful narrative of a life passed in times which are, for the most part, too distant for the writer to draw much on his own re-collections, and yet too recent to be studied in the pages of history. Not that I have endeavoured to write what is commonly called a 'Life and Times,' a combination which generally results in doing justice to neither the life nor the times. My aim has been to write the life of the man, to make him the central figure throughout, and to touch upon surrounding events only in proportion as they concerned him, only in order to indicate the exact position which he occupied relatively to them, and to show how far he affected them, or how far he was affected by them. As far as possible, I have made him speak for himself, by his letters and diary, by extracts from his speeches and published writings, and by such fragments of his conversation as I or others could recollect. The difficulty of selecting and arranging copious materials of this kind, covering a period of more than half-a-century, can hardly be conceived by any but those who have made a similar attempt; and some indulgence is due, from which I hope not to be exempted, for defects in the execution of such a task.

To those who have aided me in it, and without whose aid it could not have been accomplished with that measure of completeness to which I trust it may pretend, I beg here most gratefully to acknowledge my obligations.

Foremost amongst these must be placed my uncle, Lord Hatherley, and my wife's aunt, Miss Hook. They not only supplied me with a vast quantity of valuable letters, but their full and exact reminiscences of distant events have been an unfailing source of trustworthy information. Besides the letter embodying his reminiscences, which Lord Hatherley has been good enough to write expressly for this Memoir, I have inserted a few letters addressed by him to his friend between the years 1830 and 1834, not only on account of their intrinsic excellence, but as illustrating the variety of subjects on which the two friends corresponded.

I must thank the Rector of Whippingham, the Rev. Canon Prothero, for endeavouring to glean some local information relating to the time when Dr. Hook was curate of that parish.

To the Vicar of Holy Trinity, Coventry, the Rev. F. M. Beaumont, I am much indebted for introducing me to some of the old inhabitants of that city, more especially W. Odell, Esq., and Luke Dresser, Esq., whose communications have been exceedingly useful.

In Leeds my thanks are very particularly due to the Rev. E. Jackson, Incumbent of St. James's, and Honorary Canon of Ripon, whose recollections, as the intimate and confidential friend of the Vicar during the period of his greatest activity, have been especially valuable to me.

My thanks are also due to the present Vicar of Leeds, to T. Pridgin Teale, Esq., M.D., to G. B. Nelson, Esq., and others, and, last but not least, to Mr. Edwin Moore, Registrar of the parish church, who rendered me immense aid in the toilsome work of searching out notices bearing on my subject, contained in the local contemporary journals.

In conclusion, I beg to thank collectively the large number of persons who have placed letters at my disposal, many of which are regarded by the possessors as very precious treasures. One word of caution may here be given to the readers of these letters. They must bear in mind that the writer was a man of very strong feelings and impulses. He wrote, and especially to the great friend of his life, in the most spontaneous manner, out of a very full heart, about whatever was uppermost in his mind. This, indeed, in a great measure, constitutes their peculiar charm; that they are the freshest and most artless expressions possible of the writer's thoughts and feelings at the moment when they were dashed off; but for the same reason they must not always be taken as representing the deliberate and final conclusions of his mind upon the matters of which they treat.

The life which it has fallen to my lot to portray was a singularly noble life. I would fain hope that not a few of those who shall read the record may be stirred up by the perusal to emulate the life.

WOOLBEDING RECTORY : *September* 27, 1878.

CONTENTS

OF

THE FIRST VOLUME.

———•◦•———

CHAPTER   PAGE

I. EARLY LIFE AND EDUCATION. A.D. 1798–1821 .   1

II. ORDINATION. LIFE AT WHIPPINGHAM. A.D. 1821–1826 49

III. LIFE AT MOSELEY AND BIRMINGHAM. A.D. 1826–1829 114

IV. STATE OF THE CHURCH—RISE OF THE 'TRACTARIAN' SCHOOL—LIFE AT COVENTRY. A.D. 1829–1837 138

V. THE ELECTION TO THE VICARAGE OF LEEDS, 1837 295

VI. SETTLEMENT AT LEEDS. JULY TO DECEMBER 1837 369

VII PART I. PUBLIC LIFE FROM 1838 TO 1840 . 415

LIFE

OF

WALTER FARQUHAR HOOK.

—◦—

CHAPTER I.

EARLY LIFE AND EDUCATION.   A.D. 1798–1821.

WALTER FARQUHAR HOOK was the eldest child of the Rev. James Hook and Anne his wife, and was born on March 13, 1798, at the residence in Conduit Street, London, of his maternal grandfather, Sir Walter Farquhar, Bart.   He was eleven months older than his only brother Robert, who died in 1873.   Their only sister, Georgiana, who was several years younger, has survived both her brothers.

His paternal grandfather, Mr. James Hook, who was a composer and teacher of music at Norwich, married Miss Madden, a lady eminently skilled in painting.   Out of a numerous family by this marriage, only two sons lived to manhood, James, who was born in June 1771, and Theodore, who was seventeen years younger than his brother.

James inherited the talents of his father and mother, and added to them very considerable literary powers of his own. It was truly remarked by one of his friends that had he devoted his whole attention to painting, music, or literature, he would have achieved a high reputation in either of the three professions. His two novels, indeed, ' Pen Owen ' and ' Percy Mallory,' entitle him to a high place among the writers of fiction. Some of his juvenile sketches were shown by his mother to Sir Joshua Reynolds, who was so much struck by the genius of the young artist that he strongly recommended the boy's parents to have him trained for the profession of a painter. A series of caricatures of the leading public men of the day, statesmen, lawyers, actors, and divines, drawn and coloured when he was a school boy at Westminster, aged fifteen, remains in possession of the family. They are inimitably good, not being in the least overdone, though full of humour ; and their value as portraits, sketched from the life, of such men as Pitt, Fox, Burke, Lord Thurlow, Boswell, Kemble, Munden, and many more, has been pronounced by connoisseurs to be very high indeed.

In music he had the same aptitude as his brother Theodore for playing impromptu on the piano, and was superior to him in execution and general knowledge of the art ; but although a ready versifier, he did not improvise verses to his own accompaniments, the accomplishment for which Theodore earned such a remarkable reputation. His artistic tastes in fact were rather discouraged by his mother, who feared that they might dissipate his mind and allure it from the higher pursuits for which his more solid abilities, as she thought, fitted him. James Hook, indeed, enjoyed the inestimable advantage of the training and influence of a sensible and pious mother throughout his youth, and to the loss of this blessing at a very early age the follies and foibles of his younger brother were doubtless very largely owing.

In the latter part of the last century Westminster and Eton were the two great rival schools of England, and a brisk fire of epigram and satire was continually going on between the two through their magazines, the Etonian 'Microcosm' and the Westminster 'Trifler.' Hook was the artist of the 'Trifler,' and one of his drawings represented the boys of the two schools as being weighed by Justice in a pair of scales. The Etonians, it is needless to say, were high in air, although George III. and other weighty personages were trying to depress their scale; the Westminsters on the other hand touched the ground. This affront was retaliated by an epigram in the 'Microcosm' from George Canning, then an Eton boy:

> What mean ye by this print so rare,
>   Ye wits, of Eton jealous,
> But that we soar aloft in air
>   While ye are heavy fellows?

But his antagonist was as ready with his pen as with his pencil, and retorted in the 'Trifler' in a similar strain:

> Cease, ye Etonians, and no more
>   With rival wits contend:
> Feathers, we know, will float in air,
>   And bubbles will ascend.

During some of his holidays Hook wrote the

libretto for two of his father's operas which were brought out in London. But notwithstanding his inclination for artistic and literary occupation such as has been indicated, his mother, who was anxious that he should enter Holy Orders, carried her point, and after taking his degree from St. Mary Hall, Oxford, he was ordained Deacon by the Bishop of Sodor and Man in 1796, and he married in the following year.

Those were the days when pluralists flourished and abounded, and through the interest mainly of his father-in-law, Sir Walter Farquhar, who was the confidential friend as well as the physician of the Prince of Wales, preferments were heaped upon Mr. Hook in rapid succession. He became Rector of Sadington in 1797, Chaplain to the Prince of Wales in 1801, Rector of Epworth in 1802, of Hertingfordbury in 1804, and of St. Andrew and St. Nicholas, Hertford, in 1805.

The early childhood of Walter Farquhar Hook was spent at the Rectory of Hertingfordbury, and to this the home of his earliest recollections he ever looked back with the fondest affection. A very few years before his death he made a journey with his youngest son expressly to see it ; to pace once more the pleasant lawn and garden, and to see if the names were still legible which in his boyhood he had carved upon some of the trees that shaded the path by the river side—the names of himself and of his friend William Page Wood, together with the names of Shakspeare and Milton, whom they both loved with a passionate devotion.

While the sensitive tenderness and affectionate-ness of his nature was inherited from both his parents, the vein of comic humour which equally distinguished him, and which sometimes burst forth into rhyme or frolicsome mirth after the manner of his uncle Theodore, was derived from his father. On the other hand like so many men who have been good as well as great, he thankfully acknowledged that whatever moral virtue he had was largely due to the careful training in early life of a pious mother. ' How much,' he writes in 1829, ' my dearest mother, do I owe to you. How often do I trace all that is good in me to the blessing of the Holy Spirit upon your labours, when in my grandfather's bed-room you used to inculcate so pleasantly the truths of Revelation into the hearts of dear Bobby and myself; those dear square, red books of Mrs. Trimmer out of which you read to us —how well I remember them, and how I wish I still possessed them !'

The two brothers, Walter and Robert, learned all the rudiments of knowledge, including Latin, from their mother till they were about eight or nine years of age. A summary of their progress and remarks upon their character which she wrote, seemingly for her own private use, at the beginnings of the years 1805 and 1806, are striking proofs of the truth of the saying, 'the child is father to the man.' Walter is described as being very fond of reading, inquisitive, and anxious to have everything explained ; persevering, and resolute in conquering difficulties, with a strong idea of principle, and a warmth of religious feeling rare in so young a child. His principal defects are said to be a shy and awkward manner, and an impulsive and irritable temper, easily exasperated by opposition, coupled, however, with a keen sense of remorse. On the whole his mother considered that his character was one which required moderate, judicious encouragement, but was unable to bear much praise. Those who knew him best will easily recognise in this description some of the qualities which were most conspicuous in him throughout life.

When he was about nine years old he was sent with his brother to a school at Hertford, kept by Dr. Luscombe, and from this school he writes to his mother in February 1810 a letter which is the earliest piece of his writing that I have discovered.

'Dearest Mother,—I wish June was come and I had to tell you that I was in the Fourth Form. I am very sorry that I am not in the Third Form, but you know I tried very, very hard. It is an ill reward for my fagging ; but it is the will of God that I should not go into the Third Form, and the will of God must be done.'

Soon after this the two brothers were removed to Tiverton in Devonshire. Their recollections of this school were not pleasant. The teaching was indifferent, the discipline severe, and the food scanty. They saved up their spare pence to buy buns and loaves from time to time to alleviate the pangs of hunger. In the letters, however, written by Walter at this time there are no complaints ; and in his handwriting there is very great improvement. The style of his letters becomes curiously grand and sententious ; but they are written then as ever after in pure, sound English. In one too long for transcription, bearing date November 1, 1811, he begins :—

'My dear Mamma,—You will with me pity that wicked boy, Henry George Salter, who is now publicly expelled from this school : and his master, Master Richards, blotted his name from the Register, October 30, 1811, that it may be handed down to generations.' Then follows an account of how this 'wicked boy' enticed another to run away with him, having borrowed a watch which he afterwards sold, saying they would go to London where he would persuade his grandmother to leave him her immense fortune, which he would divide with his companion. The runaways were captured, and Salter wrote a contrite letter upon which young Walter observes, ' Well, so far one would think him to be penitent Salter, but *I* say, Salter the hypocrite ; ' and he then goes on to relate how this naughty boy repeated his escapade, borrowing and selling another watch, after which he was expelled in the awful manner described at the beginning of the letter.

In 1812, the year after this tragical occurrence, the brothers were removed to ' Commoners ' Winchester. Their father had become a Canon of Winchester, and this circumstance probably led to the selection of the school. The narrative of Lord Hatherley [1] placed at the end of this volume and the letters which I have added render it unnecessary for me to trace at length Hook's school career, and I shall confine myself to some general remarks upon his character and conduct at this period.

In the first place having been ill taught at Tiverton, he was very backward in scholarship, which at that time was the beginning and ending of

[1] Formerly William Page Wood.

education at a public school. At the instigation and with the help of his friend, William Page Wood, as will be seen, he ultimately obtained a fair position in the school ; but it may be doubted whether under the most favourable circumstances he would ever have made a finished scholar. His mind was not of that critical order which delights in nicely balancing various forms of expression and determining their precise shades of meaning. He always read books for instruction or pleasure, and if he got this from them he cared little about the mould in which the contents were cast. Lively, ready, and original, too, as he was in writing and conversation, he was always rather slow of apprehension, he had great difficulty in committing to memory, nor was his memory, especially for words, very retentive. He was never a rapid reader, and those who read aloud to him—a luxury of which he was very fond in later life—were always required to read very slowly and sometimes to repeat a passage, not seemingly obscure, several times before he could take it in.

On the other hand, even when he came to Winchester his delight in reading the best English poets and historians, and the extent of his acquaintance with them were very uncommon for a boy of fourteen. His admiration for Shakspeare and Milton grew into a passionate enthusiasm for which it would be hard to find anything like a parallel. Scarcely any letter written throughout his school or college days is without some reference to or quotation from these favourites. To read them he neglected his school work, and withdrew from the ordinary sports of his schoolfellows. He complains in one of his letters,

September 1813, that the racket and bullying out of school are so great that he can get no time to pursue his favourite studies and meditations ; that he has discovered a new hiding place, a hollow space about six feet deep enclosed by stacks of timber, on a wharf, into which he retreats to read, but that like all the rest of his haunts he fears it will soon be detected. Probably it was for the same purpose of undisturbed reading that he chose to ' take a tunding,' that is, a severe thrashing, twice, rather than fag at foot-ball. It will readily be supposed that to a boy so averse alike from the ordinary work and pastimes of the place, school life was anything but a time of enjoyment. In fact he often said that but for his friendship with Wood it would have been insupportable. His lamentations are poured forth in letters which are at times really pathetic, but still more often irresistibly droll, from the incongruity between the tragic tone of despair in which they are written and the actual circumstances of the case.

In October 1813 he writes to his brother, who for some cause was absent from school : ' I hate this place more and more every day. I was licked yesterday more severely than ever before. I cannot run or hollow out loud even now without hurting my side, and I am to be licked again to-day for writing this : yet I should not be able to write at another time as I go "at top of hall"[1] and get so much to do. I begin to fear my licking. If I am killed, which I think I shall be, tell Etheridge[2] to send you my

---

[1] A technical Winchester phrase, signifying that the boy so placed was liable to answer any demand for fagging.
[2] The school butler.

books, and hope that I am in heaven happier than all of you ; if for my sins I am condemned to hell, pity me, dear Robert, pity me.[1] Let Milton be buried with me, as he has gone through all my hardships with me.'

Writing a year later he says that though he still hates the place, he is not so rebellious as he used to be, and regards his prison house from a more philosophical point of view. ' I endeavour to find out the comforts, if any there be, and not the miseries of this place, for as my dear and beloved bard, the honour of England and of the whole of this terrestrial orb says, " the mind is its own place and can make an Heaven of Hell, an Hell of Heaven." Combined with his love of reading in retirement was a habit of meditation and reverie from which, though in itself of rather a melancholy nature, he seems to have derived a peculiar kind of enjoyment. Writing to his grandfather, Sir Walter Farquhar, in 1816, he says, ' I would have you know that if you think nothing ill will turn out from this melancholy I should still like to be possessed by it, as I am exceedingly happy when I have it, owing to the amusing thoughts which come into my mind at such times.'

His grandfather, indeed, who had won his way from obscurity to the top of his profession by hard industry and talents of the most practical order, although he had formed a high opinion of the abilities of his grandson, was much exercised by fears lest he should become too poetical and dreamy to make his way in the world. The following letter written a short time before that of his grandson's

---

[1] How Robert was to know whether he was condemned to hell or not, does not appear.

just quoted, is a quaint illustration of this dread, and savours of that shrewd worldly wisdom, frugality, and caution, to which he, in common with so many of his countrymen, mainly owed his success in life.

Conduit St.: June 8, 1815.

My dear Walter,—Your passion and steady attachment for Milton and Shakspeare, I admire, but as I have not one single particle of poetic fire in my mind and never had, I am not a judge of the justice of your adoration, and therefore you must forgive me for not entering keenly into your indignation at your tutor's presuming to correct Shakspeare. The word 'beteem' I certainly should not have understood without your explanation, and I should have been considered a great blockhead by you enthusiasts, whom I, on my part, a man of plain common sense, deem a little mad when you get on your hobbies. However I don't mean to stop you full gallop. You may run on, and I will every year add to your library books worth ten guineas, as I am pleased that you have made so good an use of my first present. I therefore desire that you will rummage your poetic and critical brain, and let me know the authors that your next passion lead you to, and before 1815 is at an end I will furnish the next shelf in your library. Sometimes I would wish you to descend from the flights of poetry, and study those things that may be useful to you in life, and teach a poor man how to live comfortably upon little, and I shall therefore add to the list you send me of books, Cocker's 'Arithmetic' and Euclid's 'Elements.' Spare half an hour now and then to look into them. You have a first cousin W. Mathison who has shown some talent for figures, mathematics, &c. I have consequently made him a present of Euclid's 'Elements,' and if you get over the fifth proposition, the Bridge of Asses, I shall conceive that with your assiduity and application you may even become a mathematician as well as a poet. My love to Robert. I don't know what he has done with his ten guineas, and when he tells me this, I shall then tell him what further I mean to do for *him*. I want to make him a plodding Dutchman, by which means he may make fortune enough to assist you and your family before you get rich in the Church, or become a Bishop; as a poet you will run the risk of dying in a garret excepting you bestow a little time occasionally on Cocker, and learn how to make a little money go far, and to manage the sober, dull realities of life in place of being in the poetical clouds for ever.

I have had a severe attack of cold and cough and been confined to my room, but I am now much better. I am not quite clear that you would have had so long a letter if I had been able to trudge about as usual.

I am with great attachment, my dear boy,

Your affectionate Grandfather,

W. FARQUHAR.

There was not, however, in Walter Hook any of that sickliness and softness, either of body or mind, which is so commonly found in boys of a pensive, meditative disposition, who have no relish for the ordinary amusements of their companions. Although tall, gaunt, and so old-looking for his age that one of his school friends now living says, that his face in mature manhood always seemed to him much the same as what it was in boyhood, yet he was muscular and vigorous in no common degree; none could swim further or dive deeper; and an audacious bully who once dared to say in his presence that Shakspeare was a fool, was instantly felled to the ground by the fist of the muscular devotee. Some soldiers also on one occasion having tried to usurp a bathing place belonging to the boys, he was selected to fight one of the intruders and made very short work of his antagonist. Few, if any, of the boys had such a

peculiar kind of droll humour, and to spend an evening
with Walter in the holidays was considered by his
young cousins more amusing than a visit to the theatre.
The matron who took care of the boys' linen at
Winchester was celebrated for affecting knowledge
on all conceivable subjects of enquiry, and it was his
delight to put such strange questions to her as would
elicit equally strange answers. ' Pray ma'am,' said
he one day to her with an air of exceeding solemnity,
' What is your opinion of Charles XII. of Sweden ? '
' Well, Mr. Hook,' she replied, ' I haven't been able
to read the papers lately and of course I am not
personally acquainted with him.' No one watched
with a keener vigilance for the extraordinary and
ludicrous blunders made by one of the old minor
canons of the Cathedral in his sermons. Two of
these especially were never forgotten, and were often
repeated by him, or as will be seen referred to in
his letters ; and indeed they were worth preservation
as specimens of the stuff sometimes tolerated in our
cathedral pulpits at the beginning of this century.
One was, ' What is impossible can never be, and very
seldom comes to pass ;' the other, ' O tempora ! O
mores ! what times we live in : little girls and boys
run about the streets cursing and swearing before
they can either walk or talk.'

Again, although his religious feelings, and his sentiments of affection for his relations and intimate friend
are expressed in fervent rapturous language most uncommon in a schoolboy, yet there is nothing unnatural,
unhealthy, or effeminate to be detected in them. They
were the genuine offspring of a heart warm indeed and
tender, yet manly and courageous. He was, in fact,

in boyhood and throughout life eminently English and
eminently Christian ; qualities which in their highest
manifestation are incompatible with any tinge of
morbid sentiment in the character. And one of the
reasons why he regretted the rigid restriction of
school work to the study of Greek and Latin was
that boys grew up knowing more about Rome than
England, more about Paganism than Christianity.
Not that he was narrow in his tastes : he read any
history with great interest, and in good poetry he
delighted in any language in which he could read it ;
but English history and English writers had a charm
for him which the history and the writers of other
nations could not excite. Having been brought up,
too, in the strictest and straitest school of Toryism,
he fully believed that the British Constitution, alike
in Church and State, was the most perfect piece of
machinery which could be found under the sun, and
in the beginning at any rate of his school days he
was prepared sturdily to uphold the virtue of the
Prince Regent and the wisdom of Lord Castlereagh
against all assailants. In like manner he would
scarcely allow a blemish in the moral beauty of Mr.
Pitt or a redeeming virtue in the moral blackness of
Mr. Fox. In June 1816, he writes to his mother,
' At a party at Mr. Rickett's, in the course of conversation Mr. R. said that drinking was the chief thing
which killed our great statesman Mr. Pitt. I thought
at first he made a mistake and meant that fellow
Fox, so I just asked him over again to see if he
really meant what he said, but afterwards I asked
everyone who was present, when Mr. R. had left
the room, not to mention what had passed in

Commoners for it would cause much laughter against me, as I always call Fox a " drunken beast;" and now I mean to ask you to petition grandpapa to dictate a few lines as Pitt's doctor and send them to me stating what really did kill him.'

Combined with his intense love and admiration for everything English, and partly as a consequence of it, was an antipathy and contempt for foreigners and foreign institutions. He was quite prepared to accept the saying of Sam Johnson, ' For all I can see, foreigners are fools ;' and he was fully persuaded of the truth of the old popular tradition handed down from the days of Agincourt, that ' one Englishman was a match for fourteen Frenchmen.' Of course his estimates of public men and historical characters in many cases underwent great alterations with his advance in age, study, and experience, but foreigners as a whole he always regarded with aversion ; and there was one eminent person of whose character his opinion never changed, and that was Napoleon Buonaparte. His only complaint, he says in 1816 of Scott's ' Life of Napoleon,' was that he had ' profaned British paper with the name of ex-Emperor,' and to the end of his life he never spoke of Napoleon by any other name than Buonaparte, regarding him as an unprincipled tyrant and a heartless ravager of the earth, colossal indeed if measured by an intellectual standard, but morally one of the meanest of mankind.

Although he did not obtain any classical prizes, except one for getting into the Sixth Form by a special effort, the nature of which is described in Lord Hatherley's narrative, he twice gained the silver

medal for recitation on the Speech Day. The first
was in 1816, when he recited the celebrated speech
of Antony upon the death of Julius Cæsar. His
voice already possessed much of that rich, melodious
softness and flexibility, combined with great volume
of tone, for which he was afterwards so remarkably
distinguished, and although he did not inherit any of
his father's or grandfather's musical talents, and could
not tell one tune from another, he was at this time
as always very pure in his pronunciation, and skilful
in the modulation of his utterances. His hearers on
this occasion seem to have been completely captivated and enchanted. Canon Nott writes to his
father : ' Your son's speaking was admirable. It was
neither acting nor declamation, but a chaste medium
between the two. He himself felt and made others
feel the beauties of his poet. You know the speech :
the *gradual* introduction of the sneer, " For Brutus
is an honourable man," was admirable. Had it been
a sneer from the first, it would not have been in
nature. Antony did not venture to insinuate anything against Brutus until he was certain he should
not offend, and this he could not have been in the
first instance.' He gained the medal also in the
following year for his recitation of Satan's speech to
the Sun in Milton's ' Paradise Lost.'

The perseverance with which he worked for the
special examination already alluded to, in order
to obtain his remove into the Sixth Form, was
the first indication of that energy and industry
in study which were afterwards so eminently
characteristic of him. He sometimes rose at three
in the morning to read his Greek play ; and Dr.

Gabell told his parents that the progress which he made while working for his remove was beyond what he could have thought it possible for any boy to make in the time. Having, moreover, once won his way to the highest form, he showed much anxiety to maintain his position with credit ; and the miscellaneous reading which had impeded his progress upwards in the school where so much depended on technical scholarship, now became an advantage and a help.

His mother writes of him at this period with mingled anxiety and pride.

His irritable, choleric temper, his fits of melancholy, his tendency in many ways to impulsiveness and eccentricity, caused her some uneasiness ; but on the other hand the warmth of his affection, his deep sense of religion, and the capacity which he had lately shown for working with dogged resolution when once convinced that duty demanded it, filled her with hope. Dr. Gabell also and all the masters spoke of his general character and conduct in terms of the most unqualified praise, and even admiration.

It had been intended that he should leave Winchester at the end of the year 1816, but at the urgent recommendation of Dr. Gabell, who thought that the delay would enable him to enter upon his Oxford career with better prospects of success, it was decided that he should remain another half-year. His grandfather obtained a nomination for him from the Prince Regent to a studentship at Christ Church, and in December 1817 he was admitted a member of that House.

Save for the parting with his deeply beloved

friend, he quitted Winchester without a pang of regret. But that parting was a very severe trial to both. They had lived a life there which was all their own ; a life bound by the closest ties not only of common interests but of reciprocal obligations, for each had helped to supply what was lacking in the other. And though both felt sure that the friendship never could be broken, yet frequent intercourse was now to cease, and, as it turned out, for a much longer period than either could have anticipated. Their favourite walk in meads, the old tree beneath which they had compared their youthful attempts in poetry, and Hook had read his tragedy of James II., the chalk pit in which at 'Evening Hills' they used to sit each with his Shakspeare and read the dialogue by turns, the stroll home by 'Goddard's walk'—all these scenes were to be abandoned, all these incidents of daily life were to be brought to a close, and bitter was the grief.

$$\pi \acute{o} \nu o \iota \; \kappa o \acute{\iota} \nu o \iota \; \lambda \acute{o} \gamma \omega \nu,$$
$$\acute{o} \mu \acute{o} \sigma \tau \epsilon \gamma \acute{o} s \; \tau \epsilon \; \kappa a \grave{\iota} \; \sigma \upsilon \nu \acute{\epsilon} \sigma \tau \iota o s \; \beta \acute{\iota} o s,$$
$$\nu o \hat{\upsilon} s \; \epsilon \hat{\iota} s \; \acute{\epsilon} \nu \; \acute{a} \mu \phi o \hat{\iota} \nu \; o \grave{\upsilon} \; \delta \acute{\upsilon} \omega, \; . \; . \; . \; .$$
$$\delta \iota \epsilon \sigma \kappa \acute{\epsilon} \delta a \sigma \tau a \iota \; \pi \acute{a} \nu \tau a, \; \kappa \acute{a} \rho \rho \iota \pi \tau a \iota \; \chi a \mu a \acute{\iota}.[1]$$

He began his residence at Oxford in Lent Term, 1818. A letter from his grandfather written soon after cautions him against allowing himself to be drawn into discussions about the character of the Prince to whom he owed his studentship ; advises him to keep a commonplace book, and to practise declamation before a looking glass that he may study grace of action as well as eloquence in public speaking. Encouraged by his grandson's success in reci-

---

[1] Greg. Nazianz. *De Vitâ Suâ*, vol. ii. p. 8, C.

tations at Winchester, Sir Walter Farquhar was at this time anxious that he should prepare for the Bar; and no doubt with this view the recommendation to the rather gaunt, ungainly youth to study gracefulness of action was not undesirable. His awkwardness was no doubt increased at this time by extreme shyness, of which the following letter, describing his first appearance as a Freshman in Hall, furnishes an amusing specimen.

Christ Church, Oxon.

My dear Brother,—When you went away I called on Mr. Goodenough; but finding him out, I had an audience with Mrs. Bright, who was bright as usual in her conversation, promised to give me advice, and lend me 'Anacharsis,' &c. I then saw Mr. G., but all the information that I could get from him was, that I was to dine in Hall, go to Chapel, and hereafter write a Latin letter, all which I knew before; about an hour after this, I was seized with a violent fit of what we Wykehamists call 'funk,' occasioned (as learned physicians tell me) by the prospect of dining in Hall; the symptoms at length began to grow alarming, for about one o'clock I could not read, write, or think, save of going up into Hall. About half-past, my memory began to fail, so much so, that I quite forgot whether the dinner hour was a quarter to four or a quarter after four; so I went to dress. Somewhere about three the bells began to ring for Cathedral, and as by this time I had entirely lost my memory, I began to fear that I must have made a mistake, and taken four for three when I was told the hour. Consequently, I sallied forth, cap and gown, &c., &c. when finding no dinner, or thought of dinner, I retired again into my lurking hole, peeping out of my bedroom window to see if I could see any men going to dinner; at a quarter to four I hurried out again; no dinner ready; looked out of window for another half hour; quarter past four sallied forth again, and in about five minutes walked

' with stately pace and slow,' into Hall, astonishing the weak
minds of the inhabitants, who gazed with silent admiration
on me, either captivated by the brilliancy of my head or
the beauty of my person. Mortal dull at dinner. Nobody
to talk to ; there were only two more Commoners besides
myself ; blushed, looked sheepish ; tried to carve some veal
for myself, failed ; at length pulled off some meat ; blushed
again, looked more sheepish than before ; took courage at
length, and called like a hero for some cheese ; looked for my
cap, could not find it ; at length the servant discovered it ;
I marched out of Hall, and here I am. This, my dear Bob,
is all that I have done to-day, which amounts to nothing.
I am very dull indeed, I should like never to speak to any
one, as far as convenience goes, for it would enable a man
to study double tides ; but it seems so horridly stupid,
that I do not like it. I am rather grumpy, but I wrote this
in good spirits, having just performed a wonderful adven-
ture : but I am beginning to have a second attack, for how
am I to know where to sit in Chapel to-morrow, and various
other things. I wish very much that I knew somebody or
other ; it would be very convenient, to say the least of it,
but ' nihil est ab omni parte beatum,' and I am so delighted
with my room that I know not whether it does not make
up for other inconveniences.

His life, indeed, at Oxford was more peculiar
and isolated than it had been at Winchester ; and of
course there were more opportunities for seclusion.
He had no sympathy with the ordinary course of
study, and had no longer a friend at hand to stimu-
late him in uncongenial work. He soon, therefore,
abandoned all attempts to read for honours, and
fell back with zest upon the study of his favourite
English authors, to whom he now added Hooker
and Jeremy Taylor. But his beloved Shakspeare
still reigned supreme in his affections ; and it is not
too much to say that the characters in Shakspeare's

plays were by far the most real companions and friends of his Oxford life. With Newman he had little or no acquaintance. With Pusey he had some degree of intimacy, yet his name is very rarely mentioned in his letters. Keble, who had taken his degree eight years before, he beheld with a kind of distant reverence and awe. The one unalterable friend to whom he turned for sympathy in all moods, whether of joyousness or depression, was his Shakspeare. The following letters will forcibly illustrate the truth of this observation, which indeed is corroborated by the countless allusions to the same subject with which his letters teem during this period. The first letter, from which an extract is here given, was written on hearing that his grandfather was recovering from a serious illness.

. . . . 'You cannot imagine how truly happy your kind letter made me. It set me quite in spirits. The minute I opened the letter and saw the news I pulled down my Shakspeare and had a very merry hour with Sir John Falstaff. I was determined to laugh heartily all that day. I asked Sir John to wine with me. I decantered a bottle of my beloved grandfather's best port, and Sir John and I drank his health right merrily. Perhaps you will want to know how my old friend Sir John drank my grandfather's health. Why I took care to find out the place where he drinks Justice Shallow's health. And so when I said " Here's to Sir Walter," I looked on the book and the knight said " Health and long life to him." But perhaps you will think me a little cracked for opening my " oak " to you, so I will talk more seriously. . . .'

The next letter written to his father a month later illustrates yet more vividly the manner in which he peopled his solitude with the characters of Shakspeare, so that never did anyone more completely make good the saying, ' Nunquam minus solus quam cùm solus.'

Christ Church, Oxford : April 27, 1818.

Corckran has gone out sailing to-day with Mr. Barrington, a son of Lord Barrington, so that I stay at home ; for to tell you the truth till Corckran comes, since Halliday left, I have taken no walks in the day-time, for it is impossible to take a solitary walk, as in whatever direction you go, you must meet some man, and therefore it looks so spoony to be by yourself, that I do not like to walk out ; and I do not like to walk with any man I know here, for with the exception of Duncombe, Sandford, and Napier, who perhaps think the same of me as I do of my other acquaintance, the men I know are such raffs in look and manner, that I do not like to walk with them, lest I should be judged by my comrades. I therefore go out at about eight o'clock, and run for about an hour up and down Christ Church walk (not meads), which is always deserted about that time, except once I met a man not of the University there ; but I do not think exercise agrees with me, for I had almost forgotten what a headache was till to-day, and yesterday I walked about seven miles with Corckran, and am fit for nothing but a long letter ; and yet I am as happy, if not more so (one single thing would make me more so), than I have ever been, except last summer. I have got into a very dissolute set of men, but they are so pleasant that they make me very often idle, when I otherwise should not be so. It consists of one Tuft, H.R.H. Henry Prince of Wales, and a gentleman Commoner named Sir John Falstaff, and a Mr. Poins, and we have several inferior associates such as Bardolph and Pistol, and some others; and with these I spend most of my time :

I breakfast with them, drink tea, and sometimes wine with them ; of course they sit at a different table from me at dinner.

Sir John, or as I call him (being great 'cons' with him), Jack, is very fond of a capon ; and I 'sported beaver' the other day, and went into the market to find one, but could not succeed. I have likewise been made acquainted by Mr. Richardson of Edinburgh with a Danish Prince, and I begin to think that I have mastered a knowledge of his character, which is most amiable. However it is my intention to take all these to Whippingham, and there leave them till I have taken my Degree, as they make me very idle. I shall miss them much next term, for nobody at Oxford can suit me like them.

The general charm of his letters at this period is that they are not filled with the ordinary gossip of an undergraduate about Oxford work, Oxford politics, Oxford amusements, but with subjects altogether peculiar to himself.

The characters in Shakspeare's plays being his most intimate friends, he was naturally very jealous of Shakspeare's honour, and watched with the keenest interest the manner in which he was represented on the stage. A mutilated version of 'King Lear' which had lately been produced having come into his hands, he writes in a fury of indignation to his mother, November 1818 :

'It is the veriest trash I ever read. Had I time I could point out hundreds of absurdities in it. I could turn myself into a brute beast, and gaze with pleasure at the men who pass off such stuff for our Shakspeare's, were they hanging on the next tree. This has plagued me more than you can imagine : it has been in my thoughts day and night since I

first discovered it. I feel the pride of an Englishman in thinking that we can boast of Shakspeare,
and consequently I feel indignant and exasperated
at seeing our Shakspeare altered to the miserable
taste of the French, who have no theatre of their
own but only a corruption of the ancients. . . .
This preys upon my mind, and in good sooth makes
me quite unhappy ; let us quit the subject.'

The event, however, which most powerfully excited and absorbed his interest during a portion of
the year 1818, was the great rebellion of the boys
at Winchester, which led to the temporary dissolution of the school. His interest was owing partly
to the intrinsic importance and extraordinary character of the event, but more especially to the part
which his friend Wood played in it. I have selected
the following letter out of many which he wrote
upon the subject because, taken together with the
account given in Lord Hatherley's narrative, it forms
an interesting original piece of evidence respecting
a very curious episode in the history of Wykeham's
great school.

Christ Church, Oxford : May 12, 1818.

My dear Mother, ... Grievance upon grievance
irritated them ; but the immediate cause was Gabell's
threatening to expel Porcher for setting watches to find
out when he was approaching, a custom handed down from
our ancestors, and daily exercised during the six years
which I had the honour of spending at Winchester. They
tried remonstrance, which as usual only irritated Gabell.
The spirit had been long concealed in the school ; this
made it break out. Several patriotic songs were sung, and
thus the lion in each boy's soul having been , roused, a
rebellion was openly proposed. Every single boy in Com-

moners assented. A message was sent into College, and all except —— unanimously agreed. This was on Wednesday; it was proposed to be carried into execution on Monday; consequently deputies met, and everything was privately agreed, and notice given for each boy to supply himself with a small pickaxe and a large club; but on Thursday information was given that Wickham, the surgeon, knew of the schemes, consequently open war commenced at a quarter to four. Thursday evening every boy was armed with a club; a patriotic song was sung. Etheridge was seized, licked, and the keys of Commons taken from him; the Commoners rushed into College, took the porter and his keys, and locked the great gates of the inner quadrangle. They closed them to all the masters and everybody, except David Williams and his wife, who passed unmolested on condition that he would bring nobody else in with him. A patriotic song was then sung, three cheers given, and they fell to work with their pickaxes, and dug up the great stones of the quadrangle, took possession of the towers, carried their stones to the top of them, and everything was prepared for a general siege. The Warden's door was blocked up, and all his windows broken. These proceedings went on admirably during the night, and College was so admirably defended with such regularity and order, that though Gabell, with John Williams as his aide-de-camp, and some constables, made several attempts to break into College, they were repulsed entirely. These particulars I have from Wood's letter to me, and Deane's (who did not join) to Heathcote. What happened in the intermediate time I have not yet heard, as Wood had not time to write a long account. All night those who were not on duty sat on the top of the different towers of the Chapel and College, singing patriotic songs. On Friday, Bernard, the brother of the Prebendary, came down to say that the military was called out, and all afterwards found resisting would be sent to prison. A conference was afterwards held with Urquhart from one of the Warden's windows, the boys, except those on duty, standing on the tower, in which he told them they might go whithersoever they liked. Afterwards they made an unfortunate sally, intending some of them to have a dinner at the 'George,' and then return ; but they were met (notwithstanding the promise of being unmolested) by a body of soldiers, by Mrs. Heathcote's house. A little skirmish ensued. Two or three who had dirks rushed into the middle of the soldiers, and fought as brave men should do ; they were, however, taken prisoners, and secured in the Cathedral. The rest were then put to flight. They were persuaded to meet Gabell, who expelled a certain number, and the rest (having bound themselves to be expelled if one was) likewise went ; but some were taken by the constables, and some were persuaded to go back. However, the next day, most of them rushed up to the 'George,' where sixty of them dined, and the rest went home. There are still between eighty and ninety who cannot escape ; but who have broken every window in Commoners, and refuse to go to chapel and school, who are only watching for an opportunity to keep their oaths. If I had been the leader, I should have managed better. There is a room in College where all the wills and deeds of College are kept ; having got them once in their hands, they could have threatened to destroy them, and made College listen to any conditions. A party of Wykehamists met last night, and drank the health of the rebels in three times three.

In another letter he writes that he was quite intoxicated with joy at hearing of the rebellion. ' All yesterday I was in such a fever of delight that I have now no small headache. I was running all over Oxford to get news, and then retailed them with a little bragging to all the men of Eton and Westminster that I know. The Etonians are full of admiration : the Westminsters are thunderstruck. Winchester will now be looked upon as *the* only school ; it beats every other school in everything, except Westminster in rowing and Eton in putting on a neckcloth.'

In the following year, 1819, we find him just after passing his ' Little Go' more averse than ever from classical studies, more thoroughly wedded to his own peculiar and secluded ways of life. In a letter to his mother he declaims vehemently against mere scholarship, and declares his conviction of his utter inability ever to become a scholar in the technical sense.   He would have written before but he had been reading hard, and his faculties and feelings seemed blunted by the labour. ' I hate verbal critics,' he proceeds, 'even on Shakspeare, and though they may be a useful, they seem to me to be a rather despicable, set.   I shall never become a scholar, my memory is so wretchedly bad and I am so deficient in the art of acquiring the idiom of language ; these, together with an inaccuracy as un-accountable as it seems incurable, and a slowness almost inconceivable in reading, are powerful enemies, and I am striving to conquer them, but hitherto in vain.'

The quaintness and oddity of his habits are indicated in the following letter to his aunt Mrs. Mathison, written in the same year.   There is a tone of philosophic irony also in his remarks upon the ways of ordinary men as contrasted with his own which has a Shakspearian ring about it, and sounds like the utterance of a disciple of the 'melancholy Jacques' in 'As you like it.'

Christ Church, Oxford : 1819.

Not many years ago I thought when I arrived at the age of twenty-one I should entirely put away childish

things. But I really find in myself no alteration from
what I was twelve years ago. I know nothing, even the
most childish thing, in which I used to delight and find
amusement then, that I could not do just the same now.
And my mind is just as wandering and unsettled. My
ideas are more extensive, inasmuch as I know more ; but
they are cast in the same mould and run on the same
subjects. I used to find great pleasure in taking a stick
and flogging trees as if they were my schoolboys, and now
I can find just as much pleasure in taking a stick and
fighting through a hedge as if it were an army and I an
Orlando ; and there is not one of the many games which I
used to invent for myself then that I could not enjoy
equally now. And when I reflect coolly upon these things,
I think that half the world, discovering the little things in
which I can find amusement (which Heaven forefend),
would put me down as the most consummate idiot and
fool. And yet when, as I said before, I reflect coolly on
the matter, I think there is no more folly in them than
there is in the sports of hunting and shooting. I therefore
think 'that all the world's a fool ; its actions show it. I
thought so once, but now I know it.' And I shall never
look for wisdom in any man ; I shall only respect the man
who has less folly than others.

He had to live frugally at Oxford, for his father,
notwithstanding his preferments, was a needy man.
In the summer of this year, however, just before the
end of term, he had an extra pound of pocket money
sent him, and determined to spend it in making a
pilgrimage to Stratford-on-Avon. What the delight
of this visit was by anticipation the following letters
will most clearly show ; but I have not discovered
any which were written soon after it had been made.
I only know that in spite of the adverse circumstances
mentioned in the second letter, he did succeed in

getting to Stratford ; and the ecstasies of the enthusiast must be left to the imagination.

Oxford : June 1819.

My dear Mother, ... So Mrs. Siddons has been on the stage. How unlucky I am never to be able to see her. I, who feel a filial affection for the stage, corrupted, depraved, and odious as it now is, yet I cannot but feel more than ordinary interest in it, and still hope that the time will come when the abominable, unconstitutional monopoly of the two theatres will be done away with, and that all theatrical talent will be employed in developing the beauties of the real English drama ; and then Shakspeare will shine forth in all his pristine glory. Indeed, it is not my least ambition to be able some day or other to acquire money enough to become a manager of some great theatre, as Sheridan was ; and I am vain enough to think that it would be a national benefit if I were to be so, as I should enter heart and soul into the cause, and that, not for the sake of filthy lucre, but merely to improve the taste of my country and enhance the glory of Shakspeare. On Friday week I start for Stratford, God willing, and return to Oxford Monday, to Winchester Tuesday. I might go on Thursday to Stratford, but I shall not, because I shall be more likely to meet an Oxford face on that day, and I shall want to settle many things. I have calculated the expenses on a liberal scale. It is more than I expected it would be ; but thanks to the kindness of my friends I shall be able to support it.

I shall not go to the ' White Lion,' which is a very excellent inn, and that at which the jubilee was celebrated. The ' Shakspeare Inn ' is about the third. I did think once of going to that, and may now. But the house that Shakspeare was born in is divided into a butcher's shop and the ' Swan,' a public-house. Now if this last can give me only a clean bed, without bugs, which I hate, I mean to go undoubtedly to that. The only objection is, that it may make my friends think that they are justified in charging me with going there from some foolish feeling ; whereas I merely go in a quiet manner to look at the place, just as some people come to lionise Oxford. Now, I mean to take with me a Dutch cheese, which will save the expense of dinners ; for at breakfast I shall have two eggs, and cut off a large slice of bread, which I shall eat with my cheese, and my drink shall be the water of the Avon, which Shakespeare, I make no doubt, drank many a time before. I do not suppose that I shall find all the pleasure which I expect. In thinking of it even, I have been so pleased, till pleasure turned to pain, and I ended with a headache. It is very foolish, but I always anticipate pleasure in this manner. I cannot read properly now from the very thoughts of it, and have not been able for a fortnight.

Believe me, my dear Mother,
Your affectionate Son,
W. F. HOOK.

He worried himself as people so commonly do in the prospect of great pleasure by the dread of something occurring to prevent or mar it. ' I am always thinking,' he writes, ' of the many things which will happen to thwart me, and most of all I fear bad weather. I am something like my mother who is angry at every fine day in town lest the weather should turn out badly when she gets into the country. So I am terrified at this most delightful summer weather.' Curiously enough his forebodings of evil weather were verified, as the following lamentable letter proves.

Journey to Stratford-on-Avon.

Shipston : 1819.

My dear Mother,—Was ever anybody so unlucky ? but I am not at Stratford. How do you think I intend spending my father's pound ? Why, even by sporting myself a chaise to Stratford. I started at twelve last night from Oxford, and arrived here at five. As it began to rain prodigiously hard, and I was outside, as moreover I like to be quite by myself on my entrance to Stratford, I determined upon breakfasting here, ten miles from Stratford, and proceeding per chaise; still, however, this rain will continue pouring. What shall I do? I want not to enter Stratford till it is fine. It is now one o'clock; the rain has set in, and the provoking people here will not even say a kind word about the weather. When I ask them whether it will clear up, they with one voice answer, 'That it looks black.' Just heard of a return chaise; must start. I almost believe that this weather, beginning the very day of my intended excursion, is intended as a punishment for me, on account of some crime I have committed, or else some demon is willing to drive me mad with vexation. I have two days; one of them will, I hope, be fine. All my dreams have vanished with this, and I never shall again trust to the prospect of delight in this world. I knew it would be thus: I was sure of it. Well, all I can say is, that if Shakspeare's spirit could govern the clouds, I think it would for me; for I verily believe he has few more sincere admirers. Still, however, I feel a glow at approaching his birthplace, and I am as puffed with pride and vanity as I well can be. I despise the whole world, and now I feel as if I were a being of superior order.

In June 1820 he had looked forward to a meeting with his great friend Mr. Wood, who had just returned to England from a two years' residence at Geneva; but his father was averse to his meeting the son of a man who had so earnestly advocated the cause of Queen Caroline, and in fact for a time he forbade intercourse between them. His mother could not put herself into direct opposition to his father's commands, but seems to have done her best to mitigate the severity of the trial to him. Of

course the enforced separation only added to the
warmth of the friendship, and the following letter
shows that he was already emancipating himself from
the thraldom of that political school in which he had
been brought up, and that even King George IV.
was to him no longer such an impeccable being as in
the simplicity of boyhood he had once believed him
to be.

Christ Church, Oxford : June 15th, 1820.

My dearest Mother,—I have to entreat your forgiveness,
and my father's, for not having viewed the subject, which
I certainly did not, in the same manner in which you have
done ; and, though with the deepest and most acute sorrow, I willingly give up that to which for two long years
Wood and myself have fondly looked ; a meeting in June.
But, I wish you to understand, I give it up on policy, not
on principle ; for you tell me that I must not let my feelings overcome my principles.   But what are, and (I appeal
to you) ever have been, my principles ?   Certainly to love
my friend ten thousand times better than my king : and a
friend too, whom I think to be one of the cleverest, I know
to be one of the best, and most pure in mind, of human
beings, before a king of whose purity and virtue (though I
yield to no one in loyalty and gratitude to him) I would
not wish to speak.   But I see thoroughly the impolity of
it, though it struck me not before ; and I yield to your
superior judgment without a murmur.   I like consistency
in politics, as in every thing else, and surely Alderman
Wood may do the same.   For years he has supported the
Queen : and although he may have given her bad advice,
and we may lament it, we surely are not called upon to
abuse and insult him, as many papers have most illiberally
done.   I am not his advocate, and I agree not in his
politics ; but as I abhor the Opposition when they charge
every action of the Minister to corruption, so in common
justice, I blame his advocates, when they call that man a

rascal, who (with views never proved to be wrong) acts injudiciously. I have long determined never to meddle with politics and, by tying myself to a party, barter my liberty. We live in dangerous times ; there are revolutions all over the world, and doubtless England will suffer in her turn. It will therefore be my object in life to be friends with all—Tory, or ultra-Whig, or Radical. So may I live, in virtuous ease, like Atticus of old ; and surely his life was happier than Cicero's ; and, moreover, he had the privilege of dying in his bed, while Cicero fell a victim to the prevailing party.

I am of that disposition that I cannot live happily without a friend ; my chief discomfort here has been the want of the presence of one. The society of many, I neither seek nor like ; but that of one, who will be as devoted to me, as I to him, is the pleasure of life, and such a friend, for nearly eight years, have I found in Wood. And thus, though I will submit to almost anything, I cannot desert him who has ever been faithful to me, the only one person (out of my family) whom in this world I have found so. I know, my dear father and mother, you never would desire it, and I freely confess I would much, much sooner see the King hurled headlong from his throne, which God forbid, than act in such a manner. I willingly forego a long, long anticipated pleasure, on policy not on principle. It is for this reason and this only, viz. that he is my father's friend, that I like the King. If such had not been the case, I should not much have admired his character.

I remain, my dearest Mother,

Your most affectionate, attached, and grateful Son,

W. F. HOOK.

It was very probably owing to the bitter disappointment caused by the prohibition of this long desired meeting with his friend, joined to his increasing repugnance to Oxford life and studies, that he conceived about this time a very singular project, that of offering himself for the situation of second master in a school at Enniskillen in Ireland, which he had seen advertised as vacant. In a long letter to his parents he dilates on the advantages of this scheme. The salary was 240*l.* a year, which would be wealth to him and would make him independent of them ; then he should take a quiet curacy in addition, study the habits of the Irish, become editor of some country journal and raise the tone of the local press : he would have leisure for pursuing his favourite studies, and executing his favourite design of bringing out a new edition of the sonnets of Shakspeare. In short, the unpleasant state of politics, and the degenerate state of the theatre, which he considered the disgrace of England at the present time, made him long to escape into a serene atmosphere of reverie and study all his own. I have not found any reply to this curious proposal or any further allusion to it in his own letters ; yet he was clearly very much in earnest about it at the moment.

The vigilance with which he continued to watch the condition of the stage in his jealous anxiety lest injustice should be done to his beloved Shakspeare, was intense. ' I am waiting,' he writes (March 1821), 'anxiously for the arrival of the newspapers to learn how Richard III. succeeded last night. Upon this depends everything to me. If the master spirits of a better age are once more to tread our stage, England will gain more true glory than she has done from all the victories of Wellington ; but if she refuses them she will be a degraded nation and a fit subject for the speculation of the Radicals.'

Next to Shakspeare there was no author whom he read at that time with keener relish than Walter Scott. He writes in several letters with enthusiasm of ' Kenilworth ' which had recently come out. Pilgrimages were being daily made to Cumnor from Oxford, and a subscription list had been set on foot to present the landlord of the ' Sun ' with the sign of the Bear and Ragged Staff. ' Undoubtedly,' he writes, ' " Kenilworth " is the finest poem of that " arch knave " and " mad wag " Watty Scott, and I shall not grudge my seven and sixpence to view the scene of Dudley's love and Amy's fate.' Besides the study of his favourite theological writers, he also gave considerable time to English history. He begs his father to get some copies of Malmesbury, Monmouth, and other early chroniclers, and declares that he will never again read the ' tasteless Hume.'

Greatly did he groan over the drudgery of reading for his degree during the spring of 1821 ; but that, to him, dreary season was brightened by one brilliant gleam. He put into a raffle for Boydell's illustrations of Shakspeare, and won it. His raptures of joy must be given in his own words :

Christ Church, Oxford : April 1821.

My dearest Mother,—I have only one moment to tell you some good news; I am almost intoxicated with joy. There was a raffle for Boydell's illustrations of Shakspeare, and though I could ill afford my guinea, with an almost superstitious feeling I did put in, and have just won ; it is most glorious ; if I believed in fairies, I should swear that Oberon and Titania and Puck guided my hand as I threw the dice. It is a glorious thing, bound in blue morocco;

and if I had the text, it would be worth a hundred guineas. The bookseller has offered me twelve for it, but considering the manner I have won it, it would be sacrilege to part with it. You will blame me for hazarding a guinea; but since I have won, it does not signify. When I can afford it, I shall have my Reid's Shakspeare bound to match. I once thought of making my father a present of it, because it seems too magnificent a book for me; but I cannot make up my mind to do it, because I am so desirous of having everything belonging to Shakspeare. I threw the dice with so much confidence, I was actually superstitious about it, and I am now quite drunk with joy, so that you must excuse more. With most affectionate love to my dear father, to whom I cannot give the book without he wants it very much,

I am your most affectionate Son.

W. F. HOOK.

In Easter Term, 1821, he went into the schools. He had resolved to place himself in some way under the protection of Shakspeare as his tutelary deity. He therefore took with him a small head of the poet carved out of his mulberry tree—a precious relic which he had brought from Stratford-on-Avon— to hold in his hand during *vivâ voce*; and in his paper-work he adopted a singular device which the following letter will explain, and which it appears had been a practice of old standing with him.

Christ Church, Oxford : June 1821.

My dearest Mother,—I have only time to tell you that my cares are at an end and, as you would say, my education finished. I did not take up enough books for a class, I am afraid; but I did what I did take up better than I could have expected, and was thanked and praised for my Divinity.

By the bye, I must tell you a circumstance which amused the examining masters not a little. I have had a custom of writing the name of W. Shakspeare on every paper which I think of importance, from ancient times. You will see it written at the corner of this sheet in very small letters, ˜⸝⸜⸍⸌.[1] which very few people would discover ; but it so happened that Mr. Cardwell, one of the examining masters, observed that this little Shakspeare was in all my copies, and they called me up to know if I meant it as a charm ; which I could not quite deny, and it afforded them great amusement. This I have not told to any of my acquaintance here who would think me a bit of a fool for my pains ; but the report about the University is, that I was cutting jokes with the examining masters all the time. They, however, behaved very good-naturedly to me, except this morning, when one of them, to the great amusement of all the rest, made me prove the errors of the Roman Catholics in worshipping relicks, and the folly of the Jews in wearing phylacteries ; the absurdity of superstition, and inutility of charms, all of which subjects I knew pretty well ; and this, with something about the doctrine of the Trinity, made up the whole of my examination in Divinity.

Now I must beg you not to tell this to my friends in town, but keep it to yourself, for some of them would think me an idiot ; I am afraid it will be soon spread over the University, for Cardwell seemed to think it a very good joke, and will tell it, I make no doubt. If so, I shall depart immediately from this place. It is my intention to stay here ten or twelve days, since, to my deep and unfeigned sorrow, I shall not be able to see dear Gilbert. I can come up directly if you wish it, but I shall write fully to-morrow. I shall not take my degree, I think, till just before the long vacation, when I shall return to Oxford. I am at this moment too happy to write sense. I am afraid the examining masters will think me a bit of a fool, but they showed that they thought it innocent and laughable folly. I would not, however, have yesterday over

---

[1] Facsimile of the original ' W. Shakspeare.'

again, really for a hundred pounds, poor though I am ; I
never was so miserable.

Classical honours he had neither desired nor
sought.   But there was just one prize upon which he
had set his heart : the Newdegate prize for English
verse, and he resolved to compete for it.   The
subject for 1821 was Pæstum.   'With trembling
hands,' he writes, 'and a throbbing heart have I
consigned the child of my hopes to the Registrar.'
He thought his good fortune in winning the Boydell
Shakspeare in the raffle a bad omen ; it would be
impossible to have another great piece of luck in the
same year.   And his apprehensions were fulfilled.
His lines, which have come into my hands, are
smooth, melodious, and free from the insipidity of
thought and turgidity of language which are so
common in Newdegate poems.   But the prize was
gained by the Hon. Mr. Howard, afterwards Lord
Carlisle, who also carried off the prize for Latin verse
in the same year.

His failure to obtain this prize was perhaps the
most poignant disappointment of his life.   At least
there was none on which he expressed his feelings
at the time in such inconsolable terms, although of
course the trial could not have been a very lasting
one.   'With indescribable sorrow ' (thus he writes to
his father) 'I sit down to inform you that all my
hopes of gaining distinction at Oxford are now at an
end ; I feel after all my failures that I should like a
little quiet and retirement.   I cannot pay my London
visits.'   And so he proposes to go to Whippingham,
of which his father was now rector.   The sweet air

and scenery of the Isle of Wight would restore his spirits. ' I cannot now look,' he proceeds, ' for distinction in life, but a quiet and humble one is perhaps after all the happiest. I wish you and my mother would decide for me what line I should take, and I will endeavour—may God grant with success—to perform its duties.' And in another letter, ' I long to escape from this most odious place : I am disgusted with Oxford, and my heart leaps with joy at the thought of quitting it, I might almost say, for ever.'

LETTERS FROM 1813–1821.

An Ideal Country Parsonage.

Winchester : November 7, 1813.

Dear Brother, ... I have only got to stay here two years more, though two years is no short time ; then, I suppose, I shall go to Oxford and, when I am twenty-three, be made a parson. I do not intend to be minor canon, for when I get a living I must still be minor canon ; but I intend to have a living just in such a village as ' sweet Auburn ' was before it was deserted ; but instead of ' passing rich with forty pounds a year ' I intend to have a thousand ; and I shall divide it thus : three hundred for myself, three hundred for the poor, and four hundred for books. I intend to keep a horse, tax-cart, and donkey, one man servant, and one maid servant. I intend to have a good library, and there shall be one corner which I will call Poets' Corner ; and in my grounds I intend there shall be a hill, and I shall build a sort of place like a temple at the top, that I may sit and read at the top in summer. I shall call it Mount Parnassus ; it shall be something like Grongar Hill which Dyer so well describes. I shall have

the busts of Milton, Dryden, Pope, Young, and Thomson
there.   In the morning I shall get up at seven in summer,
eight in winter, and take a walk in the garden for half an
hour ; come home to breakfast ; then I shall go to visit my
poor people, and at ten come home and write some of my
sermon ; at eleven go out riding, or driving in my tax-cart ;
at twelve take luncheon, and go to Parnassus till two ; at
three dine ; after dinner go to Parnassus, except in winter,
when I shall sit over the fire with wine on the table, reading.   At eight I shall have prayers in my private chapel,
when all those poor people who come I shall put down in
my pocket-book to be attended to.   At nine I shall go to
bed.   My library will be open to all poor people.   I shall
recommend Milton to them ; and I shall build around me
a large place like ' St. Cross ' for poor people who are too
old to work.   I shall be very glad to see my dearest
brother Bob, mamma, papa, or any of my other good
friends.   I shall always have a bed or two, not like Dr.
Wavell's, but all well aired, for my servants shall take it
by turns to sleep in them.   I shall sport tolerable dinners ;
I shall have apples, and grapes, and all fruits, and gooseberry wine and currant, and meat when my friends come.
I shall plant potatoes, and shall have a dog, a cat, some
rabbits and tame pheasants, and shall feed all young birds
that choose to come.   My sermons will be on an average
about an hour long, never more, but generally as long.   I
shall preach very good sermons for the poor people, but
not learned ones, as I do not want to be more learned.   I
shall have a pair of cotton stockings to go to dine with the
squire or charity schoolmaster.   I shall have a new coat
once in three years.   I shall have one hat and one pair
of boots.   My servant will have all my old clothes for his
livery.   I shall have a bank at the church, and be the
warden to the charity school, which must attend my private
chapel to answer the responses.   I shall have a hand
organ, and the clerk shall play it.   I intend to have a river
in my garden, and shall have written in large letters on a
bit of board, ' At Parnassus.   But mark what I areed thee,

now avaunt!' That is to say, that nobody must disturb me when in solitude at my Parnassus. I shall keep wine to give to the poor people that are sick, and shall always have plenty on table at dinner, though I shall never drink more than a glass or two at the very most, for two reasons : one, because it would not be right to drink more, and the other, because it would be too expensive. I shall often go to the public-house to see that nobody is getting drunk. My dog will dine with me, except when I have company. Perhaps if it is not too expensive I will keep a mastiff too, to guard the house, and a Newfoundland. I shall have little or nothing to be robbed of except my books, so the mastiff will live in the library. I shall have no plate, but will have pewter spoons ; perhaps I may have a few plated ones, in case I should have company. I shall write to my dear Robert, and papa and mamma often. I shall always give the clerk a Christmas-box, and they shall sing the Christmas carols from Milton. I quite forget the beginning (you must remember) ; in the middle there is, 'Thou sun, of this great world both eye and soul ; ' and there is at the beginning, speaking of God, 'To us invisible or dimly seen in these Thy lower works, yet these declare Thy goodness beyond thought and power divine.'

I shall have a moss house beside my river, and I intend that there shall be trees about it, that my dear mamma may be able to sit there when she comes. Dear Robert, you shall have the best bedroom but one when you come to see me, because papa must have the best. I shall introduce you to the schoolmaster and the squire, and one or two of the farmers ; and if grandpapa will be so kind as to come to see me, I daresay I shall be able to make up a rubber of whist. Now, dear Robert, you see how I intend to live. I shall wish you good-bye. Perhaps you may be Lord Mayor some day or other ; but I hope never to be more than a country parson. Give my best love to papa, mamma, and receive the same from

Your very affectionate Brother.

A Schoolboys' Debate.

Winchester : May 2, 1816.

My dear Mother, ... By the bye, I had an argument
of an hour and a half's duration one day on politics : I and
another of our club were the only ones against five col-
legians, all Opposition. They were very abusive of the
Prince, whom we defended most properly : we drew up the
Opposition one side of the table, my colleague and myself
on the other ; we always, except once, called each other
honourable gentlemen, but in the heat of argument, I could
not help breaking through the rule, and saying the honourable blackguard opposite, which gave great offence, and
was thought very vulgar. We at first agreed to conduct our
debates as in the House of Commons, but I was the first
who arose, and they declared (though it did not seem so
to me) that I spoke for half an hour ; so they thought I
should go on all night, and made it fair that we might
talk as we chose, which brought us down to common
argument. There were many boys standing round who were
very much amused with our earnestness, but particularly
with mine, for one of the fellows opposite asking, Can any
one who admires the ministers ever so much, say that the
Prince is not a fat, disgusting, and sinful, drunken beast ? I
cried out so loud that Mr. Williams, who was at the bottom
of the school, sent for me for making a noise, and I with
difficulty got off an imposition. As we went on, I asserted
that he did not drink at all ; for grandpapa told me he did
not, but as I did not feel at liberty to mention his name,
my assertion went as nothing, and one member of the
Opposition bench quoted Bloomberg that he did drink
manfully, and does so still. Now will you ask grandpapa if
I may use his name next time we meet, which may be, by
the bye, to-day in school as we have nothing to do at that
time, but talk or read ; but I must tell you who I was
compared to—no less than Mr. Pitt, while my colleague
was Mr. Canning. The leader of the party was Mr. Fox,

because, owing to the violence of his action, he broke the boards of one of my friend's books. I would not trouble you with this, but that I want to get leave to quote grandpapa, if they dare to touch on that head again. I was laughed at much, and it put me in a great passion, for while I was praising my Lord Castlereagh, one of the fellows asked me if I thought with papa on the Catholic question, for they remember his sermon on that head, I was glad to find ; I answered in the affirmative, and they triumphed much, in saying that Lord Castlereagh did not. Will you tell me how to defend the noble Lord ? . . . .

To his Brother,[1] 1816—*Lord Chesterfield's Letters—The Spectator—Sam. Johnson—Poetical Justice.*

My dear Robert,—You say you have of late been reading Lord Chesterfield ; he is an author of whom I am enabled to judge only by extracts that I have met by chance, and by quotations that I have found from other authors, but from what I have seen, he is very far from being a proper author for you to waste much time in studying, far from it ; indeed, I should think that my mother would have a very reasonable objection to your reading it, and if, as you say, you have read it and cannot unread it, nevertheless, I am far from wishing you to pay so much attention to it as will, and must naturally, be the case in translating it from the French : he seems a mean, worldly, despicable nobleman, and he seems to instruct a person in a kind of egotism. Now if I were to advise you what to read, I should propose the ' Spectator ; ' that would not only exercise you in French, but would likewise improve your English style, for the style of the amiable Addison is truly divine, and were the Gods to talk English, it would without doubt be the English of Addison ; you would by that be able to see the whims and fancies and foibles of the last century, and see what we have improved, what corrupted. You would be able when you read Milton, to understand him, too, better by far after the annotations of the amiable,

[1] Then in a house of business in Holland.

learned, and unpedantic Addison, whom I like far better
than Sam Johnson, who, though he was of good men
perhaps the very best, cannot have so much said of him as
a critic; a sound moralist he was, but far, very far, from
being a good critic. You have heard him extolled, so have
I, not as the greatest moralist and wisest of the men of
England, but as a superior critic. I must dissent from the
general opinion, and as I write to you, I doubt not but you
will excuse a boy objecting to the opinions of the learned,
but I have had a close intimacy with the Doctor, and tell you
that I think he is (and it is the greatest fault in a critic)
most partial ; witness the criticisms on Milton, Gray, and,
on the other hand, the unfortunate but unprincipled Savage.
From his criticisms on our greatest poets, he seems not to
have been able to feel any pleasure in the higher flights of
poetry, and when he looks at verses on lesser subjects, on
love, &c., he blames them for being unnatural, if they
happen to mention a heathen god, not perhaps as a deity,
but as a personification ; this he does with our poet
Hammond, who seems to be a very deserving bard, being
the only person who has succeeded in the way of Ovid and
Tibullus. But these are his lesser faults ; as a critic in the
higher flights, he was rigid, most rigid. If poor Horace
was to have such a critic, one might well cry, 'Alack, poor
Horace!' He believed in the divine right of kings—abominable! but he insists on poetical justice—worse and worse!
In dear Shakspeare's 'Lear,' he quarrels with the 'Spectator,' who blames the alteration, and making of the piece
end happy. May I ask what can be more unnatural and
improbable than justice as administered in poetry ? does
the good man always go on well in this world? would not
everything then be good, and shall then the poet of
nature forget to be natural? Heaven forbid ! if this should
be debated in the House of Commons, and my Lord
Castlereagh—should even that great, that wonderful man
defend it with his Pitt-like eloquence, I would sit on the
opposite benches.

Anxiety to hear from his Brother.

Winchester : May 12, 1816.

My dear Robert,—It is so long since any letter has
been received from you, that I cannot refrain from writing,
if it is only to ask and intreat you to write to us soon, to
me, or to some other branch of the family. Any letter
received from you, or known by me to have lately been
received from you, would greatly ease my heart, for I
must own to you that I am most excessively uneasy about
you ; the length of time that has expired since you last
wrote is prodigious—write soon, I pray you—and your last
letter told us of your having an asthma, so that I think
there is ample room for my being uneasy about you. I hope
to goodness that before you read this I shall have heard
from you, or of you, my most darling brother. I did not
intend writing to you before I heard of you, at first, but
now I must write to beg you not to allow us to be any
more uneasy about you. To-day is a holiday, and I have
leave out to your friend, Mr. Woodburn, for papa and
mamma ('Alack the day!') are going from hence about
the visitation business ; you can easily guess how very and
truly unpleasant it is to me to lose their society. I should,
I trust, be more happy than I am to-day, for I am at
present in a low state, feeling very uncomfortable for more
reasons than one, but what always comes topmost to my
soul is the anxiety I feel on your account, my dearest
Robert ; I think it will do me good having leave out, it
will raise my spirits. I was forced to stop a moment, for
names have been just called in the hall to my great detri-
ment, for my stupid fool of a fag left my boiler in the
way, and Gabell has taken it as usual ; he took all my mess
things away the other day, and now the boilers, but I shall
not lick Elliot (whom you remember), for he is my fag.
I should have been bankrupt had it not been for the
enormous goodness of my most beloved mother ; for she

made me a present of a pound when she went away, of which, when I pay for this boiler, I shall have only six shillings left, and that I must pay for a cheese, as I am 'in course' with that to-night for the rest of the half-year.   It is really such nonsense of Gabell, allowing boys to have things, and taking them away when he finds them ; but don't mention this in your letters, for this one I mean to seal with my own arms, which my most dearest mother has presented me with.   I have shown it to most fellows here, and they all admire it so much, you cannot think, so that it won't be seen and read, for I should not like them to know of my extravagance, and by the time I want some more very urgently, I shall beg for an advance of my holiday money, which mamma is always kind enough to give me.   You must mind to admire my seal, it is most beautiful, and the impression is magnificent.

Would to heaven that the time was come when I am to see you dearest, most beloved Robert again ; pray, pray write, I long so much to hear from you, and tell me how your asthma is.   If you knew the agony of mind which I now feel on your account, my sweet Robert, you would not delay an instant.   You will think me a fool, but you cannot do so more than I myself do, on that account, but do what I will, the most horrid ideas haunt me in every place, so that I may justly feel desirous of hearing of you or from you, and that too, soon.   Now I shall leave off writing. With my very best love to you, and praying you to write soon,

I shall remain, most dear and darling Robert, upon my honour, your most dotingly affectionate Brother.

Christ Church, Oxford : February 1821.

My dear Sister,—To so devoted an admirer of the fair sex, as you know I am, and every true and loyal knight must needs be, the letter of 'your naughtiness' was of course most acceptable, but I will confess that I shall find some difficulty in endeavouring to answer it, since its subject was nearly uniform, and that subject being my own praise, I am in modesty bound to be silent thereon. I beg leave, however, to state that though you should certainly have the most dutiful respect and veneration for the character of your elder brother, yet there is no necessity to make it the subject of your letters to him or of your conversations with anybody else, so that, in future I shall hope to hear more of papa and mamma, and less of myself; and indeed I shall have no very great objection to hear something about yourself (though you are nobody), and to know whether you are improving in your studies, and are more or less naughty than you were a few weeks ago. You must beg mamma to let you read the account of our good King's reception at the theatres. I have just been reading it, and it has rejoiced me so much that it has given me a headache, or I am not quite sure that you would receive this letter. It was one of the most glorious receptions, as represented in the new 'Times,' of which I have read or heard. There are, however, one or two points that have grieved me, but on which I will not dwell here.

You may nevertheless tell my father that the King of England gave his royal sanction to, and manifested his royal approbation of the vile interpolations which disfigure the 'Twelfth Night' as now performed.

This is so unworthy George IV. that I quit the subject. I like your idea of keeping my letters to show my grandchildren, they will no doubt form a fine red-headed family; and I hope that I shall be able to exhort them to follow the good example of their Aunt Georgiana. But if you are an old maid, I give you notice beforehand, that I will not permit you to enter into my house, with a whole aviary on your shoulders, and a pack of dogs of all sorts and sizes at your heels. And now my dear Demoiselle, your true faithful Sir Walter of the fiery plume has neither time nor inclination to write any more, but having assured you how highly I appreciate the honour of having opened a correspondence with the fair sex, and having desired you to give my most devoted love to my dear father and mother, I beg you to

Believe me to be, my dear Miss Hook.

Your most attached and very affectionate Brother,

W. F. Hook.

CHAPTER II.

ORDINATION. LIFE AT WHIPPINGHAM.
A.D. 1821–1826.

IT had been Sir Walter Farquhar's wish that his grandson should study for the Bar : but it was wisely determined that he should be allowed to choose his own profession after he had taken his degree ; and in the course of the summer of 1821 he declared his fixed and unalterable desire to enter holy orders.

He went to London in July and witnessed the coronation of George IV., but party spirit ran so high in reference to the Queen's case that he was not permitted by his father to meet his friend Wood ; a privation to which he submitted, but with resentment which he did not attempt to conceal. ' I lament,' he writes, ' that party spirit has now come to such a height that private intercourse between friends must be sacrificed to political feeling. It does not speak well for the times, and I could bring many instances to prove that there is no necessity for friends to part on account of diversity in their political sentiments ; though that of Addison and Steele will suffice.'

In fact his disappointment on account of his failure as he called it at Oxford, his dissatisfaction with the tone of politics and with the state of the

English drama, and the continued prohibition of intercourse with his friend, all concurred to make him turn with a sense of relief from the world, especially the world of London, to quiet preparation for holy orders in the retirement of his father's rectory in the Isle of Wight. In the latter part of the summer the curacy of Whippingham became vacant, and his father was anxious that he should fill the situation and be ordained without delay. He was examined by his father and privately ordained by the Bishop of Hereford, who was also Warden of Winchester, in the chapel of the college on September 30, and preached his first sermon in the Parish Church of Whippingham on the following Sunday.

And now being no longer shackled and fretted by uncongenial studies, he threw the whole force of his intellect and affections into the work to which he had been called. While his well-beloved poets and writers of fiction were still the companions of his leisure hours, theology and ecclesiastical history occupied the foremost place in his attention. He had long delighted in these subjects, and he now pursued the study of them with increased ardour, because he felt it to be his duty as well as his pleasure. But although everyone who knew him intimately, believed, notwithstanding the comparative failure of his career at school and college, that his abilities were of no common order, probably no one had discerned the prodigious capacity for study and the immense practical energy which were to be manifested as soon as they had got a fair field for action. Probably also few were aware what a deep

fund of tender, genial sympathy there was in one
who had hitherto lived rather after the manner of a
shy recluse, and few could have then foreseen what
a spell he would henceforth exercise over the hearts
of those who were confided to his pastoral care.

I propose to make a brief sketch of his character
and manner of life during the six years of his curacy
at Whippingham, reserving for a more particular
account the only episodes of importance in this quiet
period ; one of which was also the first event that
brought him into public notice.

His father being Archdeacon of Huntingdon and
Canon of Winchester, as well as a Royal Chaplain,
fond also of London society, a keen politician and
writer of political pamphlets, was frequently absent
from Whippingham, and when he was there seldom
could take much part in parochial duty from increasing ill-health and infirmity.   His son, therefore, was
practically curate in charge, and was often the only
inmate of the rectory for weeks or months together.
He seems thoroughly to have enjoyed his seclusion
and independence, although he had no lack of society
if he wished it, being always a welcome guest at many
houses, more especially Northwood, the residence of
Mr. Ward, near West Cowes, and Norris Castle, the
abode at that time of Lord Henry Seymour.   Quiet
English country scenery had always a peculiar charm
for him, and he enjoyed it to the full in the Isle of
Wight.   An early bathe in the Medina which flows
at the foot of the hill on which the rectory stands,
study from early morning till the beginning of the
afternoon, visits to his flock, evenings spent with his
kind and pleasant neighbours or in the society of his

fondly beloved Shakspeare or Walter Scott or Miss
Austen, nocturnal rambles on soft summer nights
sometimes prolonged till nearly dawn to listen to
the nightingale and watch the silvery light of the
moon upon the river or the sea; these made up the
ordinary incidents of his daily life, a strange con-
trast in its calm and sweet repose to the years of
turmoil and excitement in great smoky cities which
were in store for him. Often and often in those
later years, as will be seen, did he pine for the tranquillity of his Whippingham days, and look forward
to the time when he might be able to retire to some
peaceful home in or near the Isle of Wight. And
one great reason of his contentment in old age with
the Deanery of Chichester was its proximity to the
island which he loved so well.

A few extracts from his letters at this time will
best illustrate the foregoing remarks. Writing to
his mother from Oxford where he was staying for a
while to attend Lloyd's Divinity Lectures before
taking priest's orders, he says, ' My bowels yearn
for our lovely island. To peace and quiet, to the
parish that I love and the studies I delight in, to
pursuits which are congenial to my soul and to that
retirement for which I am best adapted, to divinity,
to Shakspeare and the Muse, to green fields instead
of dirty streets, to the calm of the country instead of
the noise of the town, to the love of my simple flock
instead of the heartlessness of the world, I shall
return with increased joy and redoubled zest, there
to lay deep the foundations for future distinction in
the vocation to which I am heart and soul devoted.'

Although he was now sociable on the whole in

his disposition, yet at times the impulse to spend
part of his day alone with no society but that of his
beloved poets came upon him with a force curiously
sudden and irresistible.   In a letter dated March
1823 he describes how he started one evening to
dine at Northwood 'in my best hosen, best trousers,
and best coat; but when I had walked half-way to
Cowes it occurred to me that it would be much
preferable to return to my own fire-side and read
Shakspeare, which I accordingly did ; and I had
the satisfaction of hearing the rain come down in
torrents just about the time I should have been
walking home after my dinner.'

Those who know the Isle of Wight will recognise
in the following letters a very fresh and life-like
description of the sweet sunny days in spring, and
the blustering rainy south-westers, for which the
climate there even in summer is equally notorious.

June 21, 1824.—'I arrived here cold and chilly
on Friday night at a house where I was not expected.   Next day I woke early, intending to enjoy
the delights of the country, but found it pouring in
torrents ; I therefore tried to go to sleep, but failed.
I know not anything more miserable than my condition that day : without any pursuit, all around dull,
dark, and dismal, a strong south-wester howling and
the pattering of the rain incessant.   I was a perfect
"energumen," if being possessed with "*blue* devils"
as well as others entitle one to the name, and would
have thanked our Bishop most heartily had he been
at hand to exorcise me.   Raining as it did, I was
forced to go out in self-defence.   I found the farmers
grumbling because of the hay lately cut, and the

labourers surly and wet, the matrons coming from
market sulky and the maidens cross, the invalids
doubly ill, and all the parish out of humour. When
we do have bad weather in the island I verily believe
that it is worse than anywhere else in the whole
world. But now I have hit upon my line of reading,
and it may blow tempests and rain cats and dogs for
all I care.'

May 2, 1822.

My dearest Mother, ... This is not Whippingham,
it is Paradise ; and if you wish to form any idea of what it
now is, dismiss all recollection of it from your thoughts,
and read all the fine descriptions of gardens that you meet
with in the poets, particularly in Shakspeare and Spenser ;
and then you may be able to form some (though a very
slight) idea of what it is. I think all the birds in England
are on a visit to the island—at least I will be bound to say
that you never heard such a choir as we have here. One
feels all this the more by living alone ; and, as I have no
one else to talk to, and Heaven forbid that I should have
any, I may truly say with my friend the duke that I find
'tongues in trees, books in the running brooks, sermons in
stones, and good in everything.' Uncle Theodore would
say that it would be more convenient if I could take the
last assertion but one in a more literal sense. But really,
you cannot think what an interest I take in inanimate
Nature, and animate too. I begin almost sometimes to
think that I shall grow sentimental, which is the very last
thing I desire, and perhaps be inclined ere long 'to hail
the gooseberry bushes,' which I trust you have already
done at Sydenham. I generally take a stroll in the neighbouring fields about five o'clock, and return home to dinner
between seven and eight ; and then read till about ten or
eleven, when I go out again, and flirt with the moon and
listen to the nightingale till one or two ; the moon is on
the water about that time. Alas, yesterday morning I
was wandering close to the Nashes (where there is a night-

ingale) between one and two o'clock, but never a youth or a lass did I meet going to the woods a-Maying; all was as still and silent as ever. And yesterday I could not resist the temptation of galloping over the country in quest of a Maypole, but not one was to be found; and I must confess, with all my attachment to the island, I could not conceive a place where there is less reverence for old customs, less of what you may call rural and poetic feelings in the peasantry, than there is here. There never was such weather as this is since the days of Dan Chaucer, and I do sincerely hope it may last. I was made to live alone; and certainly if one can converse with trees and brooks and stones, they must be the most pleasant companions, because they cannot thwart you, dispute with you, or quarrel with you. And hence I am miserable at the intended visit of Duncomb and Pollen; at least, if it continues fine like this; however, if they come, why then we must do as well as we can. Did you ever read 'Pride and Prejudice'? I sent for it a few weeks ago when I had a cold, which stuffed up my nose and caused a ringing in my ears, and the weather was rainy, so that I was too poorly to read anything serious, and not in a humour for poetry. It amused me very much; it is a regular gossip throughout. I found myself in a pleasant family circle, and listened to the gossip without having the trouble of joining in it; and at last became so interested in their welfare that the mamma herself could not have been more anxious about marrying her daughters than I was. I loved Lizzie; but I should have married Jane if I had had my choice. Altogether, for a bad gloomy day, and with a cold about one, it is a very good kind of book; but as to reading it in such weather as this, and in the merry month of May, it would be not only absurd, but impossible. Indeed, I suppose all the world, except people of fashion and business, are reading poetry and nothing else, without it is divinity.

Believe me,

Your most affectionate Son.

His solitude at the Rectory was relieved by the periodical visits of his parents and sister, and occasionally of his aunt, Miss Farquhar—Aunt Eliza as she was called, who seems to have been quite a type of the old maiden aunt of a family—very kind, but rather exacting, and somewhat overwhelming in her ecstatic affection and fussy anxiety for every member of the family ; qualities which could not fail to provoke playful sallies of humour from her nephew. The following letter written during his mother's convalescence after a severe illness in December 1824, puts the worthy aunt completely before us :

I have no news whatever to tell you. Aunt Eliza was a little disgusted at my not bringing back particulars enough concerning you. Let Georgiana therefore inform us how many hours you usually sleep, how much pheasant you generally eat, and whether Lady Charlotte's society does not *particularly*, in a kind of indescribable *peculiar* way, suit you. She must tell us also whether you read, and what you read, and whether you feel exhausted after reading, as is sometimes the case, or whether, as is also sometimes the case, you do *not* feel exhausted. Because, if you do *not* feel exhausted, it will do you good ; but if you *do* feel exhausted, Aunt E. ' *hopes to God* ' that my father will prevent your reading too much. Aunt E. will not believe me when I tell her that you do not like to read. She says it is all very well for me to say so, or even for you, but with your *peculiar* temperament she knows that it is impossible. In short, Georgiana must send us more particulars.

P.S. Quarter past three o'clock.—Tell Georgiana that I am happy in knowing she will write a most beautiful hand. Aunt Eliza can perceive it even now; there were some letters and some words quite perfect in her last note.

Aunt E. descanted on it for three-quarters of an hour 'by Shrewsbury clock' yesterday, and was quite angry with me, even to the stamping of stick authoritatively on the floor, when I was rather sceptical.

P.S.—I open my note once more to say that Aunt E. says it is only just three, not a quarter past.

Some time after this, when his mother was still in delicate health, he accompanied her on the journey from Whippingham to London. East Cowes, the place of embarkation for the main land, is about two miles distant from Whippingham, and whilst waiting for the boat the following report of their progress was sent back to the anxious aunt: words underlined after her own style.

Most confidential.

My dearest Aunt,—As it will be satisfactory to you to know how we are proceeding on our journey, I cannot resist the temptation of sending you word that we have advanced as far as Cowes most prosperously. My dearest, most beloved mother has borne the journey very well indeed.

Your most devotedly, adoringly affectionate Nephew.

Besides this playful kind of humour which was an essential part of his nature, and which, as will be seen, was constantly bubbling up and overflowing into all the action of his life, he at this time still practised many of the more whimsical kind of frolics which, as he mentions in one of his letters transcribed above, he had invented for his own amusement. His sister, who naturally came in for a full share of his raillery and banter, and whom he frequently addressed with mock solemnity as

> Demoiselle buxom, blithe, and debonair,
> With a naughty look and auburn hair,

used often to accompany him in his walks and rides. Now and then he would suddenly dart from her side, make a furious rush at trees or hedges and thrash them with tremendous violence, pretending that they were enemies.

As his sportive freaks were always of the most innocent and childlike character—the mere exuberance of animal spirits, so also his jocosity was now and always utterly free alike from coarseness and sarcasm or satire; it never jarred either with the amiability or earnest piety of his character, but blended itself with these qualities and enhanced their charms.

> His mirth was the pure spirit of various wit,
> But never did his God or friend forget.

And this absence of discord in his character makes it the more easy to turn from the contemplation of him in his lighter moods to the consideration of that serious work as a pastor and a student to which he was now heart and soul devoted. The parish of Whippingham was at that time very extensive, and included East Cowes about two miles distant from the Rectory and Parish Church, containing a poor maritime population. No direct and separate provision for ministering to the spiritual wants of these people had been made. Many lived in a condition of godless ignorance; a few who were more religiously disposed attended their parish church sometimes in the morning, and very commonly some dissenting chapel in the evening. Mr. Hook obtained the use of a large sail loft in which he held an evening service on Sundays, and catechised the children. These services were very largely attended by sailors, fishermen, and other poor people, and were productive of excellent results. When he was paying a visit to Whippingham after he had become Dean of Chichester, and was walking with the present Rector, Canon Prothero, about his old parish, an aged man came up and anxiously enquired if he remembered him. He said he did, and afterwards told the Rector that the man was one who had been a loose liver in his youth, but had been induced to attend the Sunday evening services in the sail loft and had become an altered character.

Any man who has made the experiment will be ready to acknowledge that it is no small labour after two full services in one church to walk two miles to conduct a third service in another place, and then to walk home; and this not once or twice on special occasions, but every Sunday and all the year round. The number of communicants also increased so largely during his administration that on great festivals the intervals between his services on Sundays were very short. In May 1825, he writes, ' On Whitsun Day I was properly worked. We had a very fine attendance at the Altar. I was not out of church till a quarter to three o'clock; went in again at three; had five christenings and a funeral, and was not out till five, when I had to start immediately to be in time for the school at East Cowes at six, from which I was not released till eight.'

His zeal, however, was well supported by physical strength to match it, and he seldom, if ever, complained of fatigue.   One very hot evening, however, in June 1825, he arrived at Northwood rather weary and very hot after his service in the sail loft.   His friend, Lord Henry Seymour, happened to be there and proposed that a chapel of ease should be built at East Cowes ; a practical suggestion which not long after, though not in Mr. Hook's time, was carried into effect.

As he always looked back to Whippingham with gratitude for the leisure which it had afforded him to lay deep the foundation of his theological and historical learning, so also did he regard his residence there as the period in which, more than in any other, he had acquired the pastoral tone of his mind and formed the pastoral habits of his life. When he was not in his study he was constantly engaged in visiting his people, and the parish, though extensive, was not so large as to prevent his becoming in this way the intimate friend of every member of his flock.   His power of sympathy, the most indispensable qualification of a successful pastor, was in this manner continually being drawn out and strengthened, and became then and ever afterwards a principal, if not *the* principal, source of his extraordinary influence over the hearts of those amongst whom he ministered.   It was his belief that the larger scale on which work has to be carried on in towns, the multiplicity of business in which town clergy are involved, and the consequent distraction of their energy and sympathy into a variety of channels, rendered a town parish an unfavourable school for learning the duties of the pastoral vocation. ' I say without hesitation,' he writes long after he had become Vicar of Leeds, ' that the very worst training a man can have is that which he receives if appointed early in life to a town parish. The strong pastoral feeling is generated in the country, and I attribute what little success I have had entirely to my country breeding.' Two or three extracts from his letters written during the Whippingham period will suffice to show how completely he had learned in the most genuine and literal sense to identify himself with the joys and sorrows of his people, to rejoice with them that rejoiced, and to weep with them that wept. The first is to his mother in December 1824.

' Your permission and recommendation to have the feast on Christmas Day in the barn is in every respect agreeable to me. The children will think more of it—and if it had been given at the school the parents would have thought that it was done by subscription, and have claimed as a right what they ought to receive as a favour. It really was gratifying to see the many happy faces which were there yesterday when I gave notice of our intentions, and it was comical to see the doubtful ones of those who were not quite sure but they had exceeded the number prescribed of bad tickets. I doubt very much whether the children enjoy the thoughts of it more than myself. I wish to heaven we could feed the whole parish, and that every day.'

In like manner, attendance at a village club dinner, which to so many clergy is a vexatious and irksome business, was to him a real pleasure. ' On Easter Monday it would sadly grieve me not to

preach to the club and dine with them. It is one
of the days I enjoy most in the whole year.'

Then to take the other side of sympathy : the
following is a specimen how thoroughly he entered
into the trouble of others as if it was his own, and
how his affection for his people and theirs for him
had its root in the discharge of his pastoral duty
amongst them ; so that it was essentially the love of
a pastor for his flock and of a flock for their pastor.
'The Tassels are going to Bideford ; they start to-
night. You cannot think how sorry I feel at parting
with them, for I had trained both of them for Holy
Communion, and he took it for the first time on
Christmas Day, and she on Whitsun Day : and she
was a convert of mine from the Dissenters. Poor
Tassel : he cried like a child at parting with me,
and so to keep him company I cried too.'

When he first made up his mind to take Holy
Orders he declared his intention of dedicating two
years entirely to a deep study of divinity, and to the
foundation of his style. This intention was more
than fulfilled, for he was a most industrious and
laborious student during the whole six years of his
curacy at Whippingham, laying up stores of knowledge and thought during that period which were of
incalculable value to him throughout the rest of his
life. In fact, whenever he was not visiting in his
parish he was engaged in study, and in order to
ensure complete privacy he had a little wooden hut
erected near the corner of the churchyard, in which
he used to read. He once asked his uncle Theodore
what he should call it. 'I should call it Walter'S cot,'
was the reply of the ever ready punster. In this cot

or hut he worked at his books, often as many as
nine or ten hours, sometimes rising very early and
reading on, with only the interval of breakfast, till
two or three o'clock in the afternoon. Sometimes but
more rarely he sat up late at night, but in any case
he usually spent a considerable part of the evening
as well as the morning in this retirement.

In the first year after his ordination as deacon
he appears to have read chiefly with a view
to his ordination as priest, which took place at
Christmas 1822, and also to fill his mind with
matter for sermons which for a considerable time
caused him no little anxiety and trouble. He
was indeed so exceedingly distrustful of his powers
that at one period he did not venture to preach his
own, but having written one which he preached on
behalf of some charity at Newport, and which was
much commended, he plucked up courage and
writes, May 1822, to his mother : ' I am now in such
good humour with myself that I shall take to writing
my own sermons again, for during the last two or
three months I have not dared even to attempt one.'

In 1824 he embarked on a course of reading
according to a plan of his own, and completed it in
1826. The annexed chart of this course is a singular monument of industry, when the necessary
avocations of parochial work and occasional interruption from other causes are taken into consideration.
The piles of note books also, in my possession, all
bearing date within the space of these two years, are
an evidence how steadily and solidly the work was
done.

A COURSE BEGUN BY W. F. HOOK JUNE 1824, AND FINISHED OCTOBER 1826.

Books of Reference.	The Course—Historical.	Digressions, or Works read on the different Controversies referred to in the History.
Patrick, Lowth, and Whitby, Theophylact 'Critici Sacri'; Schleusner; Cruden's 'Concordance'; Critnell's 'Concordance'; Horne's 'Introduction'; Calmet's 'Dictionary'; Jenning's 'Antiquities'; Spencer; Jahn; Lowman; Lock's 'Commonplace Book of Scripture'; Josephus' 'Antiquities'; 'Horæ Paulinæ'; Elsley and Slade; Godwin.	The Septuagint; Greek Testament; Shuckford; Prideaux; Josephus' 'Jewish Wars.'	Bishop Marsh; Bishop Jebb; Butler's 'Analogy,' and his 'Rolls Sermon'; Isidore of Pelusium; 'Kyphi Krebsius'; Pearse; Campbell; the Apostolic Fathers; Justin Martyr; Tertullian; Cyprian; Laurence's 'Lay Baptism Invalid'; Wall on Infant Baptism; Waterland and Young on Justification; Waterland; Bishop Bethel and Archbishop Laurence on Regeneration.
	Bingham's 'Antiquities'; Eusebius; Socrates; Sozomen; Theodoret; 'Evagrius Scholasticus.'*	*On the Church and Divine Institution of Episcopacy.* Hooker; Hickes's 'Constitution of the Catholic Church,' and his 'Christian Priesthood'; Hugh's Latin Preface to Chrysostom 'de Sacerdotio'; 'History of Episcopacy,' by Peter Heylin, under the name of Thomas Churchman; Bishop Hall's 'Divine Light of Episcopacy'; Archbishop Potter on Church Government; Law's Answer to Hoadley, and Lesley's Tracts, or the Scholar Armed; 'Church Considered as an Apostolical Institution,' by a Layman, published by the Society.
Du Pin's 'History of the Church,' and particularly his 'History of Ecclesiastical Writers'; Care's 'Primitive Christianity,' 'Lives of the Fathers,' &c.; Mosheim; Milner; Bishop Kaye's Tertullian; Hammond; Mede; Saye's 'Cyprianic Age	Jeremy Collier's 'History of England.' * Irenæus I was unable to procure.	*Liturgies.* Brett's 'Ancient Liturgies'; The Apostolical Constitutions; Ancient Liturgy of the Church of Jerusalem; St. Cyril's account of the same in his

'Mystagogical Catechism'; Clementine Liturgy; Liturgies of St. Mark, St. Chrysostom, and St. Basil Comber's Scholastic History of; Bennet on Precomposed Forms of Prayer; Sparrow's 'Rationale'; Comber's 'Companion to the Temple'; Wheatley; Sharp on Rubric and Canons.

Eucharist.

Johnson's Unbloody Sacrifice, Law on Waterland on; Jeremy Taylor; Mede; Skinner's Scotch Service; Waterland's 'Charges'; A Refutation of Transubstantiation, by Bishop Drummond of Edinburgh, in a Dialogue between Philalethes and Benevolus: Ridley's Protestatio in Randolph's 'Enchiridion'; Stillingfleet.

Catholic Doctrine.

Some of the Tracts of Athanasius; Bishop Gastrell in the 'Enchiridion'; Bishop Stillingfleet on Mysteries, in the 'Enchiridion'; Allix's 'Judgment of the Jewish Church'; Bishop Bull, and Burgh's 'Enquiry,' and Burton's 'Testimonies of the Ante-Nicene Fathers'; Dr. Waterland; Bishop Horsley; Archbishop Magee.

On the Holy Ghost.

Ridley; Nolan; Gregory Naz. 'De Spiritu Sancto.'

On Tradition.

Bishop Jebb's admirable Appendix to his 'Sermons'; Kaye's Tertullian; Bull's 'Defensio'; Van Mildert's 'Bampton Lectures,'

and Vindication'; Lardner; Pearson on Creed, *notes* Suicer; Lloyd's 'Church History'; Bede; Lewis's 'Life of Wickliffe'; Sleidan; Mosheim; Paolo Sarpi's 'Council of Trent'; Wordsworth's 'Biography'; Strype's 'Cranmer,' Parker, Grindal, Whitgift, 'Annals,' Foxe's 'Martyrs'; Burnet's 'History'; Bishop Lloyd's 'Formularies'; Jewel's 'Apology.'

F   N.B. Two or three of the books in the above list appear to have been added at a later date.

His primary object in following out this course was to obtain a clear and comprehensive view of the principles of the Church Catholic from the earliest times, to trace the introduction of errors into the Western Church during the period of Papal domination, and to measure the extent to which these errors were renounced by the Reformers of the sixteenth century, especially in our own country.   And as the result of his researches pursued on this historical method, he was led to the conviction which all his subsequent studies strengthened, and to which he ever held with a tenacious grasp, that the Reformed Anglican Church was a pure and apostolical branch of the Church Catholic : that she was essentially Catholic as being on all vital points of constitution, doctrine, and practice in harmony with the primitive Church, and on the other hand essentially Protestant, as opposed to the pretensions of the Papal power and to the corruption in teaching and practice of the Middle Ages.   The close of his career of study at Whippingham left him with his antipathies matured against the Romanist who would corrupt the Church, against the Puritan who would destroy it, against the Latitudinarian and Erastian who would sacrifice its principles to considerations of expediency and worldly interest.   And it was his destiny to carry on, throughout his life, a manful and almost incessant contest with these three great elements of danger to the purity and integrity of the Church of England.

After this general sketch of his life at Whippingham, into which it seemed desirable to enter in order to show how strongly and deeply the foundations of his future career, both as a pastor and an ecclesiastical historian and theologian, were laid, it only remains to relate in a few words the two incidents by which alone the calm seclusion of this period was interrupted.

His father had been appointed to preach at Newport, the chief town in the Isle of Wight, on the occasion of the Bishop of Winchester's visitation in the summer of 1822 ; but as the time approached he began to shrink from the exertion owing to the feeble state of his health. He determined to propose his son as his substitute, to the no small dismay of the young man, who, as has been seen, was extremely diffident of his powers of composition if not of delivery at this time, and who was as yet only in deacon's orders. Remonstrances, however, were in vain : the Bishop gave his consent ; the young deacon set about his task with the energy and perseverance which always distinguished him in a case of necessity or duty. July 2 arrived. The Bishop (Tomline) passed the night at the rectory, and on the following morning Mrs. Hook, full of maternal anxiety, drove him to Newport in her pony chaise.

The excellence of the sermon in itself, the perfection of the young preacher's utterance, and the musical tones of his voice made a very great impression upon all who heard him. The Bishop was especially warm in his praise of it, and made an exception to a rule from which he said he very rarely departed in requesting that it should be printed.[1]

---

[1] It may now be found in vol. i. of the *Church and her Ordinances,* a selection of Dr. Hook's sermons recently edited by his son, Rev. Walter Hook, Rector of Porlock, published by Bentley and Son.

The sermon is entitled 'The peculiar character of the Church of England independently of its connexion with the State.' A certain stiffness and formality of style betray the youth of the author and the painfulness and care with which he wrote at this time; but the argument is neither crude nor feeble. It is sustained with the confidence of one who feels sure of his ground and sees his way. That it is the duty of Englishmen to belong to the Church, not because it is established but because it is a pure branch of the Church Catholic; that such a Church can exist in purity and vigour under any form of government, either severed from the state or in alliance with it; that the continental Reformers in their intemperate zeal founded new churches, whereas the English only cleansed and repaired the superstructure, leaving the old foundations intact; that many of the leading foreign Reformers became as dogmatic and exacting as popes, whereas in England individuals, however eminent, had not assumed any such overbearing authority; that the most dangerous enemies to the Church were still, and always had been, the conforming Puritans, men who adhered to the form but rejected the spirit of the institution, who, in the words of South, 'live by the altar, but turn their back upon it; catch at the preferments of the Church, but hate the order and discipline of it:' these are the principal topics of his discourse. These were positions which he maintained to the end of his life; and the clear and bold assertion of them at this period proves that the laborious plan of study on which he was about to enter did but deepen convictions at which by previous reading he

had already arrived. When the sermon was published, the congratulations which reached his parents
from persons well qualified to judge of its merits were
numerous and hearty. Mr. Norris, Rector of South
Hackney, writes :

' I can only express my thankfulness that in a day
of rebuke and of blasphemy, when Gebal and Ammon
and Amalek, and the confederation of aliens, are setting
the battle in array against the Church, there are men
rising up and enlisted under her banner who have so
eminently qualified themselves for her defence. The
sketch taken of the important subject is a most
masterly one : indeed I cannot conceive of one more
masterly within the same compass . . . . I never
passed half an hour so much to my satisfaction as
that of which I am now detailing to you the impression.'

The second episode in the Whippingham period,
occurring near the close of it, was a matter of much
more importance.

An old friend of his father's, Dr. Luscombe, who
had once kept the school at Hertford in which, as has
been related, Walter and his brother Robert began
their education, had been resident for five years in
France, engaged in tuition from 1820 to 1825. It
was reckoned that about fifty thousand English were
then sojourning in that country; but the supply of
clergy and places of worship for such as belonged to
the Church of England was extremely inadequate ;
they were not licensed or subject to any regular
supervision, much laxity of practice prevailed, and
young people grew up without receiving the rite of
Confirmation. It appeared to Dr. Luscombe that

some recognised, authorised bond of union was highly desirable to hold together these scattered congregations, and keep them true to the principles of the Church of their mother country. Such a tie he conceived might be found in the appointment of a bishop, or at least an archdeacon, for the express purpose of overlooking and organising the clergy and their flocks. He consulted his friends in England on the subject as early as the year 1821, and there were none of them who entered so warmly into the project as Archdeacon Hook and his son.

It was at first thought that the design might be effected by the appointment of a suffragan to the Bishop of London, to whose spiritual jurisdiction all British residents on the Continent were nominally subject. Dr. Howley, then Bishop of London, and other prelates, as well as Mr. Peel and Mr. Canning, the Home and Foreign Secretaries of State, were consulted, who after much deliberation and correspondence expressed themselves adverse to the proposal. They entertained fears that the sending of a bishop by the Established Church of England to minister in France might be regarded by the Government of that country as an unwarrantable intrusion, and occasion jealousies and suspicions, if not difficulties of a more serious kind. The project accordingly languished and seemed likely to be abandoned. But meanwhile the young curate of Whippingham had been following out a line of study which, as we have seen, led him to discern clearly and to value deeply the essential principles of the Church independently of any connexion with the State. He had consequently learned to take a peculiar interest in the disestablished Church of Scotland, and the unestablished Church in America. In the former his interest had been more especially excited by a brief account of it in the memoirs of William Stevens, Esq., written by Judge Allan Parke, a friend of his father's, by whose advice he proceeded to read Skinner's ' Ecclesiastical History ' and the ' Annals of Scottish Episcopacy.'

The past sufferings and the present poverty and obscurity of the Scottish Church kindled in him feelings of the tenderest compassion ; its purity and zeal, feelings of the warmest admiration and respect. Suddenly it occurred to his mind that this despised and insignificant branch of the Church Catholic might execute the design to which the Church of England, hampered by its connexion with the State, had not dared to put its hand. Not only would a measure which he considered most salutary be thus accomplished, but also a visible proof would be supplied of the vital power of a true branch, however small, of the Reformed Catholic Church, and of the thread of unity which tied all such branches together. As by the consecration of Bishop Seabury, the first American Bishop, in 1784, the little Church of Scotland had become the parent of a large and flourishing Church in the New World, so he trusted she might propagate another on the European continent. A request was therefore forwarded at his suggestion to Dr. David Low, Bishop of Ross and Argyle, that he would sound the judgment of his brother bishops on the subject. After much correspondence lasting over several months, and relating chiefly to the question whether an election on the part of the English clergy in France should be required, and also how far it would be prudent or gracious for the Scottish Church to send out a bishop to minister to British subjects without the direct sanction of the English Church and Government, the College of Scotch Bishops proposed to consecrate Dr. Luscombe himself as their missionary bishop to British residents on the continent of Europe : he on his part pledging himself to renounce all offers of preferment in England. Intimations were received from the Archbishop of Canterbury, and Mr. Peel and Mr. Canning, that no obstacles would be raised by the Church or Government in England to this plan. Sunday, March 20, 1825, was fixed for the consecration, which was to take place at Stirling ; and Dr. Luscombe requested his old pupil, now Curate of Whippingham, to accompany him as his chaplain and to preach the sermon.

His visit to Scotland was always regarded by him as one of the most memorable events in his life. He deeply valued the friendships which he then formed, more especially with Bishops Sandford and Low, Mr. Walker, afterwards Bishop of Edinburgh, and last but not least with the learned, warm-hearted and deeply pious Bishop Jolly, a model of primitive simplicity and poverty in manner of life, of whom Bishop Hobart the American remarked, ' Men go from the extremity of Britain to America to see the Falls of Niagara, and think themselves amply rewarded by the sight of this singular scene in nature. Had I gone from America to Aberdeen and seen nothing but Bishop Jolly as I saw him for two days, I should hold myself greatly rewarded. In our new country we have no such men, and I could not have imagined such without seeing him.'

Just as Mr. Hook was starting on his journey an offer was made of a church in Regent Street, London, or rather a request that he would become a candidate for the incumbency by the detestable plan then not uncommon of preaching in the church as a specimen of his powers. His friends and, to some extent, his parents, who wished to push him forward at a speed in excess of his inclinations, were very anxious that he should accede to the application, and even after his arrival in Scotland he was pestered with entreaties to return to London for the purpose. But he never wavered in his refusal. At the beginning of his journey to the North, then an affair of several days, he writes while still in London : ' I think that a clergyman ought to preach anywhere when he is asked, either to instruct a flock, or to assist a brother clergyman, but most decidedly *not* to show his qualifications any more than to gratify his vanity ; and with respect to London I never can fight my way in the world. If the State divorces the Church I shall have little doubt of becoming a great man in it: but I do not understand the ways of the world.' And after his arrival in Edinburgh he writes to his father with a decisiveness intended to put a stop to all further solicitations : ' I have finally and completely made up my mind to abandon all thoughts of the church in Regent Street. I am very willing and very desirous to take a high ground, but I never will do so unless I am sure that I can keep my footing at least with satisfaction to myself, if not with advantage to others. I willingly volunteered my services on the present important occasion because I had the vanity to consider myself qualified to a certain extent to fulfil it without disgrace. I do not feel myself competent for the situation offered in London. It would necessarily lead to a superficial reading for a temporary purpose, and I should be unable to enlarge that platform upon which I mean to build my hopes. Besides which I should not choose to undertake any office which would, as it were, limit my services to only a particular and inferior branch of my calling (viz. preaching). In addition to this, I have no notion of being chosen like a public singer or actor. . . . Here therefore ends this matter.'

His father indeed had been a little fascinated by the prospect of his son's abilities being displayed in London, but his more sober judgment was adverse to the step. 'Walter's advance,' he writes, 'in his pursuits is extraordinary. He is up at six o'clock every morning in this month of February and lights his own fire, and I think it would be injurious to him should he be interrupted before he has completed the course of study by which he promises to become a most eminent theologian.' His father thought also that, with the exception of Bishop Andrewes, few men had risen to distinction as divines who had begun as preachers only.

The following group of letters will furnish the best record of his visit to Scotland. The first extract, which is from a letter written at York, I merely introduce as an illustration of the wide difference between the tongue of the North and South of England before the days of railways and education acts.

'You will be glad to hear of our arrival here, having travelled a day and a night, or rather twenty-six hours; if indeed this be York we are in. For I rather suspect that while asleep in the coach last night they must have carried me over to Germany, since the language here talked may be German or Danish, but certainly is not English. I heard the "Cryer" just now pursuing his vocation, but I would defy those who live nearer the sun than York to understand what he intended to give notice of.'

To his Mother.

Whippingham : December 20, 1824.

I am so full of ideas all bearing upon my Scotch sermon that I grudge every moment that I am not reading. I wish for a dozen eyes and a dozen brains and a dozen such memories as Woodfall's, for I could name a dozen books, all of which I want to read at once, and the difficulty is which first to choose; for as soon as I sit down to one I immediately wish that I had taken up the other. Had the good Bishop Low consulted me how best he could have gratified me, it would have been by coupling my name as he has done with my dear father's. There is a kind of beautiful rhythm in the sentence: 'To the two Hooks, father and son, though entirely unknown to me, I could wish my respects to be made through you for the public and honourable mention which they have made of our poor but still respectable Church.'

To that poor but respectable Church I last year became a subscriber of 1*l.* annual subscription, which when I become a Bishop I mean to make 100*l.* I think the correspondence which has taken place between the Scotch Bishops and Dr. Luscombe speaks volumes in praise of the former; the readiness, the zeal, the kindness, the true

Christian feeling with which they have one and all
entered into his views remind one of former and better
times ; of days when a Bishop was almost another name
for a martyr.   There is no single office that I would so
gladly undertake as that of preaching Dr. Luscombe's Consecration Sermon, and I am sure there is none for which at
present I am so well prepared.

*His Vexation at the Application of Bishop Gleig to the
Government for its Sanction to the Consecration of Dr.
Luscombe in Scotland.*

Whippingham : December 28, 1824.

I look upon the whole business as now at an end.   I shall
now cease from collecting materials for my sermon and
return to my regular pursuits.   I should have thought that
experience would have taught Bishop Gleig the absurdity
of applying to Government for its decision on a subject
purely theological ; a subject on which most of its members
are probably ignorant, and in which in these days of
liberality and conciliation they would certainly not willingly
commit themselves.   Is Government friendly to the Episcopalians of Scotland ?   When has it proved itself so ?   Has
it not always been the policy of every Government, Whig
or Tory, to oppress, persecute, exterminate the Episcopal
Church ?   Was not even their present bare toleration
merely wrung from it, with a Lord Chancellor haranguing
vehemently against them ?   But even look further, when
the greatest and wisest and best of our prelates, when
Wake and Potter and Secker, names ever to be honoured,
were earnest with Government to permit Bishops *without temporal rank* to be sent to our colonies—what did
Government do ?   It treated the application with contempt ;
or was deterred by political circumstances.   It has been
the work of *nearly a century* to wring from Government permission to send Bishops to our colonies.

He then goes on to admit that Dr. Luscombe
being a presbyter, not of Scotland but of England,

Bishop Gleig was quite justified in applying (privately) to the Archbishop of Canterbury for his permission to consecrate. 'It is strictly according to the courtesy of the Catholics (true Catholics, I mean) not to ordain ministers of another Church without permission from the Bishop at the head of it. As Demetrius, Bishop of Alexandria, was justly offended when the Bishops of Palestine ordained the celebrated Origen.'

Edinburgh.—Stirling.—Consecration of Dr. Luscombe.

Stirling : March 20, 1825.

My dearest Father,—I was delighted to find a letter from my beloved mother awaiting me here, and containing so good an account, on the whole, both of herself and you. I have seen much, and been much interested since I wrote last. I know not when I spent a pleasanter day than that in which I dined with Mr. Walker, who is a man superior both for his learning and piety. Bishop Low has been our constant companion ; Dr. Russell, also, has amused and instructed us by his conversation. On Friday last I went to church at Bishop Sandford's, and was surprised to find a congregation of perhaps 150 persons attending, dressed mostly in mourning. This is the good old way of keeping Lent. The church is a most beautiful one, and the light is pleasing and solemnly deadened by the painted windows. It holds, without galleries, about a thousand persons : it is not so large as Mr. Alison's chapel. There is close to it an ugly, tasteless kirk in which Sir Henry Moncrief officiates ; Bishop Low says it is compared to a bandbox in which Bishop Sandford's Church came down from England. Bishop Low is old enough to remember when the penal laws, the 'accursed '46 and '48,'[1] as they are

---

[1] By the Acts of 1746-48 anyone officiating as Minister in any episcopal chapel in Scotland without receiving his letters of orders from some Bishop of the Church of England or Ireland, registering them, taking all the oaths required by law, and praying for the King

called, were in full force ; and the marks of the chains are still left upon his mind.   The true Episcopalians appear to be fond of dwelling upon the sufferings of their ancestors in the holy cause.   Among the sufferers was old George Rose's father ; he lived at Brechin in Forfar, and having a second charge fourteen miles off in the Highlands, he had to trudge there on foot, through rain and snow, with only a crust of bread and an onion in his pocket.   He was apprehended after the '46 for reading Prayers to more than four persons, and put on board a man-of-war in his old age, during the winter months.   When Bishop Horne was told of this, 'Ah ! ' said he, ' I should not have guessed George Rose's parentage from his principles.'   Aunt Eliza will like the following anecdote of Mr. Skinner the historian, grandfather of the present Bishop.   He prayed for the Elector of Hanover by name, and as King ; yet for reading prayers to more than four persons he was put in prison ; he used to read the prayers aloud to himself at the prison window, and all his congregation assembled below to catch the words as they fell from him, and for this these Presbyterians actually wished him to be punished still further.   Talk of the Papists ! where was such persecution as this subsequently to the days of Constantine ?   The Church is little better off now.

Poor old Bishop Gleig is seventy-two years old, breaking by age, and otherwise afflicted ; but he is too poor to be able to have an assistant   This is permitted by a Government which intends to provide for the Papists ; by a Government which yearly gives 8,000*l.* to the English Dissenters, which has long made an allowance to the Papists and Presbyterians in Ireland.   Many Highland congregations are without ministers, because there are no funds to pay them with ; congregations which would rather become Papists than Presbyterians.   The case is at present before Government,

and Royal Family by name, was for the first offence to be imprisoned for six months, for the second to be transported to one of His Majesty's plantations for life.   These laws remained unrepealed, though not actively enforced, up to 1792.

but with little prospect of being attended to. Lord Bexley
has interested himself warmly in it. This is creditable to
his Lordship, as the Bishops here run into such an
extreme against Calvinism as to be charged with Pela-
gianism by their enemies, but unjustly. Will you believe
it? an application was intended to be made to the Society
for Promoting Christian Knowledge for assistance with
respect to the Highland congregations, when upon sounding previously some of the English Bishops, two of them
dared, in the hardihood of ignorance, to start an objection
so infamously Erastian as to say that the assistance ought
not to be afforded, since the Episcopal Church was a
dissenting Church in Scotland. One blushes with indignation and shame, but I much fear that too many on the
Bench are little better than Erastians. In our journey
hither we had much to interest us. On the Pentland Hills
of Covenanting infamy, the snow was lying. We passed
through Linlithgow, the favourite Palace of James IV.; we
passed Falkirk and Bannockburn; of Bannockburn the
Scotch are still most proud. Two Englishmen were
wandering on the field and called to a country lad, to
show them some particular spot in it. He recounted all the
deeds of that day of Scotland's glory with the accuracy of
a bard. The Englishman then offered him half-a-crown.
'Na, na,' said the clod, 'keep your siller to yoursel, the
English have paid dear enow for Bannockburn before this.'
Bishop Gleig has just sent to ask me to drink tea with him,
so I must obey. Sunday: I have just returned from
church, and I am able to say that at last Dr. Luscombe is
a Bishop. We met at Bishop Gleig's Bishop Sandford;
he is the most delightful loveable old man you ever saw, I
never knew anyone who looked more truly what one would
wish a Bishop to look. His voice is so soft, his manner so
gentle, his demeanour so gentlemanlike, that he must win
all hearts. He is always in full dress, with his short
cassock and buckles, as all the Bishops here are accustomed
to be. I never knew a more striking and solemn ceremony
than that which I have witnessed to-day. As a sight, it

would have been more affecting if it had been at Edinburgh in one of the magnificent chapels there. Stirling Chapel is an ugly building, much about the size of our Church at Whippingham, with rather a larger congregation. My sermon was about forty minutes long; I was sorry for it for Bishop Sandford is a great invalid, and could hardly remain out the service. Bishop Low was very much pleased with it; and Bishop Gleig said he could promise me that he never heard a sermon more to his liking upon such an occasion. Bishop Gleig, though a most eccentric character, is a great divine; so I consider this a great compliment.

Visit to St. Andrew's.—Dr. Chalmers.

St. Andrew's : March 24, 1825.

My dearest Mother,—I am writing this in an apartment which once formed part of the palace of our unfortunate Archbishop Sharp. It is rather remarkable that the first thing which met our eyes upon entering Edinburgh was a placard, announcing the exhibition of Allan's picture of that most fiendlike act of Presbyterian intolerance and bigotry, and upon our arrival at St. Andrew's we were forced into the house of that unfortunate martyr. Whether it forbodes ill to Bishop Luscombe or me, I know not ; but I believe that, as far as I am concerned, I could suffer martyrdom very decently, but then I should like it to be in the more regular way; by the halter or the stake, not by the knife of the assassin. The first thing we did this morning was to wait upon Dr. Chalmers, Professor of Moral Philosophy, a friend of Dr. Luscombe's, to request permission to attend his lecture ; he received us very civilly ; we shall meet him at a small party this evening. I was glad to attend his lecture, as it would be contrary to my principles to hear him preach. His lecture was a very good one, showing how the discoveries which have been made by geologists tended to the corroboration of revelation. He availed himself largely of Professor Buckland's works ; but it is rather surprising that while he referred to

Cuvier by name, he omitted to mention that great English geologist. His style was rather too figurative; one or two splendid sentences towards the close produced great effect. I was not aware that the force of a few words would be so great, for it was not the matter, but the words, which told. I shall in future endeavour to close my sermons with a few strong sentences. I understand that Chalmers has in his former lectures praised our English divines, and pronounced the hierarchy of England to have been the great bulwark against infidelity. Upon the whole his lecture was a good one; but I doubt much if it had been delivered by an Englishman, whether it (or any of his works, if the works of an Englishman), would have obtained for the author that fame which the Whigs have bestowed upon Chalmers. He gave me the idea of a person who spoke more for effect than utility; to produce admiration for himself rather than to afford edification to others. We afterwards viewed the ruins of the cathedral; dauntless did I stand under them, for I am convinced, God be thanked, that I have not in my veins one drop of the blood of John Knox; if I had, I would draw it from my body, at the risk of my life. I refer to a story which was told me by Bishop Low. When Dr. Johnson was shown the ruins of St. Andrew's, they pointed out to him a part of them which was likely to fall, and for fear of its doing mischief, they were thinking of taking it down. 'No,' said the good Doctor, 'let it stand for the present, it may chance to fall upon the head of some descendant of John Knox.'

The Episcopalians here are not numerous, but, as is the case everywhere in Scotland, they are the most respectable inhabitants. The present chapel is a room fitted up for the purpose, and by far too small for the congregation. The new chapel is nearly finished; it is a small, handsome, Gothic building, in the shape of a cross. I have recommended that at each gable end there should be erected a small cross on the exterior of the building; and I am particularly urgent to have a slight alteration made by which the altar may be placed at the east, whereas they

were going to place it at the north. Bishop Luscombe was
not warm upon the subject at first, but now, just as I am
cooling, he takes my view to the full extent. I say that I
do not esteem it quite so essential as I did, because,
although the early Christians did almost invariably worship
to the east, and particularly look to the east when professing their faith, there is, if I mistake not, an exception
to the rule mentioned by Eusebius in describing the
Church of Paulinus, which lay, I think, north and south,
instead of east and west ; but Eusebius mentions it and
remarks upon it as an exception to the rule. The Episcopalians are much delighted in having about a fortnight
ago carried a point which was thought impracticable. For
three centuries no service has been performed at the grave
of an Episcopalian. The holy service was always performed in a room, a little dust being brought in a plate to
be thrown upon the body. About a fortnight ago, an
Episcopalian lady died, one who was universally respected
and deeply lamented. Bishop Low was determined to
'take the bull by the horns,' and came over from Pittenweem
to perform the last service for his departed friend himself.
No disturbance was offered, although many Presbyterians
were present. The established ministers regard our Church,
which never wilfully interferes with them, with greater
feelings of hostility than any of those sects which are most
violent against the establishment. For the ministers of the
other Dissenters rank below the established ministers, but
the Episcopal Clergy always above them.

Doctor Chalmers—Presbyterian Theological Parties.

Edinburgh : Tuesday before Easter, 1825.

My dearest Mother, ... As I told you in my last, I
was much pleased with my visit to the kingdom of Fife.
On the evening of the day upon which I wrote last I had the
pleasure of meeting Dr. Chalmers, who, although he never
dines out, came in the evening and partook of the whiskey
toddy (most odious beverage). Both he and Dr. Nicol,

the Principal of the University, gave precedence to Bishop
Luscombe, who was called upon to say grace. With Dr.
Chalmers I had some conversation *tête-à-tête* in the drawing-room. He is an unassuming man, and in close correspondence, evidently, with our Evangelicals ; however, I did
not want to enter into controversy with him, but talked
upon his experience on the management of the poor at
Glasgow, the nature of which I remembered to have read
in the 'Edinburgh Review.' His idea is this, that if you
teach the poor to look for no assistance from the rich, they
will, from the mere feeling of self-preservation, lay up for
themselves a sufficient store for their old age ; and that by
the mutual interchange of good offices among themselves,
they will not only make themselves more comfortable and
independent, but the very disgrace which will attend the
acceptance of favours, without the possibility of returning
them, will operate in a great measure to prevent any kind
of distress ; except such as results from casualties, which
is the proper object of charity. This is, as far as I could
understand, his theory, and very good it seems to be. But
these theorists, when they come to practice, are found at
fault. I asked him what he would do, if, as is sometimes
the case in England, he found a sick person lying on a bed
without a blanket, and in a room without a fire. 'Oh !'
quoth the professor, 'I can prescribe nothing for that false
state of society in which you are in England.' So that, in
fact, his theory is only applicable to a new country. Dr.
Chalmers is a 'high flyer,' a leader of the party ; the 'high
flyers' answer to our Evangelicals. Principal Nicol is the
leading man of the moderate party, a great speaker at the
General Assembly. The moderate party, I am grieved to
say, incline to Socinianism in general. But the Principal,
who was really most kind to us, by the indignation he
expressed against the English Presbyterians who have
lapsed into that Deistical, horrible heresy, is, I hope and
trust, free from all taint. The Principal himself showed us
the two churches. In one I was much surprised to see the
monument of Archbishop Sharp ; and truly a matter of

surprise it need to be to find such a record of Presbyterian atrocity in a Presbyterian kirk.   But the secret came out afterwards; they had intended to pull it down, but it was found that the best estate belonging to the kirk was left upon condition of the monument being permitted to remain.   Our host, Mr. Binny, knew my uncle Walter very intimately, and spoke of him with great affection; he was acquainted with uncle Robert also in India.

Bishop Luscombe has gone, with my prayers for his success.   It was necessary that I should spend a week in Edinburgh, for I have not seen all the lions of the city, and I have to see those of the vicinity.   My father advised me to do all that was necessary to do at first, but I have not followed his advice strictly on this point, for this reason. In this Presbyterian land they do not commemorate the day of our Saviour's death.   I would not choose, therefore, to be in the country during Passion week, especially when most of the families of our persuasion are coming to town to celebrate the great festival which succeeds.   Many persons, very wrongly in my opinion, go to kirk in the country, but, not acknowledging the capability of a Presbyterian minister to consecrate the sacramental elements, go during the great festivals to some place where there is an Episcopal chapel.   So here I stay till Easter Monday, and here do you direct till you hear again.

Your devoted Son,

W. F. HOOK.

Visit to Bishop Jolly.

Aberdeen : April 12, 1825.

My dearest Mother,—When I wrote to you last I was about to start for Fraserburgh, from which place I reluctantly tore myself away yesterday morning, being under an engagement to dine with Bishop Skinner here.   Not arriving at Fraserburgh until ten o'clock on Saturday night, I did not wait upon good Bishop Jolly till the following morning.   I knew that the Bishop rose at four o'clock; and therefore I called at nine : but I knocked at the door in vain. I was told by a passer-by that if I walked on the opposite side of the road, the Bishop would probably see me, and speak to me from the window. No one however appearing, I began to fear that he was gone on a visitation ; I knew that he kept no servant, and that an old woman in the neighbourhood took care of the house, who after shutting the shutters and so forth of an evening, very often locked the Bishop in, and took the key with her to her own house. For this woman I enquired ; she refused to disturb the Bishop before ten. I accordingly gave her my card to deliver to him when she went to him. He immediately sent me a note requesting me to call upon the Rev. Mr. Pressley, who would respectfully conduct me to the Bishop. At half-past ten therefore I saw the good old man. He was dressed in his canonicals, with the whitest and largest wig in Christendom. His room was small, with a small round table and a desk, and various books of reference on the surrounding shelves. He seemed truly glad to see me, and said ' I am to understand that you are the son, the reverend and worthy son, of a dignified Archdeacon of the honoured Church of England.' He afterwards asked me whether that good worthy man, the Archdeacon, were well. I set him right, of course, about my father's age, and told him that he had lately been very ill ; he then adverted to the grand day at Stirling. ' I can assure you,' said he, ' my heart was with you. I read through the whole of the Consecration Service, on that morning ; and my reverend assistant, Mr. Pressley, and myself prayed together heartily that the grand design might turn out to the glory of God.' He then informed me that it was impossible for him to leave his parish during Lent, or he would have been at Stirling on that grand day, as he was preparing his young folk for Confirmation. In his own parish, he has an annual Confirmation ; in the diocese it is only triennial. In his own small parish he had nineteen persons to confirm, out of whom eleven were converts from Presbyterianism. The Bishop did not seek first to convert them, but they made the advance. Now this is very glorious.

and very striking. I asked him whether he did not think it necessary that they should be first baptized; he said that he would confess to me, as I was a friend, that they all were re-baptized, and this at their own request, since they had scruples about lay baptism, and of course, when they were converted they regarded, as we do, the ministers of the Scotch Established Church merely as laymen. Be careful not to talk of this; for although it is always done, it is done under the rose, since the ministers of the Establishment are very irate indeed when they discover that we re-baptize the quondam members of their communion. The bishop would not permit me—a reverend clergyman of the honoured Church of England (and he said 'we are very like the Church of England, almost the same,') —to sit without the rails of the altar, but I sat within with him, and read the Epistle. In the afternoon Mr. Pressley said it would be 'brotherly to read prayers,' which I did. Between the services, I was delighted with the conversation of the good, dear Bishop; a biscuit and a glass of wine was all his dinner; in general he takes a basin of soup, but, in honour of me, he had some wine that day, which made his dinner. He has perhaps as good a divinity library as any clergyman in Great Britain; some most scarce and valuable books are in it. It has been the collection of fifty years; many of them presents, or bought when books were cheaper than they are now. It shows what a man may do on a little; for this most apostolic Bishop has only 60*l.* a year to live on, having by ill health been obliged to procure an assistant at 40*l.* per annum; this 40*l.* is exclusive of the 60*l.*; of this 60*l.* he spends half in charity. You can form no conception how he is beloved. It is a beautiful sight to see the children running across the street when he appears, and holding down their little heads while he lays his hands upon them and blesses them. Many of the grown up people kneel down and receive his blessing also. Last year when Mr. Walker was at Fraserburgh, some fishermen, going out on the whale fishing, walked six miles before they sailed, to receive his blessing. It was the old custom in England, long retained in Scotland, for any person when waiting on a Bishop, to kneel down and beg his blessing. I lament, however, to say it is going out here, and is retained only by Bishop Jolly, except on particular occasions. Mr. Pressley told me that he always knelt down and received his blessing on Sunday morning, or when he waited on him on clerical business, or to pray with him. This worthy young man, Mr. Pressley, is treading in the Bishop's steps ; he was ordained deacon at nineteen ; he is now only twenty-four. His reading has been so extensive that he would shame many first-rate divines in England ; all our great English authors he knows well ; he has read the Fathers, that is the best of them ; he can refer to any sentence of Scripture, mentioning even the chapter and verse ; he can read any book in Latin, Greek, or Hebrew ; and this good young man is living contentedly on 40*l.* a year, out of which he has to contribute to the support of his parents. He is educating two young men gratis (for they cannot afford to pay him) for the Episcopal Church, and has a gentleness and urbanity of manners which is perfectly wonderful, considering that he has never been farther south than Aberdeen. For a few years Government allowed 100*l.* per annum to each of the Scotch Bishops ; it was called a regium donum. Five years ago it was stopped, with no reason assigned, by this very Government who mean to pension the Papists. Mr. Pressley says this stoppage necessitated Bishop Jolly so much to curtail his charities that it weighed much upon the good man's spirits, and he has stinted himself ever since. At six o'clock I went to drink tea with the Bishop. The old woman brought a teapot with the tea made from her own house, wrapped in a pocket handkerchief, and having laid it on the table, begged a blessing and departed. The Bishop and I (for Mr. Pressley was gone to a Sunday school) then got the cups and saucers from the closet, and drank our tea ; he said 'You see I am a perfect monk, not from choice, but a wonderful train of Providence placed me in the situation I am in, and I am perfectly happy.' He talked of the reception the bishops met with from the good King George, a print of whom was given him at Edinburgh. ' But,' said he, pointing to a print of Prince Charles, ' he has been over my fireplace for forty years, and I could not find it in my heart to depose him.' So he has placed the king in the next honourable situation, between the effigies of Archbishop Laud and Archbishop Sancroft. I said that I wanted a copy of the Scotch Episcopal Communion Service, and asked where I could get one ; he said he had one by him, and would give it to me. ' I am ashamed,' he said, ' to give you only a little sixpenny pamphlet, but,' looking with affection on his books, ' these are to be a legacy to our poor Church, so I cannot part with them.' I insisted on his writing his name in the little book, and this is what he wrote : ' Accepted with much goodness by the Rev. W. F. Hook, from Alexander Jolly, Bishop, whom he delighted by his company in Fraserburgh, Low Sunday, 1825.' I need not tell you that to my dying day, I shall value this little book. I could write on this subject for ever, but my paper warns me to conclude. After shaking hands with the dear old Bishop, I knelt down, and never, never shall I forget my feelings when, laying his two hands upon my unworthy head, he said, as if from his heart of hearts, ' My son, may God Almighty bless you by His Holy Spirit, preserve you from sin and danger, direct and prosper you in all your studies and holy duties, and keep you in His love and favour evermore.' I must add that he wishes that whenever that worthy and venerable man, the archdeacon writes to the now Bishop Luscombe, he will state that he (Bishop Jolly) will think of him every morning, and pray in great truth for his success.

The four consecrators of Dr. Luscombe were : Bishop Gleig, the Primus ; Dr. Sandford, Bishop of Edinburgh ; Dr. Skinner, Bishop of Aberdeen ; and Dr. Low, Bishop of Ross and Argyll. The very sight of Dr. Skinner was interesting, for he was a direct link between these peaceful times and one of the most suffering epochs of the Scottish Church. His grandfather, the Rev. J. Skinner, for sixty-four years pastor of Langside, had been imprisoned for six months under the oppressive Act of 1748 for the crime of reading the English Liturgy to more than four persons, although he had taken the oaths of allegiance to Government. Large crowds, however, used to gather on Sundays round the Tolbooth, to whom he preached from the grated window of his cell. His son was afterwards Bishop of Aberdeen, and father of the Bishop who assisted in the consecration of Dr. Luscombe. The object which the Scottish Bishops had in view in consecrating Dr. Luscombe will best be understood from the concluding words of the Letters of Collation which they delivered to him : ' He is sent by us, representing the Scotch Episcopal Church, to the Continent of Europe, not as a Diocesan Bishop in the modern or limited sense of the word, but for a purpose similar to that for which Titus was left by St. Paul in Crete, that he may "set in order the things that are wanting" among such of the natives of Great Britain and Ireland as he shall find professing to be members of the United Church of England and Ireland and the Episcopal Church in Scotland, and to these may be added any members of the Episcopal Church of America who may chance to be resident in Europe. But as our blessed Lord, when He first sent out His apostles, commanded them, saying, " Go not into the way of the Gentiles, and into any city of the Samaritans enter ye not; but go rather to the lost sheep of the house of Israel," so we, following so divine

an example . . . . do solemnly enjoin our right
reverend brother not to disturb the peace of any
Christian Society established as the National Church
in whatever nation he may chance to sojourn, but to
confine his ministrations to British subjects and to
such other Christians as may profess to be of a
Protestant Episcopal Church.

'And we earnestly pray God to protect and
support him in his arduous undertaking, and to
grant such success to his ministry that he may be
among those who, having turned many to righteousness, shall shine as the stars for ever and ever.'

The sermon preached on this occasion[1] elicited
great praise from the Scottish Bishops and others
who heard it, and was the first production which
brought the author into public notice. It is entitled
'An attempt to demonstrate the Catholicism of the
Church of England and the other branches of the
Episcopal Church.' In force and freedom of style
and weightiness of matter, it is a very great
advance upon the sermon of 1822. The practical bearing of the sermon upon the matter in
hand consisted in demonstrating that, if there was
an essential unity between all branches of the
Reformed Catholic Church, the appointment of a
Bishop by one branch to minister to members of
other branches hitherto destitute of such provision
could be no intrusion or usurpation. Notwithstanding differences of nationality and position, such as
the Church being established in one country and
disestablished in another, yet in itself was it one and
indivisible ; consequently the English, Scotch, and

---

[1] No. 2 in vol. i. of *The Church and her Ordinances.*

American members of the Church, clerical and lay,
sojourning on the Continent might freely acknowledge the authority of a Bishop duly consecrated
and sent forth by any one of the three branches.
Neither was there any fear, as some had supposed,
that such a Bishop would disturb the foreign Protestants or the Roman Church.

The following wise words might well be weighed
by those Dissenters, on the one hand, who seek to
upset the Church of England as at present established, and on the other by those members of the
Church who dally and coquet with Nonconformists,
whether Protestant or Romanist. 'We seek not to
interfere with, much less to overthrow, any Christian
form of worship which may be established by its
civil constitution, so long as it tends to promote (as
every Christian mode of worship *will* in a greater
or less degree promote) the great ends of virtue,
morality, and religion. For ourselves, we lay claim
to the privilege of worshipping the Almighty in the
manner we conceive to be prescribed by him, and
of keeping clear from what we consider to be error
on the one side or on the other, whether resulting
from the innovations of the Protestant or of the
Romanist. In this country (Scotland) grateful for
the toleration which is afforded to the Reformed
Catholic Church, its pious ministers, while they
vindicate its doctrines and maintain its discipline,
seek not to interfere with the Presbyterian establishment: but although they cannot enter into its
communion or attend its services, they duly appreciate its merits in contributing to rear and foster a
thinking and religious people. The same sentiments

influence us when resident in a country where the
Church of Rome is established. Far be from our
views that misdirected and fanatic zeal, which would
seek at all hazards the downfall of even an erroneous mode of Christian worship, reckless of the
consequences; which in removing one stumbling-
block may open the door to a thousand others, and
let loose passions which war against the spirit of
Christianity itself.'

The mission of Bishop Luscombe, however,
harmless as such a proceeding would be considered
in the present day, excited a great deal of controversy at the time, and was viewed with displeasure
and alarm by many good Churchmen on the very
grounds which were combated in the sermon
quoted above. Many persisted in thinking that a
Bishop consecrated by a disestablished Church,
could have no right to exercise authority over the
members of an established Church, although residing
out of their country; and also that his introduction
into the dioceses of a Church which was in alliance
with the State, and was also a branch, although a
corrupt one, of the Catholic Church, could not be
justified. Mr. Norris, rector of South Hackney,
was one of the most eminent who held these views
on the subject, and he expressed them in an article
in the 'Christian Remembrancer' for December 1825.
Had Christianity itself been in danger, then, since
salus Ecclesiæ suprema lex, he thought the irregularity would have been pardonable, but not otherwise.
To this article and other adverse criticisms, Mr.
Hook replied in the same journal, May 1826. He
points out that of the Catholic Church it had been

an invariable tenet that the Episcopate was one,
and that consequently a member of the Church owed
allegiance, not merely to the prelates of the country
in which he was born, but to the duly consecrated
Bishop of the place in which he might happen to
reside. 'With that Bishop he is bound to communicate, notwithstanding differences in rites and
ceremonies, except where, as in the case of Greece
and Rome, they have degenerated into heretical and
idolatrous superstition ; for there, as it was ruled by
Cyprian and thirty-six other prelates in the case of
the Spanish Bishops, Martialis and Basilides, the
clergy and people are not only authorised, but in
duty bounden, to renounce their allegiance ; and the
orthodox Bishops of a neighbouring nation, acting
not in their ordinary but in their Catholic character,
are permitted to send one of their number to preside over those who may continue in the primitive
faith. . . . If the Church of England were merely
a sect, then indeed it would be necessary for the
English abroad on all occasions to apply for sanction
to the authorities at home ; but being in fact, when
once they have quitted the shores of England, members of the Church at large, their allegiance becomes
due, as I said before, not to an English diocesan,
but to the Ordinary of the place wherein they reside ;
if in Scotland to the Scottish Bishop, if in America
to the American Bishop, and so on. When, however, they are resident on the Continent of Europe,
there are few places where there is an authority
established which they can conscientiously acknowledge, for, as Theodoret observes, " where Christians
are given to the worship of angels," (*a fortiori* of

saints) "they have left the Lord Jesus Christ."
They must therefore in this case apply to proper
ecclesiastical authority for the appointment of an
Ordinary, qualified for the discharge of episcopal
functions.   The question then is, In whom is that
authority vested ?   "Simplex"[1] would answer that
they could only apply to the Bishops of England,
whereas I contend that though I should prefer it,
yet this is by no means necessary, and in some cases
may be an inexpedient course. Suppose, for instance,
I were resident in a town in France, in which there
were also resident several Scottish and several
American Episcopalians, "Simplex," if not an Erastian, will allow that we should be all of the same
communion, and that if any one should refuse to
hold communion with the others we should be schismatics.   Suppose also an American clergyman were
to come to reside among us for the purpose of performing divine service, and that, convinced of the
irregularities arising from want of an Ordinary, and
desirous of securing the rite of Confirmation for our
children, we should determine to apply in the proper
quarter for the redress of the grievance ; if the
Englishman should contend that application should
be made to the English bench, and the Scotchman
should plead for the Episcopal College in Scotland,
the American would think it necessary to uphold
the dignity of the prelates in the United States.
Each party would, in this instance, be acting on the
narrow principles of a sect, and Catholic unity
would thus be destroyed.   But sinking all national
distinctions they would, if they acted properly and

---

[1] One of his critics who wrote under this name.

as *really Catholic* Christians, come to the determination of applying to *any* lawful authority, capable of judging of the expediency or inexpediency of granting their petition and relieving their wants. Referring to the records of the Church in its primitive and purest ages, they would find that the Christians in those days, when they were in want of a Bishop, did not think it necessary to apply to any particular Church, but to a synod of neighbouring Bishops canonically convened.'

It only remains to say, that Bishop Luscombe met with a most cordial reception in France, from the British Ambassador at Paris, and from all members of the Reformed Church abroad; and if his mission was not ultimately so successful as had been hoped, the failure was due to causes which were not connected with the nature of the mission itself, and into which therefore it is not worth while to enter here.

LETTERS, 1822–1826.

Renewal of Intercourse with his Friend William Page Wood.

Whippingham, Isle of Wight : March 1822.

My dearest Mother, ... I shall now proceed to my own business, which is, of course, quite and entirely confidential between you and me. After nearly eleven years' friendship, the better half of Wood's life, and no small portion of mine, it would be useless to deny that we are both of us impatient to meet once more. If, therefore, the same objections do not still exist, I am sure you, my kind mother, will endeavour, if possible, to procure and accelerate that meeting. Had you not kindly mentioned the subject when last here, I should have given it up as a hopeless case for the present, but since by your mentioning it there must be a possibility, I cannot restrain my feelings so far as not to express my wishes, and to strive to promote an object I have so much at heart. This point, however, I leave to my father's decision of course. If it is thought expedient that we should not yet meet, then I shall remain here ; for, except for that purpose, I would not sacrifice the solitude, peace, and quiet which I am here enjoying in perfection. But if (as God grant it may be) it is possible, or rather expedient, for me to see Wood, I will tell you the plan which sometimes flies athwart my brain as I compose myself to my evening's nap ; though it will never be put in execution, forasmuch as I have already enjoyed it in anticipation. I should like to get a parson's holiday, and spend three days with you in town, that I may make a solitary expedition to the Tower, and pay my usual visit to Poet's Corner, and see the Panoramas, and go to Astley's or one of the minor theatres, which is a thing I want to do for sundry reasons. Then I should like to spend three days with dear Aunt Mathison at Hampstead, and after that, to go with my father to the visitation ; from thence to Cambridge. All this is very fine talking, you will say, but it is prodigiously dissipated for a parson, and very expensive. And yet, if you except the three days in town, when I shall be on a visit to you, the week at Cambridge is not much after four years' absence, to those who, for nearly seven years, were scarcely ever four hours absent from one another in a day.

Your most affectionate Son,

W. F. HOOK.

Invitation to be Steward at a Ball.

Whippingham : April 1822.

Mr. H.'s note did not arrive till yesterday, but the answer was in time ; what it was I suppose you have anticipated. I should verily as much have thought, nay, even more seriously, of going to Jericho than of becoming steward to a ball. I should be worried and bothered my-self, and worry and bother everybody else ; and as to my qualification, if I were to dress up one of my father's cows she would perform the duties with infinite more grace and good humour than I should. Besides the plague of it would be so great that I should die under it, and it would look very ill upon my tombstone to see 'Here lies Walter Farquhar Hook, B.A., student of Christ Church, chaplain to his Grace the Duke of Argyll and sometime curate of this parish. He died of a ball, universally regretted, on the 23rd day of April 1822, in the 25th year of his age.'

Detestation of French Characters.

'Conduct is Fate' I cannot read. I am too much of a John Bull to take any interest in Monsieurs and Madames and Mademoiselles, and I suppose the heroine is a French woman ; and how could I take any interest in the adven-tures of a woman born and bred in that country where Buonaparte tyrannised, and that atheistical villain Voltaire spat his dirty venom at Shakspeare.

Law's 'Serious Call.'

Whippingham, Cowes, Isle of Wight : May 5, 1824.

My dearest Brother, . . . I have lately been reading a book the Dean of Winton gave me, Law's 'Serious Call.' I had not read it for several years ; it is a book exquisitely written, and written in such a manner that I defy any body to read it without being interested. Dr. Johnson when he was at Oxford took it up, expecting to find it a dull book, and perhaps to laugh at it. These are his own words, but says he, 'I found Law an overmatch for me, and that was the first occasion of my thinking in earnest of religion, after I became capable of rational enquiry. Now of this book I intend always to read a chapter every morning ; I am sure it will be of advantage through the whole day ; and if you will do the same, you have only to order it at Rivingtons, and place it on your bookshelf as a gift from a devotedly attached brother. You will think the first day that he commands impossibilities, but you will on the second day think those impossibilities less impossible ; and I pray God to grant us both His grace that we may both go on thus improving every day. You will, I am sure, take in good part this wee-bit prose. You know me, you know how weak I am, how easily I have yielded, and still yield, to temptation. You have always been my friend and confidant. I tremble often at the thoughts of the future, and I have been tempted to despair of the mercy of God ; but on that mercy I have now learned wholly and solely to rely, through my blessed Redeemer, and humbly I pray that I may finally be triumphant over those evil thoughts and wicked passions which too often assail me. I pray the same for you, my dear Robert, and I entreat you to join in the prayer. Believe me, my dearest Robert, to remain

Your devotedly attached Brother,

W. F. HOOK.

The three letters which follow relate to a visit to London to see Dr. Hobart, the Bishop of New York, and will perhaps be better understood if prefaced by a few words of explanation. Before the declaration of Independence in 1783, the Church in America had nominally been subject to the episcopal supervision of the Bishop of London. Commissaries were sent over by him from time to time, and very ineffectually as a rule did they discharge their work. After the establishment of the Republic it became necessary for the American Church, if it was to be episcopal at all, to obtain Bishops for itself. Dr. Seabury was sent over to England in 1785 to seek consecration from the Archbishop of Canterbury ; but the prelates of the Established

Church were afraid of taking the step lest it should involve the English Government in difficulties with the American Republic, which had just been recognised. Dr. Seabury accordingly was consecrated by the prelates of the Scotch Church. Three other Bishops were afterwards consecrated in England, the political impediments having been surmounted. The American Church, thus refounded, set about adapting itself to the altered condition of things with laudable zeal and wisdom ; but for some time it had to contend against misrepresentation, obloquy, and suspicion, and it was sinking into an unsatisfactory state of supineness when in 1798 John Henry Hobart was ordained to the ministry. He quickly began to rouse the Church into vigorous action, and in 1811, at the age of thirty-six, he was consecrated Bishop of New York. I will conclude these remarks by an extract from a lecture on the American Church given by Dr. Hook in Leeds, in which he alludes to the visit mentioned in the letters below.

' For several years the moral persecution which Bishop Hobart had to endure depressed his spirits, but never for a moment slackened his energies. Every kind of falsehood was invented to blacken his name, and for a time he had to fight almost single-handed the battle of the Church. But by degrees friends rallied round him, they increased in number, they gave him their confidence ; he lived down his enemies. Long before his death he had the happiness—and a greater happiness man can scarcely enjoy—of counting among his supporters and friends some who had been at one time his bitter opponents.

H 2

Even among those who still thought it their duty to
pursue a course of conduct different from that which
suggested itself to him, many regarded him in private
with feelings of friendship ; and in the various denominations which at one time had gone out of
their way to oppose him, many so much admired his
wisdom, his foresight, and his energy, that they were
now ready to admit that they were prepared to take
him for their model, and to bring his principles of
energetic action to bear on those very denominational
peculiarities which he most condemned.

'In 1823, worn out and fatigued with his many
anxieties and cares, he visited Europe ; and he was
received in England with those feelings of admiration
and respect which he so fully deserved.

'I was at that time a curate in the Isle of Wight.
There were no railroads and very few steamboats,
and travelling therefore was expensive ; but though
I could ill afford it, I journeyed to London on a cold
November day on the top of the coach to receive at
the end of my journey the blessing of a man whom
I admired, respected, and revered. I found him in
the grandeur of his simplicity as ready to open his
full mind to a young curate as he would have been
to a person of his own age and station. He prided
himself, and went out of his way to show it, on being
a Republican ; and the mixture of Republican with
High Church principles perplexed not a few among
those who approached him, and who confounded the
Church with the Establishment. He gave some
offence by preferring his own branch of the Church
to ours on those matters of detail in which a disestablished Church must differ from an Establishment.

He told me that the cause of the Church was retarded in America at that time by the fact that many narrow-minded persons still felt that there must be, on the part of the Episcopalians, a secret attachment to the principles of the English monarchy which was treason to American republicanism.   He wished while showing and proclaiming his devoted attachment to the Church of England to prove in his own person that he could be a loyal citizen of the United States.   From that time the progress of the Church in the United States has been rapid and satisfactory.'

Bishop Hobart and the American Church.

16 St. James's Street, London : November 1823.

My dearest Father,—I write to request a very great favour of you. The Right Reverend Father in God John Henry Hobart, Bishop of New York, has arrived in England, and is, I hear, staying at Mr. Norris's. Now, as I know that you are acquainted with Mr. Norris, I should feel, if it is not improper, the greatest possible pleasure in having an introduction given me to him. If you think this no improper intrusion, and you can send me a letter of introduction by return of post, I can easily go by the stage to Hackney some day next week. Few people, I flatter myself, in England are better acquainted than I am with the history of the Apostolic Church in America. I have been making, since I have been in town, a close abstract of Bishop White's history of that Church, published only in America, and I think I shall be able to afford you some entertainment and information on that subject when we meet. It is so interesting a history that really, were I a little older, and a deeper divine, I should instantly set to work, and from my notes, the appendix to Bishop White, and my conversations with Mr. Wheaton, I should publish a short account of it. With these feelings, you will not wonder that I would strain a point to get an introduction to Bishop Hobart. I have frequently met the Dean of Winton, and I always join him to talk a little High-Churchery. He is quite as delighted with the Apostolic Church in America as I am. I am more particularly interested in the subject, as it will cause Episcopacy to be better understood in England by the generality of persons.

Mistaken for Bishop Hobart.

16 St. James's Street : November 12, 1823.

My dearest Mother, ... I can give you but little family news. I went to Hackney yesterday. When I arrived at Mr. Norris's I was received by his servant with the most marked and peculiar respect ; he told me that Mr. N. was out, but that he would return soon, and entreated me to sit in the library while he sent to town for his master. By this time several of the other servants had collected round the door, and the maids were looking out of window. I said that I would not permit Mr. N. to be sent for, when the servant told me that his master would never forgive him if he sent not for him express. I then said I would walk about Hackney and call again in the course of an hour, when the servant begged me to leave my name. Alas ; on seeing my card, and on finding that I was a simple presbyter, all his respect and admiration vanished. He then said that Mr. N. was gone to town to fetch Bishop Hobart, Bishop of New York. ' We thought,' quoth he, ' that you, sir, were the Bishop.' You cannot think how I was flattered by this, and no Bishop, of either Scotland or America, could have assumed more episcopal dignity when surrounded by moody Covenanters or hostile sectarians, than I assumed when perambulating the streets of Hackney. I called again on Mr. Norris, who had not met the Bishop, who was detained in town by business with the American ambassador. This, and the miscarriage of his letters, in which he had arranged that the Bishop should, like the apostles of old, be ' brought by the

Church' all the way from Dover to London—that is, that he should sleep and stay at the houses of different clergy men on the road—these things, I say, had evidently put him a little out of sorts ; and although he was particularly civil, I did not get from him all that information which I expected, nor did he even offer me the loan of the official papers of the American Church.   By the way, if my father thinks it practicable, and I can get at the 'Quarterly' through Croker, I think of drawing up an article for that review from my knowledge of the American Church.   It can be done in the shape of a review on Bishop Dehon's sermons, and I think it may be rendered instructive, interesting, and useful.

Your most devoted Son,
W. F. HOOK.

Meeting with Bishop Hobart.

16 St. James's Street, London : November 13, 1823.

My dearest Mother, ... I have just come from that great and good man, Bishop Hobart. To be sure, I went pre-disposed to like him ; but my expectations were surpassed beyond expression.   His spirit, his vivacity, his judgment, are striking even in half an hour's conversation.   His sober, but zealous piety ; his strong, vehement, but tempered orthodoxy ; his veneration for our Church, his candour with respect to his own, have won my heart.   And when he told me that he had read my father's charge, in New York, I could not help giving him an invitation to Whip-pingham ; when he expressed his pleasure at the prospect of an introduction to the archdeacon, but he feared that his health would not permit him to visit us at present, as he would have to go south, but on his return he promises to come.   Alas, I fear that you will be away at that time. There is no difference in his appearance from that of a simple presbyter, nor is his exterior very polished, but there is a strong, marked expression in his face which speaks of one who has stood firm in the hour of peril, and who has fought, and will fight, the good fight, ay, and (for God is on his side) will eventually prevail over all his enemies. Gilbert says that the respect with which he is treated at New York is wonderful ; that even the Evangelicals who differ from him are forced to acknowledge the pre-eminent sanctity of his character and the sobered zeal of his religion. Nay, Gilbert has even been asked by Presbyterians, 'Have you seen our Bishop?' and they spoke of him as a great man that he must see before he left New York. Now the Right Reverend Father himself told me in conversation that it was necessary that the character of the Bishop should be upholden, as the Republicans would all be very willing to carp at and deny the necessary respect due to the office. I felt, of course, the awe and respect which a presbyter ought to feel in the presence of a Bishop ; but he was very condescending, and seemed to think that the honour was rather conferred on him than on me. I wish I was settled in the neighbourhood of town, for I long to be dabbling in High-Churchery. However, my day is not yet come ; I shall one day or other hope to be a bulwark of the Church. In the meantime, I must lay deeper the foundation, which has been too much neglected.

I shall be glad to return to you all—sweet and peaceful Whippingham, my family, the school, the parish.

Your most devoted Son,

W. F. Hook.

Whippingham, Isle of Wight : June 5, 1825.

My dearest Robert,—I do from my heart wish you many, many happy returns of the day whether, as it is doubtful, to-day or to-morrow be your real birthday.[1] To-day I dine with Lord Henry and I shall propose your health. To-morrow, to make assurance doubly sure, I will drink it in my toast and water, which is my strongest beve-

---

[1] Because Robert was born so near midnight that it was difficult to determine to which day his birth belonged.

rage, except on Sundays, when I take a glass of wine. I will do what is more, I will make peculiar mention of you, my dear, dear brother, in my private prayers, and especially to-morrow which is, I believe, your proper birthday, when I shall have an opportunity of doing so in the most solemn rite of the Church, as I have appointed that day for the private administration of the Sacrament of the Lord's Supper to a rich parishioner. And if the present dissipation of London has not too much disordered your thoughts, if you are fully prepared, I would advise you not only to form good resolutions upon your birthday, but to confirm them by receiving that sacrament as soon after as you possibly can. There is an administration of it *every* Sunday at St. Martin's. If you are not prepared then, the question is, why are you not? and I would advise you just to look at the quotation from Dr. Andrewes's sermon as given by Judge Park in his excellent little work upon the Sacrament; at the end.

Advice to a Young Man of Business.

Whippingham, Cowes : December 6, 1825.

My dearest———,—If I may be allowed to give you a little advice, it is simply this, to confine your attention almost exclusively to one point and one subject ; that is, your profession. No man ever succeeded in any one thing whose thoughts were not exclusively devoted to it. Let all your readings bear upon this point ; make yourself thoroughly master of one subject (and no man can hope to be master of more), and general knowledge will flow in wonderfully, where you least expect it. I should say that your fault is a desire to be able to say something of every thing. You have many irons in the fire, but not one red-hot. You dogmatise upon every subject, whether you understand it or not, and I think sometimes take up opinions at second hand. I was struck with this when you were with us ; there were some points on which I had intended to have gained information from you, but whenever I alluded to them, I found that you knew nothing of *particulars* ; and had only a *general*, that is to say, a confused notion upon them ; I therefore did not press them. If you wish for proof of the truth of this charge, just ask yourself upon what single point I could consult you as an authority, and yet again on what single subject would you not hazard an opinion. If you wish to succeed in any profession, the thing is, to make yourself completely and entirely master of every subject relating to it.   This is of course the work of time ; and then upon that subject you may be justified in dogmatising if you please ; on all others be silent in most instances, in all speak with diffidence.   There is another point on which I wish to prose you ; you have very good abilities and a very sound judgment, if you were pleased to exercise them, but you now seem to regard the opinion of any person of great name as a law, and im- mediately adopt it as your own.   When you are struck with any opinion or sentiment, ponder on it seriously, re- flect on it, and judge for yourself whether there be not some error in it ; until you are able to decide thoroughly upon it, never sport it as your own.   A man of real talents would never do so under any circumstances.   You should always remember that pretenders to genius are fond of starting a paradox to make fools stare ; but they never do so without supporting it with a specious argu- ment.   He who professes to hold an opinion and yet cannot support it, is considered not very wise.   Again, if a person lays down the law upon a subject, and when questioned is found to know really little or nothing upon it, that person is noted as a superficial fellow.   All this lecture amounts to this : Human nature is such that it is scarcely possible for a man to be thoroughly master of more than one subject, though he devote his life to it ; if he is not master of some one subject, thoroughly master, he will not succeed, and is not wise.   Circumstances point out the one subject to be studied ; providence has appointed you to be a man of business, and in so doing tells you

what it is to which you are exclusively (always excepting the higher claims of religion) to devote your time.

You seem to wish to have that general knowledge
which you hear great talkers lay claim to; these great
talkers are men of quickness who let fly at everything and
astonish greater fools than themselves; but they never
fail to expose themselves when talking to those who have
really studied any particular subject out of the many
which they pretend to understand. I can only judge from
my own experience. I know some men that pass for men
of talent; their knowledge of the law, of general literature,
of physics, and metaphysics, &c., &c., has astonished me;
they have had just as much pretensions to theological
subjects, the only one on which I am really capable of
judging. I have found them upon getting on that topic
overbearing and positive, but most awfully ignorant; those
men I have of course set down as empty pretenders, and I
consider them as ignorant on subjects relating to law,
physics, metaphysics &c., as I have found them to be in
theology. These people are admired at dinner parties,
and so forth, but if they had to make their bread by their
talents, they would be found lamentably deficient. Now
to shine in mixed companies, is not to be your business,
however much your vanity may desire it; it is your duty
to become a steady, unpretending, well-informed banker.
I say, unpretending; for depend upon it, where a man
knows most, there he will be most modest.

Whippingham : May 9, 1826.

My dearest Mother,—I have no patience with —— in
making such a fool of himself. A boy of sixteen, with his
head full of Ovid, Tibullus, and Catullus, would not be guilty
of such folly. I would advise him like Romeo to look out
for a new mistress in the first pretty face he meets, and
Rosaline will be soon forgotten in the superior charm of
Juliet. 'Tut, man, one fire burns out another burning; take
thou some new infection to thine eye, and the rank poison
of the old will die.' Shakspeare does well to call such

love 'fancy.' It is in my opinion all a pack of nonsense. I do not mean to say that *all* love is nonsense, but such a kind of ideal love as ——'s, unrequited and for a person whose character he does not know, is quite nonsense in any but a child. Tell —— all this, and add with my love that I think him a blockhead.

You surprise me about J. W. I think his marriage a very bad thing. He will never be a good divine, if he marries so early in his clerical life. No man should marry at all events while he is in the lower order of the Diaconate. Three or four years undisturbed by family botherations are positively necessary even to ground a man . . . . Yet I would have you know that I have a female correspondent from whom I heard only yesterday. The letter came from Cheltenham, and was franked by a Bishop. The lady has in her veins the blood of Abraham, Isaac, and Jacob. She is a steady, respectable body, rather the worse for years, not pretty, but very good. You are acquainted with her, and her name I leave you to guess.

Baptism of Converts from Anabaptism.

Whippingham, Cowes, Isle of Wight: May 29, 1826.

My dearest Father, ... Yesterday something singular and important occurred. Ryder brought his two sons to be received into the Church, informing me that they had been 'named,' by which the poor people here mean privately baptized ; but upon putting the questions to him according to the directions in the Prayer Book, I found that they had only been immersed in water by an Anabaptist teacher at an Anabaptist conventicle. I therefore administered the Sacrament to them according to that form which the Church prescribes in doubtful cases: 'If thou hast not been baptized already, I baptize thee in the Name,' &c. The children were six or seven years of age, and through ignorance, I administered the Sacrament to them by sprinkling ; but on reference to the Rubrics and the Liturgical writers, I am afraid that I acted too hastily, for by the Rubric we are directed to dip the child, unless 'they certify that it is weak,' which in the case of infants is always of course inferred. In a case like the present, the proper course would have been to apply to my Ordinary. Now, my Lord of Winton being, I am sorry to say, a very Low Churchman, would most probably be willing to allow the validity of an Anabaptist's dipping; but in this case, his would only be an opinion, and that the opinion of a fallible man in opposition to the doctrine of the Church.

But in proportion to his being low in principle, he is very strict in discipline; and should it come to his ears that I have acted on my own discretion contrary to a Rubric, he may be, and that justly, offended. Perhaps therefore, you will explain the case to his Lordship, and express my very great sorrow for this irregularity, the only one that I am conscious of having been guilty of since I have been in his diocese; he would, no doubt, have directed me to pour water on the child, which by the way I did, and always of course do; sprinkling, therefore, is a wrong term: but I ought, no doubt, to have applied to you, and you to the Bishop.

I remain, your most devoted Son,

W. F. HOOK.

Expected Meeting with Agents of Religious Tract Society.

Whippingham, Cowes, Isle of Wight : June 9, 1826.

My dearest Mother, ... I so fully expected to have seen you to-day, that I am sadly disappointed at your non-arrival. I am so full of St. Andrew's, and am building such churches in the air, that I long to talk over all my schemes with you and my beloved father. Welcome, therefore, doubly welcome will you be to this beautiful abode of black-beetles and crickets; it will certainly reconcile me to our departure that we shall at least escape those odious companions, since one or two have paid me a visit in bed.

I dread them as much 'as a sick girl.' I have much to say, but I cannot write now ; I am in what we used to call at school 'a blue funk,' for I am to be attacked by two heretics to-day, at 4 p.m.   The challenge was conveyed in the following anonymous note, received yesterday : 'An auxiliary to the Religious Tract Society having been lately formed at West Cowes, the committee respectfully present the enclosed (to wit, a pamphlet) to the Rev. W. F. Hook, soliciting his approval and assistance.   Two of the collectors will wait on Mr. H. to-morrow, at 4 o'clock p.m., to receive his answers.'   Now as I live on very good terms with Mrs. ——, Mrs. Gibbs, Mrs. Brown, &c., and even go so far as to shake hands with them, they suspect me, I suppose, of heresy ; but I shall content myself with telling them very plainly that I cannot, consistently with my principles, interfere with the religious institutions of any parish except my own ; or patronise a society established for religious purposes, unless it be under the official superintendence of my Diocesan ; and thus I shall decline all argument.   But as the Apostle tells me to beware of false prophets who come to me in sheep's clothing, because inwardly they are ravening wolves, I have ordered the deacon, on his allegiance to a priest of the Church of Winchester to attend the conference.   These little breezes in a quiet life are very pleasant, but nevertheless, as I said before, I am in a bit of a 'funk,' and can write of nothing else.

Your most devoted Son,

W. F. HOOK.

Interview with Agents of Religious Tract Society.

Cowes, Isle of Wight : June 13, 1826.

My dearest Mother, ... When I wrote to you last, I believe I informed you that I expected an interview with some schismatics ; at the appointed hour they came, and I asked them whether they had applied to the Bishop officially on their entering his diocese, and whether the

Society was placed under his direction. On their answering in the negative, I told them that I could not consistently with my feelings and principles as a clergyman of the Church of England, sanction a society professedly established for a religious purpose, unless it were placed officially under the direction of my Diocesan. I told them also that the Bishop is the ordinary minister of God over the whole diocese, and that we only preside over our respective parishes under his superintendence, and consequently that all things relating to religion through the whole district must be under his guidance. I quoted one or two passages from St. Ignatius, who was consecrated a Bishop by the Apostles themselves, to show that this was no new rule; but that, in the very first age of the Gospel the law was, that nothing was to be done without the Bishop, that we were to obey the Bishop, &c. Thus I gave them to understand that it was as much a point of conscience with me, when presiding over this parish, to oppose, as I had no doubt it was with them, to support, the Tract Society. As I said all this very civilly, wishing indeed, in a quiet way, while accounting for my own principles, to convince them of the error of theirs, they were not at all offended, but they stated, that owing to Mr. Nickson's having given his sanction at West Cowes, they had obtained so very many subscribers, that they were anxious also to obtain my support, and they hoped that (although they saw that I could not conscientiously belong to the Society) I would not oppose their proceedings, as they would pledge themselves to circulate nothing but the essentials of Christianity. I then told them that I did not intend to discuss any particular points, but I was afraid that we could not agree as to what were the essentials of Christianity; for instance, I asked them if they worshipped the same God as myself, One Being in a Trinity of Persons, the Trinity in Unity. They seemed shocked at my doubting this, and I begged their pardon, telling them that I always act firmly upon the principles of the Church of Christ, and not troubling myself with the tenets of others, I might naturally be ignorant on that point. They held also the doctrine of the Atonement. But when I asked if they held the Sacraments to be the ordinary means of grace, they were silent; and they were also silent of course, when I asked them if they believed in the Divine Institution of the Church. I then observed that these were essentials, according to my faith; and I dared not presumptuously declare which, of things that God pronounced to be essential, is the most essential, although I would by no means condemn those who were so unfortunate as not to believe all. Yet, even if my former objection were overcome, I could not support a society which taught only part of what I believe to be essential, as sufficient.

They then described the mighty good which had been done, the number of drunkards reclaimed, &c., by the Society. Without denying that much good might have resulted, I asked them whether they thought that I might do what I considered evil that good might come. Besides which, I asked them whether these persons did not owe their conversion to the grace of God, at which they exclaimed yes; 'then I believe that He would not have left them unconverted, but other means would have been found if their minds had been prepared, even if this Society had not existed.' In short I told them that it was no use talking of the good done by the Society when I thought it wrong to belong to it, for that would be, as I said before, to argue on a Popish principle (and I abhor all Popery), that the end sanctifies the means. I offered them refreshment, and lionised them all over the garden; and we parted the best friends imaginable.

I remain, your devoted Son,

W. F. HOOK.

Whippingham: August 7, 1826.

My dearest Robert,—If tears were guineas, you should be relieved from all your difficulties immediately, for I cried very much at your letter. You must, however, keep

your mind composed, for it is madness to add to real
grievances by fretting about them. Do endeavour, my
dear, to bear up like a man under your present pressure ;
and to be able to do so, address your mind to God in
prayer. It is of no use to fall down on your knees when
you are visited by misfortune, unless you determine in
your heart to lead a strictly religious life for the time
to come. Recollect that by a religious man no one single
sin is to be permitted, tolerated, or even winked at. Sins
of weakness, sins unpremeditated, committed through the
strength of temptation, will be pardoned upon repentance ;
but he who does not *intend* in all things to strive to the
utmost to do his duty, can have no pretence whatever to
be called religious. I say this, because now is the time
seriously to form good resolutions ; and because, in becoming religious, you not only lay up a store of happiness
hereafter, but secure it here. Virtue, says a celebrated
writer, is happiness in hand, and heaven in reversion.

CHAPTER III.

LIFE AT MOSELEY AND BIRMINGHAM.
A.D. 1826–1829.

In the spring of 1825 Archdeacon Hook was appointed to the Deanery of Worcester; and, although he did not take up his abode at Worcester before the following year, the pleasant home at Whippingham had to be broken up. His son's plans were unsettled for some time. It was at first proposed that he should be Curate of Stone (a country living near Worcester, held at that time with the Deanery), and also act as Chaplain to St. Oswald's Hospital in Worcester. His fancy was much captivated by this project; it seemed to offer that combination of retirement and activity which was most to his taste. In May 1826 he writes, ' I know not any situation which is so likely to suit me. Whilst living in perfect seclusion—a kind of monastery—I shall yet be able, when I find it dull at home, to enjoy a little family society at the Deanery.' This plan however, fell through.

The next scheme was to get the living of St. Andrew's in Worcester for him. To this also he was quite favourable, for he began to think that much leisure in a small country parish might foster in him habits of indolence and dreaminess, to which he still considered himself too prone. 'My wish and desire is to be guided wholly by my dear father's judgment. I am, however, sure of one thing, that it is both for my interest and my happiness to be actively engaged in my vocation : for my interest, because being naturally of a heavy, indolent habit, I want continual excitement to keep me awake ; and for my happiness, for I grow every day more and more exclusively devoted to my clerical pursuits, so much so indeed that nothing affords me pleasure except as it is connected with them. I am afraid that a small parish, much as I have speculated upon it in lazy moments would after all be the worst thing for me in the world ; for, although I should still employ myself diligently in the specu- lative, I should soon grow careless in the active, parts of my profession ; and habits are quickly formed.'

The fact is that literary occupation to which he turned with such energy and zeal in his old age was always the kind of work to which his natural incli- nation most powerfully gravitated ; but the pastoral vein was also strong, and an equally strong sense of duty being thrown into that scale turned the balance in its favour. Hence that remarkable combination of literary and pastoral activity which we shall find so conspicuous in the whole of his subsequent career down to the time of his retirement from Leeds. He was first and foremost, from the time of which we are now speaking, a diligent parish priest ; but he ever considered it a principal part of his duty as a parish priest not only to exhort, reprove, and console, but also to teach, and he never forgot that he who would teach must learn. He was, therefore, an indefatigable student, and from his study, day by day, he went out into his parish full of ideas to be imparted to others, and carried forward to some practical issue.

After the contemplation and failure of several plans, he was appointed to the perpetual curacy of Moseley, near Birmingham, to his entire satisfaction. 'At the thought of Moseley,' he writes in June 1826, 'I felt the spirit (without the powers) of Athanasius and Horsley rising within me, and a very pugnacious desire of grappling with the descendants of Priestley and jousting with the humanitarians of Birmingham.' In fact he was getting so eager for work that he hardly cared where he went. Even as late as October there seems to have been some new proposal that Moseley should be given to a cousin, and something else found for him ; upon which he writes that he was quite willing to surrender Moseley, 'only I am so tired of my holiday that a cure of souls I must and will have ere long, even though I take it gratis. I should not at all object to taking a curacy in one of those delightful churches in Birmingham ; indeed I should particularly like it. For although there are good preachers in Birmingham, the services of the Church are shamefully conducted. . . . I wish to goodness the rectors would think less of preaching, and more of having the liturgy rightly performed.'

The end of October, however, saw him fairly established at Moseley, now a suburb of Birmingham, but at that time a quiet country village nearly four miles distant from the town. He was delighted with the aspect of it. 'It is just the place,' he says, 'where I can live and die in peace and seclusion, which is all I want. We have a capital shop in the village where meat and beer, and cheese and eggs, and whipcord and thread, and tops, and gingerbread, and garden stuff, and butter and milk and cream, and almost everything are sold. Now I have turned these good people also into booksellers, and as soon as I finish this scratch I am going off to them with the Society's Bibles and Prayer Books, and as I *will* undersell the Bible Society even though the money comes, as it will, out of my own pocket, I shall persuade the "Missus" to buy them of me, offering the books at 5 per cent. below the Bible Society's price.' His stipend was only 150*l.*, and as he wished to spend liberally upon parochial matters he measured his personal expenses on the most frugal scale. He drank raspberry vinegar instead of wine, and frequently eat pork instead of beef and mutton, which were then considered very dear, he writes, at 8*d.* and 7½*d.* a pound. He declared himself a confirmed bachelor, not only, however, because he could not afford to marry, but for another and singular reason ; that he should wish his wife, if he had one, to conform to the model of George Herbert's pastor's wife, of whom one indispensable qualification was to be that she should cure and heal all the wounds and sores of the parishioners with her own hands. 'Now I never could bear to have these dressed with my wife's hands ; therefore I must remain a bachelor.'

With his sermons he began to take very special pains, being the more careful because Socinians abounded in the parish and neighbourhood, and not a few came to his church. 'I am now reading very hard,' he writes in May 1827, 'to prepare myself to state and enforce the Catholic doctrine concerning the Third Person on Whit Sunday, and that of the hypostatic union on the Sunday following. I am going to Birmingham this morning for the purpose of getting the works of Athanasius, and Bishop Horsley's tracts.'

The practical work which occupied him most during the summer of 1827 was the foundation of a village school. On June 18 he writes to his mother, 'I write a few lines lest you should be anxious, but I have not time for much. I have been on my legs since seven o'clock this morning all over Birmingham and its vicinity to persuade some landholder to sell us the eighth of an acre of land for building upon ; but I have not yet succeeded. We have a meeting on Friday, and what with computing the expenses, talking over my neighbours, preaching two sermons to convince the rich of the necessity of establishing schools, drawing up resolutions, superintending the plans and estimates of builders, applying to everyone who thinks himself a gentleman and soliciting his support, I am pretty busy ; but I never was in my life in better health and spirits, and I am sure that I never was happier, for I feel that I am just in my element.'

It must be owned that the laity of the neighbourhood seem to have been far from enthusiastic in the work, but the energy and resolution of the young curate at length succeeded in breaking down all obstacles. 'I have at last persuaded the good people,' he says, ' that what is represented as utterly impossible does sometimes come to pass.' His squire, Mr. Taylor, let half-an-acre on a lease of ninety-nine years at a guinea rent, and the building was soon begun. His first experience of opposition from members of the extreme Evangelical party began in connexion with this undertaking. They are commonly designated the 'saints' in his letters of this period. There was no kind of opposition which irritated and vexed him more than this; but he met it with much forbearance, and for the most part foiled his assailants with considerable dexterity. 'One old Saint,' he writes, 'has annoyed me much. He appeared to approve the plan until the day of our meeting, and then all at once he sent me a note containing a statement of sundry difficulties in the way of the proposed establishment, and resigning into my hands the accounts of the Sunday school and evening lecture. As to his objections I passed by them with contemptuous silence; and as to the accounts I returned them, stating that I had no intention to take upon myself the office of treasurer to the Sunday schools; that if he wished to call a meeting of the subscribers and resign his office into their hands, I should have no objection to permit a notice to that effect to be given in the church, and, upon *their* appointment, to take the office; but even then I would not receive any unaudited accounts, which has brought Mr. Saint to his right senses, and pleased the subscribers because it looks business-like. I have indeed stolen a march on the " saints " by converting an old widow lately who was once their leader.' She had consulted him about supporting the Bible Society, and he had convinced her that it was based on unsound principles. He now intended to put her at the head of his list of school visitors, and employ her to counteract any interference on the part of others. It was his customary policy, as soon as he had made an impression on anyone's mind, to lose no time in giving him work of some kind to do, in which the newly inculcated principles might be strengthened by exercise.

In August of this year he paid a visit to his friends the Wards in the Isle of Wight, and assisted in the Sunday service at Whippingham, where the Rev. James Ward was now curate in charge. When he preached in the afternoon, not only the church but the churchyard was crowded ; all the windows of the church being set open, so that many persons outside, owing to his strong, clear voice, could hear most of the sermon ; and when he left the church the path to the rectory was lined with his old parishioners. An eye-witness said it was one of the most interesting and affecting sights he ever beheld.

About the same time he accepted the offer of a Lectureship at St. Philip's, Birmingham, Dr. Gardner, Canon of Lichfield, being the rector, and entered upon his duties there in September.

The stipend was 250*l.* per annum, so he was enabled to keep a curate at Moseley ; though he did not spare himself, for after walking or riding four miles into Birmingham, visiting the sick or the schools there, and returning to Moseley, he would frequently walk two miles or more about that parish.

One evil custom connected with the mode of conducting the Burial Service had prevailed in Moseley, with which he and his curate resolutely refused to comply, though it involved a sacrifice of fees amounting to about 20*l.* a year. That part of the funeral service which is appointed to be read in the church had been commonly omitted, unless the officiator received a hatband or half a guinea. The bodies of the poor were, as a consequence, very rarely taken into the church, until Mr. Hook abolished this odious and shameful distinction between poverty and wealth.

In the latter part of October 1827 Dr. Gardner was dangerously ill, and Mr. Hook thought that in the event of death it might be his duty to reside altogether in Birmingham. ' Dr. G.'s successor,' he writes, ' would do everything in his power to render my situation disagreeable,[1] and thus to force me to resign ; but of that I should be very regardless and, to compare small things with great, I should, like old Hooker, take care that if " right Geneva " was preached in the morning, " right Canterbury " should be heard in the evening . . . . Old Gabell was one of my congregation yesterday. He was quite enthusiastic in his eulogy upon my sermon, criticising it just as he used to do my prose tasks at school.'

The work in Birmingham which engaged most of his time and attention was the establishment of a Penitentiary and the superintendence of schools.

---

[1] The appointment of St. Philip's being vested in the Bishop, then an extreme Evangelical, Bishop Ryder.

An extract from a letter, descriptive of the proceedings at a committee in connexion with the former work, illustrates very well the attitude which on this and similar occasions he adopted towards Nonconformists.

' I think I have gained some credit by the way in which I have managed the committee. I have insisted that the rector of the parish in which the Penitentiary is situated shall *ex officio* be a member of any committee, and that the chaplain shall be licensed by the Bishop, which, though of slight use in the present reign, will be a wholesome check when it pleases heaven to remove our present most worthy Diocesan. . . . The " saints " want to establish a committee of ladies. This I have resolutely opposed—a female committee always causes squabbling. The " saints " thought I should oppose any co-operation with dissenters ; when I observed that if they proposed any such resolution as the one in the Bath Penitentiary, which says that the parochial clergy *and* ministers of dissenting congregations shall be *ex officio* members of the committee, I should oppose them most decidedly, because I could not conscientiously admit any proposition which would go to assert the ministerial office of a dissenting teacher. But if they excluded the dissenters from *religious* interference, I said that I should be among the first to seek the support of that respectable body of men. I added that I would never refuse to co-operate with dissenters, when I could do so without compromising the principles of the Church, but that I would sacrifice nothing.'

He succeeded in defeating the proposal for a committee of ladies, and remarks, ' My triumph was rather unexpected.   I find myself much in the same predicament as the Duke of Wellington was, last session, when he carried his amendment of the Corn Bill against the ministers.   I had no expectation of being in a majority.   I only intended to oppose so strongly that Hodson and Spooner might see they were not to dictate to us.   Hodson came down to the meeting thinking that he would be able to carry all before him, and when it was given against him, he and our chairman sat quite aghast, the latter actually forgetting to count hands.   Hodson immediately withdrew from the office of secretary, having declared a ladies' committee to be a *sine quâ non*, and the unanimous call upon me to supply his place was certainly the greatest compliment that could be paid, because it was as much as declaring me to be the leader of one side, as Hodson is of the other.'

Besides occasional shorter visits, he once a month devoted the greater part of a day to a careful examination of the schools for poor children in Birmingham.   He mentions in one of his letters, that he inspected the Blue Coat School from twelve to one o'clock, the Boys' National School from two to four o'clock, and the Girls' from four to five o'clock.   How he won the hearts of many of the children, may be learned from the following interesting letter, written to me by Mr. Peers, for many years a working silversmith in Birmingham.

I attended Pinfold Street School in 1828, which stood upon the present site of the London and North Western

Railway Station. Dr. Hook was a busy, bustling man, full of life, and a great lover and forwarder of education. Once a month he came down to our school, and after going through it and looking into everything, he examined the first class. I was in that class, and we always did our best, because we knew the man and loved him. His examinations were thorough and searching; he warmed to his work, and so did we. When he had finished, he would say, 'Well done, my boys, you are a credit to the school.'

I never saw the good man again, since the last time that he examined the school, but he always took an interest in any of the scholars. He sent me his portrait some years since, which I often look upon with pleasure. God bless him! I trust we shall meet again in heaven, where he is gone.

Since I received this letter, I have found another amongst Dr. Hook's papers, addressed to him in 1864 by the same person. It was called forth by a letter which had appeared in the 'Times,' and had been copied into the 'Birmingham Daily Post' on the relation of political parties to the Church. This will be mentioned more particularly in its proper place. The first part of the letter from his old Birmingham scholar is concerned with that subject; but in the latter part he refers to his boyish recollections of the Curate of Moseley.

If I mistake not, sir, I have very old reasons to respect you. I can remember when I was a little boy, and you took a great interest in the Birmingham National School, and when you had examined the first class, in which I was a scholar, you used sometimes to show how pleased you were by emptying your pocket of all your loose silver to be divided among us. Oh! those were glorious times. It sometimes came to as much as $2\frac{1}{2}d$. each ; and then the consultation as to what we should do with so vast a sum! No Privy Council was ever more solemn in their discussion ; nor did the Rothschild family ever feel the weight of their riches more than we did ours.

But somehow the 'hot suck' shop, at the top of Lease Lane, generally got the lion's share of the money. Only once, I remember, we marched in a body to an empty house in High Street, which had been converted into a theatre, to see the 'Babes in the Wood.' That was my first view of scenic representations, and I have to thank you, sir, for many an hour's enjoyment, for it set me reading, and reading has been to me like an extra sense given by the Deity.

I think you were at the examination when two books were put up as prizes for competition, and I won the first prize. It is lying by my side as I write, and the date is July 20, 1829. I often think of you and the years gone by, and when you bring out a new work, I read the reviews of it in the papers with interest, as I am too poor to purchase the books themselves.

May God give you His blessing, and may you be led by His hand still higher in His Church, to do good to His people, is the sincere wish of your humble servant,

A. PEERS.

In February 1828 his father died, and the family was left very ill provided for. His mother and sister resided with him for a short time at Edgbaston, and afterwards took a small house at Leamington. His mother was extremely anxious to obtain a living for him, but he earnestly deprecated, and finally forbade her application to the Lord Chancellor, the Bishop of Lincoln, and other patrons with whom she had some acquaintance. He had

enough, he said, to support him as long as he remained unmarried, and did not wish to have a rich
living.

Lord Lyndhurst, however, the Chancellor, who
was an old schoolfellow and friend of his father's,
would have given him the rich living of Stone, had
it not been promised to Mr. Peel, a brother of the
Home Secretary. ' I am extremely sorry,' he writes,
' that it is not in my power to give you the living of
Stone, which I should be desirous of doing, as well
from the respect I bear for the memory of your father,
as from the very favourable report I have heard of
your own character and acquirements.' He offered
him the living of 'Stoke Bliss,' in Herefordshire
(which was declined), and added, ' I shall be glad if
it is in my power on a future occasion still further to
assist you.'

His Birmingham friends, meanwhile, were in
great dread of losing him. A 'round robin' was
largely signed in May 1828, entreating the Bishop
to give him the living of St. Philip's in the event
of Dr. Gardner's death, which then seemed im-
minent. The committee which organised the
movement was a mixed body of leading Tories,
Whigs, and Dissenters ; a very remarkable coalition
in days just preceding the Reform Bill, when party
strife was carried on with unprecedented bitterness. ' It is a curious thing,' he writes, ' that I am
popular with the Dissenters, and a great number
of them always form part of my afternoon congregation.'

In August 1828 a letter appeared in one of the
Birmingham papers urging that the stipend of the

lectureship at St. Philip's should be augmented by
annual subscription lest the present lecturer should be
lost to the parish from the necessity of his seeking a
more amply endowed post, 'In my own circle,' the
writer says, 'I am acquainted with at least a dozen
who eagerly wait for an opportunity of this kind to
testify their admiration of the greatest genius that
has ever graced the pulpits of our town. Let but the
appeal once be made, and I am fully satisfied that
it would not be made in vain.'

But if the people of one town were anxious not
to lose him, the people of another town were equally
anxious to gain him for themselves. Early in the
autumn of 1828 the living of Holy Trinity, Coventry, became vacant, and some of the parishioners
lost no time in seeking an interview with him,
and begging him to apply to the Lord Chancellor
for it. After going over to Coventry with his friend
Wood to survey the church and parish, he determined on making an application to Lord Lyndhurst,
through his uncle, Sir Thomas Farquhar. The
Chancellor wrote to him in very friendly terms on
October 3rd, offering the living, 'I am informed,'
he said, 'that it is a situation which requires great
exertion and much discretion on the part of the
incumbent. I trust, and have no doubt, that
you will fulfil the opinion which I entertain of you
in making this appointment. Yours very truly,
Lyndhurst.

Having now completed those early stages of his
life in which, first as a schoolboy, and afterwards as
a curate, he occupied a dependent and subordinate
position, two features in his character may be noticed

which specially distinguish it during this period. First, his humble and reverent submission to authority; the more remarkable in one whose natural disposition was fiery and impulsive. However much his wishes were at variance with the decisions either of his schoolmasters or his parents in early youth, he never questioned the superiority of their judgment, and never hesitated to comply with it. And in like manner as a curate, first under his father and afterwards under Dr. Gardner, he never would act on his own responsibility, but before every step he took he had consulted and obtained the consent of his chief. Secondly, whatever position he was called upon to fill he made the best of it; he saw all its advantages and few of its drawbacks, and discharged the duties of his office with a cheerful persuasion that of all duties in the world they were the pleasantest which could be assigned to him.

LETTERS, 1827-1828.

To his Father.—Meeting with Mr. Wilberforce, the father of Bishop Wilberforce.

June 4, 1827.

And now you will wish to know how I, of all men in the world, should have fallen in with Mr. Wilberforce, or Mr. Wilber, as his intimates style him. Since I have been at Moseley, conciliation has been the word with me, as well as with his Majesty's ministers, but not, as in the case of the latter, with the sacrifice of principle. And the 'saints' and I are on the best possible terms—I, on the one hand, hoping to convert them, and they expecting, on the other, to pervert me; so a whole gang of their sanctities having come to Birmingham to a Jews' Society on Thursday, I was invited to meet the leaders at dinner at Mr. Palmer's on Friday. I accepted the invitation, and we really had a pleasant and even cheerful party. Mr. ——, the leading 'saint' of Birmingham, and chaplain to my Lord Bishop, had previously called upon me. He is a most delightful man, and I should have some hope of him if his wife were not as full of spiritual pride as an egg is of meat. I wished to have a little conversation with Mr. Wilber after dinner, and we gossiped together for some time. He began by recommending me not to study or to take exercise directly after meals, but to take up one of Scott's novels! which I must own made me stare. We talked on till he alluded to the London University, which he said he had not supported because there was not provision made for religious instruction, although there was to be admission to all parties. He thought those evidences might be admitted to which even Socinians would not object. I told him that I hoped he would not consider me presumptuous, but I could not go so far with him as that, for the objections would not be removed in my mind if a false religion were allowed to be taught; that the step he proposed seemed to me to go towards the establishment of Socinianism; and that, besides, a Christian has no right to preach part of the truth—he must preach the whole or none; he must not only preach Christ, but Him crucified. So that I amused myself by attacking the *pseudo-Evangelical* on really Evangelical grounds, and almost to make him appear as the advocate of Socinianism! He then said that he would agree with me to a certain point, but he thought that since we could not do all the good we wished, we might nevertheless do all that was possible for us to do. To this I replied that I agreed in this doctrine, as long as we could do this good by lawful means; and here, I told him, appeared to me to be the grand difference between his principle and that of those whom I considered to be right; namely, that we do not solely regard the end, but also attend to the means—that to do a great good we do not consider ourselves justified in acting even a little wrong. He would not allow that such were his principles, but he could not prove the contrary. I then showed him that on his own grounds the good he proposed could not be obtained. The object he hoped to gain was this—that evidence should be brought to prove the Scriptures genuine and authentic, and that then, this point gained, we might afterwards convert them by reasoning from Scripture genuine religion ; but, I said, suppose the genuineness of the Scriptures to be proved, a Socinian lecturer would persuade his auditory that our version is incorrect, and if they could not refer to the original they would then have recourse to Mr. Belsham's Bible, and thus be more hardened in their Socinianism. I concluded by stating it as my principle to do right, according to the rules of the Church, and I leave the rest to Providence. He seemed to be much interested in the conversation, for we stood for a long time by ourselves, and we then went to other sub-jects. He shook me heartily by the hand at parting. Miss Wilberforce received the Sacrament at my hands yesterday. I am afraid, however, that she will take but a bad account of me to her papa, for I gave them a most strong sermon against trusting to religious feelings, and showed that if a zeal for the promotion of religion was not accompanied with the regular discharge of other duties, or even if it led us into schism, it might be inspired by a lying spirit, and that by our conduct only we could judge of the influence of the Spirit.

Prospect of a Lectureship at St. Philip's, Birmingham.

Moseley, Birmingham : September 18, 1827.

My dearest Mother,—My spirit is quite up with respect to the Lectureship of St. Philip's, and many are the mighty castles of orthodox utility that I have been building upon the subject. I intend to recall, if possible, the remnant of Dr. Story's scattered friends ; I shall volunteer my services as secretary to the Society for Promoting Christian Knowledge, and by my activity compel the Bishop to give it more decided support. When I am licensed, I shall speak to his lordship about establishing a branch of the Society for Propagating the Gospel. I intend to take the blue-coat school (which has been much neglected by the clergy) under my fostering wing. I shall tell Hodson that on all points where we do not differ, I will go hand in hand with him ; and thus get my footing in the national and infant schools. I shall take also great pains with my sermons, and thus by exertion and prayer I hope to obtain God's grace, and to do some good in my generation. All this, however, will occupy my whole mind so completely as to render it necessary for me to decline engagements as much as possible, and my visits to Worcester will be like angels', 'few and far between.' I am not quick, and require deliberation ; in a bustle and confusion, also, I can do nothing ; I require calm and retirement to collect my thoughts. I intend to devote all the energies of my mind, by God's blessing, to my new appointment, and I long to begin. I shall be obliged to keep a horse for myself and curate, which I think I can do at a neighbouring farmer's for six or eight shillings a week. I shall also get my curate to take a lodging with two bed-rooms, and by paying him a small sum for one of them, I shall have an apartment in Birmingham ; and I shall get Dr. Gardner to give me the key of the parish library, which can be my Birmingham study, in which I will make a point of passing one day out of the seven, so that people may know where to find me. Whateley tells me that my appointment has given much satisfaction, and that Dr. Gardner is very much pleased with it.

Your devoted Son,

W. F. HOOK.

Hard Work.

8 Colmore Row, Birmingham : November 2, 1827.

My dearest Mother, ... I have now so much on hand, that you must not expect me to be a very good correspondent ; indeed, I am quite awestruck at my temerity in undertaking what I have done. A semi-saint told me, upon my saying that I respected Mr. Hodson's character, though I disliked his principles, that he knew Mr. Hodson and Mr. Garbett also respected me, inasmuch as they are afraid of me, both as being steady in my principles and having much influence in the neighbourhood. I am here almost single-handed. There are many persons who will act orthodoxly when put up to it, but they cannot advise as to the line to be taken, and there is a prevalent wish to yield as far as possible to the 'saints' on one side ; and, on the other, one or two persons are so violently opposed to them that they put themselves in the wrong. I have another difficulty to overcome : my Moseley people, I hear from all quarters, are very angry at my leaving them. With all these difficulties I am expecting my new schoolmaster and mistress from Bath, and I have to attend a sub-committee for forming a penitentiary, of which I am the only member who even pretends to orthodoxy. If I can get through all these things well, I shall not care ; but I must own that I regard my present position with fear and trembling. Besides all this, I have sermons to write or to correct with the greatest care, for people discuss points on which I have spoken in the pulpit, and seem to watch me very narrowly—in fact, I find myself placed in a very prominent situation, too prominent for my time of life, and it is with no ordinary diffidence and fear that I look forward to the future.

Your devoted Son,

W. F. Hook.

Blunders in Bishops' Titles.

8 Colmore Row : December 10, 1827.

My dearest Mother, ... I wish a certain person would not trouble himself in matters ecclesiastical ; he has made the most ridiculous blunder in censuring the writer of the 'Times' for calling the Archbishop of Canterbury the 'Metropolitan'; thinking, I suppose, that the Bishop of London, being Bishop of the civil metropolis, must naturally be so of the ecclesiastical one.   He said not long ago that the Bishop of Winton had refused the Metropolitan see, meaning the see of London.   A censor of others ought himself to be correct.   I see the papers continue to speak of the reconsecration of the Bishop of Rochester ; I wish very much to know whether this is true.   If it is, all I can say is, that it is the most infamous, shameful act of barefaced schism that has ever been committed in the Church of England since the Reformation, degraded as she has too often been, and still is, by those careless Bishops and Archbishops, who have not scrupled to violate at will the fundamental principles and canons of the Universal Church of Christ.   I have not time for more ; I expect some staunch friends to meet me here for the purpose of arranging places for Wednesday.   I have just been reading the last report of the S. P. C. K., where the reply of Bishop James to the address of the Bishop of Gloucester is given.   I am still more convinced than ever that there could not be a more unfit man than Bishop James for the Church of India ; evidently not a divine, and also evidently an egotist.   He will be unable to meet the Greek Christians in the way in which they ought to be met ; and, ignorant of the nature of the Church, he will be unable to propagate Christianity in the way in which it ought to be propagated.   He is a semi-saint, and if the Church Missionary Society and Bible Society ply him, as no doubt they will, with flattery, he will soon be a red-hot one.

With best love to my father, of whom I shall still be anxious to hear,

I remain, your devoted Son,

W. F. HOOK.

Letter from Bishop Jolly on the Death of Mr. Hook's Father.

Fraserburgh : March 24 (Annunciation Eve), 1828.

My very dear reverend Brother,—Ever thinking of you with affectionate esteem, I felt how you must have been affected upon the demise of your most venerable and worthy father, now for ever happy. A heart so tenderly filial as yours (and the best hearts feel most) must have smarted under the stroke, while you kissed the rod with entire submission and resignation to the holy will of our Heavenly Father. I pretend not, therefore, to suggest topics of consolation to you, who have them for your own use in abundance, and minister them to others. And indeed, at present, I am very unfit to write anything upon any subject, being, upon the back of a heavy cold, under particular oppression and languor. But having a letter from our mutual dear friend of Fifeshire, in which he kindly writes of you, I could not forbear to give you the trouble of my line of condolence with the best wishes of my heart, which begs your prayers for me in return. The very title which your excellent father most worthily bore was endearing to me. His ever memorable predecessor, great and good Dr. Hickes, in his preface to Bishop Campbell's book on the intermediate state of the soul, writes and states that scriptural and truly primitive doctrine so as, in my opinion, to yield a vast fund of consolation under our momentary separation (and that only in respect of bodily intercourse), from our deceased friends. Bishop Hickes I consider and rank among the best writers against the corruptions of the Church of Rome. The truly Catholic practice of prayer for the advancement of the final consummation of the bliss of the faithful departed, plants a barrier strong against some of its most dangerous doctrines and practices.

That quondam dean, with whom the late good dean now is, drew up a prayer to be used for himself after his decease, which he put for that purpose into the hand of a friend ; from that friend our excellent Bishop Rattray received it in London, 1717, and I have it in the hand-writing of Bishop Alexander, Bishop Rattray's successor. As my paper may, I think, contain it by compressing, I will transcribe a copy which you will receive as a curiosity. I entertain no doubt upon the point ; and my great favourite, Dr. S. Johnson, used such prayer, and would probably have done it with more confidence had he been as well versed in the ancient fathers as Dr. Hickes was. The phraseology is that of the Apostolical Constitutions.

'O God, who by Thy nature art immortal and ever-lasting, by whom all things mortal and immortal were created, and who madest Thy rational creature, man, the inhabitant of this world, subject unto death. but hast pro-mised him a resurrection unto eternal life ; O God, who wouldst not suffer Enoch and Elias to undergo the sentence of death ; O God of Abraham, Isaac, and Jacob, who art the God of men, not as they are dead but as living ; because the souls of all live unto Thee, and the spirits of the just, whom no torments can touch in any degree, are in Thy hand, they being all holy in Thy sight ; do Thou, O Lord, now look upon this Thy servant, whom Thou hast chosen, and taken from this into the other state. O Thou lover of men, forgive him all his offences, which he hath committed willingly or unwillingly against Thee ; and send Thy benevolent angels to him to conduct him into the bosom of the Patriarchs, Prophets, and Apostles, and of all Thy righteous servants who have pleased Thee from the beginning of the world ; into that region of light, where there is no sorrow, no grief, no lamentation, but a calm and quiet place of bliss and blessed spirits, and a haven of rest, free from the storms and tempests of this world, and where the souls of the just converse together in a joyful expectation of their future reward, and behold the glory of Christ. In whose name, we beseech Thee, O Father of spirits, to accomplish the number of Thine elect, that we with this Thy servant, and with all who are gone before us, and who shall follow us to their promised rest, may have our consummation of perfect bliss, both in body and soul, at the resurrection of the just ; through our Lord Jesus Christ, who rose from the dead, and ascended into Heaven, from whence He shall come again with glory to judge both the quick and the dead. To whom, with Thee and the Holy Ghost, the Lord, and Giver of Life, be all glory, honour, worship, thanksgiving, and adoration, now and for ever. Amen.'

In the above I do most humbly think there is nothing but what results from the blessed apostle's prayer for his dear Onesiphorus which we read last evening, 'The Lord grant unto him that he may find mercy of the Lord in that day.' The final blotting out of sin awaits His coming from Heaven to raise and refine the body also, and make it a fit companion for the soul in eternal glory! meanwhile, although the body lies insensible, the fellowship of souls in the Communion of Saints, remains uninterrupted, and defecated of corporeal affections, is the more spiritualised. The translation of our dear departed friends elevates our hearts more to the heavenly state, and to think of the bliss of Paradise. I ever read those words of St. Cyprian (in his sweet little book, 'De Mortalitate,') with tender emotion. 'Magnus illic nos carorum numerus expectat ; parentum, fratrum, filiorum, frequens nos et copiosa turba desiderat, jam de suâ immortalitate secura, et adhuc de nostrâ sollicita. In horum conspectum et complexum venire, quanta et illis et nobis in commune lætitia est !'

Accept now, my very dear reverend sir, this poor attempt of my goodwill to express the cordial attachment of your very respectful

ALEXANDER JOLLY.

I earnestly request a place in your prayers.'

[1] The good Bishop lived ten years after the date of this letter, and died aged eighty-two. I cannot forbear relating the affecting circum-

stances of his last illness and death as recorded by his chaplain the Rev. Charles Pressley. A lay friend visited him in the summer of 1838, when a general synod of the clergy was about to take place. 'Tell Dr. Walker' (Bishop of Edinburgh), he said, 'that I am dying, getting weaker and weaker. I trust to his taking care that things are so managed at the synod that the principles of the Church may be preserved unimpaired. I am more and more convinced of the awfully responsible situation of the clergy, and I greatly fear that (not excepting myself), they fall far short of what they ought to be.' His friend remarked that if all the clergy performed their duty as he had done his, they might have confidence : to which he replied that he had no confidence in anything but the merits of his Saviour, on which alone he trusted. A few days after this, on the evening of St. Peter's Day, he seemed better than usual, and was left alone for the night about nine o'clock. When his attendant returned in the morning about seven o'clock he found the Bishop dead, lying in the most easy posture with his hands folded across his breast, and a most serene expression of countenance. Sutton's ' Disce mori ' (' Learn to Die,') lay by his side.

CHAPTER IV.

STATE OF THE CHURCH—RISE OF THE 'TRACTARIAN
SCHOOL—LIFE AT COVENTRY.   A.D. 1829–1837.

WE have now reached the period when the subject
of this memoir begins to occupy a conspicuous place,
not only as an eminent parish priest, but also as an
actor in the great ecclesiastical movements of the
age.   In order, therefore, to form a just estimate of
the character and value of his work, it seems desirable to take a brief survey of the condition of
the Church of England at this epoch.

She had but lately begun to shake off the lethargy
by which she had been oppressed during the eigh-
teenth century.   The causes of that depression had
been manifold.   The unfortunate attachment of a
considerable body of the clergy to the dynasty of the
Stuarts excluded for more than half a century many
men of ability, learning, and earnest piety—men
devoted to Catholic doctrine and practice of the
purest type—from positions of influence in the Established Church.   In the reigns of the first two
Georges, the energy of the Church, such as it was,
had to contend, on behalf of the first principles of
faith and morality, against a flood tide of Deism,
Atheism, and profligacy.   It was as much as she
could do to stem the torrent ; she did not advance,

and in many vital respects she slipped back. Whilst the reason was occupied with evidences and demonstrations, the religious sentiments and emotions were comparatively uncultivated and the love of many waxed cold. It was the policy of the State to depress the Church, and to convert it as much as possible into a servile implement for political purposes. Worldly-minded ministers conferred bishoprics on worldly-minded men, under whose misrule fearful havoc was made in the doctrine and discipline of the Church. Laxity and listlessness in the discharge of spiritual functions pervaded, with some noble exceptions, all ranks of the hierarchy. In days when a Bishop of Winchester made one visitation only in the course of twenty-one years—when an Archbishop of York confirmed but once—when a Bishop of Llandaff, who never resided in his diocese, complacently thanked God that he had not spent his time in idleness, but had been usefully employed in writing many 'seasonable publications,' and building and planting on his estate in Westmoreland— when candidates were admitted to ordination, after a few hasty questions put by a chaplain, sometimes in the cricket field, or after his return from hunting, it is not surprising that parish priests, especially in rural places, were to be seen smoking their clay pipes with village gossips outside the alehouse ; that they caroused with their squire or farmers over the punch bowl ; and that on Sundays they preached, what Samuel Pepys would have called ' lazy, dull sermons ' in mouldy churches, to scanty congregations.

Such scandals were not extinct at the beginning of this century, but they were rapidly diminishing ;

for during the latter half of the former century, a
noise and a shaking had been going on amongst the
dry bones.

That great apostle of Christ, John Wesley,
and his disciples, kindled a flame of piety in the
land, although the Church in her coldness and
pride repelled it. The spiritual work which the
Wesleyans conducted, after their secession, outside the Church, was carried on by the Evangelical
school which grew up within the fold. But the
Evangelicals were unable to revive the Church,
for the simple reason that they did not comprehend or enforce more than a part of her doctrine, while they were comparatively regardless of
ecclesiastical discipline and liturgical ordinances.
They had a zeal for God, but not according to knowledge.   Their theology was based, rather on the
teaching of Wesley and Whitfield, than on a study of
the primitive fathers and the history of the Church,
or the great divines of the English Reformation.
The sum and substance of it was the doctrine *con-
sciously* embraced of man's inability to save himself,
a total abnegation of his own merits, and an absolute dependence on the merits of Christ's sacrifice
for salvation.   They were powerful in showing the
work done *for* us by our Redeemer ; where they
failed was, in showing the work which he does *in* us,
more especially through the Sacraments, and (in
their measure) through other ordinances of the
Church as divinely appointed means whereby men
may become partakers of the Divine Nature. By
their neglect of discipline and ordinances they confused the lines of demarcation between the Church

and Dissent, and fed the ranks of Nonconformity instead of recruiting from them. A very marked increase in the number of sects is visible after the rise of the Evangelical movement. Thus, while the Church is indebted to the Evangelicals for an infusion of piety, she is also unhappily indebted to them for the creation of much schism and confusion.

The revival of the Church was to come from men of another stamp; from men who understood and taught and, as far as possible, practised the principles of the Church in their integrity and fulness. From the time of the Restoration onwards, such men had never been wanting; even in the darkest days of trouble and rebuke and blasphemy and coldness they were to be found, although like the seven thousand in Israel, who had not bowed the knee to Baal, they were often unnoticed and unknown.

Religious societies, which lasted from the Restoration to the reign of the Georges, had been formed for the avowed object of 'promoting holiness of heart and life,' including amongst the means to this end daily services, weekly celebration of Holy Communion, a strict observance of the fasts and festivals of the Church, monthly conferences of the clergy, the establishment of schools, and various other agencies for reclaiming the vicious and ignorant. There were about thirty-nine of such societies in or near London, with branches in other parts of the country. These societies gave birth to the 'Society for Promoting Christian Knowledge' whence proceeded the 'Society for the Propagation of the Gospel in Foreign Parts.' They were stifled soon after the commencement of the Hanoverian rule,

but they had bred a race of men which never died
out.   Such, amongst Bishops, were Wilson and
Butler, Wake and Potter, Gibson, Berkeley, and
Louth ; amongst the second order of clergy, Bingham
and Waterland ; amongst the laity, Samuel Johnson.
They were the successors, though at long intervals,
in thought and feeling, of Collier and Ken, and
Nelson and Horneck.

And when we cross the boundary which divides
the last century from the present, the number of
such men, especially amongst the laity and the
inferior ranks of the clergy, largely increases.
William Stevens, the Treasurer of Queen Anne's
Bounty ; Jones of Nayland ; Bishops Van Mildert,
Lloyd, and Jebb ; Alexander Knox, Joshua Watson
and Henry Handley Norris, are only the most conspicuous and able amongst many who studied, loved,
and reverenced the principles of the Anglican Church
and of the Church Catholic as it was constituted
before the disruption of Eastern and Western Christendom.   In this succession, for at present it was
a succession rather than a definite school or party,
the subject of this memoir is entitled to be placed.
Bishop Jebb, indeed, Joshua Watson, and Mr. Norris
were his personal friends in early life.   He was a
connecting link between such men and the Oxford
Tractarian School, which was yet unformed.

The great and good men whose names I have
just cited did much—some by their writings, others
by their practical exertions—to promote the knowledge of sound principles and to engender that
corporate feeling and action on the part of the
Church in which she was as yet very deficient.   By

their efforts, the National Society for Promoting the Education of the Poor in the Principles of the Established Church was founded in the year 1811, and the old Societies for Promoting Christian Knowledge and Propagating the Gospel were quickened into fresh life. But much remained to be done. By the end of that period to which the present memoir has been brought down, the organisation of the Church was still very incomplete. Episcopal Visitations and Confirmations were in many instances very irregularly performed. Agencies for sustaining the corporate life of the Church were in abeyance. Convocation, suppressed in 1717, was still silent. Congresses, conferences, and even ruridecanal meetings were as yet things unknown. There were not those large bodies of hearty supporters of the Church which are to be found among the laity of the present day, although there were earnest and enlightened laymen who have never been surpassed in their attachment to it.

The clergy also were as a body very deficient in activity and such learning as pertained to their vocation. It was remarked by Dr. Hobart, the Bishop of New York, when he visited England in 1824, that while the best educated among the English clergy were well versed in scholarship or divers branches of science, they were very commonly ignorant of the theology and the history of the Church. There seemed good ground for such complaint, when for a long time it was found impracticable to get support for a journal of sacred literature. ' The country clergy,' wrote Mr. Norris, 'are constant readers of the " Gentleman's Magazine," deep in the antiquities of the signs of inns, speculations as to what becomes of swallows in winter, and whether hedgehogs or other urchins are most justly accused of sucking milch cows dry at night.' It was not till the year 1818 that Mr. Norris and Joshua Watson induced Mr. Iremonger to start the 'Christian Remembrancer.'

The diocesan supervision of the clergy, in fact, was so imperfect, and they so rarely met in those voluntary conferences in which experiences are compared and emulation is kindled, that if a country parson was inclined to lapse into the easy-going country gentleman, there was no strong force of public opinion in the Church to hinder him. Sydney Smith's rhyming summary of Bishop Blomfield's first Charge in the Diocese of Chester in 1825 is a burlesque, but it indicates truly enough the kind of amusements to which the country clergy in that part at least of the kingdom were addicted.

> Hunt not, fish not, shoot not ;
> Dance not, fiddle not, flute not ;
> But, before all things, it is my particular desire,
> That, once at least in every week, you take
> Your dinner with the Squire.

Moreover, even amongst High Churchmen, so called, both clerical and lay, the idea of the Church as a divine institution, rather than a merely political institution or department of the State, was very imperfectly formed ; while, even as a department of the State, its growth and action were hampered and impeded at every turn. Most of the parochial endowments remained as they had been in the days when the clergy were celibate, and the value of

money was five times as great as it is in the nine-
teenth century. Out of a total of some 10,600
parochial benefices at the beginning of this century,
the incomes of more than half were under 50*l.* a year.
The number of the parochial clergy was 10,300,
actually smaller than the number of parishes to be
served; hence a vast number of pluralist incumbents,
parishes without parsonage houses, curates dividing
their time between several cures, often considerable
distances apart, Sunday services cut down to one in
a fortnight, sometimes to one in three weeks, or on
accidental occasions; holy communion celebrated
at rare intervals, and in some instances altogether
dropped for several years. There were indeed
churches where divine service was still carried on
daily, sometimes even twice a day, but this was for
the most part in towns where special endowments
existed from ancient times for the purpose, and they
were mere ghosts of what they once had been in
days when the religious societies were in full
activity. It was suggested by some, as one induce-
ment amongst others to Mr. Hook to take the living
of Trinity, in Coventry, that the Wednesday and
Friday services had been dropped since the death of
the late Vicar, and that there was no need to resume
them.

In the distribution of the clergy, there was the
same kind of disproportion relative to the population as that which prevailed in Parliamentary representation. Just as great manufacturing towns where
the population had risen to 50,000 or 100,000 souls,
returned only one member to Parliament or none at
all, so very commonly were they provided with but

one or two pastors. This was not the fault of the Church; for before the Church Building Act of 1818 it was not possible to divide a parish without a special Act of Parliament, the cost of which was ruinously great. After the passing of this Act and the establishment of the Incorporated Church Building Society, a great spring in the direction of church extension took place. During the first seven years of this century only twenty-four churches were consecrated in the kingdom, whereas between 1821 and 1830 the number was 308, and Bishop Blomfield between 1828 and 1856 consecrated more than 200 in the diocese of London alone.

But while the Church had been heavily clogged in her endeavours to keep pace with the population, Dissent had been free; Dissent, never powerful in the country, stepped into the great waste places in large towns, and established strongholds from which it is now only beginning to be dislodged. During the first two or even three decades of the century, Dissent did not assume a very hostile or aggressive tone towards the Church, because the Church was too feeble and inactive to provoke jealousy or alarm. It was not until the Church began to shake herself free from her slumber and her shackles, and to do her duty by the nation as she never had done it before, that Dissent began to clamour for disestablishment and disendowment. While the Church 'was dying' as Sydney Smith said, 'of dignity,' Dissent was quiet and content. Thus it will be seen that the most active opposition which Dr. Hook encountered in the earlier part of his career proceeded, not so much from the Dissenters outside the Church, as from the more fanatical of the Evangelicals inside her walls. This indeed was also due to the principle, which he always advocated and practised, of absolute toleration towards them 'that are without' : he neither denounced them nor molested them in any way, but left them to pursue their course without interference, and whenever it was possible, without compromising his principles, he worked with them. 'There is a line between us,' he used to say, 'but across that line we shake hands.'

The state of the country when he became Vicar of Trinity, Coventry, was not such as to render the pastoral charge of a large manufacturing parish agreeable or encouraging. The repeal of the Corporation and Test Acts in 1828, and the passing of the Roman Catholic Relief Bill in 1829, had indeed removed two irritating causes of political discontent, but the social condition of the people was one of deep and deplorable distress. The long exhausting war with the French, which ended in the victory of Waterloo, had left the nation burdened with a huge debt. The population rapidly increased after the establishment of peace, while the duties on the importation of foreign corn hindered a supply of food adequate to the increased demand. In addition to this the poor laws were ill devised and ill administered, while, to crown all, Parliamentary representation was so unequal that large masses of the people were unable to seek redress for their grievances through natural and constitutional channels. From all parts of the country during the years 1829 and 1830 innumerable petitions poured into Parliament representing the pitiable state of depression and distress which prevailed in every department of industry. Agricultural labourers were found starved to death. In spite of landlords' reducing rents and clergy foregoing payment of tithe, wages fell. The peasantry in their dense ignorance and mad despair took to breaking machines and burning ricks, and night after night the sky was lit up with the ruddy glare of the flames which were destroying the nation's food.

The distress of the manufacturing districts was less severe and was more patiently endured; but frequent strikes, and occasional disturbances of a violent character proved that it was keenly felt. The returns of the Coventry Union at this time illustrate the state of things in that city, and may be taken as a sample of the condition of large towns all over the country. The number of families receiving relief in Coventry in the year 1827 was 280; the number in 1830 was 1,312. The number of paupers in the house at the close of the year 1827 was 183; the number at the beginning of the year 1830 was 456. These statistics moreover were a very imperfect representation of the distress in Coventry. It is an ancient privilege of the inhabitants in that city that any man who has served an apprenticeship of seven years at one trade is entitled to the franchise, and the holders of this franchise are at all times very reluctant to forfeit it by falling upon the parish. Hence the distress of the operatives in Coventry, especially the weavers, during a depression of trade is always peculiarly great.

Although the clergy, speaking generally, did their utmost by the most charitable and self-denying labours to relieve the misery by which they were surrounded, yet their popularity as a body was at a low ebb, owing to the unfortunate opposition which, with some exceptions, they offered to the demands of the nation for Parliamentary Reform. The Bishops, who consistently voted against the Reform Bill in the Upper House, were insulted and threatened in public; and in the riots of Bristol in 1831 the Bishop's palace was rifled and partly burnt. By not heartily throwing themselves into the cause of Reform the clergy lost a magnificent opportunity of attaching the people to the Church, and were too commonly regarded by the vulgar mind as opponents rather than champions of the great Christian principles of liberty and justice. The interests of Liberalism and Dissent came to be considered identical, although there is no natural or necessary connexion between them. Deeply beloved as the Vicar personally was by the poor of his parish in Coventry, he owns in one of his letters that it was a rare thing to get a civil answer from a working man, if he was a stranger. Although theoretically a Tory, and as such opposed to the Reform Bill, yet he abstained from taking part in any public opposition to the measure; he was not slow to recognise the justice of it when it had become law, and as time went on he became, especially on social and educational questions, a Reformer himself of a bold and advanced type. From political agitation of any kind he always held aloof on principle, and he was of too large and independent a mind to attach himself irrevocably to any party leader in the affairs of either Church or State. ' *Nullius addictus jurare in verba magistri* ' was a motto which he was accustomed to quote in reference to himself.

The throes and struggles by which the country was convulsed during the slow and painful birth of the Reform Bill, amongst other good results, completely woke up the Church. The events which her foes hoped, and which some of her friends feared, would effect her downfall, really turned out in many ways to her advantage; they led to the removal or rectification of abuses, they caused her truest-hearted members to rally round her in force, to 'lengthen her cords and to strengthen her stakes.'

All kinds of schemes of Church Reform, some reasonable, others violent and wild, were afloat. While some persons would have been content with the abolition of Church rates and the readjustment of ecclesiastical revenues, others demanded the expulsion of the Bishops from the legislature, and others the complete separation of Church and State; while others, such as Dr. Arnold and Lord Henley, though they did not agree in details, would have united all sects with the Church by Act of Parliament, on the principle of each retaining its distinctive doctrines, and all using the buildings of the Church in common, just as one sometimes sees cats, dogs, mice, and all manner of birds confined within one cage. The proposals for alterations in the Liturgy were countless, and would, if acted upon, have improved that venerable compilation off the face of the earth. The usual lies were diligently circulated concerning the 'enormous wealth' and 'State pay' of the clergy; the usual 'scandals' were industriously sought out, or fabricated, for the purpose of

disgracing a whole order in the eyes of the world
by parading the delinquencies of a few unworthy
members.   On the other hand the attachment of
many to the Church was wholly or mainly political:
they viewed it as a department of the State, and
were profoundly ignorant of Church principles.

The alarm of the friends of the Church, already
excited by the Roman Catholic Relief Bill and by
the Reform Bill, was brought to a height by the
suppression of ten Irish Bishoprics in 1833.

It was then that a small knot of friends, men of
mark indeed in the Universities but otherwise little
known to the world, began to take counsel together
to devise means for helping the Church in the hour,
as it was believed, of extreme peril.

At the beginning of the Long Vacation of 1833
the Rev. W. Palmer of Worcester College, Oxford,
and Mr. Hurrell Froude met in the Common Room
of Oriel, and resolved to form an association for the
purpose of vindicating the rights of the Church, and
restoring the knowledge of sound principles.   The
design was communicated by Mr. Palmer to Mr.
Hugh James Rose, then Rector of Hadleigh in
Suffolk, and by Mr. Froude to Mr. Keble.   Mr.
Newman was at that time absent from England, but
joined the party on his return from the Continent.
The Rev. Arthur Perceval also was soon afterwards
added to the number.   A conference of the friends
was held at Hadleigh, and they parted comforted in
spirit and strengthened in purpose, more especially
by the influence of the learned, large-minded, warm-
hearted Rector, Mr. Rose, ‘ who,’ to quote the words
of the most illustrious of that company, ‘ when hearts

were failing, bade us stir up the gift that was in us and betake ourselves to our true mother.'

Mr. Rose had started the 'British Magazine' in 1832, a periodical which, under his able editorship, and afterwards under that of Dr. Maitland, helped much to cultivate a spirit of churchmanship, and to extend a knowledge of sound Church principles. Some articles by Mr. Palmer had lately appeared in the Magazine calling attention to the increasing feebleness of Dissent, more especially as betrayed in the tendency to endless subdivisions of sects, the ignorance of many of their ministers, and the estrangement from their ranks of the higher orders of society. In July 1833, Mr. Hook had contributed a paper to the same journal, in which the absurdity and impracticability of Dr. Arnold's scheme for identifying Church and State by the simple expedient of including all denominations within the lines of the Church, were ably exposed. He pointed out that any such attempt to secure the Establishment by sacrificing the fundamental principles of the Church would involve the loss of nearly all the best of the clergy, who would never consent to minister in a Church so constituted, and that (to quote his own words) 'the sight would not be edifying of ejecting the most learned and devoted of the clergy to turn their churches into parochial Exeter Halls.'

He was not present at the conference at Hadleigh ; but from letters written to him by Mr. Rose, Mr. Palmer, and Mr. Perceval, it is clear that he was kept well informed of the proceedings of the newly-created party. After the conference at Hadleigh, frequent meetings took place at Oriel College between Mr. Newman, Mr. Keble, Mr. Palmer, and Mr. Froude, the first result of which, and of correspondence with their friends at a distance, was that a formulary was drawn up entitled, 'Suggestions for the Formation of an Association of Friends of the Church,' which was printed and extensively circulated in all parts of England in the autumn of 1833. The objects of the Association were defined to be :

'1. To maintain pure and inviolate the doctrines, the services, and the discipline of the Church : that is, to withstand all change which involves the denial and suppression of doctrine, a departure from primitive practice in religious offices, or innovation upon the apostolical prerogatives, order, and commission of bishops, priests, and deacons.

'2. To afford churchmen an opportunity of exchanging their sentiments, and co-operating together on a large scale.'

Mr. Palmer visited several of the large towns to enlist the sympathy of the clergy in the Association, and from none did he meet a heartier welcome or receive more cordial promises of support than from the Vicar of Holy Trinity, Coventry, and such clergy belonging to that city or neighbourhood as were under his influence.

One of the most direct fruits of the Association was an address signed by about 7,000 of the clergy, and presented to the Archbishop of Canterbury (Howley) in February 1834. This address was a declaration, that amidst the growth of Latitudinarian sentiments and ignorance concerning the spiritual claims of the Church, the signatories wished to express their devoted adherence to the apostolical doctrine and polity of the Church, and their deep-rooted attachment to the Liturgy as an embodiment of the primitive faith ; but that while they deprecated any rash innovation in spiritual matters, the primate might rely upon their hearty and dutiful support in carrying into effect such wholesome reforms as the times might require, especially such as would tend to revive the discipline of ancient times, to strengthen the connexion between the bishops, clergy, and people, and to promote the purity, efficiency, and unity of the Church.

This address was signed by Mr. Hook. It was not long afterwards followed by a declaration on the part of the laity, which was mainly composed by Joshua Watson. Its language was similar to the address of the clergy, save that it insisted more forcibly on the importance of protecting the Church as an establishment, asserting that 'the consecration of the State by the public maintenance of the Christian religion is the first and paramount duty of a Christian people.' Many laymen, zealously de-voted to the Church, abstained from signing the declaration on account of these strong expressions, and among them Mr. W. P. Wood. It received, however, the signatures of about 250,000 heads of families. The activity of the Vicar of Holy Trinity in obtaining signatures in Coventry may be esti-mated from the fact, that in his parish 1,120 names were appended to the document, whereas in the adjoining parish, though nearly double in population,[1] the number was only 529.

Although he did not object to the declaration

[1] The population of Holy Trinity Parish was about 10,000.

notwithstanding the prominence which it gave to the duty of supporting the Church as an establishment, yet he thought that many High Churchmen at this time dwelt too much on that aspect of the Church, and overlooked its higher and more commanding claims as a Divine Institution. On the other hand, he fully allowed and, with advancing years, became increasingly convinced of, the value of an Established Church in keeping religion alive in places where, without it, the people would probably relapse into total godlessness. Writing to Mr. Wood, in June 1834, he confesses that at one time he had been too much in favour of disestablishment, and says, 'My error consisted in thinking only of the purity of the Church. I would far sooner myself live in a Church unshackled by the State ; but then we must look to the indirect good ; to the forming a religious atmosphere. It is something to provide a religion for quiet, unreflective classes of society, who, but for an Establishment, would be respectable Nothingarians.'

The same argument is worked out at length, and with very considerable force, in the second of two sermons which he preached about this time on the 'Church and the Establishment.'

'It is true,' he says, 'that even though the Church were not established, religion would still have its influence. I will go even further, and add, that so far as regards those who are churchmen in *deed and in truth*, the Church itself would be benefited by a separation from the State : for she would regain those undoubted rights from which, for the sake of harmony, she now recedes : the right, for instance of

legislating for herself on all occasions, and of electing her Bishops without the interference of the civil
power.   The question with the legislator is not
whether the Church would do *much* good, though
unconnected with the State, but whether by an
alliance therewith she cannot do *more* good ; and the
question with the churchman is, whether, for placing
in abeyance some of her spiritual rights, the Church
does not receive compensation by the indirect influence she is enabled to exert.   The Church may be
less free, but is she not more efficient ? . . . It is,
indeed, not as churchmen but as patriots that we
deprecate the desecration of the State ; that is to
say, we deprecate it for the sake, not of those who are
within the pale, but of those that are without : we
deprecate it not because the Church would be a less
efficient minister of grace to the *faithful* if, driven
from her glorious cathedrals, she summoned her
children around her in the upper room of a hired
house, or the caves of the desert, but because she
would be a less effectual preacher of morality to the
unenlightened and the unbeliever.   Her voice would
still be the voice of the charmer, but it would not
reach so far. . . . The strong would have their meat,
but how would the babes be supplied with milk ? . . .
In short, where there is no national establishment
they who require instruction least receive it most ;
and they who require it most receive it not at all.
And, therefore, whether we look at the fact with
the eye of the legislator or of the Christian, the
circumstance of stationing a man of education,
respectability, and religion in each parish where the
inhabitants are too poor to support, or too ignorant

to desire, an instructor, is an advantage to the country which will only *then* be properly appreciated when it is lost.'

Thus he held the balance between those who, in their zeal for the Establishment, underrated the claims of the Church, and those who in their zeal for the purity of the Church undervalued the advantages of an establishment. This last was the error, he conceived, of Mr. Hurrell Froude and some other enthusiasts of the new movement, who were amongst the writers of ' The Tracts.' These Tracts, which afterwards became so celebrated under the name of ' Tracts for the Times,' began to appear towards the latter part of the year 1833. Mr. Newman was their editor, and in a great measure at first their author. Dr. Pusey made his first contribution to the series by the Tract on Fasting in the end of December. The writers were generally known to be Oxford men, and the tracts themselves were commonly designated the Oxford Tracts. The originators of the new movement had always contemplated the necessity of employing the press for the revival of those principles which they had at heart ; but when the Tracts began to appear Mr. Palmer, Mr. Perceval, and some others, were anxious that they should be subjected to a committee of revision, and thus go forth stamped with the authority of the whole school or association. Mr. Newman, however, Mr. Keble, and Mr. Froude were wholly opposed to this proposal. ' If we altered to please everyone,' wrote Mr. Newman to Mr. Palmer, ' the effect would be spoiled. They (the Tracts) were not intended as symbols *e cathedrâ*, but as the expression of individual minds; and individuals feeling strongly, while on the one hand they are incidentally faulty in mode or language, are still peculiarly effective. No great work was done by a system; whereas systems rise out of individual exertions.'

From this point the leading men of the new movement, although maintaining now and long afterwards the most friendly intercourse, were fairly divisible into two main classes. There were those who by age, position in the Church, or family associations, were closely connected with the old school of High Anglicans. They were men who, although they would not surrender to expediency the smallest atom of what they deemed essential, nevertheless valued the Establishment; and in all matters relating to the revival of forgotten doctrines or abandoned customs were inclined to proceed with caution and judgment. Such were Mr. Palmer and Mr. Le Bas. Some of them, especially those who were incumbents of parishes, were eminently practical in their views of things; they were men of tact, accustomed to feel the pulse of their people, and knew the risk of putting new wine into old bottles. Eminent in this class were Mr. Rose, Mr. Paget, and the subject of this memoir.

Amongst the men in the other class, were some who had been originally brought up in the Evangelical school, and who now embraced High Church principles and sentiments with all the ardour of those who have discovered a new treasure; others were young, few of them had pastoral cures, some of them were resident in Oxford. Amongst these were the Tract writers. Full of intellectual vigour and learn-

ing, full of earnest piety, full of hope and even
confidence that they were destined to work out a
second Reformation of the Church, they wrote freely
and fearlessly, unfettered by restraints, especially such
as are felt by men who, moving in a practical sphere,
have to consider not only the best possible, but also
and primarily, the best practicable. Hence although
it was a long time before Mr. Hook and others
like-minded publicly expressed their disapproval of
any of the Tracts, believing, as they did, that on the
whole the dissemination of them was most salutary;
yet even in the earlier Tracts, which were the least
open to objection of any, they detected expressions
which they regretted as unseasonable, incautious,
and liable to misunderstanding, if not in themselves
objectionable. They watched them as they came
out with interest, with much sympathy, but with no
little anxiety. In the earlier numbers, Mr. Hook
for the most part rejoiced, as teaching what he had
long been endeavouring to inculcate; he distributed
them, but with caution, among his flock, and warned
those who read them against particular parts which appeared to be inconsiderate or overstrained in expression. Nevertheless, he seems to have been regarded
by the Tract writers for some time as the principal,
almost the solitary, instance of one who worked out
in a large parochial sphere fully and freely the principles which they taught. Mr. Newman, in a letter con-
gratulating him on the recovery of his health in the
latter part of 1834, begs him not to risk it by a repetition of overwork. 'Your being obliged,' he says,
' to retire from parochial duty, would be a calamity
we ought to try to prevent, as we have no specimen

(so far as I know) but that which you supply of the influential nature of true Church principles on a town population.'

On the other hand it must be carefully borne in mind that he was neither a colleague nor a disciple of the Tract writers. He was for a certain time *with* them, but he was never *of* them. He had advanced some distance upon his career, with clearly formed principles and aims, the result of patient study and practical experience under guidance, long before many of the most eminent of the Tract writers had settled their opinions and line of action. Presently they came up with him ; he welcomed them as fellow travellers, and for a while they journeyed side by side. After a time when, as will be seen, they diverged from his path, and got into difficulties, he defended them as long as he conscientiously could ; and when their most illustrious leader fell away from the ranks of the Church, when the Tracts came to an end and the party was shaken to its foundation, he went on his way at the same steady pace and with the same undeviating straightforwardness of movement as before his connexion with them. The uncomfortable and painful contact into which he was afterwards brought at Leeds with some extreme disciples of this party will be narrated in its proper place. It will suffice to close this general sketch by remarking that to extremes in every direction he was always steadily opposed. Whichever school was for the time being most dominant, aggressive, and dangerous to the highest interests of the Church, whether it was the Puritan, the Latitudinarian, or the Romanising school, received the full force of his attack. And this was the reason why, whilst really being in the mean, he often appeared to superficial observers to be gravitating towards one of the extremes ; so that when he attacked the Puritans or Erastians he was denounced as a Tractarian, and when he attacked the Romanizers he was upbraided for deserting the ranks of High Churchmen ; whereas, in fact, he remained steadfast, only facing first in one direction and then in another. As Bishop Wilberforce once happily expressed it, ' Hook is like a ship at anchor, which, without moving from its anchorage, always swings round to turn its breast to the tide.'

The letters written during his Incumbency at Coventry are so numerous and full that they supply a chronicle of his life, almost month by month, and I have not found it necessary to do more than to add a few details which they do not contain, or to explain some matters to which they refer.

He read himself in at Holy Trinity, Coventry, on Sunday, December 14, 1828, and on January 4, 1829, he preached his farewell sermon at St. Philip's, Birmingham, on the text 1 Cor. xiii. 1, 2, 3. One of the Birmingham papers, in reporting the sermon, re· marks, ' We can give the matter of his discourse, but the charm of his manner and voice must be left to the imagination or the memory, for it is indescribable.'

In the same month the congregation of St. Philip's presented him with a service of plate, bearing an inscription, which stated that it was given ' in testimony of their respect and of their gratitude for his zealous services as Lecturer during the past fourteen months.'

On February 15, he preached his first sermon in the Church of Holy Trinity, Coventry, and began to enter on his pastoral labours there.

He had now a sphere of work adequate to his powers, and those powers were soon to be alike quickened and chastened by coming under the influence of her to whom not only the happiness but also the success of his future life was very largely owing.

He had become acquainted in Birmingham with Dr. John Johnstone, a physician of very high reputation, a man of great ability and scientific knowledge, a Fellow of the Royal Society, the intimate friend and biographer of Dr. Parr. Dr. Johnstone's eldest daughter, Anna Delicia, was only seventeen years of age when Mr. Hook was appointed to his living in Coventry, but beneath the most girlish playfulness and sparkling vivacity of manner, was a deep fund of sound practical wisdom and earnest piety. He had not been slow to discern and to be captivated by this combination of high qualities, but her extreme youth and his own want of means until he had obtained a living deterred him for some time from declaring his attachment.

In February 1829 she wrote a valentine in verse to a lady with whom he was acquainted, under the assumed name of ‘ John Bright.’ The handwriting however was detected, the verses were shown to Mr. Hook, and he composed the following reply for his friend, which was in fact the first approach to an open declaration of his sentiments. It is dated February 15th, the very day on which he officiated for the first time as Vicar in his church at Coventry, and it is therefore a curious illustration of the natural and innocent way in which he passed from things grave to gay.

Lady, I think that you are right,
When valentines you would indite,
Under fictitious names to write ;
And upon none could you alight
So well appropriate as ‘ Bright.’
Between yourself and all that's bright,
You thus comparison invite ;
Let us examine then your plight.
Winning the heart of many a wight,
Those soft dark eyes are beaming *bright*,
And far eclipse the orbs of night ;
The Pæstan roses are less *bright*
Than th' hues which on your cheek unite.
Upon that neck—(itself as *bright*
As alabaster's purest white)
The locks that hang in ringlets light
As ebony are black and *bright* ;
When you are smiling with delight,
Your smile is as the sunbeam *bright*,
Revealing to the enraptured sight
Those teeth than ivory more *bright* ;
While the two pouting lips they bite,
Are as the coral red and *bright*.
But brighter far, O far more *bright*,
The charms within! if brought to light,
They'd prove that you're perfection quite :
A mind with wit and talent *bright*,
A soul so pure, that well it might
Be deemed the soul of angel *bright*.
Hence, lady, I must think you right
When you assume the name of *Bright*.

It was perfectly true ;—‘ Brightness ’ was eminently characteristic of his future wife. The fresh-

ness and buoyancy of her spirits never forsook
her to the end of her life, although that life was
shortened by care, anxiety, and toil which overtasked
her physical strength.   Naturally elastic, however,
as her spirit was, the invariable and equable cheerfulness which she exhibited was partly sustained
from a sense of duty.   Her husband was attacked
with some alarming epileptic fits soon after his settlement at Coventry, and she was then informed by
the doctors that his future health and, perhaps, his
life would depend upon his preservation from those
moods of undue depression to which impulsive and
irritable temperaments, such as his, are especially
liable.   Thus her original and natural disposition to
cheerfulness was cultivated and trained into a habit,
but at times the maintenance of this habit, as one of
the duties of daily life, was a severe strain.   There
was no doubt a considerable fund of common sense
and practical wisdom in her husband, but there were
also some of the eccentricities which belong to that
order of mind which we call genius, and the very
warmth of his affections and vehemence of his
impulses which, on the one hand, constituted his
strength, on the other overbore at times his calmer
judgment, and hurried him into acts of which the
consequences were embarrassing.   By her superiority
in discernment of character, and in the affairs of
practical life, his wife was constantly engaged in
saving him or extricating him from the awkward
positions into which his reckless generosity and his
violent fits, either of affection or antipathy towards
individuals, were constantly urging him.   To make
both ends meet with a large family and small means,

to mediate, to conciliate, sometimes to soothe and
encourage, sometimes to warn and repress, was the
daily task of her life, and nobly did she discharge it.
He himself knew his failings, and he had prepared
her mind for the work she would have to do.   In
one of his letters, written before their marriage, he
says, 'I never can or will intentionally hurt your
feelings ; but I am rather an uncouth being whom
you must polish and tame.   I am a kind of Cimon
and you must be my Iphigenia.'   Having to deal
with one who was always very irrepressible in the
expression of his feelings, and occasionally allowed
them to outrun the bounds of discretion, she was as
a rule reserved and undemonstrative, although this
habit was partly also due to the circumstances of
early life.   'I was very timid,' she writes, 'in my
early youth, and used often to get put down if ever,
conquering my shyness, I uttered anything sentimental ; and these early influences wear deeper into
the character than people are commonly aware of,
even to quenching sometimes what was originally a
prominent part of it.   I think there is a great deal
of self-knowledge required to discover how far we
may indulge our feelings, and when we ought to
repress them ; but perhaps in this we may take our
common duties as a measure, and whatever unfits
us for them we may suppose to be undue.'   How
admirably and wonderfully these 'common duties'
were discharged, alike in the household and in the
parish, cannot be adequately understood save by
those who actually witnessed the execution of them ;
but the depth and fervour of her religious feelings may be known to all who read the 'Medita-

tions for Every Day in the Year,' which were composed by her, or ' The Cross of Christ,' which she compiled, although, appearing as they did under the editorship of her husband, they have commonly been ascribed to him. There are few women who could turn from the drudgery of account-keeping and other matters of domestic or parochial business to the composition of manuals of devotion, which have been the refreshment and consolation of thousands of pious Christians. In a letter written late at night from Leeds, she says, ' I have a great bundle of proofs at my side, and account-books frowning at me in the distance and threatening an hour or two of calculation and puzzling. How I hate them! being in a constant apprehension of spending too much and not having enough to meet all demands.' The close juxtaposition of her Book of Meditations and of her account-books alluded to in this letter is not a bad key to the character of the writer : she was eminently devout and at the same time eminently practical.

And this union of qualities was the great secret of her remarkable influence alike within the circle of her family and beyond it. She was, indeed, at once the fresh and cheerful companion of her children, entering with keen relish into their amusements and pursuits, especially music, in which she was uncommonly skilled ; and also the counsellor on whose sound judgment they could always rely for instruction and advice respecting their duty in this world, and their preparation for the world which is to come. And in like manner, outside the walls of home, the curates who looked up to her as a mother, and a

large number of friends, young and old of both sexes,
were wont to turn to her before all others for the
Christian sympathy and the wholesome counsel which
were never asked in vain.

Few, indeed, have more nearly fulfilled the
description of the virtuous woman drawn long ago
by the Wise Man :

> She openeth her mouth with wisdom, and in her tongue
> is the law of kindness.
> She looketh well to the ways of her household, and
> eateth not the bread of idleness.
> Her children arise up and call her blessed ; her husband
> also, and he praiseth her.
> Many daughters have done virtuously, but thou excellest
> them all.

And not less applicable to her are the words of
one of our wisest and noblest poets :

> A being breathing thoughtful breath,
> A traveller between life and death,
> The reason firm, the temperate will,
> Endurance, foresight, strength, and skill :
> A perfect woman, nobly planned
> To warn, to comfort, and command :
> And yet a spirit too, and bright,
> With something of an angel light.

I have dwelt thus long upon the character of
Mrs. Hook not only because it deserved some
special notice, but also to impress on the reader of
this memoir that, although comparatively few direct
allusions to her may occur in the following pages, it
must never be forgotten that, while her husband is
the prominent actor in the foreground, she is always

a controlling regulating principle in the background, and that without her it is probable that he never would have become what he was, or have accomplished the things which he did.

They were married on June 4, 1829, and in the latter part of the summer the bells of Holy Trinity Church rang to welcome the arrival of the Vicar and his young wife. They took up their abode in one of a row of small red brick houses in a by-street called St. Nicholas Place. The street itself is rather gloomy, but the situation is high, and the back windows command a good view of the ancient city of Coventry, out of the midst of which rise conspicuous the two noble churches of St. Michael and Holy Trinity with their graceful and lofty spires. The house soon became too small for their needs, and they then moved to a larger one in the Leicester Road, just outside the town. Soon after the Vicar and his wife had settled in their home it was broken into by burglars who were probably tempted by the hope of getting the service of plate which had been presented to him by his flock in Birmingham. As they did not succeed in robbing the house of any valuable contents, the incident would be hardly worth recording but for the singular and ludicrous circumstance that the thieves drank a quantity of ink under the impression that it was port wine, and one of them was afterwards detected by the stains of ink upon his clothes.

As the temporal condition of the people of Coventry was deeply depressed when he entered upon his pastoral charge, so also was the spirit of churchmanship at a low ebb. That kind of irre-

verence towards holy places and holy things which
is bred partly of ignorance, partly of that indifference
which is the result of ignorance or at least of low
and feeble ideas on the whole subject of religion,
was prevalent and startling. He found that it was
the custom at vestry dinners to propose as the first
toast, ' Trinity in Unity,' which was considered a
pleasant punning allusion to the dedication of the
Church to the Holy Trinity ; and no one seemed to
have any perception of the profanity of the practice
until the new Vicar pointed it out and put a stop
to it. On such a subject he could speak with a
dignified sternness and a force of resolution which
few dared to resist or disobey. On one occasion
a vestry meeting was so numerously attended that
it was adjourned from the vestry to the church.
Several persons kept their hats on. The Vicar
requested that they would take them off, but they
refused to comply. ' Very well, gentlemen,' he replied, ' but remember that in this house the insult is
not done to me, but to your God ; ' and the hats were
immediately taken off.

In the internal arrangements of the church, the
principal alterations which he made consisted in removing a painting at the east end, which represented
a kind of Moorish Temple, and placing a simple Rere-
dos in its stead ; filling the east window with stained
glass, detaching the prayer desk from the pulpit,
beneath which it had stood confronting the people,
and turning it round so that the officiating priest
faced eastwards. On this subject there is a very excellent letter by him in the ' British Magazine ' for
October 1833, in which he points out that ' confined

in a narrow box, the officiating minister cannot perform his various offices as he ought to do ; with his
face always turned to the people, most of the people,
listlessly rolling in their seats, seem to think he is
reading *to them.*'   The points on which he mainly
insists are : that when the priest is praying he ought
to be as low as possible in position, provided he can
be heard ; and when preaching only so high as conveniently to overlook his flock.   He also proves that
the chancel is the proper place in which to say the
prayers ; but concludes, ' I am not visionary enough
to suppose that in these days we shall be permitted
to go back to the chancel, though I trust that I have
shown that if we *must* have a reading desk, we ought
not to make it look like a pulpit.'

As regarded the services of the church, he found
that it was a common practice with his parishioners
to attend church on Sunday morning and to go to
some Dissenting chapel in the evening.   He therefore began evening services on Sunday during the
summer of 1830.   These were very largely attended,
nearly 2,000 being generally present ; and the people
were so unwilling they should be dropped, that in
the month of August a meeting was held in the
vestry, at which it was resolved that the church
should be lighted with gas.   The resolution was
carried into effect, and on November 7, 1830, evening service was held for the first time in the newly
lighted church, being the first church ever opened
for evening service in Coventry.

In Lent of the following year he gave a course
of lectures, which were delivered on the morning
of each Wednesday, and so great was the interest

which they excited that, as I have been told by an aged parishioner, who was then a young man in a house of business, he and many others similarly occupied used to get permission from their employers to leave their offices to attend them. Others, who were unable to quit business at that hour, entreated the Vicar to deliver the lectures in the evening instead of the morning. Several anonymous letters to this effect have come into my hands. In one of these the writer concludes, ' with many, many thanks for your increasing attention to our spiritual and also our temporal welfare, and trusting that you may long be spared to dwell among us, I remain, reverend sir, Your dutiful servant and parishioner.' And this is only a specimen of others expressed in the same style of admiration and gratitude.

In Holy Week of the same year, or as it was then more commonly called, Passion Week, he delivered day by day the lectures which were afterwards published under the title of the ' Last Days of our Lord's Ministry.' This was his first literary venture, and not one of the least successful. He was encouraged to undertake the work by the learned and pious Bishop of Limerick, Bishop Jebb, who had now been residing some time for the sake of his health at Leamington, where he had first formed in 1828 an acquaintance with Mr. Hook, which had soon ripened into a close and affectionate friendship. The Bishop corrected the proofs of the volume, suggested the title, and in part composed the dedication which runs thus: ' To William Page Wood, of Lincoln's Inn, Esq., late Fellow of Trinity College, Cambridge, this volume is inscribed as the record of an early and unintermitting friendship.' He received letters expressing high admiration of the work from Southey, Wordsworth, Joshua Watson, Mr. Le Bas, Dr. Butler, afterwards Bishop of Lichfield, Bishop Monk of Gloucester, and Judge Alan Park, who took a kind of fatherly interest in his career.

But perhaps the testimony which he valued most of all was that of good Bishop Jolly, who in writing to thank him for the copy which had been presented to him, said, ' You have traced the adorable steps of our Divine Redeemer dying for us, in such a manner as has affected my heart and repeatedly sent me to my prayers.'

And the following acknowledgment of a similar gift from one of his churchwardens, who made it his special business to keep all the parochial accounts, was just the kind of evidence that he had not laboured in vain, in which his pastoral heart especially delighted, and which stimulated him to further exertions more than any other kind of praise.

' If at any period I have in the least degree contributed to your comfort and convenience, I am amply rewarded by your confidence and esteem, and by the advantages which I have derived from your ministerial instructions.

' That you may long continue to be our pastor and guide, is the earnest prayer of your devoted, faithful servant, JAMES WALL.'

The preface to a new and cheaper edition in the year 1863 pointing out, as it does, how uncommon the delivery of such a course of lectures was at the period when they were originally published, bespeaks

for them a kind of historical interest, apart from
their own intrinsic merits, which are of a high order.

'The author of this little volume,' he writes,
'was in Edinburgh in the year 1825. . . . During
Passion Week he occasionally assisted Dr. Sandford,
the earnest-minded Bishop of Edinburgh, who
preached every day on the events of that sacred
season. Deeply impressed with what he heard, the
author determined if he ever had a parish of his
own to follow the example of the pious prelate ; and
in the Passion Week, 1831, the following sermons
were delivered day by day in the Church of the Holy
Trinity, Coventry. At that time there was not
perhaps any other parish in England, certainly not
in the large towns, where this course was pursued.
Now, after the lapse of thirty years, we are able
to affirm that there is not perhaps a large town in
England in which a daily course of sermons is not
delivered during the Holy Week. We bless God for
this increased attention to public duty which indicates an increased devotion of mind to the things of
God. Many things to which a pastor, thirty years
ago, had to call especial attention, are now regarded
as truisms ; a pleasing circumstance which is stated
to account for the fact that some things in the notes
to these discourses are proved or explained which in
the present day would be taken for granted.'

In fact this course of lectures, like so many other
things which he said and did, would scarcely deserve
special mention, save as an illustration of the manner
in which he led the way in the reformation and
revival of the Church, anticipating to a great extent that more general revival which was afterwards

the result of the Tractarian or Oxford movement.
And this indeed is the impression which his ministry at Coventry seems to have left most deeply en
graven in the minds of those who lived under it.
Aged parishioners, to whom I applied for information respecting his work amongst them, while in
some instances unable to recall many particulars of
it, were all unanimous in saying, ' He was the
beginner of all things here ; he set everything a
going.' And this is a truth which cannot too constantly be borne in mind in reading the record of his
early life. Sunday evening services, frequent com-
munions, Saint's day services—these are wonderfully
common things now, but they were rare novelties
then. The voice of the Church had been almost
dumb during the season of Lent, and

> He was the first that ever burst
> Into that silent sea.

How scanty, indeed, were the services in a large
number of our parish churches at this period, may
be gathered from a letter by Dr. Burton in the
' British Magazine ' for May 1832, in which he re-
commends that sermons should be preached at
evening as well as morning services, and that where,
as was most common, the Holy Communion was
celebrated *four times a year*, at the great festivals,
an additional celebration should be held on the Sunday following each of those festivals. The editor in
a note observes that, ' in *one* large village known to
him there was an early communion at eight o'clock as
well as at the usual hour on the great festivals.'

The multiplication therefore of services and sermons by the Vicar of Holy Trinity may well have been deemed amazing. He did not, however, mul· tiply services without seeking in a corresponding degree so to instruct and train his flock that they might comprehend and value them. This he did by frequent explanations in his sermons of the several offices in our Prayer Book, more particularly in the year 1834 by a complete series of lectures on the Liturgy. His Sunday evening sermons almost always consisted of an expository course upon some subject, or upon some book of Holy Scripture. For several years he was engaged in this manner upon St. Matthew's Gospel, and the sermon afterwards so notorious, ' Hear the Church,' was originally composed for this series.

Thus he gathered around him a body of *intelligent* as well as devout worshippers ; persons who felt the influence of his learning as well as of his piety. How intense his own devotion was, those who saw and heard him minister in the services of the Church could best understand ; and how deeply he felt his responsibility as a leader of the devotions of others may be gathered from the following letter to Mr. Wood.

I find it always wise to keep quiet in my study on Monday. The increasing excitement and fatigue during twelve hours on the Lord's Day demand that kind of rest which I can only find in my study. A layman is not aware of what a High Church parson goes through on a Sunday. To say nothing of the noise of schools, and the fatigue of catechising and preaching, a layman has in church to do little else than join in the devotion. But a clergyman, besides praying, has also the excitement of endeavouring to set off the glorious services of the Church

to the best advantage. Even if he does not officiate at
the prayers, still he has to respond loud, and to take the
lead, so as to excite others to do their duty—that duty
which Protestants so sadly neglect. Then if you find your
congregation joining well, there is the excitement of joy :
if not, there is the annoyance ; and all this coexisting with
one's own devotions, with the feeling that you are in some
degree responsible for the deficiencies of the congregation ;—
all this quite knocks me up, *not* on the Sunday, but on the
Monday morning, and I consequently feel it quite important to remain quiet.

The Sunday schools and catechising, to which
reference is made in this letter, occupied a great
deal of his interest and attention ; and in the administration of this department he had an able assistant
in his wife. Writing soon after their settlement at
Coventry, he says, ' She has taken possession of the
Girls' Sunday school, and is to have the management
under her husband and pastor of the Girls' National
school. In fact she is a very notable person, and I
really like her tolerably well.' The rapid and steady
increase in the number of children attending the
Sunday schools is a powerful indication of the progress made in this most important branch of pastoral
work. In the summer of 1829, when the Vicar entered on his charge, the total was 120. In August
1834 the number had risen to 524 boys and 407 girls ;
fifty-two adults also were instructed on Sunday evenings, and before the Vicar quitted Coventry in 1837
the total number of Sunday school children considerably exceeded 1,200. His old scholars retain a lively
impression of his teaching and catechising ; he was
never dull and heavy, and whilst severe in the re-
pression of levity or irreverence, he at times rallied

the interests of the children and won their sympathy by mingling fun with his reproofs. 'Why, what
is the matter with you?' he said one cold winter's
morning, when he thought the children of his class
were slow in answering, 'I think the frost has got
into your throats.' There was something in his tone
and manner, as he said it, which tickled the fancy of
the children, and their wits and voices were effectually
thawed for the rest of the school hour. How complete was the control which he exercised over them,
and how promptly and instinctively they responded
to his admonitions, was curiously illustrated one day
in church. They had been noisy and ill-behaved
during the service, and consequently in his sermon
he addressed them in a particularly grave and earnest manner, ending with an appeal to their good
feelings, and saying, 'I am sure, my dear children,
you won't do this again;' whereupon they stood
up in a body there and then and replied, 'No, sir;
we won't.'

Besides reviving and extending the Sunday
schools, he was the principal founder of other useful
institutions, some of which continue in a highly
flourishing condition to the present day. 'I am
endeavouring,' he writes in 1830, 'to establish an
infant school, a dispensary, and a savings' bank; on
the first I am opposed by Dissenters because I insist on the master being a member of the Church,
but I have triumphed gloriously, as I have raised
300*l.* and they only 100*l.* On the second, I am
opposed by the doctors; and on the third, by the
bankers, publicans, and brewers. We are all,
however, very good friends.'

The infant school was opened in January 1831. The dispensary was started in 1830, but owing partly to the depression in trade and the secretary becoming insane, it remained for some time almost in abeyance. At length in 1834 trade having become more prosperous, Mr. Dresser, a gentleman, who to this day takes an active part in the management of the institution, suggested to the Vicar that the opportunity was favourable for reviving it. The Vicar took up the matter most warmly, and became himself one of the six trustees. The thing was established on a sound, self-supporting basis, and is perhaps the most thriving institution of its class in the kingdom. The free members subscribe a penny a week ; the number of free members is about 13,000, and their subscriptions amount to 1,500*l.* a year, enabling the committee to pay three surgeons at the rate of nearly 300*l.* a year each.

Some few years ago a debt of 600*l.* was incurred in building another house. It was proposed to the free members, who now principally manage the concern, that they should provide for the discharge of the debt. This they did by a voluntary rate of one shilling a head payable quarterly, which not only cleared off the debt, but left a surplus which was invested and produces interest to the amount of 120*l.* a year.

The savings bank also was established mainly through the exertions of the Vicar in 1834. The balance in the first year was 124*l.*: the present amount of deposits from 7,300 depositors is about 225,000*l.* with a surplus fund of 4,300*l.* Of course the lasting prosperity of these and similar institutions has been due not only to the sound principles on which they were originally based, but also to the skill and energy of those who have been concerned in the management of them ; but all who recollect their foundation agree in attributing it to the activity and perseverance of the Vicar. In matters of this kind his power consisted not in working the practical details of business, for which he never had any aptitude or liking, but first of all in discerning and securing the right workmen, and then interesting them in their duty and animating them with zeal and courage to fulfil it.

The institution in which, from the nature of the case, he took personally the most lively interest was the Religious and Useful Knowledge Society, which was founded in May 1835 for the purpose of forwarding and extending such knowledge by means of a library, classes of instruction, and periodical lectures. The Society for Promoting Christian Knowledge made a grant of books to the value of 25*l.*, which was the starting point of the library. The Vicar was indefatigable in securing lecturers and giving lectures himself, which were delivered during the first winter in St. Mary's Hall. The subscriptions to the society were one shilling, half-a-crown, or five shillings a quarter, and the society was so popular that in January 1836 it was resolved that a room should be built or bought in which the library might be kept and the lectures carried on. This society and the Mechanics' Institute were afterwards united under the name of the Coventry Institute, which still exists, but is used more as a reading room and club than anything else ; the Free Library, School of Art, and

Science classes having superseded the more educational purposes to which it was formerly devoted.

One of his last acts on behalf of the society before he left Coventry was to write an application for support to Sir Robert Peel, as being an owner of land in the neighbourhood, to which he received the following reply.

'I am afraid my local interest in connexion with Coventry is too remote to enable me *on that ground* to accede to your request without the establishment of rather an inconvenient precedent.   But the insufficiency of that claim on my contribution is amply supplied by my respect for your character and for your unremitting and successful exertions to promote the moral and religious instruction of the people committed to your spiritual charge.   I have with pleasure, therefore, enclosed the sum of 10*l.* in aid of the object in respect to which you have addressed me.'

The origin and early progress of this society are described by the Vicar in the following letter, dated June 1836, to the Dean of Hereford, who seems to have applied for information concerning it as a guide to himself in establishing something of the same nature.

Very reverend and dear Sir, . . . As this society has gradually arisen from the circumstances of this place and not from any particular plan devised by me, I must trouble you with a little history in order to enable you to perceive its nature ; and at the same time I must disclaim any wish to hold it forth as a model.   It is adapted, I think, to our position—in another place it might require various modifications.   Indeed it has been always my rule of conduct not to adopt any general theory as to the management of a parish or the regulation of schools : but (having formed certain principles from which I never permit any notions of expediency to lead me to deviate) to take the materials I find, and to mould them, not into the best shape I can imagine, but into the best that circumstances will admit. I have invariably maintained strong Church principles, and declared my resolution never to act on any others: and then I leave them to do their work. Of these principles this society is the fruit—as will now be seen.

When first I came here about eight years ago, I of course catechised the children regularly at church. As the children in the upper classes became too old for school, they many of them requested permission to stay as teachers. To this, of course, I readily consented. Their number increasing they formed themselves into a society under the superintendence of the clergy of the parish. And now we have a Sunday school of nearly twelve hundred children, managed almost entirely by these teachers, about fifty in number. The clergy have only to look into the school for a few minutes before church to see that all is going on right, and the teachers bring what classes they think fit to be catechised at church. With these persons of course a familiar intercourse has taken place ; and with the clergy of the town and neighbourhood, churchwardens, &c., we go out into the country in the summer and dine together, while at Christmas they all dine with me. These are all very zealous churchmen, and *they* are the originators of the society in question. About twelve months ago they came to me, and said they were much in want of the means of self-improvement, and that young persons who had left school had only the resource of the Mechanics' Institute, which having been started by the Political Union was managed by Radicals and Dissenters, and where all the good principles imbibed at school were destroyed. They complained also that the Church was continually attacked by persons in their own line of life, and that they had no books to refer to for the defence of their principles. They

suggested, therefore, the establishment of a Mechanics'
Institute on right principles. I accordingly called them
together, asking one or two other friends to attend, when
they proposed that the Bishop should be President, the
Archdeacon Vice-President, and that every clergyman in
the town should be *ex officio* on the committee, which
would consist besides of fifteen members. The property
was vested in four trustees, who have a veto on all proceedings of the committee. To exclude politics, the trustees
consist of two Tories and two Whigs. There are three
classes of subscribers, 5s. per quarter, 2s. 6d. per quarter
and 1s. per quarter—thus to admit all orders of society.
The first class have tickets of admission to all lectures,
transferable, and may also introduce a friend ; the second
class, transferable tickets ; the third class, non-transferable
tickets. The object here is to bring all kinds of people
together. There is a reading-room open every evening
from seven to nine o'clock, an important arrangement as
many young apprentices go to an alehouse merely because
they have no comfortable apartment in which to sit. On
the table we have the 'Saturday' and 'Penny Magazine,'
the 'British' and the 'New Monthly,' 'Chambers' Edinburgh
Journal,' &c., and any books may be had from the library.
Classes are formed for reading history, for arithmetic, and
drawing. I conduct one myself of divinity, chiefly of young
shopkeepers, and relating to Church history and those questions in religion which cannot be conveniently handled in the
pulpit. We have already about nine hundred volumes in
the library in various branches of literature. For I am very
desirous to cultivate among the people not merely a *scientific* but a *literary* turn of mind, to induce them to relish
poetry and works of imagination : for the civilised mind is
best prepared to give the heart to religion. We have had
lectures given, twelve on experimental philosophy, twelve
on physiology, two on perspective, one on the origin and progress of society, and I am now preparing one on the history
of literature and science. We have upwards of six hundred members. We have met with most violent and furious

opposition from Dissenters of all classes except Wesleyans. I have been abused most fiercely in the Radical paper, and the Mechanics' Institute, from a spirit of opposition, has increased from sixty members to two hundred. But this only shows that we are doing good. Such is our history.

The remarks at the close of this letter are eminently characteristic of the writer, and illustrate his favourite maxim, that plentiful abuse partly indicated, partly promoted the prosperity of the cause which was attacked. His parting words to the members of the society, in which he sketched the history of its progress, were to the same effect. 'At first the members had pursued the noiseless tenor of their way unmolested, an insignificant body. But the little society had grown into a large and important institution, and then like all other prosperous parties they were surrounded with a host of opponents and revilers. But the society when reviled reviled not again, and the good policy of this conduct became apparent since their opponents saved them the trouble of advertising.'

The manner also in which the society grew up, as described in the beginning of his letter, is a good example of the way in which, alike at Coventry and Leeds, he always adapted his action to circumstances and never forced circumstances to square with some preconceived plan of action. He inculcated principles and left them to work. The consequence of this wise policy was, that to a great extent the action of the Church in his parish proceeded from the laity ; it was the spontaneous fruit of the spirit which they caught and of the principles which they learned from him. Hence, also, they took an un-

common pride and interest in things which were
their own production.   Writing later in life he says,
'My plan has never been to force a practice, but
rather to have things forced upon me.   My aim has
been to lay down principles and encourage a certain kind of spirit: then, after a time, as men love
to find fault, they have blamed me for not acting up
to my principles.   The answer is then ready : " Oh !
very well ; if *you* wish it, I will do it."   Thus a choral
service at Leeds was actually forced upon me.'   And
here we have a key to the meaning of his famous
saying   many   years   afterwards   at   the   Church
Congress in Manchester where he had been asked
to relate how he managed his parish.   ' I did not
manage it ; the parish managed me.'

After this general sketch of his work at Coventry
it only remains to mention, in their chronological
order, a few incidents which seem to require a more
particular and separate notice.

First among these must be placed the remonstrance which he addressed, in 1830, to his diocesan,
Dr. Ryder, the Bishop of Lichfield and Coventry, a
prelate of extreme Evangelical views, for presiding at
a meeting of the Bible Society in Coventry.   The
letter has a twofold interest, because it was employed
as a weapon against him, seven years afterwards, by
the party which vehemently opposed his election to
the Vicarage of Leeds.

The following account of the transaction and
copy of the letter is taken from one of the local
newspapers of the day :

On Thursday, August 19, 1830, the Bishop of Lichfield
and Coventry presided at the eighth anniversary of the

Coventry Bible Society. His lordship said that although it had occasioned him some inconvenience, he could not suffer the present anniversary to pass without coming forward to express his constant and unceasing attachment to the British and Foreign Bible Society, supported, as it was, by the most respectable inhabitants of Coventry and its neighbourhood. He highly approved of the Society and the object which for five-and-twenty years it had uniformly pursued ; and it was gratifying to him that it had a tendency to promote a union of Christians of all denominations, without compelling them to compromise their principles. He would repeat, that the Society should have his unceasing support, and he wished to see it extend itself through the whole of his large and populous diocese—a diocese containing not less than 1,000,000 souls. A few days before the meeting, the Rev. W. F. Hook, Vicar of Trinity Parish, Coventry, and his curate addressed the following remonstrance to the Bishop :

' My Lord,—We feel it to be our duty respectfully to represent to your lordship the mischief that is likely to result to the cause of religion in this city, from your determination to preside at the meeting of the Bible Society on Thursday next.

' Surrounded by Dissenting teachers, your lordship will not be supported by the clergy of this town, with perhaps one solitary exception. And we do earnestly request your lordship to reflect on the impression which will be made on the minds of our people when they see their Bishop co-operating with sectarians in promoting measures uncalled for by the exigencies of the place, and inconsistent with the principles inculcated by their more immediate pastors. As far as our own parish is concerned, if your lordship's object is to supply us with Bibles, we can obtain all that we require from the Society for Promoting Christian Knowledge ; if it be to levy contributions for the speculations of the society in foreign parts, we beg to inform your lordship that the demands upon the charity of our more opulent parishioners for local purposes are already greater than can be easily met, and that the poor will be injured in proportion as the society is benefited. We will take the liberty further to observe that your lordship compels us, in self-defence, to state to those persons committed to our charge what our reasons are for declining to support a society at which our Bishop presides. If we fail to convince them that we are right, we shall expose ourselves to their contempt, and our ministrations will become ineffectual ; if, on the other hand, we succeed, we shall do what is equally to be deprecated, by rendering our Bishop obnoxious to their censures ; or, at all events, those who hold to the one side will despise those who hold to the other ; and while we are humbly endeavouring to promote harmony and goodwill in our parish, your lordship will, unintentionally, be the means of exciting a party spirit, than which nothing can be more detrimental to the sacred cause in which we are engaged. So important it is, in an extensive parish like this, to maintain unanimity and concord, among Churchmen at least, that we seriously and solemnly, in the name of our common Lord and Master, entreat and implore your lordship not to sow among us the seeds of discord.

'Your lordship is so honest in the discharge of all that you conceive to be your duty, that we feel assured you will not be unnecessarily offended at our maintaining our own principles with equal honesty and zeal, or at our endeavouring to avert what we have reason to know will be attended with the most mischievous consequences, by causing a division in our flock and by affording a triumph to Dissenters.

'On the merits or demerits of the Bible Society, we at present say nothing. Our observations have reference only to your lordship's supporting it, so far as our parish is concerned, in opposition to our wishes, and in spite of our well-known opinions and principles. With our humble but hearty prayers to Him from whom all good counsels as well as all just works do proceed, that He may vouchsafe to direct your lordship to a wise decision upon the subject, we have the honour to remain

' Your lordship's obedient servants.'

In 1831 he was attacked with fits of an epileptic nature, in which he lost his consciousness and lay to all appearance as one dead for five or ten minutes. They were attributed by the doctors to over-anxiety, and excitement of the brain. His first seizure was during the Archdeacon's visitation in June 1831. He turned faint while reading the prayers in his church, and was carried in an unconscious state into the vestry, where he recovered, and wrote a note to his mother, who was then at Leamington. Fearing lest she should hear an exaggerated account, he makes as light of it as possible, and attributes it mainly to a little worry and nervous anxiety lest the Archdeacon, an Evangelical, should say anything unorthodox in his church, and so interfere with his usefulness.

His father-in-law, Dr. Johnstone, insisted on his abstaining from all parochial work for a time, and the greater part of the summer was spent under Dr. Johnstone's roof, where he gradually recovered his nervous power. The preparation of his lectures on ' The Last Days of our Lord's Ministry,' for publication was his chief occupation during this period of enforced leisure. He was not permitted to return to his parish before September. The enthusiasm with which he was greeted by his flock filled him with delight, and made him set about his work again with renewed energy and spirit. ' On coming out of church,' he writes to Mr. Wood, ' the first evening that I preached, there was quite a mob round the

door of people rushing forwards to shake hands with
me, and my hand, though a good stout one, was
nearly squeezed to a mummy.' And the following
letter to his mother describes the occasion more
minutely.

September 1831.

My dearest Mother,—You will be glad to hear that I
am wonderfully well this morning; I only went to church
once yesterday, that is to say, in the evening, when I
preached. Delicia had made me go on Saturday morning
by way of a break, and it was lucky I did, for the manner
in which I was received as I drove through the town, and
the way all the old people came up to shake hands with
me, with tears in their eyes, quite affected me; nothing
could have been more gratifying to my pastoral feelings
than my reception yesterday; there was an immense congregation, and as I left the church there was quite a mob
collected round the door to shake hands with me, and
bless me; it was indeed one of the happiest moments of
my life; may God Almighty bless them all. How much
has poor Coventry been maligned. I was affected when
I began my sermon, but soon took courage and proceeded
right well, although to add to my nervousness someone
fainted almost as soon as I commenced. I took for my
text Psalm cxix. 71 : 'It is good for me that I have been
afflicted.' Coker Adams and his warm-hearted family
were all present, and nothing could have been kinder.
The churchwardens are to apprehend me if I go into the
town on week-day duty, and to take me before Coker
Adams as a Justice of the Peace. It was well for me that
Coker Adams was with me, for he performed the service
as if he had some fellow feeling with my people, rejoicing,
as they evidently were, to see their pastor once again. I
have not felt so well as I now do for a long time, and I
will tell you why I did not like to defer my first sermon;
the prospect of it so excited me, and rendered me so
nervous that I really think I should have been made ill

had I put it off till next Sunday; for the three or four last days I could do nothing, and the very fact of persons telling me that they doubted whether I should be equal to the exertion almost incapacitated me for it: the act itself was not very fatiguing, but the anticipation of it was both absorbing and exciting; it was on these gounds that I determined to get it over as soon as I could. I am now so calm and comfortable, and in such good temper with the world, that my sermon must have been better than a dose of physic.

He was not wholly free from epileptic attacks for three or four years, and occasionally had to suspend work to recover his strength, and for a time the thought of resigning Coventry and seeking a rural parish was seriously entertained by him and his friends. But gradually the attacks abated, until he attained that singularly robust state of health which he continued to enjoy far into old age. The recovery and subsequent preservation of his health were due day by day to his wife, in a measure which can hardly be over-estimated. By her union of cheerfulness, common sense, and piety, she exercised that calming, soothing influence which had a most salutary effect, physical as well as moral, upon his sensitive and excitable temperament. 'I am very sorry to think,' she writes during one of his absences from home, 'of you as being so languid and nervous. It is a sign of an over-wrought mind. I, too, have suffered " no end " from my nerves, and have come to an idea on the subject which, I think, has helped me more than anything else to act against the malady. It seems to me that when we are placed in a situation tolerably free from temptation of an

ordinary kind, and when God has blessed us with a
frequent and free access to the means of grace, by
which we have been enabled to subdue our passions
and submit our wills to His, He allows the devil
to work upon us in another way, by turning the
very sensitiveness which God has given for a special
blessing, into a temptation.   I have endeavoured to
battle and subdue these feelings in every way in my
power, and have found if I take them in that light,
that I can put aside the perplexing feelings.   Here
is my philosophy : and from what I have observed
of your cranky fits, I am almost sure a similar course
would answer.   Never allow yourself wittingly any
contortions of feature or body, they only add to the
misery ; and set about doing something quite in an
opposite line to that which worries you.'

By the close of the summer of 1834, his health
seemed to be re-established—his wife writes in July
that he was in ' monstrous spirits, and had not been so
well for ages,' and that he had left off the wig which
he had worn since his first attack, after which his head
had been shaved.   Some persons in Coventry have
a lively recollection of his wig, for in his fits of frolicsome mirth he would sometimes take it off and kick
it across the room.

In the autumn, however, of this year, his health
was again a cause of uneasiness.   There was a slight
recurrence of the fits, and he again went for rest and
retirement and medical care to his father-in-law's
house.   He preached two sermons at Oxford in
November, having been appointed one of the select
preachers for the University, and it is not improbable
that this effort, which seems to have caused him

much nervous anxiety, may have partly occasioned his relapse. He did not, however, betray any symptoms of weakness during his visit to Oxford, and the sermons were considered eminently successful. His cousin, Walter Hamilton, afterwards Bishop of Salisbury, writes to Mrs. Hook: ' He was looking very well, was in excellent voice, and commanded the most complete attention. I never recollect so strong an impression created. He preached in the morning on the Glory of God, and in the evening on the Special Providence of God. His matter was most eloquent, and his manner very impressive and effective. In the evening the church was crowded to excess. In short, he has been quite successful—may the blessing of God rest upon his awakening appeals.'

The following letters, however, show that his health was unsettled throughout the latter half of the year 1834, and that he still clung to the idea of retirement to a country living.

To Archdeacon Hamilton.

Coventry : August 5, 1834.

My dear Uncle,—When I was at Leamington on Friday, my mother showed me a copy of the note you wrote to the Chancellor, requesting him to give me St. George's, Bloomsbury ; and I cannot refrain from expressing to you my warmest and most grateful thanks for your consideration of me. Your kindness to me on this and very many other occasions I feel indeed most deeply. About the same time I had been privately informed my dear friend Archdeacon Bayley was trying to obtain for me St. Margaret's, Westminster ; but the Dean of Ripon will not now resign, as the Bishop of Lichfield threatens,

in the event of a vacancy, to hold it *in commendam.*
But the object of our wishes is a country living ; and if
I might name a living, it would be Hertingfordbury.
Delicia and I are quite agreed on that point ; and the
innocent pleasures of a country life are those most to be
desired for my little ones, to whom is due my first and
dearest duty.   I have been thirteen years in holy orders,
and seven of these I have spent in situations as difficult
and laborious as any in England ; and if I live for two or
three years longer I shall think myself privileged to retire, for I am come to St. Basil's opinion, that happiness
is to be found in quiet.   Fervour and zeal are providentially ordained to set us a-going on our Christian course ;
but the perfection of a Christian life is to be found in
calmness and peace.   Give my love to Walter, and tell
him how happy we shall be to see him here, though our
cool temperature will but ill accord with his boiling heat.
From what I have heard and seen of my reverend cousin,
I suspect that he has taken his place in his friend Wordsworth's boat, ' in shape a very crescent moon,' and gone up
into the clouds, looking after what he will not find, the god-
dess Perfection.   If this be so, I am glad of it ; few men are
worth anything who have not wandered a little among the
clouds ; and then by degrees they come down, and find
that men, though not perfect, may gradually pass from
dutiful sons to affectionate parents and kind masters, and
die good honest Christians, and that such are the characters to be valued.

Your grateful and affectionate

W. F. HOOK.

To W. P. Wood, Esq.—Sermons at Oxford.

Oxford : November 3, 1834.

My dearest Friend,—Although I have so much to do,
say, and see, that I cannot write a long letter, yet I know
that you will like to receive a line from me, and to hear
that I am passing well.   I preached twice yesterday, and

although I did not preach as well as I could wish, yet I hope I may have set some young heads a-thinking in the right way, which is what I aim at in my sermons, since two undergraduates have called upon me to request permission to read my evening sermon. As they are perfect strangers to me I shall refuse to lend the sermon, but I am going to their college (Lincoln), and shall read it over to them, with my comments; thus I am going to give a divinity lecture.

I have been amused (and so will you be) at finding in a French paper ('L'Univers,' just brought to me by an acquaintance at Worcester College) a quotation from my sermon on the Church, almost every word, by the bye, spelt wrong. I am classed with Bishop Jebb, Reveridge, (*sic*), Joseph Mède, Hammond, and others among the great divines of the Church of England. I was going to return home to-morrow, but having received an invitation from Dr. Burton, I thought it right to accept it. The Dean of Christ Church has also invited me, which is very civil, for Oxford is a perfect aristocracy; the heads of houses keep entirely aloof from the masters, and the masters from the undergraduates; which is, I think, on the whole a good thing. It was rather awful to sit in a large kind of chapter room, before going into sermon, and to see the heads of houses one by one come in, not deigning a look, each silently taking his place till the procession was prepared to move into church. It is a good thing to find how infinitely small one really is, after having played the great man in a parish. My reception in Oxford, after so many years of absence, has been very gratifying and, indeed, flattering.

To Mrs. Hook.

Oxford : November 3, 1834.

My dearest Love,—I can only find a single sheet of paper in the blotting book, and I therefore write a *billet-doux*. I am very well, I preached yesterday tolerably, not so effectually as I could wish, but I hope with some effect, as two undergraduates have just called on me to ask permission to read the sermon I preached in the afternoon. We went to evening service at Newman's church ; he is, my dear love, the most delightful apostolical man I ever met; I wish you could have been with me at the service ; his sermon was one of the most useful I ever heard. I have been much amused at finding myself quoted as a great divine in a French paper, called 'L'Univers.' I suppose I may now consider that I have a ' continental reputation !'

I will call on Mr. B—— (D. V.) as I pass through Leamington ; thanks for the hint. I long to be at home ; kisses to the brats, love to Miss Ross, a box on the ear to yourself.

Your reverend Husband,

W. F. HOOK.

Beaumont Street, Oxford : November 3, 1834.

My dearest Mother,—As I mentioned in my last that I had been ill, I think it right to tell you now that I continue to be well ; all the better, indeed, for my delightful little holiday. My duties yesterday were light, compared with those I have at home ; but as you probably fancy them greater than they were, you will be glad to hear that I am not at all knocked up. I preached twice, and then attended the evening service of my admirable friend Mr. Newman. Now I consider it to have been a blessed privilege to have been able to unite, both on Saturday (All Saints' Day) and Sunday, in public prayer with that apostolical man ; his appearance, his voice, his sermon, were so perfectly what they ought to be, that I could almost have imagined that one of that glorious army of saints and martyrs, whose memory we were celebrating, had risen from the grave and come among us. Mr. Palmer and myself afterwards dined in Merton Hall with Walter Hamilton ; the Fellows there appear to be pleasant men of the world, but the society was not such as to suit Palmer and me: besides, it is a waste of precious time to associate with men who are not of my own party, when I have only three or four days to spare for Oxford. I am very much of my friend Rose's opinion, that we do ourselves no good by mixing much with other people, whose opinions do not accord with our own on fundamental points.

Your devoted Son,

W. F. HOOK.

To the Bishop of Lichfield.

Coventry : December 29, 1834.

My Lord,—The kindness of your last letter encourages me to make a request to your lordship. My medical friends concur with your lordship in thinking it to be essential to my health that I should quit the noise and oppositions of this place; and although I should regret to leave a parish where I am now enjoying the fruits of my past labour, yet, with an increasing family, I think it my duty to listen to their advice.

It is not, indeed, to be supposed that anyone who has a pleasant country living, will be willing to exchange it for this ; but I have sufficient interest with Lord Lyndhurst to feel sure that, on my resigning this piece of preferment, he would be willing to present me to some other of equal value, upon my application.

The difficulty is, to know where an eligible rectory within reasonable distance of London is, or is likely to be, vacant. And my request, therefore, to your lordship is, that you will have the kindness to inform me whenever you know such to be the case. I beg to apologise for this intrusion upon your valuable time, an intrusion which may be considered as the penalty for having made me what I most sincerely am, my lord,

Your lordship's ever obliged and dutiful servant,

W. F. HOOK.

But before the offer of the country living came, he had shaken off the malady (which never returned) and was, physically, prepared for the gigantic labours which he was destined to undertake and accomplish.

On the complete restoration of his health in 1835, a very handsome and costly testimonial of plate, to which the poor subscribed in large numbers as well as the rich, was presented to him. In the course of his reply to the address made at the time of presentation, the Vicar said, ' It has been my endeavour to unite with the firmest and most uncompromising adherence to the principles of that blessed Church of which you are respected members, and of which I glory in being a minister, the greatest courtesy towards those who unfortunately differ from us, the greatest charity in judging of the motives of others, and goodwill towards all men. By this public mark of your approbation I presume that you desire me to persevere in this course, and by God's help so I will.'

The only remaining event of importance which deserves a separate notice was the visit, in the summer of 1833, of Dr. Low, Bishop of Ross, Moray, and Argyll, whose friendship he had formed on the occasion of the consecration of Dr. Luscombe in 1825.

The last relic of oppression of the Church of Scotland was not yet removed by the repeal of the Act which prohibited anyone who had received holy orders in that Church from ministering in England.[1] The Vicar of Trinity shortly before the arrival of the

---

[1] This Act was repealed in 1840.

Bishop was dining with his old friend Judge Park.
'I told him,' he writes to Dr. Low, 'with some
complacency that I was expecting a visit from your
reverence, when he reminded me of the iniquitous
Act of Parliament which prevents your officiating in
England. I replied that I should elevate a seat
within the rails of the altar for the Bishop, and
though the *State* might silence him, the *Church*
should receive him with the same episcopal honour
as she would offer to our own diocesan. You will
be received in this house by as firm and true a body
of the clergy as any in England, many of whom are
devoted admirers of your Church—some, indeed,
made so by me, for I speak of my visit to the Scotch
Church wherever I go, and I have lent all the books
bearing upon your history to the right hand and to
the left.'

The Bishop accordingly was welcomed at Coventry with all the honour which the clergy could pay
him. Besides being conducted into the church with
the reverence usually shown to episcopal visitors,
and being placed in the seat of dignity within the
sanctuary, he was also entertained at a public dinner
which all the clergy of the neighbourhood attended.
The event was thoroughly gratifying to the Vicar
who delighted in any opportunity, however small,
of testifying to the unity of the Reformed Catholic
Church by paying equal honour to all branches of it,
whether established or disestablished. To enlighten
the profound ignorance which then commonly prevailed respecting the Episcopal Churches in Scotland and America, to kindle an interest in their
welfare, and to promote their prosperity by every

means which lay within his power, was in fact one of the labours of his life. The condition indeed of the American Church about this time was viewed by him, and some of his Oxford friends, especially Mr. Newman and Dr. Pusey, with considerable anxiety. The opinions and the tone of some of the American clergy and Bishops who had recently visited England seemed to them far from satisfactory. On the subject of Baptismal Regeneration, especially, there seemed reason to fear that the American Church might split into two sections—the western taking the extreme Protestant view, the New York connexion following the Catholic doctrine. Mr. Newman thought it would be highly desirable that two or three able and learned men of sound views should go over to New York and make it their head-quarters for several years, for the purpose of propagating Catholic truth ; but it seemed impossible to find men who combined ability, leisure, and means to undertake the work. Mr. Hook proposed sending books instead of men ; and started a subscription for purchasing a complete set of the Fathers to be presented to the library of the Episcopal College at New York. 'It is obvious,' he writes to Mr. Newman in April 1835, 'that surrounded as the Church there is by papists and fanatics, our grand hope under God must rest with a learned clergy. . . . Certainly the divinity of some of our Transatlantic brethren (and fathers even) is somewhat crude ;' and in December of the same year he says in another letter to Mr. Newman :

I wrote to Dr. McVicar to ascertain what standard works of the Fathers they possessed. He stated in answer, scarcely anything ; except Cotelerius and one or two very common editions. They have Bingham and Suicer and books of that sort. I cannot contribute myself more than 5*l.*, and I expect to raise in this neighbourhood 20*l.* more. I feel anxious to assist the brethren in America, because though they have a Catholic Church, there prevails among its members very little genuine Church principle. I have watched their progress for some years, and have seen with sorrow that there has always been an inclination even among their best men to yield to the prevailing opinions of the age : see, for instance, their Rubric on Regeneration. I fear that our American fathers and brothers are too apt to consider that if they maintain the one doctrine of Episcopacy, sadly curtailed as the jurisdiction of Bishops is, nothing more is required.'

As he lived to see these fears dispelled, and to esteem some of the American clergy and Bishops, especially Dr. Doane, the Bishop of New Jersey, as distinguished ornaments of the Church, it was no small pleasure to him to reflect that he had ever striven to promote intercourse between the English and American members of the Church, and had thus helped to keep the Transatlantic branch stedfast in the faith.

The year 1836 was the last of his ministry at Coventry, although, his health being now re-established and all idea of seeking a country living being abandoned there seemed every prospect of his remaining where he was for some time to come. He was thoroughly contented, thoroughly happy. His habit indeed of making the best of his circumstances whatever they were, which was due partly to his sanguine, manly, and cheerful disposition, partly to his trust in the Providence of God, had never failed him even when the state of his health seemed to indicate the expediency of rest and change. 'Thank you,' he wrote to a friend in the midst of that crisis, 'for wishing what I wish myself—a country parish; not, however, that I wish to leave my own dear parishioners, for I do really love Coventry from the bottom of my heart, but I long to see woods, hills, and lakes; I quite pine for all this. Nevertheless, God's will be done. Determined I am of one thing; to take things as they come, to look on the bright side, to thank my Saviour and my God, and to endeavour to show my gratitude by my obedience.' And his obedience was rewarded by finding himself, after eight years of labour in Coventry, the vicar of a grateful parish, possessed of much influence in the town and neighbourhood, and triumphant over the opposition which he had encountered in the outset of his career. This of course had proceeded from Dissenters and extreme Evangelicals, though it was never comparable in vehemence to that which he afterwards experienced in Leeds. A Nonconformist minister in the city, a man of some ability, attempted, by delivering a set of lectures in his chapel in 1834, to confute the lectures on the Liturgy which were being given by the Vicar in his church; but, as the Vicar remarked, the attack upon his series enhanced their importance, had the effect of an advertisement, and increased the number of his hearers.

On the first Sunday in each month he, at one time, omitted a sermon owing to the large number of communicants. A few malevolent Evangelicals represented this to the Bishop as a great dereliction of duty, although at that very time, being the season of Lent, he preached thrice every week.

The Bishop, however, although himself an extreme Evangelical, was a kind and fair man, and dismissed the complaint with the contempt it deserved.

There was, however, one source of annoyance to which the Vicar never was reconciled, and which, I have often heard him say, was the only reason why he really was glad to leave Coventry. The income of the living depended on a rate levied on all householders in the parish. The system was so distasteful to him that he never would push his rights against defaulters, and consequently seldom received more than half the amount to which he was entitled. The assessors of the rate were appointed at a parish meeting, and, on one occasion, soon after he became Vicar, the Dissenters procured the nomination of one of their party with a view to annoying the Vicar and keeping down the rate. But they had mistaken their man. The Vicar met him soon after his appointment, shook hands with him in his heartiest manner, saying, ' I am very glad you are appointed ; I shall trust you to do all that is just and right, and that is all I care about.' The man, however, did not relish his office and resigned.

The year 1836 ended in grief. Mrs. Hook's father died on December 28, and a few weeks before this event their eldest and, at that time, their only boy was taken from them after a lingering illness. The brief reports of his condition, written by his father from day to day to various relations and friends, are deeply affecting in their expression of passionate affection for the child, coupled with meek submission to the will of God. And now and then, even in the midst of his anxiety and distress, the irrepressible vein of his playful humour comes to the surface, as in one of the reports which is cast into the shape of an official medical bulletin, and is addressed to his brother Robert, and Mr. and Mrs. Wood, as

MESSRS. ROBERT, WILLIAM, CHARLOTTE, & CO.

Sympathisers,

London.

The invitation which he received to become a candidate for the Vicarage of Leeds, early in the following year, was a salutary diversion to the thoughts of the sorrow-stricken parents. But a more particular account of his election to Leeds and departure from Coventry must be reserved for another chapter.

LETTERS, 1829-1836.

To his Curate, Rev. E. Gibson.

Coventry : March 10, 1829.

My dear Sir,—I am extremely sorry to be obliged to quarrel with you so early in our acquaintance, and especially after the very kind and gratifying note which I have just received.

It is lucky that we are both parsons, or a duel would probably ensue ; for you have treated with the greatest contempt one part of my note yesterday—that which requested the pleasure of your company at dinner. This is a kind of insult which can only be atoned for by your making a point of dining with me in spite of any other engagement which you may have. No excuse whatever can be admitted, and therefore no further answer is required. Come you must, or we must fight in private—without seconds, to avoid the scandal.

Yours most truly.

To the same.

Rue Castiglione, Paris : June 29, 1829.

[After asking for information about the Parish]—' I am heartily sick of Paris ; hate France, and think Frenchmen the most detestable of human beings. In three weeks I hope to be in dear old England, and never shall I wish again to quit her shores. I particularly feel the want of clerical employment, and of books of reference when reading the Bible. Should I not, however, return before the Archdeacon's visitation, will you have the kindness to make my apologies, and to take care that every kind of attention is shown him ? I dislike the man's principles, and think the man himself a humbug, but I should not like him to have it in his power to say that I had shown any disrespect to his office ; I wish, therefore, to be particular on this point. . . .

To W. P. Wood, Esq.—Charitable Judgments—Character of George IV.

July 6, 1830.

My dearest Friend, ... I have just been publishing a sermon. I am afraid you will consider me rather ultra ; but you will see by my attack on the Bishops that, Tory though I am, I can still be independent. If I maintain my own principles strongly, God, who knows my heart, can bear me witness that I am equally ultra in the charity with which I judge of others. I always hold that we may condemn opinions, but that we may not condemn those who hold them. That we may, for instance, say that damnation is threatened against habitual drunkenness, but, that we may *not* say to the drunkard, ' *Thou* wilt be damned.'

I have felt much the death of poor King George, for he was so kind a friend to my father and my grandfather, that I looked upon him with something like family affection. When we consider the faults of his education, the talent which was early used to corrupt him, and the strength of the temptations to which he was exposed, I think the judgment which has been passed upon him by the London papers in general, harsh and unchristian. In such a case especially, I hold that the rule 'Judge not' is peculiarly applicable. You, of course, have had other feelings towards him than I have had, but now he is gone, I dare say you feel as I do.

What a blessing it is to have been well and piously brought up in middling life, and thus unexposed to those temptations to which the extremes of high life and low life are so peculiarly exposed. When we take eternity into consideration I think that this is a blessing, the extent of which cannot be too highly estimated. The very circumstance of being obliged to labour for subsistence is the source of many virtues, to which a higher station would render us strangers ; while the being exempted from actual penury enables us to encourage those tastes and feelings, without which the moral man cannot be brought to any degree of perfection. The more I see of the world, the more am I impressed with the advantage of being placed in that station of life which leads a man to labour in a liberal profession rather than in a trade ; though I consider a trade, in nine instances out of ten, to be preferable to an independent fortune.

To some few persons an independent fortune is an advantage ; but how many does it ruin ? while the number of persons improved by professional avocations, and even by professional ambition, is incalculable. Your Charlotte may complain that your professional business takes you too much from her ; but perhaps, (tell her not this, lest she utterly discard me) the very fact that you are obliged sometimes to leave her renders the moments you spend in her society doubly dear.

Yours devotedly,

W. F. HOOK.

To the same—Recollections of School Days—Contentment—Foreign Churches and Sects—The Bible Society.

July 19, 1830.

My dearest Friend, ... The disposition of my mind is to revert to old times and old friends with more than usual fondness ; I forget the discomforts of the former and the faults of the latter, and love to remember them, and to cherish their memory. When I think of Winchester I put out of consideration the floggings and bullyings and revilings, which rendered me miserable on first going to school ; and think only of the happy hours I used to pass with my friend, with whom I did, indeed, take sweet counsel, and who was always ready to sympathise with me under discomforts to which I was more sensibly alive than most boys of my age. And when I remember good old Gabell, I think only of his great kindness, his very great kindness to me, and of the admirable manner in which he instructed us, without reference to his occasional mismanagement out of school. I have seen him several times since, and I love him the more, from the deep interest he seems always to take in the welfare of his quondam naughty boys. Under these circumstances, nothing touched me more than the delightful picture you have drawn in your letter of the old man sitting in the House of Commons, like a patriarch, surrounded by his children. I wish I had been with you ; indeed, I wish more and more to be settled in London. I should so like to mix under altered circumstances with my contemporaries ; moreover, a little clerical and literary society would do me good, in addition to the immense advantage—leaving pleasure out of the question—which I should derive, as I have always done, from a nearer intercourse with you. I think my mind has much improved of late, and, I begin to hope that I could stand my ground in such a field as London, without disgracing myself or doing injury to the Church. I should have shrunk from it a year or two ago. But, after all,

what am I saying? I scarcely know whether I am speaking the truth; I sometimes sit me down and think that I
am the most contented of human beings, since my church
is just the kind of church I like, and my parish suited to
my abilities; while my new curate suits me in every way.
But at other times, when I try to wish for something,
I wish for London. This is a kind of contradiction, but
it is that kind of contradiction which, I presume, exists
occasionally in all minds in a healthy state. My notion
is, that we should always be so contented as never to
envy anyone else; and yet not so contented as to prevent
a proper degree of emulation. While acting from the
higher motives of religion, we are not to eradicate but to
direct the inferior motives which set human nature in
motion; character is to be continually improved, and as
long as this process is going on, no matter how it is
accomplished; for the glory is to be ascribed to God, whose
providence ordains those circumstances under which we
are placed.

With respect to your observations about the circulation of the Scriptures in Greece, &c., you, by taking a
view rather inclining to one side, and I, by taking a
view rather inclining to the other side, without materially
disagreeing, would, perhaps, arrive at an opinion in which
there would be a shade, and only a shade, of difference.
My studies have lain among the primitive writers, and in
the study of the early antiquities of the Church; and my
principle, perhaps originating from that circumstance, is
this, to endeavour to render the Church as conformable as
possible with the primitive model. Hence, I differ from
such divines as Paley; he would make such alterations
in the Church as would render it more comprehensive,
taking, if I may so say, a political view of it; and this
seems to be the object with most of the Church Reformers
of the day. For this purpose he would do away with
many primitive customs, to which those who think with
me are attached. Thus he looks to what must be impossible, owing to the lax state of discipline, a union with
Protestant Dissenters. Now we look not to this, but by (if

any alteration is necessary) even a return to some of the usages discarded at our Reformation, to conform more and more to the primitive model ; that thus, when the Roman Catholic Churches abroad gradually attempt to reform themselves, or what is yet more likely, when the Church of Greece, to which I mainly look, begins to reform, they may see that this can be done without running into that discord and confusion which is certainly the disgrace of Protestantism, and which as certainly makes it stink in their nostrils.   The Greeks abominate the Pope ; but our disunion they abominate equally.   They dread reformation on this account ; ours is the only Church which shows that the Church can be *reformed*, not as in the case of most other Protestants—I ought to except those of Denmark and Sweden—that to correct abuses it must be first overturned and then rebuilt, *de novo* ; and we prevent them from feeling an inclination to reform, by so many of our countrymen in those parts making common cause with all Protestants.   Let us leave events, say I, to Providence ; let us bring ourselves as near to perfection as we can ; nor would I ever for one moment admit it as a ground for any concession, that the safety of the Establishment is concerned.   Concede, in God's name, on all points where concession is innocent, but never from the worldly consideration of sustaining the worldly pre-eminence of the Church.   With respect to the circulation of the Scriptures in Greece, I conceive that, where any prospect of good arises, the Society for Promoting Christian Knowledge would come forward ; but the absurdity is, to commence on a new field ere half the work is done on the old ; our own colonies are lamentably destitute.   As to our liturgy, the Society for Promoting Christian Knowledge would never think it a necessary accompaniment to the Scriptures among the Christians of the Church of Greece.   But you can have no conception of the mischief done there and elsewhere by the circulation of Bibles by the Bible Society, translated imperfectly and, I may say, dishonestly, or at least, unfairly, by Socinians.

The traveller Macfarlane, whose work on Constantinople

you have probably read, asserts that the Bible circulated among the Greeks is written in such strange Romaic that they cannot read it. You will find this, and some other striking cases, stated in the third edition of Arthur Perceval's 'Reasons Why I am not a Member of the Bible Society,' a little tract which I would very strongly recommend to your notice ; it only costs one shilling.

To the same—Preparations for Sunday Evening Services— Remonstrance with the Bishop for attending the Meeting of the Bible Society.

September 5, 1830.

I have been of late rather overworked, and I foolishly consented to make a tour in Wales ; I was only absent five days, so you may imagine that I was rather hurried, but as I could not enjoy myself when absent from my beloved wife, and as much travelling does not agree with me, I returned without being much refreshed as to mind, and with a body rather the worse for wear. Then I have been busily employed in getting subscriptions for lighting my church by gas ; as I am anxious to establish a third service on the Sunday evening, which I did during the summer, and found it to be highly serviceable. This third service I *give* to my parish ; for, as your friend Irving would say, ' Silver and gold have I none, but what I have— that is my labour—I bestow.' Though even here, by the way, —since for ' none ' we ought to read ' but little '—my purse suffers, as it entails upon me the expense of a curate. In most parishes the evening lecturer is paid ; but I thus take that payment on myself. I say this, because I have been abused like a pick-pocket, not by my own parishioners, but by Dissenters and Evangelicals, because I addressed a remonstrance to the Bishop for coming to preside at a Bible meeting in my own parish, and they wish to make it appear to the world that, somehow or other, this arrange-ment will benefit my pocket.

I remain, your devoted Friend,

W. F. HOOK.

Visit to the Bishop of London.

10 Dean's Yard, Westminster : October 1830.

Wife !—Learn to treat your husband with the respect which is due to a man of his consequence. When the Lord Bishop of London invited the Rev. Vicar of Holy Trinity, Coventry, to dine with his lordship, at his lordship's palace at Fulham, who do you think was the *only* person (with the exception of the chaplain) that the said Lord Bishop thought worthy to be invited to meet the said Rev. Vicar, your honoured lord and master ? hear and be confounded—His Grace the Lord Archbishop of Canterbury, Primate of all England and Metropolitan ! ! ! ! ! ! Your poor weak little bit of a mind would indeed have been astonished and astounded to hear how these three pillars of the Church (for I consider the chaplain as a nonentity) discuss affairs ecclesiastical ; yet, without a joke, it was an awful solemnity. The poor Vicar was quite dumb-founded till he had refreshed his nerves by a glass of the Bishop's best wine. Things were going on smoothly after this, when, lo and behold ! in a meek and gentle voice the Lord Archbishop challenged the poor priest to take a glass of wine, and the said priest was again overpowered : he spilt the wine, first on the table-cloth, then on his coat, and forgot to bow to his grace. Luckily ' Piety Without Asceticism ' [1] was named, and the very thought of his dear, kind, apostolical patron, the Bishop of Limerick, inspired the poor priest once more with courage. We all chanted the praises of the work ; and then the poor priest was listened to with interest, as he could give the latest account of Ireland's best Prelate. Indeed, he could not help thinking that his grace the metropolitan seemed to treat him with more respect, when he remembered, probably, that he, the said priest, was immortalised by being mentioned in ' Practical Theology,' as Bishop Jebb's friend. At ten o'clock the three assembled pillars, accompanied by

[1] Title of a work by Bishop Jebb.

Mrs. Blomfield, went to the chapel, where upwards of fifty servants were assembled ; this was indeed a sublime and touching sight. A delightful chapel, the prayers read by a Bishop, and the Vicar kneeling at the side of an Archbishop. Well here ends the history : how I have lived to write it I know not ; but I can say no more, for by eleven o'clock I must attend the meeting of Convocation at St. Paul's, thence I shall have to hurry to the levee. I asked the Bishop whether I was to preach next Sunday ; he said ' of course,' as he never preached except by the King's command : but then he dines with the King on Saturday, when probably he will be commanded. You had better send this letter on to my mother, who will be anxious to hear how things went off at Fulham. Kiss our sweet babe for me till you are tired. I am aweary of these honours, and long to be back with my dear, dear wife, who has in me a

Most devoted Husband,

W. F. HOOK.

To his Wife—First Sermon at the Chapel Royal.

16 St. James Street, London : November 1830.

My dearest Love, ... I had the honour yesterday of preaching before their Majesties. Bob says I delivered the sermon well ; but I do not think the sermon itself was a good one. I trust, however, that I may have touched the hearts and roused the feelings of some of my congregation ; for I warned them in pretty strong terms of the danger, as well as the sin, of denying God and deserting the cause of religion. The Bishop of Chichester[1] came into the vestry after service, and introduced himself as an old friend and schoolfellow of my father's ; he said he could not mistake me from my likeness. His lordship told me that in the bidding prayer I ought not to name the Bishop of the Diocese when preaching in a royal chapel, since such chapels are considered as peculiars. ' And,' said he, ' I may without fear of offence point out one fault, when

[1] Dr. Carr.

there is so much to admire, both in matter and manner.' I made one great, uncavalierlike mistake. The etiquette is, to walk down from the pulpit backwards, and I was told of it twenty times at least ; but when the sermon was ended I forgot it all, and in my eagerness to escape, down I ran with my back to his Majesty. I have heard of various eulogies (the abuse, of course, not being reported to me) from persons who are so ignorant of ecclesiastical affairs as not to know so wonderful a person as myself, for one person to Gilbert Mathison called me Mr. Wood ; another to Mr. Tupper, Mr. Cook. But I see the Court circular, in the newspapers, sets the matter right. Upon the whole, I am not pleased with myself ; I have seldom been more discontented with any of my performances of any kind.

Your most devoted Husband,

W. F. Hook.

From *W. P. Wood, Esq.—Character of Lord Brougham.*

Lincoln's Inn : Dec. 1, 1830.

. . . . Assuredly, my dear friend, the situation of our country does not appear to be such as to inspire ambitious thoughts, and those who undertake to steer us through our difficulties are bold adventurers. I have little doubt that Lord Brougham had sense sufficient to foresee the difficulties to which the new administration will be exposed. I seriously think that he has acted most honestly in taking office. In fact, as I believe I have often said to you, I do not consider that Brougham was ever dishonest, in the worst sense of the word ; but, with a sincere desire to promote many useful objects, he at the same time is beset by no slight degree of what the American Channing calls 'self-exaggeration.' Added to this defect, he is frequently the servant of sudden impulses, for lack of sufficient fixedness of character. Whatever want of confidence may have been evinced by his associates towards Brougham, has arisen rather from his independence than his servility, and he certainly has never been guilty of an actual breach of political principle. His conduct in taking office was marked with his usual faults, and precipitancy. He refused the seals, and then must immediately make a speech to let the world know that he had declined office (for nobody of course would have supposed that it had been offered to him) : he is then told, that an administration cannot be formed without him, and he has in my judgment acted rightly in accepting office, believing of course, as he does, that a Whig administration will be beneficial to the country, and that he himself (an advantage he certainly will not underrate,) will thus be enabled to realise many of his schemes for the public benefit and his own renown. The latter object he is, I think, anxious—as most men are, and he perhaps more than many—to attain, but he fortunately couples it with the best method of attainment. He will, I think, in all probability overthrow the ministry by endeavouring to take the lead of them ; and his splendid speech on the establishment of local courts, the peroration of which I think as magnificently eloquent as any remains of ancient didactic eloquence, furnished a specimen of his probable course ; the bill being brought in, as he stated, independently of any communication with the ministry.

From *W. P. Wood, Esq.—Sympathy between Rich and Poor.*

Lincoln's Inn : May 21, 1831.

. . . . I do not intend to trouble you with politics, but I am sure that a great proportion of the troubles which disturb old-established governments arise from the want of sympathy between the rich and poor. I mean that real sympathy which consults the feelings, and the mental as well as bodily wants of the sufferer ; that truly Christian spirit of benevolence which prompts the more favoured individual to lower himself as far as possible to the level of the poorer classes in his intercourse with them ; to convince them that he regards himself standing before God as humbled a creature as the meanest of his brethren, and that he feels his worldly wealth only entrusted to him as a means of effecting the most extensive good ; whilst, after all the good which he can effect, he is but an unprofitable servant. It is not enough to say that in England more is done for the poor, than in any other country, by gifts : the question is *how* is the wealth given ? and if it should ever be shown that more of actual intercourse with the poor exists among the gentry of this country than of any other nation, yet is it after all but comparative ; and I fear we are very, very far below what might be expected, after eighteen centuries of instruction in real wisdom have been vouchsafed the world. In one respect we are decidedly behind our continental neighbours, and that is in the ineffable distance between master and servant. It is impossible you can work upon the minds of those who regard you with no affection ; and I would ask if anyone can point to more than half-a-dozen instances of attached domestics within his own knowledge. I would follow up my inquiry by asking him the reason. I do not think that foreigners, in general, sufficiently avail themselves of the advantages they have over us in this respect, by influencing the minds of their dependants ; but, I can safely say that we can never hope to effect much benefit in our families while this barrier exists. . . .

I fully agree with you in the excellent view you take of the gradation of duty. An instance of perverted feeling on this subject was shown the other day in this great mart of all extravagance. Crowds had attended meetings held in the new hall in the Strand, for *converting* the *Continent* by ' Sabbath Societies,' and various other contrivances ; but at a meeting for the promotion of 'district visiting,' the only really efficacious means of bettering the temporal and spiritual condition of the poor, but a few stragglers could be collected. Those who are thus usefully employed were perhaps better engaged than in contributing to the parade of a public meeting, but where were the customary haunters of these exhibitions ? preaching in imagination to the Chinese, or weeping tears of joy over a letter from Otaheite.

To W. P. Wood, Esq.—Parochial Work—Opposition from Dissenters.

January 31, 1831.

. . . . This letter only comes a month after the time; it ought to have been received on the first of January. I hope it will be received on the first of February, and though it would not be according to etiquette to express what I heartily wish, that you may pass a happy twelvemonth, yet, here are from me and mine, to you and yours, most hearty wishes for a happy elevenmonth. Christmas time is among the parsons, as you well know, no holiday time; much extra duty always awaits us; and the delightful task of dispensing charities, feeding the national school children, &c., &c., consumes time most voraciously. In addition to this, ours has, till within the last ten days, been the city of the plague; small pox, measles, scarlet and typhus fever have been raging around us; and God Almighty be thanked that we, of this household, have hitherto escaped. I have likewise had the very disagreeable duty of having to beg, from house to house, to get support for our intended infant schools. I am beginning to be a little vain, for I cannot but suppose, as all my friends assert, that the bitterness, I may say the fierceness, with which I am assailed by some of the Dissenters here, must arise from having emptied their shops by establishing an evening service, and stirring up the Churchmen who were before permitted to go to sleep. Every kind of abuse, the most personal, has been heaped upon me, on account of this infant school. I was told that it was expected that the Church should come forward, and that the Dissenters would contribute. Together, therefore, with all the beneficed clergy of the city, we called a meeting, only insisting that the children should be taught the Creed, Lord's Prayer, and ten Commandments, and that the master should be a member of the Church. It was necessary to do this before calling a meeting, because we knew that, while Churchmen would supply the money, the Dissenters would be able to outnumber us by resorting to measures for packing the meeting, to which we would not condescend. We thought it right, therefore, to state what we should consider a *sine quâ non*. At the meeting, if the Dissenters could not conscientiously support our plan, I intended to propose, that we should raise a subscription together, and establish two schools ; one to be superintended by the clergy, the other by the Dissenters, with an understanding that neither party would receive the children dismissed for ill-conduct from the other establishment. But a violent Dissenting teacher, abetted by as violent an Evangelical clergyman, chaplain to the Bridewell, called an opposition meeting, branded us with the title of intolerant bigots, and determined to crush us. We have let them have their way ; when reviled, we have carefully abstained from reviling again ; and the consequence has been that we have raised nearly 300*l.*, and their subscriptions are, I suspect, so inconsiderable that they have hitherto refrained from publishing them. Their funds have chiefly been supplied by the Quakers, who at first promised to support us ; by some few among the gentry at a distance, who were deceived by their assuming the name of an *anti-sectarian* infant school ; and by the political characters who have subscribed to both. All this is easily written, but it was not so easily done. It has been personally satisfactory to me, since many persons have given their five pounds, saying at the same time that they had not intended to support an infant school, but they were glad of any opportunity to show their respect for me. Thus you see how I am situated ; you cannot in Coventry take a single step in any matter without meeting with a factious opposition. I have found, however, staunch friends where I did not expect them ; while this has been balanced by an opposition, which has shown its bitterness in ascribing to me words and deeds which have not a shadow of foundation in truth.

*To the same—Foundation of a Dispensary.—Resignation of
Moseley—Parochial Work.*

Coventry : March 14, 1831.

My dearest Friend,—I lose no time in thanking you
and your wife for your kind letter of congratulation, if
it be a subject of congratulation, that I have entered
my thirty-fourth year and am no better than I am.
I am at present a bachelor, my spouse having run
away from me, with the heiress of all the Hooks, to
pay a visit to her father and mother. I am too busy to go,
and I am at present almost too nervous to write, for I am
to make my first—no, my second (after a long interval)
—appearance as an extempore speaker to-morrow. The
thought of it, strange as it may appear, in one who
preaches so often, makes me ache all over. The meeting
is called for the purpose of establishing a self-supporting
dispensary, and I am to move the first resolution. We
shall be opposed by a host of medical men ; but a dispensary of some sort or other shall be established ; they may
bully, but we are determined not to yield. You tell me
you shall write to me on politics ; remember, Sir Radical,
that I am a Tory ; so moderate your tone of triumph, if it
be from mere compassion. But in truth, I am too much
occupied in parochial details to be able to busy myself in
politics ; and the state of politics is such at present as so
to sadden my poor Tory heart that I avoid the subject as
much as possible, seeing that I could do no good. I
seldom indeed advert to them, except when I offer the
prayer for Parliament, which is offered from the heart.
But let us fly from this gloomy subject, and let me tell
you of what will probably prevent our intended visit to
London by burdening us with expense. We are about to
change our house, having found one to our liking, just out
of the town, but in the parish. And as we cannot go to
you, why will not you come to us? we have a nice airy
situation, a good small garden, and everything that can

allure you. The expense of flitting is not all ; for I have now diminished my income 50*l.* a year, by resigning Moseley. I was overpersuaded by my mother to keep it, but for the last year and a half I have been anxious to give it up, from a feeling that my being non-resident at a living so near Birmingham was injurious to the cause of religion ; I retained it, however, for the sake of my curate. That difficulty has been overcome ; for the Bishop of Rochester, the patron, having heard of my wish, sent me a letter last week stating that he wished to bestow the preferment so as to advance the cause of true religion, and to counteract the effects of the fanaticism prevalent in Birmingham and its vicinity. He consequently placed the nomination in my hands, and I have nominated my curate. This is very noble in his Lordship, since we had some misunderstanding when he took possession of the Deanery. All these things, with the small-pox raging like a plague around us ; with a dispensary, savings bank, and infant school to be established ; with lectures every Wednesday, and lectures to prepare for every day in Passion Week ; with, I am delighted to say, an improving parish, and consequent increase of parochial duty—all these things must account for the fact that Walter Hook is not so good a correspondent as he once was, that when he has time to write, his pen is employed in sermons rather than in letters ; but it will not prove to William Wood, who knows him so well, that his love and friendship are one whit the less.

To the same—Lectures on the Last Days of our Lord's Ministry —Change of House—Foundation of a Dispensary—Calumnies.

Leicester Road, Coventry : April 13, 1831.

. . . . I delivered my lectures every day in Passion Week to a very attentive and devout congregation. Indeed, I have reason to hope that they were of service, not only to myself, but to many who heard them. On one person in particular I know that they have made a serious impression, and a Socinian lady who was with me all the week presented herself at the altar on Easter day. I have indeed been very successful in my ministry of late, for two of the leading surgeons in my parish have not only become regular attendants at church but have received the Sacrament. . . . All this has been highly satisfactory, and I am in good humour with my parish. It was nevertheless hard work, for I had only written one of my lectures when I commenced, and had in consequence to sit up late and rise early; besides which, I started one evening to see my little wee bit of a wife (she is only about an inch taller than yours), and having found her as well as could be, I returned in the morning. Then I have been very busy in moving from St. Nicholas Place to this house. I have been labouring night and day to get it ready for Delicia, so that she may have no trouble or fatigue when she returns, which I hope will be on Friday. I have seldom felt so anxious for any day since I left Winchester; my feelings are just those with which we used to look forward to the holidays: I have been so busy about all this, that I have not seen her for a week. I must tell you that this house though in the parish is in the country; quite rural, with a garden and all. I have been studying the art of gardening too; I can give you the history of gardening, from that of Paradise to that described in the Canticles; and from that of Alcinous to that of Academus, and so on to Sir William Temple and Kent, down to our own times, not forgetting the hanging gardens of Babylon. This morning I have been sowing peas: but there have arisen a very disagreeable sect of Dissenters in my little plantation; they are known by the name of slugs, and have opened a conventicle in the very heart of my cabbage-bed. I am a bigoted, intolerant wretch, as you know, and mean to burn them, not with fire and fagot, but with lime. I must narrate another grievance. In endeavouring to establish a self-supporting dispensary I have incurred the wrath of all the doctors in this place; I know not whether I mentioned this before, but so it is, and thus

I am placed between two fires. In the Coventry papers the doctors are attacking me as a hypocrite, &c. &c., and all the time a Dissenting teacher is publishing every week an ecclesiastical lecture, in which he holds me up to censure for various iniquities : one, in particular, is rather amusing, he accuses me of avarice, and calls me 'the holy minister of Holy Trinity.' Now avarice is certainly not one of my faults ; and if he inquired further he would find that while by my rate here, at the lowest valuation, I ought to receive 498*l.* a year, I only in fact receive 250*l.* ; and when some of my parishioners found fault with my collector (for the business is not managed by me), he told them that the blame did not rest with him, but if anyone goes to the Vicar he not only excuses them but gives them something for the trouble of calling. However, so it is with my Dissenting friends ; many of my real faults are passed over, and things are brought against me of which my conscience does not accuse me. Now you know my sensibility, and will think, perhaps, that all these things are sufficient to drive me mad ; but no, I have found the secret which enables me to laugh at them. I have learned not to care for man's judgment, and simply to think how far I am doing what is right in the sight of God.

Infidels and fanatics are furious against me, but that only proves that having flung the stone at them, I have made the curs yelp, while my congregation has increased, and my flock, generally speaking, are devoted to me.

To the same—Abstinence from Politics.

May 16, 1831.

My poor dear Friend, . . . At Worcester you carried all before you, but I voted of course for Lygon. In Coventry I never meddle with politics. My principle is this ; to do those duties, or rather to attempt to do them, which Providence points out to us, by the circumstances under which we are placed, always remembering that the nearest and easiest duties are to us the first in importance. Thus I consider my first duty is to my family, including my servants ; my next to the parish, over which the Holy Ghost has made me overseer ; then to my diocese, my country, and so on to all mankind. It is that which our hand findeth to do that we are to do with all our might. And the mischief of the present age is, that every one is striving to do some great thing ; while those minor points, which are first to the individual, are neglected. Men are devising schemes to convert heathens, while their own families, and perhaps themselves, are quite as much in need of conversion ; they are anxious to waft the Scriptures from the Ganges to the Mississippi, but forget to make the Bible their own companion and familiar friend. It would be well for England if, instead of clamouring for reform, men would do (as Rickman, the Quaker architect, observed to me the other day) their own business, and reform themselves. It was on these principles that I voted at Worcester, having a vote for the county. I thought myself in these times called upon to exercise my privilege and, consequently, I voted like an obstinate old Tory (as Lord Lyttleton, who brought in his brother-in-law, called me). I take a gloomy view of things. It is at the same time a comfort to me to feel that you, who are so much wiser than I am, and are not a party man, at least, not violently so, think otherwise. I consider you as a thoroughly honest politician. The men I dislike are those who support the Reform Bill simply because it is introduced by their friends.

To Hon. and Rev. A. Perceval—Advantages of an Establishment.

Coventry : May 25, 1831.

I am now become a waiter upon Providence. For some inscrutable purpose the country appears to me to have been demented ; the afflicting hand of Providence is upon us, and we must diligently labour to ascertain precisely what our duty is, both in bearing and forbearing, and then seek for grace to perform it.

As churchmen, we have the blessed conviction that the Church will flourish more under oppression than at any other time. St. Hilary says ' Hoc habet proprium ecclesia, dum persecutionem patitur floret, dum opprimitur proficit, dum læditur vincit, dum arguitur intelligit, tunc stat, quum superari videtur.'

But as patriots and as Englishmen who but must weep? let the Church be unestablished and infidelity will be rampant. I am one of those who think a little religion to be better than none at all. And I regard the establishment of the Church to be one of the means appointed to lead men gradually to a serious sense of the faith. A man may love the Church at first merely because it is an institution of his country. With an honest mind, like the apostles when first called to be disciples, their principles may be too secular. Too many do not advance at all, but many more come by degrees to see how the Church is the mystical body of their Saviour, and glorying in their privilege, they not only abide in Christ but Christ abides in them. From fruitless they are pruned into fruitful branches of the Vine. That God will devise other means for bringing those who are of honest and good hearts to the truth, no one will deny, but no Christian can contemplate without sorrow the withdrawment of one of the visible means hitherto ordained for that purpose, even though the Church itself be purified, while depressed, thereby. As a Church, the Reformed Catholic Church in England will be benefited by its disunion from the State ; but, as the Bishop of Limerick observes, the question is not whether the Church be *less* pure, but the country be not *more* pure. And one of the offices of the Church is to be the salt of the earth, and indirectly to purify even worldlings. I refer our calamities to the repeal of the Test Act ; for then the State *virtually* renounced every connexion with religion. It pronounced religion to be, so far as the State is concerned, a thing indifferent.

England is now in the position of a man who has excommunicated himself. To the special protection of Providence and of grace it has no longer a covenant claim. Our legislation is in fact of *any* religion, which is the same as saying of *no* religion.

Convalescence.

Birmingham : June 14, 1831.

My dearest Mother,—Although I am mending fast, the doctor entirely disapproves of my leaving the Monument at present, and my system is, strictly to follow the advice of the doctor under whose care Providence, by the arrangement of circumstances, has placed me ; then, as our good Lord of Limerick says, if I die, it is his fault and not mine. That I am better will appear from this, that I am growing hourly more impatient to return to dear Coventry ; happy I never can be out of my parish, and I long to offer my prayers once again in my noble church. There is no church in England that suits me so well. ' Say not this is lame devotion that cannot mount without the help of such a wooden stick ; rather 'tis lame indeed which is not raised though having the advantage thereof.' This sentence is from Fuller, whose ' Holy State ' I am reading, much to my edification and delight. I am going out a-fishing to-day !! but truth to tell, I should be more in my element if I were at Coventry trying to catch men ; the fact is that I am so identified with my parish that, if too much duty knocks me up, a little duty is essential to amuse me. Without parochial duty I feel much as a dram-drinker must do when robbed of his morning draught.

An Author's Anxieties about the Publication of his First Book.

The Monument : August 1831.

My dearest Mother, ... On one point you disappointed me in your last ; you told me that you had had a long conversation with the Archdeacon about me, and yet told me not what the Archdeacon said: now this is acting the part of Tantalus. All that he said about divinity would of course be interesting to me, for he is my pope. His medical opinions you might have suppressed, because, as he has not graduated in medicine, I might be unwilling to follow his advice; indeed, I hope you will no more write on that subject. But I am very anxious to hear what he says of my lectures; from your silence I suppose he does not think them worth publishing, which annoys me. Pray let me have them back again; the only little solace I have consists in preparing these lectures for press. It is a light and agreeable study, such as Dr. Johnstone approves of; it leads my mind back to the happy period when I delivered them, and sometimes flatters my vanity by making me hope to be useful after I have been consigned to the grave. The thought of being compelled to dismount my little hobby is painful; it is as much as telling me that I am put entirely on the shelf, and then what am I to do? for I have no one pleasure, no thought, no wish that is not professional: pray send me back my poor little lectures, and pray for me that I may have health and strength to preach them yet again, and fail not to let me know at once if they are condemned; put me out of my pain, suspense is disagreeable; I have been able to do nothing at them for the last two or three days, because if those two are condemned, it is needless to go on with the others; and then poor Othello's occupation is done.

To W. P. Wood, Esq.

Coventry : December 1, 1831.

My dearest Friend, ... Now for your letter;— thank you much, for the delightful pouring out of your feelings; and believe me, that when I read the sentiments of humble piety which you therein express, I am more proud of the friendship which has ever been my honour as well as my delight. Thank God it is not on our own works that we depend for hope, as to everlasting bliss. Christ is our all in all, and to Him we can only approach by faith. Now it is on this doctrine of justification by faith alone, that I delight to dwell when I am inclined to despond ; I then throw myself without reserve at the feet of Christ. You, my dear Wood, understand me in what I say, and know very well that I am not pleading the cause of Antinomianism. Nothing is more easy than to reconcile St. Paul and St. James, when we understand the scheme of redemption as revealed in the Gospel. I only refer to that doctrine, which is our greatest comfort and consolation when we are humbled and laid in the dust. It is not the only doctrine of Scripture, and therefore we shall miss the truth if we consider it without reference to others which limit and elucidate it ; but it is the doctrine that gives life and health to the humble and lowly of heart. As to prayer, I suppose every person has some different method of elevating his soul to communion with the Deity. For my part, I find I can pray best when I am walking in my garden ; indeed, I am generally a peripatetic in my devotions, and I find the open air my most delightful temple. Again, I know nothing more conducive to bring me to a devotional disposition than to read some portion of the Bible, till I gradually sink off into a holy reverie. I throw out these hints, because when first I became seriously impressed with religious feelings, I had some of those difficulties of which you seem to complain. And even in those days when we cannot take the usual delight in prayer and praise, we ought to remember that our Saviour knows our hindrances, and that by Him, the will will be taken for the deed ; when we have struggled much without success, faith will, in this sense, be counted to us for righteousness.

From W. P. Wood, Esq.—Uses of a Belief in Angels—
Irvingism.

Lincoln's Inn : March 1832.

. . . . I thank you for your beautiful hint as to the Angels.[1] It is curious that I have two or three times said to my wife that I thought we were too much in the habit of neglecting the clear doctrine, as laid down in the Bible, of spiritual agents subordinate to the Deity, and of their interference with the events of this world. There is certainly a degree of danger in dwelling too much on such a subject if the mind be predisposed to enthusiasm ; but at the same time I think that the great caution of many preachers has led to a carelessness even as regards the restless machinations of our great spiritual adversary. You will recollect that you told me an anecdote of a Unitarian saying ' nobody could believe in the devil.' Still more may have been deprived of great spiritual consolation from the neglect of those many beautiful passages in Scripture which represent the watchfulness of the angels over those who serve God, and their great interest in all that concerns our welfare. People are very apt to imagine that their deceased friends take an interest in their conduct, for which we have no direct Scriptural authority (the parable of Lazarus being, perhaps, only a parable), and which may prove a dangerous conceit as tending to saint worship. Now the clear knowledge afforded us of the ministry of Angels ought to be no less consolatory.

My mind has been brought to dwell upon many of the deeper points of the ' mystery of Godliness ' owing to a visit from two young friends, who have been, to a certain extent, led away by the enthusiasts of Irving's school. With regard to the alleged *miracles,* I think it is at once an answer to say that no *miracle* has yet been even *stated* ; for the uttering of sounds which no one professes to

[1] That the knowledge of their sympathy should be an auxiliary to our devotions.

comprehend is so far from miraculous that any of us could do the same thing for hours together ; and I think I satisfied our friends of the wonderful difference between such quackery and the stupendous miracle of the day of Pentecost. But the greatest difficulty I met with was on the subject of election. My own views on this subject do not quite coincide with Whately's. I think a little more is meant than the simple fact of election to privileges which may be accepted or waived, and I confess I rather lean to the doctrine of those who think that God, foreseeing who will accept the conditions of salvation, and having promised that all who do so accept them shall be saved, may be said in that sense to have *elected* the *saved*. But then I am quite certain from Scripture that although God knows this, no *man* can know it, no man can see the end of his career, which God does see, and therefore no man can be assured that he will continue in a state of grace. A man may perhaps feel an assurance that through Christ's mercy, if he were to die that moment, he would be saved, but he can say nothing more. Not even St. Paul would venture on so bold (so almost blasphemous) a conviction, 1 Cor. ix. 27, Phil. iii. 11–14. You have, I dare say, observed a remarkable mistranslation in Heb. x. 38, where ' any man ' has been substituted for ' he,' and thus a strong text against absolute, certain election has been considerably weakened. Rom. viii. 29, 30–33, and some other passages induce me not to adopt Whately's views entirely, though I think the word ' election ' is often used in his sense ; for, as he has observed, there are no strict logical definitions in the Gospel. Irving, of course, adopts the most presumptuous and dangerous doctrine of the high Calvinists.

To W. P. Wood, Esq.—Christian Sympathy.

Leamington : March 1, 1832.

My dearest Friend,—As usual, I must begin my letter with an excuse. To avoid this frequent repetition, let it be fairly understood that I love you as much as ever; you must not therefore attribute my silence to any diminution of affection.   A little writing soon knocks me up ; and, consequently, I can never think of a letter until my sermons are off the stocks, and that seldom is till Saturday evening. We came here last week to visit my mother.   My brother having also arrived, we are, what we seldom are, all of us together.   I have also enjoyed the society of my honoured friend and patron, the Lord Bishop of Limerick ; he is indeed a right worthy successor of the Holy Apostles : to me he has ever been like a parent.   He has perused the manuscripts of my lectures, and what is more, with unheard of kindness, he offers to correct the press for me, and to take all the drudgery of publication off my hands.   This, he says, will be a little useful employment to him ; and it will be everything to me to be sent into the world under such auspices.   He has, however, directed me to write some notes, and has moreover advised that the publication should be deferred till the end of the year, since nobody now thinks of anything but reform and cholera.   I intended to answer your last most interesting letter fully, but I have forgotten to bring it with me.   But I remember well one topic to which you refer, which is, the want of Christian sympathy which you seem to experience when worshipping in church.   This is a subject on which I have had very many conversations with my reverend brethren in this neighbourhood ; for fifteen or twenty of us frequently meet, not to discuss, but to converse ; being happily of pretty nearly the same principles in religion, though there are slight shades of difference in our politics.   Nothing fills the Dissenting chapels so much as their being able to remedy the defect of which you complain.   When a man has seriously turned his thoughts to religion, he comes to church and finds no one sympathising with him, no one under circumstances somewhat similar, ready to communicate his thoughts.   He goes to a meeting house, he is immediately hailed as a convert ; he is flattered, calmed, and soothed.   Now we have considered whether some such

steps as these might not be profitably adopted in the
Church; it would immediately increase its popularity with
some religionists; for man is an aristocratic animal, and
sectarianism flatters the aristocratical feeling. Everyone
in religion, as in everything else, likes to be a peg above
his neighbour, and to be one of a party superior in purity
or in wisdom to those around him. If, then, we were to
consider merely the religionists, if merely the popularity of
the Church, it might be well to adopt some such classifica-
tion as prevails with the Methodists. But the Church of
Christ, I conceive, is not intended to be confined as to its
benefits and advantages to those who are true Christians:
here is the mistake with the sectarians. There is a yet
more extensive object, though less flattering to human
pride; it is to act as leaven and as salt by which the mass
of society may be gradually purified; it is indirectly to
benefit those who are without, as well as those that are
within the pale; to improve men's morals, when it cannot
prevail upon them to become Christians in very deed.
Thus it has been shown by Bishop Jebb that, in the commission of the Apostles, our Lord commanded them first
to convert individuals, and then to convert nations; to have
to do with whole masses of society. While the Church
was composed merely of individuals, as was the case till
the time of Constantine, it was in its purest state; when it
was allied with the world, its discipline was relaxed, and
consequently it became less pure. But the question is,
not whether the Church be less pure, but whether the
world by this contact, be not more pure; and of this no
one, I presume, can doubt. We ought, therefore, always to
recollect this secondary but very important character of
the Church, this leavening and salting purpose for which it
is intended, and not to administer it so as to seek the gratification of those only who are really pious in their feelings.
The advantage of this indirect influence on society is great.
Suppose I prevail upon a man no further than to respect
the common decencies of life; as to his fate we dare not
decide, God alone can judge; but this I see, that his

children being brought up morally, and orderly, are prepared to embrace the whole faith, as it is in Jesus. Pray
read Bishop Jebb's beautiful perfect sermon on transmissive
religion in 'Practical Theology'; if you have not the book,
say so, and I will send you a copy.

To his Wife—Account of Visit to Lincoln to be Installed as
Prebendary of Caistor.[1]

Lincoln : Trinity Sunday, June 1832.

My dearest Love,—I wrote to you chiefly to state my
intentions with respect to my movements. I hope to leave
this early on Tuesday morning, and to reach London the
same day; but you must not be alarmed if I do not make
my appearance till Wednesday. My journey here was
prosperous; I got on to Loughborough from Leicester, in
a return chaise for two shillings. With the collegiate
church of Southwell, I fell desperately in love; it is really
beautiful, with fine old Norman arches. I attended service
there, and found the choir well managed. The town itself
is pretty, and I should not object to have a stall there,
with a living attached. From Southwell to Lincoln, the
journey is easy; but I was obliged after all to post one
stage. Arrived at Lincoln, I found the inn in much confusion, for there was a visitation dinner. 'Whose visitation is
it?' I asked : 'The Archdeacon of Stow's,' was the answer;
and sure enough I saw his reverence at no great distance,
giving a jobation to a churchwarden. 'Give the Archdeacon this card,' said the Prebendary elect; on receiving
which, forth comes my kind friend Archdeacon Bayley,
pulls me into the room, and says, 'Gentlemen, allow me
to introduce our new Prebendary; you have all heard of
Mr. Hook;' and then a long eulogy was pronounced.
'For his own sake, therefore,' said the Archdeacon, 'and
his admirable father's sake, let us drink his good health

[1] The stall had been given him by the Bishop, who was a friend of his
father.

in a bumper.' The Dean was present, and invited me to
dine with him to-day. The preacher of the visitation
sermon gave me a bed, two miles in the country at his
pretty Parsonage. The Sub-dean has been most kind, but
unfortunately his house was full, and he could not therefore
give me a bed ; but he has forced me to stay over Monday
to meet Archdeacon Bayley, the Dean, and others at
dinner. The Dean, Sub-dean, and a brother Prebendary
dined with me yesterday at the Inn ; a very bad custom, I
think, but so it is. The Minster is grand beyond description, it beats every other cathedral, in my opinion, out of
the field, except York, and it yields not to that. The in-
stallation is a very good ceremony, it took place yesterday.
To-day I read in, morning and evening, and preached
twice ; this in fact it is that has quite decided me not to
go away to-morrow ; a day's rest will be useful. I long to
see you again, my dear, sweet little wife, and I long also to
behold our darling. May God Almighty bless you both.
I hope to find a letter at the post. Love to all friends.

Your devotedly attached Husband,

W. F. HOOK.

In the autumn of 1832 his mother and sister
spent some time in the Lake Country near Rydal.
They became intimate with the Wordsworth family,
and paid almost daily visits to the poet's house.
One day during the severe illness of his sister, Miss
Wordsworth, they found the poet sitting by her
side, where he had been for hours rubbing her feet.
Miss Hook wrote a letter to her brother full of
enthusiastic admiration for this trait of fraternal
affection on the part of Wordsworth ; to which he
replied in the following strain :

I wish you could read Quinctilian or Longinus, and

then, as in times past, I should set you a portion to learn
by heart, and initiate you into the arts of composition.
Most horrible was the bathos into which your last letter
plunged.   Having descanted not only on the genius but
the virtues of the poet, having entered into 'your little
boat, in shape a very crescent moon,' and carried me into
the third heaven, you then introduce me to the venerable
bard—surrounded by the Muses—doing what? striking
the silver lyre? no! rubbing his dear old sister's cold toes.
O fie! Miss Hook! fie! as a punishment I shall put down
my pen, and conclude this letter just when I please.   I
should not indeed write to you at all, but that I should
like to earn another such letter, excepting that part which
descants on brotherly affection towards cold feet in a sister.
I hope that you will always be able to keep your feet
warm with exercise, and your heart still warmer by enthusiasm, kept of course under the fraternal control of good
sense. . . .

The Lakes—Wordsworth.

Coventry : September 8, 1832.

My dearest Mother, ... How I do envy you your
delightful visit to the Lakes ; no, envy is not the right
word, for I should like to enjoy it with you.   I think as one
grows older, and becomes more christianised (almost all
other terms have been so wrongly applied, that it is scarcely
lawful to use them), as the natural man goes down hill, and
the moral man learns to take higher and higher flights
towards those heavenly regions where he humbly hopes
to live for ever with his Saviour and those who were
worthy of his love on earth ; so do we feel more deeply,
more intensely, the beauties of inanimate nature—that
nature to which your honoured friend Wordsworth has,
more than any other poet, given a voice ; a voice which
speaks to the very heart of hearts.   In early youth there is
an enchantment in the scenes of nature which makes
every lad worth anything, think and hope that he is born

to take station among the poets of his country. How beautifully are these feelings described in the 'Excursion.' But the boy tries his hand at expressing his thoughts, and finds in despair that language fails him : he cannot say all he feels, and rushes out from the Temple of the Muses in despair. Encouragement no one can give, for he who feels strongly will most likely feel awfully sensitive in permitting his feelings to be known ; they can only be fully opened to a person of the same age, a wife, or such a friend as Wood. Then other pursuits engage the attention, the feelings are chilled by a cold world; worldliness of mind ensues, ambition urges on to exertion, and the soul is more and more alienated from heavenly aspirations. After this comes disappointment and misfortune ; those blessings in disguise, when religion becomes once more a reality, when the soul becomes elevated, the affections spiritualised, and the mind no longer earthy ; and it is then that nature in her grand and in her calmer scenes once more speaks to the heart. Having diligently marked not only the progress of my own mind, but that of many of my contemporaries, and having also had minds opened to me by persons who have wished for spiritual consolation in my parish, I am so convinced that this is the usual process with such as become rightly religious, that the tone of my sermons is always in accordance with these notions. I don't like violent philippics against vice, or those feelings which *will* have their way. I like to paint the loveliness of religion, to call back the mind to those calm joys it experienced, before worldliness, or inordinate ambition, or the passions assumed their tyranny ; and then to show how by degrees God's grace will not only restore those amiable sentiments of childhood, but give them a vigour and a holiness of which the worldly can form no conception. Now, as I humbly hope that my mind has become spiritualised, I feel that I am just in the condition to profit by those delightful views which you and dear Georgiana so well describe. I should indeed delight to wander over your mountains, and pour out my thoughts, not in poems, but in sermons. I am weary of towns, and especially of manufacturing towns, and I sigh for the country.

Delicia and I agree that of all places we have seen Hertingfordbury would suit us best, yes, even more than Whippingham ; she likes the retirement of Hertingford-bury, and I confess that the dark, shady walk by the river has fresh charms for me as I grow older. I am, as the good dear Bishop would say, something self-complacent, at the praise you tell me has been bestowed on me by Wordsworth ; Delicia and I have guessed the truth. It is so utterly impossible that he should ever have heard of me, that we conclude thus : One day Mrs. Hook was talking to the poet, and, in the overflow of her maternal fondness, she told him that her son was the finest preacher and best parson, &c., &c., in England. Well, many days had elapsed, and the poet had meanwhile been in the third heavens. When Mrs. Hook calls on him again, the name of her son is mentioned ; ' Oh,' says the poet, ' I have heard that your son is a very fine preacher, and a very good divine.' ' Who told you ?' ' I quite forget,' replies the poet, ' but I am certain that I have heard it.' I am so convinced that this, or something like it, is the fact, that I am not vain, as I otherwise might be, at the eulogy. But I am indeed complacent at the idea of my being known, even by name, to the living poet of England. I have in my time so worshipped poets, that the very thought of being known to such a poet as Wordsworth stirs up the enthusiasm which the noise and smoke and bustle of a large town has well nigh quenched. By the bye, I do not at all approve of Mr. Macaulay's criticism ; I hate to hear people call Wordsworth 'the modern Milton,' as they so frequently do : it gives one the idea of his being one of the servile herd of imitators. Now, of all poets that ever existed, saving only Homer, and my old friend, Shakspeare, Wordsworth is the most original. He has shaped out a line peculiarly and entirely his own ; and one of the reasons that for a long time he was not popular with the mob of readers, was this very circumstance—he was so different from the namby-pamby poetasters they had been accustomed to admire, that they could not relish him ; or else, because he was so different from other poets, they knew not by what rules to try him. But Wordsworth was a true poet, and those many hearts he touched by his poetry soon learned that he was to give laws, or rather to provide materials, from which future Aristotles might frame laws, and not to receive them from pedants.

Your devoted Son,

W. F. HOOK.

To W. P. Wood, Esq.—Origin of Heathen Ideas about a Future State.

Coventry : October 3, 1832.

My dearest Friend, ... Since you left us, we have been going on as you, knowing our ways of proceeding, would expect, with the exception that I have of course had some arrears of business to make up after my happy holiday during your stay with us. I have made but little progress in the metaphysical or philosophical inquiries, if they deserve the name, on which we conversed when you were with us. I am, however, reading St. Augustine's 'De Civitate Dei,' or rather the three last books of it, which relate to the doctrine of the Resurrection. Some years have passed since I read it before, and I may trouble you on some future occasion with my thoughts upon that very extraordinary work. I am also going to read Cicero's Tusculans ; the more I consider the subject, the more convinced I am, that the better informed among the heathen held the doctrine of a future state, merely as a careless opinion, not as an article of faith, which would influence practice ; but that the doctrine was, in some sense or other, universally held by the mass of mankind, appears to be indisputable. Whence could it arise that such was the fact ? Not from the discoveries of reason, for even when a Plato reasoned thereon, he only fell into absurdities, but from a tradition which was gladly received, because congenial with the mind of man, ever looking forward, and ever ready to believe that God is just. But then, where is the revelation of the fact, which a tradition would suppose? We can only speak on this point by reference to Scripture, and Scripture does not record any early revelation. But then, Scripture does tell us of the promise to Adam of a future deliverer, and it does also tell us that this promise was handed down in many instances from sire to son. At first, the Patriarchs might have expected its fulfilment before they themselves saw death, but when their children found that their expectations were erroneous, they would look for the fulfilment of the promise after their death; but if they were to be interested in its fulfilment, this would of course induce them to suppose that they would be recalled from the dead. To confirm this expectation, the rapture of Enoch may have been intended. It seems much more likely that men should in early ages have received the doctrine, in some such way as this, than that they should have arrived at it by any metaphysical reasons. An express revelation then, of course, could not be till the doctrine of the Atonement, on which the doctrine of the Resurrection depends, was fully known. You see, I take rather a midway station betweeen Warburton and his opponents. I know not whether I have made myself intelligible, but I hope if you understand me, and any facts or arguments, *pro* or *con.*, suggest themselves to your mind, you will send them.

Your devoted Friend,

W. F. HOOK.

Publication of Lectures on ' Last Days of our Lord.'

Lichfield : November 1, 1832.

My dearest Mother, ... The work is to come out this week, and therefore your country bookseller will have no difficulty in obtaining copies from his agent in London. I think you had better send the copy to Mr. Southey, and all others, except to Mrs. Grant, from yourself; I will be your debtor for the last, and also for one which I should like to present to Mr. Wordsworth if he will accept it. Tell him that it comes from me who venerates his character and who has derived, not only intellectual pleasure, but moral improvement from his immortal writings. I am afraid, however, that neither he nor Southey will approve of what was written, not by a retired scholar, but by a clergyman, who has never known what leisure is, since he entered into holy orders, and who is therefore guilty perhaps of unpardonable presumption in thrusting himself into the republic of letters. I certainly wish for the success of the work, not because it deserves success, but because, if I am not severely cut up, I may be able to do something better. I am glad to hear you talking, or rather to read you writing of settling at the Lakes: we might easily arrange matters, so that we could spend two or three months with you in the summer, and you, two or three months with us in the winter. I only wish that we had commenced housekeeping less expensively than we did, for though our expenses are less than those of most persons in our station of life, yet they leave us not the means of travelling, or indulging our wishes on several other points. From various circumstances, our income, which I once thought would be 800*l.* a year, and thus very plentiful, has fallen down to 500*l.*, which is certainly more than many of our betters possess, but is, nevertheless, only barely equal to the many demands upon us. If I can but make 200*l.* by my book, it will be glorious. Delicia could then have a piano of her own ; I would get a Benedictine Chrysostom ; my church should be presented with a painted window ; and you and Georgiana should have our company in your visit to the Lakes next year.

I remain, my dearest Mother, your devoted Son,

W. F. HOOK.

To W. P. Wood, Esq.—Different Classes of Writers—
Letter from Wordsworth.

November 27, 1832.

It seems that we, once the most prolific of letter-writers, are now compelled to commence each epistle with an apology. But as Thompson said when writing to his sister, we know one another better than to interpret our silence into any decay of affection. It seems to me that the intellectual world may be divided into two parties ; first, there is a class consisting of those whose talents are ever ready, whose armour is ever bright and polished. Such was Shakspeare, such was our dear lost Sir Walter Scott, such are those differing infinitely in degree but not in genus, whose pen is at all times prepared to write a letter, or to chatter and gabble in society on every subject. The next class consists of those who have the pen of a ready writer, but who can only use it when the fit of inspiration is upon them. At the head of this tribe, according to his biographers, was Milton ; and, though infinitely beneath their great masters, such are they who can sometimes write with a vigour and energy and zeal and enthusiasm, for which at others they sigh in vain. In this latter class I rank myself ; my vigour is at all times but weakness, but yet comparatively it is vigour when contrasted with the listlessness and lassitude with which I am occasionally oppressed for weeks and months. Some months there are when I pen off a sermon at a sitting, and can write a fresh one every day in the week ; while there are many weeks when my poor head conceives, but brings forth nothing. So also is it with respect to letter-writing, I have been long waiting till the spirit would move me to unburden my mind to you, but alas, my spirit is for the present quite immoveable, and I therefore compel myself to write merely on the principle, that even in such friendships as ours a discontinuance of intercourse for any great length of time is dangerous. My mother and sister have also formed a bosom friendship with the great poet Wordsworth, who appears to be as heavenly-minded, as pure, and as christian in his daily intercourse with society as I think him to be pre-eminent in his poetry. At my mother's request I presented him with a copy of my lectures ; and so complacent am I at the autograph letter in which he acknowledges the present that, at the risk of being accounted rather vain, I shall copy it.

'Dear Sir,—I cannot but avail myself of the present opportunity to thank you for the very valuable volume of lectures which I have had the honour of receiving from you through the hands of your excellent mother. Having been absent from home I have not had opportunity yet to read more than the two first discourses, with the matter and manner of which I have been exceedingly pleased. The first and paramount importance of the subject cannot but recommend to general notice, at least so I trust, a work executed with so much sincere piety and fervour, and with learning and ability of so high an order. Wishing you earnestly success in the labours of your ministry, and health and life to prolong them,

'I remain, dear Sir,

'Faithfully your obliged,

'WM. WORDSWORTH.'

To W. P. Wood, Esq.—Baptismal Regeneration.

January 3, 1833.

Most happy indeed I am once more to see your dear old fist, and I hasten to assure you that my prayers for you and your Charlotte shall be as fervent as yours are for us. The feelings you express at the commencement of your letter are natural, and I fear those which we must all of us experience ; they are, however, so well expressed that had your letter come last week I should have put some of your observations into my sermon. I think you will find much comfort and much food for thought if you can read Mr. Alexander Knox's letter to the Bishop of

Limerick, published in the introduction to Burnet's 'Lives,' just edited by his lordship. It will not take five minutes to read, and probably, therefore, you will be able to borrow it of your bookseller. In every sentiment there expressed I fully agree; but I am inclined to quarrel with some of his expressions, and especially with his reference to the text, 'Except ye be born again, ye cannot enter into the kingdom of Heaven.' It is not fair to quote thus partially, for our Lord says, 'Except a man be born *of water and of the Spirit,*' a passage which Dr. Wall shows was invariably interpreted by the ancients as relating to baptism. I conceive the doctrine to stand thus: We are not by nature entitled to eternal life; it is important that this should be constantly borne in mind; nothing can more strongly impress this upon us than a rite by which we are translated from a state of nature and placed in covenant with God. This fact declares that our only trust, even with respect to innocent babes, is in God's free, undeserved mercy: even for them we do not *claim* Heaven as a matter of *right.* The Holy Ghost, the divine Person, under whose superintendence the Christian Church is, receives us in the ordinance appointed by our Saviour as children of God; and thus as heirs, not for our own merits but through God's mercies in Christ, of heaven—heirs, not possessors. As children of God we are, moreover, entitled by the covenant to the assistance of the Holy Ghost, *if* duly sought. Woe to parents and sponsors who teach not their children how to avail themselves of this great privilege. If we avail ourselves of it, then the Holy Ghost renews or renovates our souls; this is a process to go on to our dying day; we, with the assistance of the Holy Ghost, are to go on improving our souls, until they become entirely changed from what they would have been if left to nature. An effectual change *must* take place, but whether it be slow or not will depend on circumstances. Whenever by repentance we replace ourselves in the covenant with God, the Holy Spirit still stands ready to effectuate this change; the change, as I said before, is not complete till we go hence and be no more seen; but it may be very marked and discernible, especially in those who have not been religiously brought up, I believe till the days of Calvin there had been no dispute on this subject; and it is a most important one, since as you will easily see it is an effectual check upon fanaticism, to which a weak mind, holding the doctrine of the Spirit's forming a new heart within us, may incline, and still more, as silencing the doubts of those who would otherwise begin to despair of their election. Whether there be any other election than this is not for us to know. That point has, in my mind, been quite set at rest by Archbishop King's admirable sermon on Predestination, edited by Whately. If you have not read it, it will amply repay all trouble. In Mr. Knox's conversation with a member of your profession, now dead, you will see what appears to me to be a useful remark on the advantages of an Establishment in keeping up a low tone of religion among those who otherwise would have *no* religion, and in thus preparing the way for *true* religion.

' *Judge not.*'

March 22, 1833.

My dearest Brother,—I must beg to thank you for your great kindness in writing to me, notwithstanding the many claims upon your time. In all your excellent sentiments I most cordially agree. Christianity, while it enjoins us to threaten with severity the living, teaches us to hope for the best, with respect to the dead. ' Judge not,' says our Saviour. His words are not, Judge not harshly, but ' Judge not '—judge not at all. And why? Because, as you very justly observe, you cannot tell what disadvantages, from internal weakness or the force of external temptation, another person has had; you cannot tell what disadvantages were opposed to his apparent advantages. You can tell, to a certain extent with respect to yourself, what advantages have been afforded you, and you know that for the neglect of them you will be punished: but the

Searcher of hearts, and He only, can tell this with respect to others. Be this, however, as it may, sure I am that the wretched sinner who dares to judge another with respect to his eternal state places himself on the same footing as the most determined profligate ; and certainly, unless he re-pents, excludes himself from any part in Christ. As to our poor dear uncle, the speech to Mr. Cooper, which you related in your last, proves that he had been thinking of his latter end ; but, however, that may be, he who dares to judge him is no Christian. Thus perfectly agreeing with you, my beloved brother,

I remain, your devoted Brother,

W. F. HOOK.

To W. P. Wood, Esq.—Calvinism—Wesley.

April 13, 1833.

My dearest Friend, ... So much have I to say to you, that I know not where to begin. In your first letter I perfectly agree with you in your opinion touching those dogmas which are usually called Calvinistic ; but which might perhaps with equal propriety be called Augustinism, as Augustine was their first promulgator. I think that, even admitting them, they need not perplex a humble-minded Christian. But alas ! this is not always the case ; a clergyman finds in his intercourse with his flock that these opinions lead to the most fatal consequences. I do not think much of what polemics say against them, with respect to their encouraging men in sin. However theo-retically this may be a legitimate consequence from the doctrine, it is not practically found to be the case, or, at least, not often.

The way they operate for evil is through the awful despair to which they depress some, and the awful presump-tion to which they excite others. If all men were men of sense it would not much signify ; we could easily satisfy them. But you can have no conception of the difficulty we sometimes find in quieting unnecessary alarms. I have heard it said that men of business lay it down as a rule that when they deal with a man they always treat him as a knave. Sure I am that a pastor must, if he wishes to do good, treat men as fools. It is not till men arrive at my age that people unburden their minds to their pastor; but I have now had many consciences, the consciences of educated persons, laid open to me, and have had in some degree the advantages of a confessor; and I am inclined to think that the fools far surpass the knaves. Oh, the difficulty of knocking a foolish idea out of some persons' heads; it is quite surprising. It is only surpassed by the difficulty of knocking in a right idea. So that you must not always think that a poor parson is fighting a shadow when he is combating a doctrine, which to you may appear to be a matter of indifference; for it is not for the wise alone that we write and preach and think. Still, I regard these points merely in the light of preventing persons from enjoying those comforts of religion which they would otherwise have. So long as a person is brought to Christ, and gives his heart to Christ so that it may be prepared for heaven by the Holy Spirit, so long, I think, he is safe; though the devil may have power for awhile to torment him. A clergyman, in my humble opinion, is to be regarded as much as a comforter as an adviser.

I like what you say of Wesley. Intellectually and morally, he was a great man; his latter days were his worst, for this plain reason—he was worshipped as something more than human; and whose head would not be turned by such adoration? A great man of the world feels that most of his worshippers are worshipping him chiefly with a view to their own interests; but Wesley must have felt that among his adorers were some of the best of God's creatures. That he erred, grievously erred in his conduct, I think. That religion, before his day, had become too much a business of the head alone, I admit; and that he was a main instrument of restoring it to the dominion of the heart, must ever be acknowledged. But the believer in a providence must ascribe the consequences of all events to God, and God alone; he must not permit the good that has been deduced from an action to bias his judgment in deciding on the nature of the action itself. Wesley might have been as much the instrument of good without his schism as with it. We can never too constantly bear in mind that we are not to look to the end, but, leaving all events in the hands of God, take the circumstances which He provides for us, and then ask, What under those circumstances is my duty? *That* it is which God tells me to do: in *that* way it is that I am to advance His glory.

To the same—Importance of Encouragement—Pusey's Criticism on his Lectures.

May 8, 1833.

. . . . I think that the system adopted by Evangelical preachers, and to which Benson would seem to incline, is a very bad one, viz. to divide their people into two parts, the saints and the sinners. For my part, I know that my own growth in grace has been very slow and gradual; and, therefore, I am desirous of encouraging others, who, though perhaps not quite so far advanced as I am now, are still going on, and yet feel something like despair at the slowness of their progress. Few are they who come regularly to church who have not some feelings of religion, some wishes to improve. Encourage, excite, animate such persons; don't say to them, 'You must be damned, because you are not better than you are;' but say, 'I am glad to see that God is so merciful to you: now try if you cannot make a little further spring in the straight and narrow path.' O encourage, encourage, encourage one another! I hate your preachers that are always dealing in hell and damnation; I am sure that they can have never experienced the difficulties with which most people have to contend, and I am doubtful how far you can account that as a virtue which it has required no difficulty to acquire; while I am quite certain that the wickedness is great to regard with self-complacency what is merely a gift. For a man to say, I am never in a passion, therefore, how much better a man I am than so and so, is, of course, absurd, if he has never been tempted by the passion of anger. But he who, being naturally an ill-tempered man, has overcome the wicked passion, may say, God has given me proof that He is assisting me with His grace on this point, and, therefore, I have full confidence, that confidence which experience gives, that He will likewise assist me on others, where now I am almost inclined to despair. I have been interested in what you say about the critics and criticism of my poor volume, which, except when it is re-verted to by you, I have well nigh forgotten. It is clear that Pusey is disappointed with it; he tells me he agrees with what I say of Church government in my first lecture, but thinks it unduly pushed forward on such an occasion; it takes too prominent a place. Here I plead guilty; it is undoubtedly a fault; but when a man gets on his hobby, his hobby will be frisky. By the bye, I have told you why I insist so much on this point; of course I should insist on anything that I believe to be truth; for we are to be the guardians not only of *saving* truths but of *all* truth. But the reason why I think it expedient to bring forward this matter so much is that, it seems to me, we are in these days hurrying to a very dangerous extreme, which our wise Reformers providentially avoided. All the writers on Church reform seem to take it for granted that our first step ought to be a step for which everything is to be sacri-ficed; to conciliate Protestant sects. Now I maintain that the Reformed Episcopal Church ought to present to the world a system which will conciliate the good opinion of other parties besides Protestants. The day will surely come when the Greek Church will awaken to a sense of her errors; surely it will be not a little important to let them see that reformation is not incompatible with the most steady adherence to ecclesiastical discipline and tradition. So with respect to those foreign Churches in connexion with Rome; it is most important to show that we can retain what is Catholic, while we renounce what is Popish. It is in some such manner as this that I expect union to be restored to Christendom. When Catholic Churches, Greek, Roman, and Reformed, all purified of their grosser errors, are united in one sacred bond of union, then may we hope that sectarianism will fade away.

To the same—Extremes in Religious Feeling—Over-esti-mate of Preaching—Keble's ' Christian Year.'

June 1, 1833.

. . . . You can hardly imagine the difficulty there is in keeping people just at the right heat. It is a fact, that Dissent generally abounds in those parishes where the clergy are most active, and insist earnestly on the necessity of sanctification ; and I conceive the reason to be that they warm up the cold hearts to a certain heat, and then many of them boil over. Of persons whom I have been permitted to be the instrument of awakening to a lively sense of religion, I feel morally certain that several, though so attached to me that they will not desert me so long as I remain among them, would, in the event of my leaving them, seek ' to sit under ' an Evangelical preacher. You will not misunderstand me in what I have said. I do not like the one class of preachers more than the other, for I think the medium between the two that which is right. But if driven to the choice, I would prefer him who is rather too cold to him who is rather too warm, as giving though not the most pleasant, yet the most wholesome food. For, after all, the right religious heat is to be kept up in our own hearts by ourselves, and chiefly by the Sacrament of the Lord's Supper. It is a dangerous down-falling in the present age to exalt the ordinance of preaching unduly, and to make it, as some do, a third Sacrament. The being moved at a pathetic discourse is no more proof of our being in a right religious tone of mind, than the crying at a tragedy is proof of a tender heart. Buonaparte could deluge the world with blood for his selfish purposes, and yet weep over the sufferings of a wounded soldier. Sensibility does not necessarily imply a kind disposition. Talking of sacred poets, I hope you have read and often recur to the 'Christian Year,' written by a most holy man, an acquaintance of mine at Oxford, Mr. Keble. He is a man the most meek, the most humble, and yet the most gifted with genius and learning, of any I ever met with. He went to Oxford at fourteen, and carried away all the honours and prizes ; and lately refused to stand for the Headship of his College, though almost certain of succeeding, that he might be the comfort and support of his aged father, and relieve him from the cares of his parish by acting as his curate.

From W. P. Wood, Esq.—The Philosophy of Jeremy Bentham.[1]

10 Dean's Yard, July 3, 1833.

. . . . I will at once tell you all that occurs to me respecting the Utilitarians or Benthamites ; but in the first place you would, I think, do well to ascertain whether this pestilent sect abounds at Oxford as much as at Cambridge. I know but few Oxford men, and I do not think that among those few there is one Benthamite, and of course if the error be not rife, then your lectures would be directed, comparatively speaking, against a phantom. At the same time the principle which I term the principle of 'refined selfishness,' and which is in fact pure Epicureanism revived, is one that may readily find its way to the corrupt portion of our hearts ; and though few have the patience to explore it through all its intricacies as traced in Bentham's work, yet most men have some *practical* acquaintance with it, and are glad, at some time or other, to find the dictates of an unregenerate heart dignified with the title of Philosophy.

If you have had time to look into Bentham's work

---

[1] Mr. Hook was thinking of introducing some criticisms upon Benthamism into his Oxford Sermons.

which I mentioned to you, you will find that he assumes that there are only three principles of action, 1. asceticism, 2. sympathy, 3. utility. There is a misplaced attempt at facetiousness involving a gross misstatement of the first of these principles at the outset of the book ; for it is a bad introduction to a work professing strict philosophy to lay down that the principle of asceticism consists in supposing the 'misery of His creatures to be gratifying to the Creator.' The principle, though carried to an excess, was in itself good and true, namely, the subduing of sensual appetites as a means of freeing the mind from their bias. Like every other device of man, this principle failed with the monks as it had failed with the Stoics, and I think that on inquiry it would be found the radical vice of the system was its leading men to dwell too exclusively on *self*, by which in the first place pride, and in the next indifference to the happiness of others, became gradually engendered in the ascetic.

The principle of 'sympathy' is dismissed with nearly the same flippancy by Bentham. If you want to see what can be made out of that principle, you should read Adam Smith's 'Theory of Moral Sentiment.' You will find there a conviction equally strong with that of Bentham of the inadequacy of the *principle* as a guide of moral action, but on different grounds, for I ten thousand times prefer it to Bentham's substitute, and think a man much more likely to act right in following the dictates of a refined sympathy such as is delineated by Smith, than in acknowledging no guide but his own self-conceit ; that is, I prefer the heart to the head even in the natural man, though I see no necessity for separating feeling and reason, the great but opposite error of the Sympathetic and Utilitarian doctors.

Before proposing his own doctrines, however, Bentham, in one of his most obnoxious passages (chap. ii. § 18 and note), tells us he utterly discards the theological principle, and that which refers right and wrong to the will of God, which he says cannot be the revealed will as contained in the Sacred Scriptures, for that is a system to which nobody ever thinks of recurring at this time of day, for (what do you think?) *the details of political administration!* and even before it can be applied to the details of private conduct, it is universally allowed by the most eminent divines of all persuasions to stand in need of ample interpretations, else to what use are the works of those divines? (!!)   In time, Bentham's own argument may recoil upon himself, for his disciple Mill has already published pretty ample exposition of his master's principles which, therefore, are insufficient, 'else to what use' are the said Mill's works?

He then proceeds in a note to tell you his notion of God's will. 'The principle of theology refers everything to God's pleasure, but what is God's pleasure?   God does not, He confessedly does not *now*' [ergo, I suppose He never did.   Q. E. D.] 'either speak or write to us.   How then are we to know what is His pleasure?' [now the grand arcanum of Utilitarianism is to be revealed] 'By observing what is our own pleasure and calling it His.   Accordingly what is called the pleasure of God, is and must necessarily be (revelation aside) neither more nor less than the good pleasure of the person, whoever he be, who is pronouncing what he believes or pretends to be God's pleasure.'   Here is, you will observe, Atheism in all its hideousness, and an acknowledgment that, *revelation aside*, there is no medium, a result at which Bishop Butler, I think, satisfactorily arrives in his 'Analogy,' though happily for him he embraced the opposite alternative, and did *not* set revelation aside.   I think these parts I have pointed out by far the most vulnerable of Bentham's work.   He is an acute logician, and like Spinosa, from whom he borrowed largely, you must attack his first principles, or you will find his deductions unassailable.   It is true there is a moral *reductio ad absurdum* in some of his conclusions on legislation, as where he considers the murder of an infant by the consent of both parents a trifling error; but although you may say at once the principles must be wrong which lead to such a result, you will find the result is correctly deduced from them, and as an 'ad absurdum' is not considered the most

satisfactory refutation, it is better to attack the principles
per directum.   Now it appears to me that the whole evil of
the system is apparent in the last quoted note.   He lays
down the principle of utility as that which produces the
greatest happiness to each individual as regards morals, or
the greatest happiness to the greatest number as regards
politics.   This happiness he considers to be composed of
certain ingredients divisible into two classes, viz. pleasures
and pains ; and he has given a very beautiful analysis of
them, borrowed, however, in a great measure from Spinosa's
third book ' De Affectibus.'   He then establishes four ' Sanctions ' (1) the physical, by which a man will avoid physical
pain, and seek physical pleasure ; (2) the moral, which
operates chiefly through the medium of the opinion of
others as to our conduct, so that he sometimes calls it
the sanction of human or public opinion ; (3) the political
sanction, namely, the pains and pleasures affixed by laws
to our conduct ; (4) the religious sanction, which he considers too weak to have any effect, on account of the distance of its proffered pains and pleasures ; for he calls those
pleasures the most desirable which are most speedy, certain,
intense and lasting, and *vice versâ* of pains.

Now one thing that stares you in the face in all this
doctrine is, what can be the use of it ?   It is our interest,
he tells us, to secure the greatest lot of desirable pleasures
with the least admixture of pains, but pray who is to tell
us which are most desirable ?   He makes a fine catalogue,
somebody else may make a different one ; or, in other words,
as he tells us in the famous note, God's pleasure (and *a
fortiori*, the wisest man's opinion) is to be judged by every
individual according to his own fancy.   In one sense, indeed,
his whole theory is only a truism ; for men will necessarily
act according to what gives the most pleasure and least
pain, and do not require Bentham's recommendation to do
so ; but if Bentham means, as he does, that the philosopher's
view of pleasures and pains is to be taken, how can he expect that any man will give more credit to his (Bentham's)
philosophy than he (Bentham himself) is willing to give to

others who assert what God's pleasure is? Each man will answer, 'I am my own philosopher, and know best what will give me the most pleasure and least pain.' The thief, the drunkard, the debauchee may say, 'It is very true our pleasures are short, but they are intense, and make up by their intensity for want of duration,' and so on. To sum up. Men will always in one sense seek pleasure and avoid pain, but you say, 'We mean philosophical pleasure and philosophical pain;' then I answer 'Every man will be his own philosopher, and as for your sanctions how are they to act upon men whom you teach at the outset to despise any rule of conduct but that which their own good pleasure suggests?'

Now to turn to the more pleasing picture. What is the peculiar beauty of Christianity? It affords ample scope for the exercise of the reason, but at the same time teaches us that there is a divine reason which, unlike ours, coincides with the affections; perfect wisdom and perfect love being identical. It teaches us that our hearts are desperately corrupt and widely removed from the guidance even of natural reason, for what we would not that we do. How is this corruption to be cured? By the eradication of the selfish principle which regards neither God nor man, and the implanting of a faith which enables us in some sense to see the union of wisdom and love. But how can such eradication be effected? By no other means than a child-like submission to Him whose works proved His authority, and who spake as never man spake, and by giving up our whole affections also to Him as the undoubted fountain of light and love. We are thus at once enlightened in our understandings, and corrected in the depravity of our hearts, which, no longer dwelling on ourselves, expand in benevolence to our fellow-creatures *as such*; that is, as the offspring of a common Father, who must, as indeed He tells us, love them, and whom He *therefore* commands us to love.

I will only add one hint. Take the three principles of love, fear, and mere selfish calculation, and how quickly can the advantage of the first be perceived as enforcing action, whether the object loved be present or absent, with equal energy and uniformity; whilst fear, independently of its slavish effects on the mind, will not operate without the strongest conviction of the power and presence of the person feared; and selfish calculation is irregular in its results, depending on the caprice of passion and the changes of sensibility.

Hearty Greeting on Return to his Parish.

July 15, 1833.

My dearest Mother, ... My dear flock rallied round me yesterday in grand style, as if glad to see me after even one Sunday's absence. I certainly intend to take a month's holiday, or rather absence from my parish; I know few things more delightful than the return to one's parish after a short absence; the smile of recognition, the friendly nod, sometimes even the extended hand, as one walks up the aisle to the vestry, which awaits one from the earlier comers to church. Then the clerk, the sexton, the beadles, all activity and bustle, the bolder few pressing into the vestry to say they are glad to see the Vicar back; the triumphant voluntary of the organist, the responses rather better made than usual, the charity children seeming as if they *would* speak if they *dared*, the poor ' God blessing you, glad to see your reverence back ; ' then, when in the pulpit, you look round upon the well-filled pews, their inmates seem to look back a ' How d'ye do ? ' All these are joys which a pastor's heart only can feel; and feeling them, he feels himself more than repaid for all his troubles. These joys I have experienced, and I hope to experience them again. And now having given you this pretty picture, I will send to you a parson's blessing, if you will send a mother's blessing in return to

Your devoted Son,

W. F. HOOK.

From W. P. Wood, Esq.—Christian Ethics—Brewster's
Life of Newton.

Lincoln's Inn : August 1833.

. . . . I agree with you certainly on the point of conscience, and detest Paley's chapter on the Moral Sense.
The question is not, whether it be thought right in one
country to kill your aged parents, and in another to
cherish them, but whether there be, or be not, a principle
within us, which occasions uneasiness when we do that
which we *think* wrong, however erroneous our estimate of
right and wrong may be. I have not read Brown's ' Philosophy of the Mind,' but have read his ' Cause and Effect,'
a work undoubtedly of great merit and some originality,
but falling into the general error or vice of the Scotch
school—abusing Berkeley, and at the same time pillaging
him most unmercifully, so that one cannot but suspect
them of Voltaire's course with Shakspeare—thieving, and
throwing filth upon their booty to conceal it.

I like your suggestion of Scripture Ethics, the more so
because, in my vanity, one of my favourite plans if ever I
became rich, and free from the necessary drudgery of a
profession, has been to write on what I meant to term
Christian Ethics. . . . My scheme would be to draw out
a system, as near as possible resembling those of the
heathen authors, whose *heads* were by no means deficient ;
and thus to point out more clearly, in what they were
really deficient in each branch of duty ; for though my
principles would be essentially different, and therefore the
results would be correspondingly modified, yet, no doubt,
the *principle* of conscience has been too strong to be, in
fact, obliterated, and therefore the details of right and
wrong in the several relations of life would not vary so
much as might be at first imagined. . . .

I have been pleased lately with the Life of Newton,
by Brewster. Brewster is, I am happy to find, a sincere
Christian, and as such takes great pains to clear up the
question of Newton's alleged insanity, of which some

infidel French philosophers, (as they style themselves) have made use, in order to effect a wider breach than already too often exists between intellect and religion, and to prove that none who have eaten of the tree of knowledge can ever be desirous of approaching the tree of life. These miserable men seem to envy the blissful serenity which religion alone was able to impart to Newton's naturally irritable temperament; and have asserted, first, that he was mad during the latter half of his life; second, that he wrote his theological works during that interval. Brewster has demonstrated from published and unpublished documents, first, that he was never deranged, though he suffered a short attack of extreme nervous excitement, occasioned by the loss of his papers by fire; and second, that one of his principal theological works was written before even his alleged madness, and that he was also before that time in correspondence with Locke on the Book of Daniel and the Book of Revelation.

Zeal for God, not according to knowledge.

Birmingham : August 23, 1833.

My dearest Brother, . . . The error of —— lies not in his religious principles, but in weakness of judgment, and consequent obstinacy of character; it is his logic, not his religion which is to blame; not his principles, but his wrong application of them. His position is true, that if the commands of his God and the wishes of his father are at variance, the former are to be obeyed rather than the latter; but he does not see that it is, in the first place, important to be morally certain as to what the command of God in any particular case is; for a man may (as he has done) mistake for a command of his God what is, in fact, merely the surmise of his own mind. He thinks it to be his duty to God to attempt the conversion of his sisters; but, who commissioned him to do this? who gave him authority over his sisters? If he looks to the Bible, he may be certain that it is his duty to honour his parents; if he appeals to his common sense, he must perceive that he cannot dishonour them more than by leading their children to infer that they have neglected their education, in the most essential of all points. He thus neglects a duty of which he may be certain, to perform a duty which he cannot prove that he is commissioned to perform. For again I ask, who gave him such commission? all he can say is, that he *feels* it to be a duty; but I remember a poor man who felt it to be a duty to send the first good man he met to heaven, and consequently he killed him. To trust to mere feeling is absurd; we are always to do what our conscience thinks right, but we are to enquire whether that is right which our conscience thus thinks. That it would be his duty, if he had children of his own, to seek for God's grace to instil into their minds the doctrines he believes to be true, there can be no doubt; that he is thus to promote God's truth wherever Providence affords an opportunity for doing so, without the violation of any known duty, is also not to be doubted; but here Providence does not open a door to him; he cannot attempt this without dishonouring his parents. As Lady —— observes, the children are theirs not his; if God intends him to be the means of awakening them (supposing that they are not awakened to a proper sense of religion), he will call their parents to himself and put it into their minds to leave him as their guardian. Then what is now presumption will become a duty. He is now acting as if he were without faith in the special providence of God. I say all this because I am sure he will only be confirmed in his errors if they are ascribed to his religion. Religion has nothing to do with them. He would be indignant at the idea; but I think that between his religious principles and mine, there can scarcely be a shade of difference; the grace of God has softened and sanctified his heart, and his affections are right with his Saviour. It is the head that is the source of all the mischief, I have known him quote texts of Scripture in a sense directly opposed to what is correct, from mere ignorance of the

Greek ; he converses on religious topics only with persons as ignorant as himself : he learns to dogmatise on his own imaginations ; he becomes self-sufficient and soon learns to think all the world wrong except the few weak but well-meaning characters who love his virtues and have not the skill to discover that he is no wiseacre. Now all this might just as well have happened to him if he had given up his mind to banking instead of religion ; he would then perhaps have undertaken, on some hypothesis of his own, to set you all right in the mode of doing business. Depend upon it, my dearest Robert, that the fault in all this matter is to be traced to a weak head, not to a pious heart ; his piety only renders his obstinacy and self-sufficiency less than they would otherwise have been ; and I doubt not but that these faults, venial faults, will gradually diminish in so bright and almost perfect a character. But let the language of his friends be to him, not 'you are too religious,' for then he will think himself a martyr ; but ' you are a bit of a blockhead ;' he may then perhaps seek for advice. I take it, his education was defective ; not being of an energetic character, he did not work, I suppose, at Eton ; and it may be lamented that he had not been sent instead to a good strict tutor, who would have compelled him to study. When he was with me, I wished to persuade him to study Adam Smith, but he had no powers of application, and soon laid aside what could only be mastered by deep thought. I think now the best thing would be for him to have a separate lodging, and not to live in his father's house, where his morbid feelings would be increased, and if it were possible to find a really religious friend of great abilities, who would urge him on to deep study, even on theological matters, I think all would come right. The worst of it is, there are no really learned and clever men whom he will tolerate ; men of his sort can only put up with flatterers, with persons who entirely agree with them.

Your devoted Brother,

W. F. Hook.

From W. P. Wood, Esq.—Berkeley's Philosophy.

Lincoln's Inn : December 7, 1833.

. . . . I am glad you are about to read Berkeley. There was never, I think, any man since Plato who was gifted with imagination and reasoning power in so high a degree ; and if he, like Plato, occasionally let his imagination run wild, yet I question whether Plato ever, like Berkeley, practically acted on the views which were deemed visionary, and thus gave evidence of sincerity and singleness of heart. I am always in love with Berkeley when I think of his proffered resignation of the bishopric to ameliorate the condition of the unhappy Bermudians. . . . You will feel the great value of Berkeley as giving a sound resting place for the mind amid the bewilderments of metaphysics. It is quite false to say that Hume has demonstrated that there is no such thing as spirit ; on the same principle Berkeley had shown that there was no such thing as matter. In the first place, Berkeley makes no such assertion, but simply that matter, considered *independently* of *mind*, is a nonenity. That all those sensations we daily experience from objects termed external, are *real*, Berkeley, who is eminently an experimental or Baconian philosopher, was never absurd enough to deny. For external, read independent of *us* or *our* minds, and you will have Berkeley's notion of matter as regards man ; but he boldly asserts that matter cannot be conceived of by us as independent of *a* mind. The Scotch metaphysicians to a man either wilfully or stupidly jumble *a* mind with *the* mind, meaning each individual's mind, whilst by *a* mind, Berkeley means *some* mind or other ; and admitting that the table at which I am now writing will exist when I do not think of it, the question is, Can it exist if there be no mind to limit out its nature, which is but an aggregate of sensations? Berkeley says, No ; and experience, I think, demonstrates that what can only be known as an object of sensation, owes its existence to a sentient power ; not mine or yours, because experience shows the sensations to exist independently of your will or mine, but to the Eternal sentient power by whose will our minds perceive it as that which is created or willed by Him. This is always to me the most beautiful demonstration of a God, and most satisfactory refutation of the eternity of matter which is, according to Berkeley, an absurdity, matter being but the stage in which certain volitions of the Supreme Mind are exhibited to man. The resurrection of the body also becomes thus at once intelligible, because He who wills us to perceive the efforts of His will in a certain manner now, may cause us to perceive them in a similar manner at any future time, blessing us probably with additional pleasure by a more thorough perception of the beauty of His work. By '*us*' you will see I consider the mind alone, regarding the material *about us* as no other than a combination of God's impressed thoughts (if I may so say) which affects our minds with various impressions, such as pain and pleasure and their infinite varieties. . . .

I have not time to write to you about Miss Martineau's Tales, of which of course you have heard, and we have read many. Some are, I think, excellent, and all are powerful where her imagination comes into play. Her reasoning is not and does not pretend to be original. It is taken verbatim from Malthus and McCulloch, a bad school, and her sectarianism not unfrequently peeps out; but I would recommend you strongly to read the 'Manchester Strike,' which might I think be useful to your poor people at Coventry hereafter, if the time should come when any such folly should be meditated.

To W. P. Wood, Esq.—Plain Sermons—Optimism—
Mode of Conducting Divine Service.

December 9, 1833.

And now, my dearest friend, I am determined to sit down to have a little gossip with you. When one's hands are full one thinks it impossible to write a long letter, and, therefore, neglects to commence one ; an unwise course, seeing that a short letter is better than none, and that, in this respect as in some others, one frequently finds that what is 'impossible, does sometimes come to pass.' I believe Seneca is right when he says, ' Scis quare non possumus ista ? quia nos posse non credimus.'

In the first place let me ask whether you think Rose has done justice to your brother's sermons. The slight censure makes the praise doubly valuable, and I incline to agree with the critic, that there is something rather objectionable in the sermon on our Saviour's sufferings. I wish he could be prevailed upon in another edition to give us more than twelve, or rather, to send out a second volume. I really have never read anything better fitted for its intended purpose than that volume. ' Dispeream si quid legi unquam sanctius, aut si quid potuit populo tradier utilius.' I hate the title ; it would be better were it to describe the sermons as addressed to a congregation entirely agricultural ; 'plain sermons,' &c., plain everything I dislike, because the term has been used so much, that it seems to savour of affectation ; it as much as says, I, the author, could do a great deal better, but behold how I condescend to men of low estate. Now it is well known, and admitted on all hands, that really plain sermons, such as his, are the most difficult compositions in the language. Tell him to go on ; I wish he would learn the art of weaving, and send me some sermons for my manufacturers ; I am such a 'thick' that I cannot, for the life of me, understand the art of weaving, and I seldom venture beyond a quotation, to remind my people that their days are swifter than a weaver's shuttle.

I am a bit of an optimist, I always look to the bright side of things ; though I sometimes croak, as I sometimes scold Delicia, not because she deserves a scolding but, as I tell her, to keep her up to duty-mark (a very wholesome exercise, take my word for it). You will, of course, rub out the parenthesis before you show this to your wife. But I really like to trace good out of evil ; you know how

I disapproved of Roman Catholic Emancipation, but now that the measure has been carried, instead of looking on the attendant evils (as I think them), I look to the good which will result, and one great good in my opinion is, that we shall no longer attempt to club together, and to hold up general Protestantism against Popery. Take Protestantism in general, that is, all sects not popish, and I think there is quite as much error on one side as the other. I would side with a Papist rather than a Unitarian ; I hope that henceforth the question will simply be between the Church of England and the Church of Rome ; so far as we, who are members of the Church of England, are leaving other Protestants to fight their own battles, we have a very strong case. As to theirs, I fancy they must fight hard to obtain the victory. In like manner, the attacks which are made on the liturgy will do good, by inducing persons to examine the subject yet further, and thus to appreciate its excellencies more highly. The clergy have, in my opinion, been very careless as to their mode of performing divine service, reading prayers instead of performing service. The officiating minister ought to have two objects always in view ; his own devotions and a desire to excite the devotions of others, and to do justice to the glorious services of the Church. The latter object is too often lost sight of ; for my part, I continually keep it in view, and even when I am not officiating myself, I always in my own church appear in my official character, and take as much pains to lead the responses as the clerk. Justice is very seldom done to the liturgy ; I had some remarks on this subject in the October number of the ' British Magazine.'

To the same—Attitude towards Dissenters.

December 20, 1833.

During the season of Christmas—sermons, sacraments, and holy rejoicings, you cannot expect a long letter. But yet I cannot refrain from expressing to you how heartily and entirely I concur with you in all you say in your last.

The comparison between the worshippers on Mount Gerizim and the Dissenters is admirable, and is precisely the view I have always taken of the question. We are, moreover, always in speaking of an action to make the distinction between what is absolutely and what is relatively right or wrong. It is for the intention only, *i.e.* the relative rightness or wrongness, that a man will be judged, if he has properly enquired, as far as his abilities permit, as to the absolute nature of the action. That schism is a sin, we know, but that every schismatic (so called) is a sinner, I by no means admit, for he may not act with a schismatical intent. And yet it may be charity in me, in some instances, to tell him that I think him a schismatic, in order to awaken him to enquiry. In *some* instances I say ; for my rule is never to disturb the faith of those who have been educated in Dissent, if they hold the doctrine of the Atonement, *if* they are persons not qualified to judge of the differences between us. Believe me, my dearest friend, that you have quite mistaken me, if you think I regard Presbyterians, Wesleyans, &c., in the light of heathens. μὴ γένοιτο. I regard them just as you do ; they look only to the end, without sufficiently thinking of the means ; they labour to bring men to Christ, and they do well, but they forget that besides this there is another object which ought not to be overlooked ; to wit, the preservation of the purity and unity of the Church. I believe that our position is this : you *may* be going in the right road, and I hope you are ; but I feel more certain that this is the right road, and, therefore, I remain in it ; my assurance is stronger.

To the same—The Good and Evil of the Established Church.

February 4, 1834.

. . . . I perfectly agree with you in thinking that a man may be attached to the Church, and opposed to an establishment ; Bishop Hobart was so, and most of the very high Churchmen in England are so : it was indeed chiefly with a view to them that I have printed the second sermon.[1] If you look to the religious public only, I should agree; but, looking to the irreligious also, I do not agree. I know that you think an establishment tends to secularise the clergy; but I see quite as much, and more, secularity among the Dissenting ministers. If the clergy are too much inclined to Toryism, the Dissenting ministers are to radicalism, and some of the Dissenting meeting-houses in this city are, every Sunday evening, converted after service into political debating societies. Is not the Dissenting teacher as secular when seeking to fill his pews by preaching, *not* truth, but popular doctrine, as the clergyman who makes unworthy compliances to conciliate a patron? Both are to be condemned; but while the world lasts some degree of secularity in twelve thousand men there must be; the only question is, whether it matters how it shows itself? Mind, my dear friend, I do not quarrel with you for taking just the opposite view, I only state what occurs to me : my prejudices may induce me to exaggerate the advantages of an establishment, and yet the time was when I preferred being without one.

From W. P. Wood, Esq.—*Advantages and Evils of an Established Religion.*

Lincoln's Inn : February 1834.

. . . . I think you have brought forward every argument in favour of an establishment with the greatest force. You tell me you hope to convert me, and will, I dare say, think me an obstinate creature if not *quite* a convert. However, I will acknowledge that you have confirmed my perhaps hesitating opinion that where we find a Church established we ought not to lend any assistance towards *un*establishing. I am not a lover of change at any time for the sake of change (though you may smile at this, looking to my radicalism); I ever consider change as a positive evil, for assuredly happiness consists

[1] 'On the Church and the Establishment.'

in tranquillity, and He who is all wise and all happy is immutable; but there are cases, as all must admit, where the evils of abiding in your actual state and the advantage to be derived from a change fully justify the effort and sacrifice required for alteration.   Such, however, is not, I think, the case with regard to the establishment. Amongst the evils, which I cannot but yet think incident to the compulsory support by the State of any religious doctrine, there are to be found unquestionably great and perhaps counterbalancing benefits, and I would not root up the tares lest the wheat be rooted up also.

Of course I do not think an establishment unscriptural, that is, forbidden by Scripture, or I should consider the question settled.   'Unscriptural' is one of those convenient words for controversy, which allow the opponents of the Church the widest possible field by keeping off any close attack.   In one sense, unquestionably, the Establishment is unscriptural; that is to say, the early Christian Church as delineated in Scripture rested, from the necessity of the case, upon no support from the State, and this the Dissenter falls back upon, when pressed by argument.   I think your argument as to the Jewish Church a very good one against the Establishment being unscriptural in any other sense, but I do not think it equally good as a positive reason to urge us to an alliance of Church and State, for there was a direct temporal covenant between God and the Jewish nation.   The government remained in some sense a theocracy even after St. Paul's conversion, and where God was the temporal monarch it was almost a necessary consequence that His ministers would be temporal governors also. My objections, or rather I should say my difficulties, as to establishments are several; first, political, the difficulty of choosing your establishment, for I incline to think that the forcing of six millions in Ireland to pay for the maintenance of the religion of one million is almost unscriptural in the worst sense.   In Scotland we have acted differently; treating Ireland as a conquered country, that is, by the rule of force.   I think an establishment of our Church in India,

supported by forced contributions from the natives, would
be monstrous. To this I know you will answer that the
tithes are a gift by Christian possessors. This may, and
I think, does apply to England ; but consider how the possessors acquired their property in Ireland—by nothing in
fact but brutal violence done to the large majority of
that nation, though a weak minority as compared with the
overwhelming forces of England. My *second* objection to
establishments is, their effect on the clergy, but I will
not enter into a long disquisition on this point ; and my
third objection is, the effect on the laity, who become
members of a Church because it is established, and make
no further enquiry. I admit great force in the arguments
you bring forward as to the indirect effect on families,
and I admit also the difficulties entangling the whole
question, but I should ever wish, above all things, to see
the questions kept separate, for there are not many who
have your liberality in thinking one can belong to the
Church of Christ without being over anxious as to the
seats of bishops in Parliament, and the other consequences
of a union between Church and State ; and this species of
bigotry is itself one of the evils of that union, for I fear
many give the State at least *equal* consideration.

To W. P. Wood, Esq.—A busy Week.

Coventry : Easter Monday, March 31, 1834.

I write to you to thank you for your kind letter, though
I cannot write much ; for although my hard work of
Passion Week is over, yet my feasting work of Easter Week
has begun. My curate, Mr. Crawford, this day regales the
girls of our blue-coat school ; to-morrow our vestry dine
together ; next day I feast fifty young operatives, who
assist in the management of our Sunday schools ; Thursday, I suppose, I shall be sick with all this festivity ;
Friday, I must visit my poor ; Saturday, write my sermon ;
so, you see, though very pleasant, my hands are very full ;
and, to add to my calamities, my wife is going to desert

me ; she is to pay a visit for ten days to her parents, at the Monument ; I hope to join her for two days next week, and then I intend (D.V.) to take a *bonâ fide* holiday, by skipping a Sunday and spending a fortnight at Leamington with my mother.

To W. P. Wood, Esq.—Correspondence of Alexander Knox and Bishop Jebb—Henry Martin—Lucas on Happiness.

September 22, 1834.

. . . . I exhort you very earnestly to read the correspondence of Knox and Jebb, because it is a book well calculated to calm your mind at the present time, and to set one a-thinking in the right line. I am rather urgent upon this subject, because, moreover, while Mr. Knox frequently reminds · me of you, while he was to Bishop Jebb nearly as much as you are to me ; their system of Christian philosophy is one peculiarly adapted to you. I think that of late (and under your present afflictive circumstances it is natural that it should be so) your views with respect to religion have taken a less bright turn than I could wish ; I mean that you seem to despond too much about the capabilities of renewed human nature and, falling a little into the spirit of the age, to rate too highly the active, and too lowly the contemplative life. On all these points the words of Knox and Jebb appear to me to be the words of soberness and truth. We are not to underrate, and we are not to overrate, the persons of active life, the practical men as they are called ; but the meditative Christian may, perhaps, be able to draw nearer to perfection than the other ; though the meditative Christian philosopher would scarcely, in these days, be called a Christian at all. I would not have you measure yourself by Henry Martin, nor would I have held you up to Henry Martin as a model. I think that Martin, by the bye, committed a grievous error in throwing himself out of that sphere to which Providence assuredly called him ; and hence, probably, his want of success. I wish not to detract from the virtues of so admirable a man ; but I should say to another, if God has caused you to be born in a Christian country, has put it into your parents' minds to give you a learned education, and has so far blessed your exertions as to enable you to become a senior wrangler, you should read in that circumstance His command to serve Him as a man of learning and reading. Practical work may be performed by an inferior intellect, not only as well, but better ; the religious cultivation of intellect is a duty to those who have the time. Again, I would say that those who find themselves engaged in a secular profession ought not to torment themselves, because they are not directly engaged in God's work ; they may do more good by the rhetoric of their good example. Knox and Jebb are great perfectionists ; religious *edification*, not religious *excitement*, was what they sought ; and feeling sure that the Scriptures could not urge an impossibility, they fully expected to reach, and I really believe they did reach what the Scripture means by perfection ; although, because not a bustling, busy, practical man, Bishop Jebb was much abused by the Evangelicals. If you wish to see what the Scripture means by perfection, I would refer you to a book recommended in their letters, the second volume of Lucas upon Happiness ; a work which is so strictly devotional that it would be a good one for your Sunday readings. I delight in it ; you will there find it, I think, satisfactorily proved that when the Scriptures speak of perfection, they mean habitual righteousness. Conversion begins, perfection completes, the habit. Habit is second nature, therefore the habitually righteous are called new creatures, partakers of the divine nature, &c. Lucas shows how a man, in this world, can live without sin, that is, mortal sin ; venial sin or imperfections of course there are, but these he would style frailties : I perfectly agree with him. If you look upon sin as unconnected with a Saviour, there can be no such thing as venial sin ; sin is the transgression of the law, and the soul that sinneth it shall die. But what has Christ done for us?

He has procured heaven for the habitually righteous ; they
are thus freed from the penalty of the original law ; and
being under the Gospel their occasional infirmities are
either not to be called sins, or to be classed as venial sins,
not having in them any longer the sentence of death.
Connected with this subject Lucas and the correspondents
would open a *via media* with respect to Romans vii.,
neither agreeing with those who would apply the passage
to the renewed Christian as long as he is in the flesh,
nor agreeing with those who would have applied it to the
unrenewed. They would apply it to such as are in a pro-
gressive state, who are in progress to renovation ; to the
babe in Christ, the young man of St. John, not to the perfect man, not to the fathers.

To W. P. Wood, Esq.—Sermon-writing—Knox and Jebb—
Regeneration and Renovation.

September 31, 1834.

I avail myself of a wet day and a little *poorlytude* to
have a little coze with you. I very often feel inclined to
write to you, indeed I always do when I am in meditation
mood ; but that is the very time, of course, for sermonising
also : and as duty must yield to pleasure, so my correspondence with you flags, that sermons may exist. For my part,
I think one sermon per week for a man of moderate
abilities, and with three days entirely devoted to practical
work, during which writing and reading must be suspended,
is quite enough. I write my sermon at a sitting, at least
generally, and I find those extempore discourses tell best ;
but then I have to think it well over during the early days
of the week, and to consult commentators when there is
need ; and sometimes one cannot help feeling, as one
advances in learning oneself, that it would be pleasanter to
have a more intellectual congregation than I have here.
It is not pleasant, and perhaps not profitable, to be obliged
to check one's thoughts, and to blot out a page because
you feel it to be above the reach of any of your hearers.

But then, on the other hand, the moral discipline is very useful ; and when a man begins to think that he could do better in a more extensive sphere, the probability is that there is a spirit of pride lurking in the heart, and ‘ Get thee behind me, Satan ! ’ ought to be resolutely said with a prayer for grace.

Delicia and I are reading together the correspondence of Bishop Jebb with Mr. Alexander Knox ; it is a work which no one can read without improvement. The natural, fervent, glowing eloquence of Mr. Knox is sometimes very striking. In the use of some terms he is unfortunate ; *e.g.* he uses the word regeneration for what we should call renovation, making, as the apostle does, a distinction between the washing of regeneration and the renewing of the Holy Ghost. Both are needful to make the complete Christian, but the renewing of the Holy Ghost may not be, as we too sadly see, where the regeneration has been. Regeneration was the term applied to baptism by all the Fathers ; by every writer, I believe, till the Reformation, and it was used to denote, not the final triumph of grace over the heart, but the primary operations of the Spirit in the scheme of man’s redemption. The Puritans used the term to signify the final triumph of grace over the heart ; and then, giving a new meaning to the term, abused the Church for using the word in the old sense. I believe that much of the difficulty which some persons have as to the true doctrine is to be traced to their considering, perhaps, without acknowledging, grace to be indefectible, and to their forgetting that by the neglect of the person or the parent the Spirit may be quenched. I look upon the doctrine as important, as it at once puts an end·to idle fears as to election. We can say to the penitent who has been baptized, ‘ You are elected, so far as the Scripture says anything of election ; ’ and it enables us to tell others, ‘ If you fall, the fault will be yours, since the Holy Ghost has covenanted to create a new heart in you, if you will but apply to Him.’ While on this subject I will mention a new argument, which I have lately met with on infant baptism. Christ blessed infants. Was His blessing an idle ceremony? No; if He blessed, He sanctified them; but how could He sanctify, except by imparting to them a portion of His Spirit? How the Spirit operates we know not. I would add, with respect to infant baptism, that I apprehend doubts on the subject may be traced to our regarding the Lord Jesus as an *instructor*, rather than as 'the way, the truth, and the life,' through whose merits a being who comes into the world condemned may obtain salvation.

To W. P. Wood, Esq.—Summoned to Preach at Oxford.

October 9, 1834.

I suppose you will soon be settled again in London, I therefore write to you a hasty line—a *hasty* line—because I have much to do. I have within the last few days received a notice from Oxford calling upon me, as select preacher, to preach on the first Sunday in November. The suddenness of this (as I did not expect to be called upon before Christmas), has quite shaken my nerves; and I begin to feel, that in consenting to become a select preacher before the University, I have presumptuously taken a position far above the reach of my abilities. Who am I, that I should address a learned body, being so unlearned myself? I really do feel that I have been guilty of unheard of presumption. When I know myself to be really in my place, I have no fears; but I do fear much, fear lest I should injure the cause I have at heart; and also, lest I should do discredit to myself, and thus interfere with my usefulness in many ways, when I thus put myself, as it were, out of my place. Now with these feelings it would be an inexpressible comfort to me if you would read my sermon; having your sanction, I should have confidence, for I know you would not flatter. I rejoiced to hear from Mrs. Wood that you are very busy; but as you never work on Sundays, I am thinking that you might kindly permit my discourse to form part of your Sunday readings, either next Sunday se'nnight, or the Sunday following. We so cordially agree in our views on metaphysical and theological subjects, that your opinion would be to me more valuable than anyone's else. The only point I believe on which we differ, is on the necessity of the State's having a religion. I did once entertain your views, and prefer the state of things in America ; and I believe that these are the highest Church views, and lead one more closely to investigate its spiritual claims. I cannot enter now into the arguments which have made me think differently, but I will (D.V.) some time or other ; I only allude to the circumstance, because there are one or two passages in the sermon, which I have now nearly finished, bearing upon that point.

To Rev. J. H. Newman—Suffragan Bishoprics.[1]

April 11, 1835.

Our friend, A. Perceval, I find, prefers the division of the Diocese to the restoration of Suffragans. I confess I agree with you rather than with him on this point, because I think it most important that there should be frequent intercourse between the people and the highest order of pastors, and this under existing circumstances can only be done by the reinstitution of Suffragans. Of course we should all prefer the establishment of twenty or thirty new Dioceses, but of that there is no hope.

I am not so fearful of an open attack as of a system of undermining. Hating the Church as they do, I verily believe that the Whigs will attempt to ruin it by preferring unworthy characters. And surely we ought to be prepared for action, we ought to be prepared to petition generally throughout every Diocese against such an ap-

---

[1] The Church Commission issued their first Report this year, containing proposals for the formation of some new sees, and the readjustment of diocesan boundaries and episcopal incomes.

pointment, and to adopt every lawful means to prevent
its confirmation, if made. I think too we ought to get up
petitions without loss of time, praying the King to make
some alteration in the mode of appointing bishops. I
suppose you have read Perceval's pamphlet on the subject.
. . . I fear that the majority of Conservatives in Parliament
are influenced by little better than party feelings with
respect to religion.

*To W. P. Wood, Esq.—Suffragan Bishops—Admission
of Laymen to Convocation—Church and Dissent.*

April 1835.

. . . . I cannot help saying how entirely I agree in all
the sentiments you so well express, except in your allusions
to the Bishops. I consider it important in this age, when
political power is everything, that there should attach some
degree of political power and consequence to the heads of
the Church. I do not say that the attachment of the peer-
age to the bishoprics is not attended with some evil, but
I think the good preponderates, and I hope that there will
be instituted suffragan bishoprics, for which the constitution makes provision without peerages, and this will bring
the bishops and the people, as you wish, into closer communion. I perfectly admit what you say touching the
propriety of an occasional national synod ; say, a synod to
be held once in three years, together with annual diocesan
synods ; and I should wish to have the laity represented
in them. My former objection was to Convocation, which
is, in fact, not an ecclesiastical synod, but, merely a convention of ecclesiastics, originally called by the King to
tax themselves, and afterwards—first from convenience and
then from custom—formed into an assembly for the discussion of spiritual affairs. I am an advocate for the
introduction of laymen, though I think the proportion is
too great in the American convention, to the constitution
of which there are some objections. It is a curious fact

that, when the attention of the laity is called to such matters, the laity always become higher Churchmen than the clergy, the latter generally I suppose, feeling a fear lest they should appear to advance their personal claims when defending the rights of their order.   Our two great High Church authorities are, Robert Nelson, Esq., and Henry Dodwell, Esp. ; and it is a curious fact that, when it was lately proposed in America that the pulpits of the Church should be opened to all sectarians holding the doctrine of the Trinity, the clergy yielded, but the laity resolutely resisted the shameful proposition.   So again, when it was proposed to let the Wesleyans unite with the Church on condition that their existing ministers should not be episcopally ordained, here also the clergy, looking to the immense accession to their numbers (not of course to their principles, or what ought to be their principles) which would thus occur, gave ground ; but the laity would not consent.   Anything which would bring these subjects under discussion would be a good, at least in our opinion, who believe that we have the truth ; and it is lamentable to see how ignorant the clergy are, even good, pious, hardworking men, on the commonest points of discipline. I agree with you also in what you say of Brother Jonathan ; with all his faults he is our brother, and if I am driven from England, I shall hope to abide with him. America is the next best country to our own, and as to what travellers say of the Americans, we may always reply : the wonder is, not that they are behind us, but that so new a country should have come so near to us.

To W. P. Wood, Esq.—Calmness and Confidence in the Discharge of Duty.

Leamington : May 6, 1835.

. . . . The cure of twenty thousand souls would not be to me more arduous than that of nine thousand, for why ? in either case it is impossible to attend to them all,

and God does not require impossibilities at our hands.
I should feel then as I feel now, 'All that the Father
giveth to me, will come unto me'; there will be a special
providence over those who are prepared to embrace the
means of salvation, and either they will be led to me, or I
to them.   It is the fault of the present day, to think and
to act as if man could do everything, and certainly to
forget God's special Providence.   Hence that busybodyness
which distinguishes the religious world, and prevents that
depth of piety which is the result of sober, calm reflection,
and which shows itself in doing calmly, and unostentatiously,
not what seems likely to be attended with the greatest
results, but simply the duty our hand findeth to do.   What
does God require of me? is the question to be asked, and
the answer is, nothing that can interfere with any immediate
duty.   Your immediate duty, for instance, of a Sunday
afternoon is, as you say, with your father; you would be
wrong then to omit this, even were the entire welfare of
the school to depend on your individual exertions; for God
can provide teachers for the school without your aid.   In
the morning, no immediate duty claims your time, and you
therefore devote it to a work of charity.   Now with these
principles, I should not feel any fears in undertaking any
parish; and though I do not see any objection to the plan
you propose, of licensing rooms for divine service, yet I
would never do anything irregular for any object whatever,
under the conviction that the times and seasons are in
God's own hands.

To W. P. Wood, Esq.—Youthful Dreams—Advice to Young Poets.

October 14, 1835.

. . . . Yesterday I returned, and this my first holiday I
dedicate to my friend; for though, after a day of labour, I
cannot sit down to write a letter, because the stooping tries
me, I know no recreation greater than that of writing to
you.   I always in doing so regain some portion of that

boyish enthusiasm for which, as we advance in years, we so often sigh in vain. I remember well the days when the highest object of my ambition was that we should be famed in story as the modern Pylades and Orestes, and appear as twin authors, the rivals of Beaumont and Fletcher. Those were days when I thought no one worthy of consideration except a poet; and I fondly dreamed what I found out, to my great comfort, in good time to be only a dream, that I was born to be one whose eye should be always in a 'fine frenzy rolling.' I have this day thought of this the more, since I found awaiting my arrival from Oxford a small volume of poems by a very youthful poet, requesting me to give my advice as to the publication of them. This kind of thing has often occurred to me, and it places one in a most awkward predicament. If you advise the author to publish, you only send him to the flogging form to be scourged to death by the critics; and if you tell him honestly that the thing will not do, you seriously hurt a mind which must be sensitive (*must* be, or it would not overflow in poetry), and do injury to feelings which are for the most part amiable. I do cordially enter into the feelings of the poor young writers, for I have felt as they feel, and had I been in their situation of life with a friendly pastor to consult, I should most likely have written the same kind of warm-hearted, respectful, tremulous letter as those are which I am frequently in the habit of receiving. The volume now before me is accompanied by a letter, which, as it gives me archiepiscopal honours (bishops having succeeded poets in my love), styling me 'most reverend Sir,' is very flattering. But poor lad, what am I to do for him? with much poetical sentiment he has much bad grammar, with no power of expression:—that is, he is born to admire poetry, not to write it; although he expects clearly that when his volume sees the light, some future Johnson will contend for his admission into the assembly of British poets. I must do to him as I have done for others: after a civil word or two, I must

assume the look, not of a critic, but a friendly adviser, of a
Mœcius or a Horace, and say of the poem,

> . . . . nonumque prematur in annum,
> Membranis intus positis ; delere licebit
> Quod non edideris.   Nescit vox missa reverti.

This must be the text, and I must expound it ; happy I,
that my *protégés* understand not Latin, or perhaps their
minds would go a little higher up the page and understand
my hint too clearly, upon seeing.

> Qui nescit, versus tamen audet fingere.

Luther and O'Connell compared—Catholicism most potent against Popery.

October 1835.

My dearest Mother, ... I am glad that Georgiana so
thoroughly understands the principles of the Church of her
Saviour, and is not ashamed of them.   The danger now is,
not from Popery, but from that snare of Satan, ultra-
Protestantism.   Perhaps, if she had read as much about
Luther as I have done, she would have floored her antagonist by stating her abhorrence of that man's principles.
I am amused to hear those who abuse O'Connell eulogising
Luther ; for Luther's line of conduct, his violence, his insubordination was precisely similar to that of O'Connell.
Luther was certainly a most ultra-radical, and he certainly
permitted the Elector of Hesse to marry two wives in
order that he might secure him for a political partisan.
Both he and O'Connell have made religion their pretext ;
but whether they were not both rather influenced by a
factious spirit, may be doubtful ; the only difference
between them is, that they have taken the opposite
extremes.   I am a lover of truth wherever it leads, and
therefore I will not seek to whitewash Luther merely
because he was a useful instrument against Popery.   I am
rather amused at your saying that you would not receive

the Sacraments from a Popish priest, and in the same sentence professing admiration of the Church; for if the ministrations of Popish priests be not valid, how do you prove the validity of our own orders, descended as we are, in regular line from Popish priests?

Let Georgiana glory in being called a Papist, while she holds not Popish, but Catholic principles. All the great divines of the Church of England, from the blessed martyr Laud, down to Bishop Butler, and from Bishop Butler down to our own times, to Mr. Rose, all have been called Papists, though they have hated the Pope, and done more service against Popery than all the Ultras, who really act on Popish principles. Tell her that when a man in argument urges *extreme cases*, it is a sign that he is a blockhead, and I always cut the matter short by saying: 'Pray, what would you do if you were a horse? When you have made up your mind on that point, then I will tell you what I should do were I placed in circumstances in which I never expect to be placed.'

Your devoted Son.

Contentment with Coventry.

Coventry : October 21, 1835.

My dearest Mother, ... As to any change in my preferment, I speak the sentiments both of Delicia and myself, which we often express to one another in great sincerity, that we should contemplate any change with sorrow. Here we are, as perfectly happy and as nearly contented as mortals can be. Two hundred a year, to enable me to buy a few more books and her to have a little carriage, would be the very summit of our wishes; and if that wish were granted, other evils would attend. If we improve our condition in one way, we should only injure it in another; we have here a union of perfect retirement in one respect, with just sufficient excitement in another. I hope you will persevere in your course of saying nothing about me or my affairs; as the good old Bishop used to say, 'The less we hear of ourselves, either in praise or dispraise, the better.' As regards myself, my system has always been to act according to my own views, to do what I think right, without the least regard to the opinions of others, to evil report, or good report; this is the only way to obtain peace of mind and consistency of conduct. I find now that those who were at one time very angry with me, seeing they cannot alter me, are beginning to praise me; to wit, our kindhearted Bishop. I will not budge a step to go over to others, and therefore many others of my acquaintance have come over to me, while all do me the favour of leaving off any attempts to convert me. I have always determined to be independent, to go my own way to work, and consequently, I am as obstinate as a pig; unless a friend chooses to call my obstinacy perseverance in a good cause. I never care for censures, and when I am praised, my chief rejoicing is, if I know myself, that my principles have prevailed. For as to the praise of man, I know its worthlessness, for I find in general when it is bestowed upon me it is a bitter satire, alluding rather to what it is supposed I have done than to what is really the case.

I heard to-day from my friend, my very kind friend, Mr. Rose; by the way, his is a very flattering letter, as he expresses his great wish that nothing may take me away from Coventry. When people say this, it is a real compliment; and dear, dear Coventry, I never wish to leave thee. I confess I feel what the good Bishop would have called a little sinful pride, at having the title of 'Mr. Hook of Coventry': my ambition is, to be known in after times in the catalogue of our Vicars as 'the painful preacher of Coventry.'

To W. P. Wood, Esq.—Sermons, Means of Instruction rather than of Grace—Dr. Moberly—Sermon at Oxford.

November 21, 1835.

. . . . I do not look upon sermons, as people in the present day too frequently do, as direct means of grace, but simply as means of instruction. The ultra-Protestant notion, that preaching is a direct means of grace, was unknown to the ancients ; they taught men to seek for grace chiefly in the two Sacraments, and then in prayer. The relative merits of the ordinances may be seen from the following outline of their penitential discipline. There were four orders of penitents : first, the προσκλαίοντες, *flentes*, whose station was in the vestibule of the church, who begged the prayers of the faithful, as they went into the sanctuary ; not daring to join in the public prayer themselves. Second, the ἀκροώμενοι, *audientes*, who were allowed to enter the church, to hear the Scriptures read, and to attend the sermon, but not allowed to stay for the common prayers. Third, the γουνκλίνοντες, *genuflectentes*, who were admitted to the prayers, and were blessed by the Bishop ; but when the rest of the congregation stood (as was the universal custom on Sundays) in prayer, they were obliged to kneel ; their station was round the reading desk. Fourth, the συνιστάμενοι, *consistentes*, who were admitted to all the privileges of the common prayer, and even stood at the rails of the altar while the faithful communicated, but were not yet permitted to communicate themselves.

When I was at Oxford, I had the pleasure of hearing the new Master of Winchester preach. He was select preacher in the morning, I in the afternoon. I afterwards met him at Dr. Burton's, and he told me he remembered my last half year at Winton ; I suppose, therefore, you knew more of him. His name is Moberly ; he is a delightful preacher ; his discourse was deeply metaphysical, on Predestination, and I thought he handled it admirably. I certainly never preached to such a mob before, not even in my own church ;

not only was the church crowded with gownsmen up to
the pulpit stairs, but the townspeople presented in the
distance quite a sea of heads. You will perhaps think I
was appalled at the sight ; but no! I am very nervous
when I preach in a place for the first time, but when I am
accustomed to it, my nerves become hardened. It is not
from nerves that I suffer so much as from great excitement, and as I am excited just as much when I write what
I am to speak, as when I speak what I have written,
sermonising does not particularly agree with me. I find
that I can put myself in precisely the same position of
mind when delivering my sermon as when writing, and
consequently can add extempore bits. And this is in fact
all that extempore preachers really do, if they are speakers
worth anything ; they have a speech by heart, of which they
are so thoroughly masters that they can add to it, take away
from it, or partially change as they go on. If the speech
is their own, the overflow of their own thoughts, they can do
this ; if, as is generally the case, they have only worked up
other people's ideas, they cannot do this, and consequently
they fail ; is not this the case ?

*To W. P. Wood, Esq.—Refusal of a joint Offer made by
him and Archdeacon Bayley to provide a second
Curate.*

December 1835.

Where I feel a little overworked now-a-days is in a
department where help cannot be given. People write to
me from all quarters requesting advice on this point or
that ; here on a parochial matter, there on a doctrinal matter.
Quarrels and misunderstandings and jealousies occur
between persons in this parish on whom I must depend,
which no one but myself can set to rights. Meetings are
proposed and societies formed in which I am compelled to
come forward, because I have some personal influence.
For instance, at the present moment some of my people
are eager to have a meeting for the Irish Clergy ; the
management of which will be most troublesome to me, as

I shall have so to arrange matters as not to give offence to our very touchy Archdeacon, to get influential people to attend, to draw up all the Resolutions, and above all to take care that it does not degenerate into a political assembly. In all this no curate can help me. Were I writing to anyone else it would seem conceited in me to say this. But I can only place the matter before you by so doing. By steadiness to certain principles, and by having gone straightforward in my course, and by the success of some of my measures, I have acquired an influence over much superior men to myself who have been wanting in perseverance. And here it is that I am sometimes a little overworked.

To W. P. Wood, Esq.—Argument—Prejudice—Religious and Useful Knowledge Society.

February 1, 1836.

. . . . You say that my argument about the Reformation is monstrous, and that it will convince no one. My dear friend, did you ever know anyone convinced by argument? it is a thing I never attempt. All that I attempt is to confirm those in their opinion, whose opinion I believe to be correct; and this you seem to admit will be done. My own conviction is, that men never entirely quit their hereditary opinions and principles, except from interest or passion; I look upon the Whig son of a Tory, or the Tory son of a Whig, as an ill-conditioned cur. All that I should attempt to do would be to modify; to make a man less vehement and violent, and so to prepare the next generation for an imperceptible change. If a Whig turns Tory, or a Dissenter a Churchman, I rejoice, but it is generally speaking merely because his family will be educated in what I think right principles, that their prejudices will be in favour of the truth; the convert himself in nine cases out of ten (mind, I make exceptions), has been influenced by some passion or pride. We inherit in like manner our religion, and it was intended that we should do so.　Christianity was taught by word of mouth, before the Scriptures were written ; what we receive by tradition, we correct and improve by reference to Scripture. No man takes his religion from Scripture only ; it would take a lifetime to do this ; he is what he was brought up, and corrects himself by the Scriptures which were given ·for that purpose.　And I look upon the advantages of an Establishment to consist greatly in this, that it secures a wide spread of traditionary religion, creates a prejudice in favour of religion.　I put down a man who pretends to be unprejudiced as a humbug.　The great thing is, to create *good* prejudices : this is what the Bible tells us to do, when it bids us bring up our children in the 'nurture and admonition of the Lord.'　It is through the spectacles of prejudice that we look upon facts the most clear ; for instance and with reference to that which has given rise to these observations, what different impressions are made on your mind and mine by certain facts.　We learn from history that the vote for the renunciation of the Popish supremacy in the Irish Parliament was unanimous, that it was received with joy throughout the nation, the clergy having been unpopular ; that in Convocation the bishops and almost all the clergy (in England I believe there were only 138 dissentients, but that is not to the purpose) assented to the Reformation ; there were only two, some say four, Bishops who refused.　From these facts (and I only regret that in my sermon I did not quote my authorities more fully), I draw inferences which you think monstrous, because you simply say you cannot believe the facts.　So it is ; I do not expect to convince you ; I should say at once 'he is a Whig, there is no hope of convincing him.'　My point is gained if I add one more impulse to the conviction of those with whom I think the truth is ; and all I can expect of you is, what you are willing to say, that there is more to be said on the subject than you before supposed.

　　As to parish business, I am at present, as I believe every active man occasionally is, in hot water, and if you were

to see our Whig newspaper and some other publications
you would think your friend a very devil incarnate. I believe I mentioned to you that just before I left home in the
summer the teachers of my school expressed a wish to
form a society for the improvement, after quitting school,
of the young people, and especially with a view to the
establishment of a library of religious books. Well, I
rejoiced at the proposal and entered into it cordially ; I got
a grant from the Society for Promoting Christian Knowledge of 25*l.*, emptied my own library of all my spare
works ; begged books of others, and the end has been that
we have now a library containing nearly 500 volumes, and
we have 600 members. The Mechanics' Institute having
gone on for years and not having above 200, our success
has excited the wrath of the members of the latter society,
against which I have never done a hostile act ; and now
they let out upon me the vials of their abuse, and even
threaten my person, which is very illiberal in liberals.
This kind of thing does not move me, for my rule never
is to oppose, but to proceed in my own course ; I never
interfered with the Mechanics' Institute, though I could
not conscientiously belong to it. I instituted our Society,
because I considered its establishment a positive good ;
and all these attacks on me do good. As I said before,
I do not hope to gain converts from them, and their
abuse of me makes those who love me as their pastor
more zealous ; while, on the same grounds, the others will
not win from us any worth keeping. That there was need
of our society is proved from this, that at the Mechanics'
Institute an order was made to admit religious books,
which was immediately rescinded, because to meet the
religious views of some of the members, it would be
necessary to admit Tom Paine's works. Meanwhile, not
conscious of having done any man wrong by establishing a
society in which religion is recognised as a branch of useful
knowledge, we are raising money to erect a building and I
am preparing to deliver a lecture on savings banks. Can
you assist me ? it is not much in my line of business, but

there are only seventeen weavers in all Coventry who put into our savings bank ; so that I think I ought to do something : pray help me if you can.

To W. P. Wood, Esq.—Accused of Intolerance—Sermon at Oxford.

Shrove Tuesday, February 17, 1836.

. . . . I am rather amused with our opponents having styled me the Rev. Autocrat of Coventry ; my autocracy simply consisting in always doing what I think to be right, without regard to consequences, and the result being, as it generally is, that, as I will not go over to others, others come over to me.   I have a strong feeling that I will not belong to a society from which my Saviour and my God is virtually excluded.   I belonged to a rather good library and reading room in this town, from which I withdrew on that account, viz. that no religious books were admissible ; the object of course being to obtain the support of all sects.   I did not state, and have not stated, this to be my reason, but simply retired, not having sufficiently examined the subject to urge the principle upon others ; but the more I reflect on it, the more inclined I am to think that I am right.   An express exclusion of the Master we serve ought to be a virtual exclusion of ourselves.   I mention this because I should like to know whether and what you have to object to it.   If things go on as they now are, I shall be obliged in self-defence to assert my principles. Our position is this ; we are accused of intolerance and I know not what all for not having acted with the Mechanics' Institute ; and as to religious works it is asked, Why could not the Rev. Autocrat establish a Church lending library ? and we are assailed with all manner of abuse. Now, it certainly seems to me that the intolerance is all on the other side ; for it is intolerance to try to compel another, no matter how, whether by ridicule, abuse, or force, to walk in my way ; but it is not intolerance for me to refuse to walk in the same path with another if I disagree with him, or if I cannot conscientiously do so. You are kind enough to ask how my sermon went off at Oxford, and I hope by the attention that is paid to me, that by the blessing of a good God my labours in the University will not be vain. My brother was there, and he was told that the church was fuller than it had ever been since ——'s memorable sermon, in which he attacked the Church just before he quitted our communion. It was indeed a grand and imposing sight, as one stood in the pulpit, and until I got well into my subject I was very nervous and, as I was afterwards told, looked deadly pale. From the pulpit you see nothing but men, and the black gowns give a sombre appearance to the scene. There is too, a most awful silence, occasioned doubtless by the absence of children, and of the rustling of silks and satins.

To W. P. Wood, Esq.—Justification—Neglect of Primitive Tradition—Interpretation of Scripture.

March 25, 1836.

. . . . Since I wrote yesterday I have found that the prayer you object to is found verbatim in Bishop Andrewes' devotions; nor did he seem to anticipate the shadow of an objection to it. The fact is, in his time the tradition of our Church was much purer and more primitive than it has been since the Rebellion. It is perhaps now peculiarly erroneous, from the fact that those who stirred up the religious feelings in the country about fifty years ago, and their successors the Evangelicals or popular party have gone, not to the fountain head, not to the tradition as it was set a-flowing by the Apostles, and jealously watched and guarded by the primitive Church, but merely to the doctors of the Reformation, who, however praiseworthy in their resistance to Popery, were not of course armed at all points, and were better skilled most of them to pull down than to build up. The doctrine may be best stated perhaps by altering the terms; Justification is by faith alone, the salvation of the justified by works, founded upon faith, and wrought through the influence of the Holy Ghost. No one may approach the Father but through the Son. He who is brought to the Father by the Son is permitted to make the offering of good works, which, knowing his own impotence, he implores the Holy Ghost to enable him to perform. Thus did the traditional religion of the Primitive Church accord with all parts of Scripture, whereas the modern ultra-Protestant ideas so ill accord with Scripture as a whole that Luther actually rejected the Epistle of St. James, thus in fact condemning the ultra-Protestant notion of justification by faith as unscriptural. And in these days for one that preaches justification by works, there are a hundred that preach justification by faith alone. Yet St. James expressly tells us that we are justified by works; why reject St. James more than St. Paul? The consequence of modern teaching has been high pretensions, but much lax morality, much fanaticism with little mortification, but the consequences are not the consideration; the question is simply, What has been revealed? To ascertain what has been revealed, it is I apprehend necessary, first, to discover what the Universal Church taught, when the means existed of ascertaining this fact; and then to see whether this tradition is confirmed by Scripture. If it be, then I conceive we may be sure that we have the truth. We shall only err if we assert as truth what I, an individual teacher, think that Scripture means. What *I* think the Scripture means, an Arian or Socinian may *not* think. I do not blame anyone for holding to the modern doctrine; for in point of fact most persons must receive their doctrines in the first instance from tradition, from what their teachers tell them, adhering to them if they appear to be proved by Scripture, rejecting them only if they are directly contrary to Scripture. But those who are able or have time to examine more deeply, to ascertain what was the traditional teaching in the Apostolic age, they are bound to correct the erroneous tradition of their own age. Thus it was that I said in my preface, the prayers published by me would not accord with the religious feelings of the present time ; *ergo*, I stand a chance of being abused, but it is my duty to throw my drop into the stream which is purifying the tradition of the time.

To W. P. Wood, Esq.—A Drifter into Romanism—Trans-missive Religion.

April 18, 1836.

. . . . And now for Minchin. I predict that he will become a Romanist, because his affections are engaged on that side. He is disgusted with the illiberality of ultra-Protestants, which is doubtless great, but he does not perceive the illiberality of Romanism, which is yet greater. See particularly Pope Pius's Creed and the Canons of Trent ; this one-sided view of that question shows the predilection, and when that is the case, Romanism has much to say for itself. My opinion is that God intends that religion shall be as the general rule transmissive ; and that we are to take the religion we inherit, and examine it by the Scriptures, adhering to it if we find the Scriptures in great degree confirming what we have received, correcting and . improving what was deficient in our father's creed or practice ; but in doubtful cases interpreting Scripture so as to lean to the side of our ancestors ; thus using our reason, but acting with humility. This makes it important for us never for the sake of peace to shrink from the assertion of truth, since it is most important to make the traditional religion of our country what it ought to be. Now it appears to me that to Minchin very little religion was transmitted ; what he learned was very imperfectly learned at Winchester. He has lived chiefly abroad, and there the religion transmitted to him has been Romanism ; it has had attractions for him, and he is much in the condition of a man who has been born and bred a Romanist. When he examines, he will incline to the side of Romanism ; doubtful points will receive force from this prejudice, he will often see the weakness of an argument on our side, seldom

on the side of the Romanists. I think, however, the best
book you can send him at present is a little work I re-pub-
lished a few years ago with notes. 'Friendly Advice to the
Roman Catholics.' It is by the celebrated Dean Comber,
and is written in a very mild, conciliatory tone. If this
makes an impression, I will think of some other works for
his edification. I like your idea of Hooker; it is always
better to explain the nature of true Churchism than to
make a decided attack on Romanism; to assert the truth
than to combat error. Palmer has a work in the press,
perhaps the most important on this subject since the days
of Hooker, and intended to meet the modern objections of
Romanism; I wish it were out. You know I am an un-
flinching asserter of what I believe to be the truth, regardless of persons and consequences, and I am therefore called
illiberal and bigoted, &c. But I never condemn an individual who piously belongs to the system I may censure and
oppose. I would stay the progress of an erroneous system,
even sometimes when I should refrain from seeking to
make a proselyte of one who belongs to the system; for
unless that proselyte can be made by sound reasoning, you
gain nothing by winning him, and perhaps injure his own
character; saving that you secure the better education of
his children, which is sometimes to be considered. I can
thus oppose Romanism, but love a Romanist; and I
should rejoice to renew my acquaintance with old Toody,
of whom I can never think without affection; even though
we could not prevail upon him not to take this false step,
to which, as I conceive, I can trace the circumstances
which led him.

*To a Young Clergyman—Opinion on Lay Baptism—Advice
about Private Life—Treatment of Dissenters.*

Leamington : July 27, 1836.

My dear ——,—The question you propose is a difficult
one to answer. So far as argument goes, it appears to me
that the line of argument adopted by you is correct, and

lay baptism ought not to be considered valid. But I am inclined to think that the practice of the Catholic Church has been on the other side, and that lay baptism, though considered uncanonical, improper, and much to be censured, has not been treated as invalid. When heretics were received into the Church they were not *baptised*, but *confirmed*, and by the act of confirmation the previous uncanonical act was made canonical. But here we may observe that all the ancient heretics had, in some sense, the Apostolical succession : they had Bishops, though not canonical ones. To this, however, it is replied that heretical orders were never regarded as valid. In short, the whole subject is a difficult one. Some divines make a distinction between *lay*, and *unauthorised* baptism, lay baptism when the Bishop sanctions it being accounted valid, but Dissenting baptism, not having secured the episcopal sanction, invalid. The Church in this country, from the period of the Reformation, and indeed before that time, till the reign of James I., undoubtedly sanctioned lay baptism by licensing midwives to baptise. When that rubric was altered and we were directed to send for a minister, it would seem to decide that it ought to be a ministerial act. I remember two strong instances in the primitive Church on the other side. St. Athanasius was baptised by his playfellows in sport, and this baptism was deemed sufficient ; and so was that of an actor who was baptised in the regular form on the stage in a play written to ridicule Christianity.

Being removed from all my books I cannot enter more fully into the subject, but you will see it incidentally discussed in Dr. Pusey's admirable treatise on Holy Baptism, published among the Oxford Tracts, to which I particularly invite your attention. You may consult also on the one side Lawrence, on the Invalidity of Lay Baptism, and on the other Bingham's ' Scholastic History of Lay Baptism.' As to the practical point I am in the habit of telling people that at least there is some *doubt* on the subject, and if they received lay baptism and are fearful on that account, I use the conditional form, ' If thou hast not been before baptised,' &c., as found at the end of our Baptismal Service, and this is the course pursued by the Bishops and clergy in Scotland when persons come over to them from the Established Church. . . . You may depend upon it that nothing is to be done in a parish without a patient care of the schools. It is by patience only, a patient continuance in well-doing, that you will be able to make your present situation an agreeable one, always remembering that permanent comfort and happiness are not intended for this world. *Peace* is the reward of our labours here, in the world to come, purchased for us by our Lord. You must also remember that you let many precious years pass by, to say the least of it, in carelessness, for which you ought to make up by humiliation, mortification, and other holy exercises. If you have not strength of mind to do this for yourself, you ought to pray that God may take the discipline of you into His own hands—that he may so order things that your pride and vanity may be mortified, that while in His hands you are an instrument of good you may not for a season witness the effects of your labours. To a man who ought like you to seek for mortification, who ought to take the lowest seat at the heavenly banquet, I should say that your present situation *because unpleasant* is a very proper one. And perhaps it may be well after a week of such fasting and prayer to ask earnestly and seriously *why* it is unpleasant. Seek not the *pretext* but the *real reason* of your present discontent. Particularly be sure that vanity, pride, presumption have nothing to do with it. I mention these faults as being those of young men very frequently which can easily be masked by an appearance of religious zeal.

I sincerely hope as you say that the cause of Catholicism is prospering everywhere, though I am inclined to take a less sanguine view of our present position than you do. As to Dissenters I literally know nothing of them. You speak of a schism among the Methodists. I am sorry to hear of it ; for all schisms, even schisms among schismatics, engender bad feelings. Sure I am that we shall

not profit by any such evil deeds. Those who quit Dissenting congregations are far more likely to turn infidels than
Churchmen. A true Churchman will feel that to him a
high trust is committed, viz. the preservation of God's
truth. It may be that in maintaining God's truth he may
have to fight single-handed against a multitude. Still he
will be unmoved. In God's good time His Holy Spirit will
bring over the people to the side of His truth, and till that
time comes we must keep our souls in patience. One of
the worst things a man can do is to try and make converts,
one of the next is to attack Dissenters, or to have anything
whatever to do with them. Keep aloof from Dissenters as
persons of a different religion, and try to build up the two
or three God sends to you in the principles of the Holy
Catholic Church.

I could say much more, but want of room prevents my
so doing.

Believe me to be, my dear ——,

Your faithful and sincere friend.

*To his Wife, during a Tour in the Autumn of 1836 with a
Lady and Gentleman in the North of England.*

I was amused with something Mrs. B. told me on the
way, which accounts for a very warm reception I met with
at the inn at Matlock. The landlord's daughter there
gazed on me with an admiration which much perplexed
me. The servants followed the mistress's example. I was
removed to the best room in the inn, and everybody
seemed delighted to serve me. They had caught my
name, and the fair daughter of the landlord said to Mrs.
B., 'Excuse me, ma'am, but I suppose Mr. Hook is the
great Mr. Hook.' 'Yes,' said Mrs. B. 'Ah!' said the fair
Maid of the Inn, 'I have just been reading his beautiful
work "Gilbert Gurney."' 'Oh!' quoth Mrs. B., '*this* Mr.
Hook is nephew to *that* Mr. Hook; and though his works

are very celebrated, they are of a different kind ;' but, alas ! my friend confesses that the young lady was sadly disappointed.

To a young clergyman—Study and Dissenters.

Coventry : November 2, 1836.

My dear Friend,—I have just received your delightful and gratifying letter, and though I am rather overwhelmed with my correspondence, having sometimes to write eight or nine letters in a day, I shall always be glad to hear from you if you will kindly permit me to take my own time for my answer. I say this because it may occasionally be agreeable to you, living in such retirement as you do, to open your mind to a friend. But I must protest against your speaking of me in the terms you do ; I can only aid you by having a little more experience and having experienced all those evils which you have to lament, and by being able, in consequence. to sympathise with you while I offer advice. . . . There are two points in your letter to which I must now address myself.

It seems clear to me, in the first place, that you require some hard study ; something rather dry. If you were near a library, with plenty of time, I would mark out a course for you. As it is, I recommend you to read *through* Bingham's ' Antiquities,' to be followed by Palmer's ' Origines Liturgicæ,' and then I would have you go on with Jeremy Collier's ' Ecclesiastical History of England.' By these means you will lay in a vast store of useful information ; you will be giving to yourself a habit of study, and you will overcome a habit of self-indulgence which may creep on us even in our studies. During the first seven years that I was in orders, I was a hard student, and I used to rise at four o'clock in the morning. This, perhaps, would not suit you, but when you are at these studies, it might be well to read standing, or in a part of the room far from the fire. This keeps up attention, and is a little useful bodily discipline. I agree with you as to what you say with respect to works on personal devotion in your particular case. Your heart *is* right, and what you now chiefly want is self-discipline.

In the next place, if the Methodists do attend church, and do *not* attend meeting, they are clearly not Dissenters. The original Methodists under Wesley were on very many points much to be admired. Their doctrine of Perfection is good, and has been of great use against the prevailing Calvinism of the day. I am afraid that in my last I did not express myself quite clearly. What I mean is this, that we ought to look with a single eye to *the truth*, not to the filling of our churches, and decreasing Dissent or anything else. What we are required as preachers to do is, to declare all the counsel of God, reckless of consequences. If people take offence, they must do so; if not, then give God the praise. Our business is to state fairly the tradition of the Church as it is preserved in our Ritual, Liturgy, and Articles (learned men go to the fountain-head at once, the primitive Church), and then to prove that the tradition of the Church is scriptural. We *receive* our religion from the Church, we *prove* our religion from the Bible.

Your affectionate Friend.

I would advise you always to read with a pen in your hand, noting down everything remarkable in a common-place book.

To the Rev. T. H. Tragett—How to Refit a Church—Catechising.

Coventry : November 5, 1836.

. . . . And now let me congratulate you on your parish—I wish it were entirely your own, as it is unpleasant to depend on the life of another; I have often dreamed of retiring upon just such a parish; about 2,000 people. Yours is doubtless a holy ambition, to make your little parish a perfect model of what a parish ought to be; such a parish I have in Utopia, and I will tell you what I would do with it. If the walls of the church are strong, I would gut it. I would beg of my friends and acquaintance till I obtained 200*l.* (if you should think of anything like this, come to me for 1*l.* 1*s.*), I would then entirely refit the interior, having no pews, and erecting in the chancel an open seat, like one of the stalls in a cathedral, for my reading-pew. I would then observe who were regular attendants at church, and at Christmas give them a good dinner. This would soon increase the congregation, and why should we not act thus? Our Blessed Lord fed the five thousand before he began to teach them; and if we can bribe people to hear us, they may afterwards stay without a bribe. But indeed, with such a parish you might give them all a good dinner of roast beef and plum-pudding, for as much as two dinners to your equals would cost; and the surest way to men's hearts, as old Hamond used to say, is down their throats; and when you have their hearts they will patiently hear you, while you endeavour to cure their souls. As to the children, they are certainly the first and grand consideration. You say you are a wretched catechist, but the art of catechising does not, any more than that of reading and writing, come by nature; but to become a good catechist you must catechise, and it is astonishing how rapid is the improvement, both on the part of the catechiser and the catechised. It is important to have by heart the answers in Crossman and Lewis, and the books with which the children are acquainted, so that when the questions you have put in other words are unanswered, you may fall back on those they have by rote, and so shame the fools. And the first boy or girl who smiles at any little pleasantry of which you may be guilty, will deserve a reward, as giving proof that the intellect is beginning to thaw. I have found it best to stick to the Church Catechism, as by a little skill you can put questions from all the books they may have learnt, without much forcing; one question leads to another. It is impossible, however, to draw too largely on the bank of stupidity, and the same questions must come perpetually over and over again ; Henderson on the Catechism is a work which will give you some invaluable hints. You ask what I did at Whipping-ham and Moseley : I laboured much at my schools, and never missed an attendance there all day on the Fridays, when I examined all the classes ; only catechising in church in Lent. I was younger then than I am now, and I should now catechise in church under any circumstances, under the expectation of receiving greater grace, and under the conviction that the fact of their being examined in church impresses it on the minds of the children that it is not knowledge, but religious knowledge, that they come to receive. In Coventry, I can only get the lower orders to attend, but next spring, (D.V.) Augusta will be catechised with the rest, and I hope this example will have good effect. At Whippingham and Moseley my schools cost me a mint of money ; not much less than 20*l.* a year, for I established a system of tickets, which came to a great deal. This was folly, but my schools there were my hobby ; still at first it is well worth while to incur some expense ; for it is astonishing how it quickens the wits, and the attention to find that attention has a marketable value. Here, again, I act on the system that we may begin with giving the loaves and fishes : thence, when you have secured atten-tion, you may proceed to higher principles, and gradually drop the bribing plan ; for once get an active stirring spirit in a school, and it will remain.

Your affectionate Friend.

From W. P. Wood, Esq. to W. F. Hook—On the Death of his Infant Boy.

Lincoln's Inn : December 23, 1836.

. . . . It is a great comfort to know that you are thus upheld in the hour of need. Doubtless our God is a ' very present help in trouble,' and it should be at once a confirm-ation of our faith and an exhortation to abide in it when we see that so severe a dispensation can be softened and tempered to you both. I sometimes ask myself under such trials, what would my situation be if I believed not in a hereafter? I am not at all surprised that the heathen should have so often resorted to self-destruction. But to the Christian the heaviest affliction is but a cloud, or at the most but as a thick mist, and if he cannot always see that God hath 'set his bow in the cloud,' yet he knows that the hour of the power of darkness is measured, while his hope is unbounded as eternity. 'Heaviness may endure for a night, but joy cometh in the morning.' . . . One sometimes feels it a happiness to be *permitted* to retire from the bustle of life under domestic affliction, though of course such feelings must not be indulged beyond very moderate limits, as we are readily tempted to sink into morbid indolence. The daily labour we are called upon to perform seems mercifully ordered in a world where death prevails, to tear away our minds from too deep and overpowering a sorrow for the dead, and to divert them also from an appalling fear of death. The poor, who have so much to contend with, find, I have no doubt, great relief in the necessity of constant occupation. You will have a comfort which none but those of your vocation can enjoy, that while your occupation will allay your sorrow, it will not tend to separate you from God. For the great danger with men of other professions is that they will try to bully their feelings by over-activity and bustle; and instead of casting their cares upon God, try to forget them, and in the experiment too frequently end by forgetting Him also.

CHAPTER V.

THE ELECTION TO THE VICARAGE OF LEEDS, 1837.

In the year 1836 Mr. William Page Wood and his wife paid a visit to the Vicar of Trinity at Coventry. Soon after their return to London they were invited by Dr. Williamson, the Head Master of Westminster School, to meet a barrister from Leeds, Mr. Robert Hall, who had recently taken a house in Dean's Yard, where they also at that time resided. When the day for dining at Dr. Williamson's arrived, Mr. Wood was unable, owing to a feverish cold, to fulfil his engagement, and his wife was very unwilling to leave him, but knowing that ladies would be wanted to make up the party, she thought it would be selfish to decline at the last moment. At dinner she sat next to Mr. Hall. He was not only an agreeable and able man, who had taken first-class honours at Oxford, but a zealous Churchman, and he therefore listened with interest to an account which Mrs. Wood gave of the great and good work which had been, and was being, done by her husband's friend at Coventry. To this conversation so accidental, as it would be carelessly called, so nearly being missed owing to the reluctance of one of the parties to leave home on that particular evening, the appointment of Mr. Hook to the Vicarage of Leeds was, under

God, primarily due, so that to the end of his life he was accustomed to call Mrs. Wood his 'patroness'; and that the wife of his deeply beloved friend should have been unconsciously instrumental in sending him to the place where he did his greatest work and won his greatest fame, was a circumstance on which he reflected with delight to the end of his life.

In January 1837, a few months after the meeting just mentioned with Mr. Hall, the Vicar of Leeds, Dr. Fawcett, somewhat suddenly died.   The patronage of the living is vested in twenty-five trustees. The senior trustee at that time was Mr. Henry Hall, father of Mr. Robert Hall, who also himself was a junior member of the body.   No sooner had Mr. Robert Hall heard of the death of Dr. Fawcett than his mind reverted to the description which he had heard of the hard-working Vicar of Coventry. He is the man for Leeds, thought Mr. Hall, if he is all that he has been represented to be.   So he instantly hastened to Coventry, verified by private enquiry and observation the account which he had received of the man and his work, and on his return called upon Mr. Wood to tell him that if his friend would become a candidate for the vacant living he would do his utmost to secure his election.   But he added that great opposition must be expected, as Mr. Hook belonged to a school in the Church totally different in thought, feeling, and practice from any which prevailed in Leeds, a school, moreover, which at that time, owing to its supposed connexion with the 'Oxford movement,' was regarded with peculiar suspicion.   Mr. Hall, therefore, was anxious that no time should be lost in ascertaining whether he would consent to be a candidate for the living, in order that the largest possible number of testimonials might be got together from persons representing various shades of opinion in the Church. How the application was made and received will be seen from the following letter to Mr. Wood. The absence of Mrs. Hook, who was staying with her mother, increased the difficulty of coming to an immediate decision.

Coventry : February 22, 1837.

My dearest Friend, ... On Sunday I received, quite unexpectedly, from Oxford a letter stating that I had been recommended in several quarters to the trustees of the Vicarage of Leeds, and that the trustees wished to ascertain through my kind friend Dr. Barnes, Sub-dean of Christ Church, whether, if the living were offered to me, I would accept it. It is a great calamity to be separated from Delicia at such a moment; but, in order that we might communicate with one another by letter, I took two or three days to consider the business, and I have now written to say that if offered the appointment I would accept it, but that I should decline presenting myself as a candidate, or adopting any steps for procuring it. My rule has been this, not to shrink from any duties to which I may be providentially called, having full reliance on the grace of my Saviour ; on the other hand, in humble distrust of myself, not to seek any responsible office. Delicia tells me that, if our family increase, we cannot go on long as we now do, and that if her health fail we have not the means of educating our children according to their condition ; I see, too, that her anxiety lest we should not be able to make the two ends of the year meet is weighing on her health and spirits ; so that I think I am justified in the step I have taken. Leeds is valued at 1,257*l.*, the average of three years before the last Parliamentary returns. If I do not obtain the appointment, my pride will be mortified, a very good thing ; I was not aware of the existence of the evil passion in me till on self-examination, I found that my chief wish to obtain the living is to prevent the mortification : it will be a good Lent exercise therefore. If I get it it will be sad, not only to quit a people whom I love, and by whom I am loved, but to leave many kind friends ; and not least, to move far away from those still loved remains, which are deposited in Trinity Church. From you and yours, to be removed 190 miles, will be like banishment ; I confess that the objections were so strong on my mind that I had fully determined to refuse the thing out and out, but Delicia, together with her mother and sister, urged the thing upon me, and I have done as I have said. I am sore perplexed ;—I dread the thing. Did I ever tell you that the Bishop of Worcester told our friend, Lord Eastnor, that there were two livings likely to be soon vacant, to the first of which he would present me ? St. Philip's, Birmingham, is one, the other I do not know ; I should like to wait for these birds in the bush, for at my time of life, just forty, I do not like breaking new ground.

The conflict of arguments and feelings in his own mind was so great that from the first he declared to his wife the decision must rest with her, not with himself.

I have, really and honestly speaking, (he writes to her on March 2) no wish upon the subject. The worldly considerations weigh not with me in the least. The only thing that makes me hesitate to say no is this—there is no Church feeling, no Catholic feeling, as I am informed in that part of the country. People there do not know what the Catholic Church is, and if I may be honoured as an instrument to introduce Catholicism there, as I have done here, I should feel that I have not lived entirely in vain. Then on the other hand we must remember that I should probably have a bad successor here :[1] one who

---

[1] The Whig Ministry being then in office.

would undo all that I have been doing during eight years
of labour, so that when the one thing is weighed against
the other I think I should not be induced on these grounds
to make the change. You now know my feelings on the
subject: yours, I repeat, must lead to the decision, for it is
mere matter of feeling not of duty.

If our sweet boy had lived, perhaps the patronage
would have been a temptation, but now I cannot expect
to live to see a son of mine labouring in the service of the
beloved Church, so that is out of all consideration. To me
the agreeable part has taken place. I am very sensible of
the honour of having been singled out, without my having
the remotest intention of becoming a candidate; and yet
these compliments are very humiliating. How humiliating
it is to find that the world thinks you better than you really
are: how much the conscience reproaches one on these
occasions. Perhaps I am more than usually sensible of this
from the self-examination to which this season of Lent
has led me. What a blessing, my dear love, it is, that
the Apostles and primitive Bishops appointed this season
for us to perform that duty which, if not compelled to do
it, we should, perhaps, put off and put off, and never perform.

Your devoted, adoring Lover.

His wife and her mother were in favour of his
consenting to be nominated as a candidate, and so
one step was gained. But the inflexible resolution
of the candidate on another point threatened to be a
formidable, if not fatal, obstacle to further progress.
He flatly refused to go to Leeds to present himself
to the trustees; still less would he consent to preach
a 'trial sermon,' or canvass interest on his behalf, as
most of the other candidates had done. Here was
a dilemma which at first caused no small vexation
and perplexity to Mr. Robert Hall and his father,

and some of the other trustees whom he had inspired with an enthusiastic desire equal to his own for the election of his candidate. Mr. Wood, however, suggested as a solution of the difficulty that some of the trustees should go to Coventry unknown to the Vicar, and he promised that he would not give his friend any intimation of their visit. Some old people in Coventry can remember the curiosity which was excited on Sunday, March 12, 1837, by the appearance in Trinity Church of six strange gentlemen at the morning and evening services, who had requested that they might be placed together in a position favourable for hearing the reading and preaching of the Vicar. Who they were and what they heard will be learned from the following letter, written by the Vicar the day after to Mr. Wood :

Coventry : March 13, 1837.

My dearest Friend,—Wearied with the labours of yesterday I cannot write *con spirito*, but still I must make you acquainted with the state of affairs. Yesterday Coventry was filled with trustees, Hall, Becket, Gott, Banks, Tennant, and one from the enemies' camp, Atkinson, to spy out the nakedness of the land.

They all in the morning spoke to me of what would happen if I went to Leeds; in the evening it was 'when you go to Leeds.' Mr. Gott said, 'I suppose you must be aware that many of the trustees are favourable to you.' 'Pooh, nonsense,' quoth Mr. Banks, 'you have the very large majority.' The prudent Mr. Hall, however, only reckons on twelve. But we were talking of Dr. Thorpe, and Sheepshanks was saying something not quite complimentary, when Mr. H. said, 'We will say nothing about that, as we mean him to vote for us ; but he is not one of the twelve certain.'

I verily believe that the sermon I delivered in the

evening, I wrote under the special direction of God; it
was written quite *extempore* and in a hurry on the Saturday, but if I had laboured to preach at the trustees I
could not have done so well. You know I am preaching
on St. Matthew's Gospel, and the text that came to me
was Matthew xxiii. 8, 9, 10, when I was naturally led
to explain in a simple manner the impropriety of choosing
for an authority in religion either the Pope or a Protestant Reformer, and how we took for our guidance, in
doubtful points, the customs of the first churches. This
explained to my friendly trustees (though I did not in
the least expect to see them) my views as they are, and
not as they are misrepresented. I then branched off into
a discourse on justification by faith, making the law our
rule of righteousness, but not our means of justification, in
a manner that could not but appease the fears of my
opposing visitor. One of the trustees, Mr. Gott, who
seemed very much impressed with the sermon, and asked
me to lend it, which I thought better to decline, said to
Sheepshanks, 'That sermon ought to be published.' 'Oh,'
exclaimed my enthusiastic partisan, 'if you think that, every
sermon preached every Sunday evening ought to be published; this is by no means the best we hear here.' Dear
good Sheepshanks is almost mad with zeal. With Mr.
Atkinson I had some conversation in the vestry; of course
I could not give him entire satisfaction, but he was more
favourably impressed than he had been before; I assured
him I did not hold the doctrine of Transubstantiation. He
is a nice, pleasant, well-informed man; I told him that I
would not discuss, but I was fully convinced of the truth
of my principles, and would answer him any questions he
might like to ask. He cross-examined me, but in a pleasant,
gentlemanlike style.

The reader will perceive from the foregoing
letter that however much puzzled some members of
the congregation at Holy Trinity may have been
by the visit to their Church of six rather inquisitive

strangers, the Vicar himself was not equally taken by surprise. The fact was that four out of the six trustees had called upon him the night before, not however so much to make known the purpose of their coming to Coventry, as to entreat that he would consent to go to Leeds for a few days, not to preach, not to canvass, but merely to be seen. Mr. Hall, indeed, had written to the same effect a few days before, ' The wish to hear you preach is given up. I find that the opinion is gaining ground that it is improper for a man to get up into a pulpit for the purpose of preaching not Christ crucified, but himself and his preferment. There is, however, a strong wish to *see* you : some of the trustees have declared their determination not to vote for a man they have never seen.'

To these solicitations, which were backed by his uncle, Archdeacon Hamilton, and Mr. Wood, he yielded, and writes to the latter that he has accepted the invitation to be the guest for two days of Mr. Henry Hall, the senior trustee, ' to exhibit my fat carcase at Leeds, and I certainly look what the people here call jolly.' But the prospect of the tremendous responsibilities which would fall upon him in the event of his election deterred him from any enthusiasm in his own cause. ' I feel interested in my success,' he writes, ' as I should do in that of the respectable Mr. Richard Roe or John Doe if they were engaged in a contest, and I was of their counsel. But when I think of the thing itself or the pang of parting with old friends, and the annoyance of breaking up new ground, my heart becomes sick, and I ask why I consented to embark in this affair.'

Meanwhile those who were eager for his success had collected a mass of testimony in his favour from very various sources, in order to prove that he was respected and admired not by one school or party only in the Church, but by many, and had 'won golden opinions from all sorts of people.'

At the request of his friends he asked Sir Robert Peel whether the letter which he had written in answer to an appeal on behalf of the Religious and Useful Knowledge Society,[1] might be used as a testimonial. To this he received the following reply. It was one of the few testimonials for which he made personal application, and was probably one of the most telling.

Whitehall : March 1, 1837.

Sir,—You have my full permission to make whatever use you please of the letter to which you refer. It contains a sincere and disinterested testimony to your character and acquirements, from one who has not the pleasure of your personal acquaintance, and who had no conceivable motive for bearing that testimony, excepting the firm impression that you had, as a preacher and minister of religion, essentially served the cause of religion and of charity, in two great manufacturing towns, and under circumstances of no ordinary difficulty, by a rare combination of ability, firmness, and devotion to the duties of your spiritual office.

I am Sir, with much respect, your faithful Servant,

ROBERT PEEL.

One of the warmest testimonials was from the Bishop of Lichfield, Dr. Butler, formerly Head Master of Shrewsbury, a man of critical mind, and not addicted to lavish praise.

[1] Quoted above, p. 180.

As a parochial minister he is considered an example, not only in the district to which he belongs, but far beyond it, of what an indefatigable, pious, and strictly conscientious clergyman ought to be. His immense church at Coventry I have witnessed full to overflowing. He has inspired into that large parish under his care, containing about 10,000 inhabitants, quite a new life; and the example has widely spread through the city, which is becoming full of attachment to the Church, though previously remarkable for Dissent. I may appear to have written strongly, but I am quite sure I have written only the truth, and I ought to say that in political opinions Mr. Hook and I do not perfectly agree; you may, therefore, feel assured that I have not been influenced in my testimony by any party feeling.

Mr. Le Bas pronounced him to be 'the fittest man in England to preside over such a parish as Leeds. Let Coventry and Birmingham be appealed to. If the former place is silent, it would only be because it could not raise its voice without danger of losing the spiritual guide who has bowed the hearts of his congregation towards him as the heart of one man.'

Mr. Keble wrote, 'I was acquainted with Mr. Hook when he was an undergraduate at Christ Church, and I believe that his conduct was then as blameless and exemplary, as his heart was unquestionably always open and generous. Since that time I have not often met him, but I have read his publications, and I should say that for eloquent persuasiveness, and soundness of principle, they certainly rank among the first of the age, to say nothing of the rare theological learning which they exhibit. As a preacher I need only refer you to the fact that no one draws such crowded congregations among the young men of Oxford :. no bad test, perhaps, of the qualities which make a person effective in that duty.'

A large number of the clergy in Coventry and the neighbourhood signed an earnest declaration of their affection and esteem. 'We have witnessed in him,' they said, 'a combination of ability, zeal, and spiritual-mindedness in the discharge of his parochial duties such as is seldom met with, and we see the fruits of it in a very greatly increased and increasing attendance in his parish upon public worship and the Lord's Supper. The younger portion of us have looked up to him in every duty as an exemplar, and in every difficulty as a kind and faithful guide, and those amongst us who are his contemporaries or his seniors have beheld with heartfelt respect and approbation his apostolic zeal for his Master's glory.' This collective testimony from the clergy was clenched by a private letter to the trustees from his great friend Mr. Tragett, who had held a cure in Coventry. 'The clergy,' he writes, 'of the city of Coventry and its extensive neighbourhood looked up to him as their head and chief ; and his learning, wisdom, and discretion formed the bond of union and zealous co-operation by which we were all enabled to act in harmony amongst ourselves, and to the general benefit of the community.'

Such are a few specimens out of a great multitude of testimonials which poured in thick and fast from persons of various positions in the Church.

There was one enthusiastic partisan, however, whose zealous activity occasioned some anxiety and

annoyance to him for whose benefit it was intended.
Mr. Theodore Hook announced his intention of
writing to Sir John Beckett, who had great influence
in Leeds, on behalf of his nephew. The nephew
deprecated the application, and suggested that it
should at least be made through Mr. Croker, a
common friend, rather than directly by Mr. Theodore Hook himself. But the uncle was not to be
thwarted, and replied to the remonstrance in the
following characteristic letter :—

> I dare say I have done wrong—I don't care if I have.
> I am sure I haven't done harm. I really don't see why *I*
> should not write to Sir John, or why I should ask Croker
> to ask him. I do *their* jobs : why the deuce should they
> not do mine ? It is not as if I asked them to prop up a
> stupid, ill-conditioned cur, because he happened to be my
> relation. It is *I* who do them a favour in giving them the
> opportunity of getting such a clergyman. If you are angry,
> I can't help it. I *will* have my own way, so I don't care.
> . . . . Come now, none of your nonsense—don't be angry
> and look cross ; the mouse may do good to the lion.

The last clause in this letter indicates the humble
respect and almost reverence with which the celebrated humourist regarded his clerical nephew. His
was a warm-hearted and generous disposition, sus-
ceptible also of religious feelings, and capable of
admiring and envying in others that strength of
moral purpose which was unhappily too much lacking
in himself.

The supporters of Mr. Hook had good reason
for making very strenuous efforts on his behalf. In
the first place there were many competitors, the
most formidable being Mr. Molesworth and Mr

Hugh Stowell, and they had been present in the
town and had preached in several of the churches
long before Mr. Hook had been brought forward as
a candidate. The election was to take place on
March 20, and it was not till the beginning of March
that his name appeared in the published lists of
candidates. And then a fierce storm of opposition
burst forth, and every endeavour was made to prejudice and intimidate the electors. The ' Record '
wrote in an agony of alarm, and sought to persuade
the religious world that he was a very monster of
Tractarian iniquity. ' He professed that kind of
modified popery with which the " Tracts for the
Times " were filled. For his fierce bigotry and
intolerance he could be compared only with Laud :
he consigned all Dissenters to the uncovenanted
mercies of God, and denied the right of private
judgment, which the " Record " considered the fundamental principle of the Reformation. A Jesuit in
disguise could not do more mischief to the Establishment than one who in spirit and doctrine
seemed as if he had been brought up within the
Holy Inquisition.' In short, it would be impossible
to imagine an appointment more fraught with disaster
to Leeds and to the Church of England.

These pleasant remarks in the ' Record ' were
followed by a sharp attack in the ' Christian Observer,' directed against his statements in two of
his Oxford sermons on the value of Catholic tradition and the authority of the Church. Feeble as
the criticism was, his supporters dreaded the effect
it might produce on the minds of some of the
trustees, especially as it insinuated that his views

were identical with those expressed in the 'Tracts for the Times,' and it was thought expedient that Mr. Wood should address a letter to one of the Trustees, exposing the fallacies and misrepresentations of the article. 'The reviewer,' he writes, 'maintains that the Bible, and the Bible only, is the religion of Protestants.' In one sense we all agree in this. All admit that nothing is to be believed which cannot bear the *test* of Scripture. In another sense it is not admitted by the reviewer himself, for in disputed points he says, 'We will refer to nothing but the Bible *and our own authorised formularies.*' What are these but the creeds, articles, catechism, &c. ? Is not the catechism taught to children before they can themselves deduce it from the Bible, and is not this transmissive religion ? The reviewer talks of our putting the Bible to the *humble* office of confirming opinion. The office of an umpire in settling disputes is not considered a humble one. If each man is to be his own interpreter, you may have Muggletonians "et hoc genus omne" without end, and " quot homines tot sententiæ." The Oxford men do not say the Church is infallible, but they believe that the Holy Spirit is promised to the Church : they believe the Church consists of men united in a faith which is cemented by well-approved formularies handed down from age to age. The Church may err ; but the chances of error in the case of individuals are infinitely greater.'

As the time for the election drew nearer, the strife of parties in Leeds waxed very hot. The papers were filled with all kinds of statements, true and false, concerning the candidates, and the trustees

were inundated with letters, many of them anonymous, until it was not easy to keep their heads clear
or their tempers cool.   Those who were known to
be favourable to Mr. Hook, especially Mr. Robert
Hall, were subjected to the most severe inquisitorial
examinations respecting his character and opinions
by the evangelical leaders in Leeds.   Mr. Hall in
one of his letters gives a specimen of a cross-ques-
tioning which he endured.   What were Mr. Hook's
opinions on baptismal regeneration ?   Did he preach
the necessity of a converted heart ?   Did he make
justification and sanctification prominent points in
his preaching, or did he merely concede them ?   Did
he support the Church Missionary Society ?   Was
he of holy life and conversation ?   Of course he did
not play cards or countenance gay amusements
himself, but did he permit his family to do so ? and
so on for nearly two hours, until Mr. Hall's patience
was fairly worn out, and he declined to be tormented
any longer.

Mr. Hook himself was so much distressed at
having become the occasion of contention and ill-
will that about this time he announced his intention
of withdrawing from the contest, in the following
letter to Mr. Robert Hall :—

Dear Sir,—I send a line, though in the greatest haste,
to acknowledge and to thank you for your kind letter.
This is necessary, because two or three days may elapse
before I can obtain a sight of the ' Christian Observer,'
which no person, that I can hear of, in this neighbourhood
takes in, and which was lately expelled from our Clerical
Society on account of the *unchristian* spirit, as it seemed
to us, in which it was conducted, especially on account of

its abuse of that good man, my dear friend, the late Bishop Jebb. Although I have never written any of the Oxford Tracts, nor indeed, have read them all, still, I am known to be a High Churchman, and it is not wonderful that I should be attacked by the 'Christian Observer,' which is the organ of *Low* Churchism or *No* Churchism.

But it may be necessary for me, when I have read the articles to which you refer, to trouble you with a few remarks in vindication of my character, and it will then be my wish to retire from this unpleasant contest. I consider it due to you, my dear sir, and to my friend Wood, not to take this step without your sanction. I wrote to him on the subject yesterday; and I now state to you what my wish and, unless you prohibit it, my intention is. I thank God that my circumstances are independent, and I am very happy here. When I was brought forward as a candidate on this occasion, I felt anxious for my success, because it is my nature to take an eager interest in any business in which I am engaged. But I am very unwilling to cause dissension among the trustees. I do not choose to have my peace of mind disturbed by the abuse of anonymous assailants, and I am unwilling to place myself in a situation which may give rise in me to those angry feelings which I condemn in my opponents. I am now able to retire without a feeling of regret, without bearing ill-will to anyone, with a sense of obligation to the trustees in general and with feelings of gratitude towards you which will, I hope, ripen into a lasting friendship. I am sorry to have caused you so much trouble, and I will endeavour to repay you for it by using all the influence I possess in favour of that candidate who is considered by you fittest for the situation.

Believe me to be, my dear Sir, with every sentiment of gratitude and respect,

Your obliged and faithful servant.

His friends, however, unanimously insisted on his retracting this decision. 'We must, if possible,' wrote Mr. Robert Hall, 'have the best man in the kingdom for Vicar of Leeds : you must therefore suffer me for the present to consider you as not having retired from the contest.' And Mr. Henry Hall wrote to the same effect : 'Attempts have been made to force upon us some clergymen of the Low Church party, and, in furtherance of this object, exceptions have been made to some of your doctrinal views ; but I assure you the misrepresentations of the "Christian Observer" have produced no effect on the majority of the trustees ; we are convinced that you will faithfully preach the Gospel to our people (this is what they look for, regardless of party names), and that you will by your "preaching and living" stop the mouths of all gainsayers.' And Mr. Wood restored the calmness of his friend by dwelling on higher considerations. 'We will not do those who have shown so much kindly feeling the injustice of supposing they will be turned from their good purpose by an anonymous attack. If we have trusted the event sufficiently to God, *nothing* ought to disturb us : if we are but conscious that *we ourselves* have not occasioned failure, either by negligence in proper exertion, or by undue eagerness, then the result will be *right* and *good*, and no scribbling in reviews or anything else can alter the case.'

Not long after this, in compliance with the request of the deputation which went to Coventry, Mr. Hook paid his visit to Leeds, and on Wednesday, March 15, he was introduced to the trustees at their weekly meeting in the vestry of the parish church. The following letters refer to the event :—

First Visit to Leeds—Machinations of the Hostile Party.

My dearest Friend,—I send just one line to say that I have returned from my northern expedition in good case. I wish I had gone to Leeds before, for my mind is now quite at ease. If I am to stay here, the comfort, a little quiet, and the regular routine of my duties, will be delightful ; if I am to go to Leeds, now that I have reconnoitred the country, I know that I shall not enter upon duties for which I am wholly disqualified. I feel quite up to the work, by God's grace ; depending on the Divine assistance, I shall embark in it, if at all, with vigour and confidence. We arrived, as Hall will have told you, on Tuesday. On Wednesday morning I saw most of the clergy, all of whom but two are on my side, and one of whom had generously drawn up a vindication of my doctrines. I stated to the trustees that I had come to Leeds at the request of certain of their body, not to canvass, but to be able at once to deny certain charges, if brought against me. To avoid all appearance of canvassing I left the town on the Wednesday evening. The clergy seemed to think me their Vicar, who is spoken of as somebody next in importance, if not to the king, at least to his prime minister. Several trustees told me that I might consider myself as elected ; even Hall seems to be in good cheer : but I know the party I have to deal with too well to feel anything like confidence. They have to meet on Wednesday for the purpose of memorialising the trustees against me ; they have represented me, as I suppose you have heard, not only as a Papist, but as a drunkard, a gambler, &c., &c. How I bless God that he has given me a heart that never bears malice or hatred; irritated I may sometimes be, but these kind of things do not irritate me. I have many, very many difficulties to contend with, from a nature desperately wicked ; but this is one of my advantages, that I scarcely notice, and immediately forget injuries. I should think that my best chance is, that the opposite party have no distinguished person to bring forward ; and the town clergy very properly say that, if they are passed over, they ought, at least, to have put over them a man of eminence ; and such, I presume, from the abuse heaped on me they suppose me to be. I suppose you have seen Stowell's letter following the attack upon me in the ' Record.' I told the trustees that I should regard an attack in the ' Record ' in the light of a testimonial. I was told that some of the opponents threatened to withdraw their accounts from Becket's bank, if they voted for me. Since writing this, the Coventry paper has come in ; by whom the Leeds paragraph was written I know not ; I suspect Sheepshanks. I am deeply gratified by the conduct of the people here ; they are all anxious for my welfare, and yet sorry to part with me. Is not this nice and kind and generous ? This, too, will render my remaining here the more comfortable, especially as they will know that it is only party violence that will exclude me.

From Mrs. Hook to Mr. and Mrs. Wood.

Coventry : 1837.

My dear Friends,—I received your letter during my solitude, and was quite comforted by it. Though I felt desperately anxious all the time the old boy was away, yet he is come back so well, so pleased, so frisky, and so tiresome, that I can hardly write a word for his coming and making impertinent remarks. His account of Leeds is satisfactory, and I feel that as a home it will be pleasant, though its distance from London must be a drawback. I suppose you will hear the result as soon as we do. I really

cannot help feeling anxious, in spite of my determination
to think either way the best.

Ever your truly attached Friend,

A. D. HOOK.

There remained only three days between his
departure from Leeds and the 20th, the day appointed for the election, and in this little interval
the opposition fired their last and largest gun. This
was a petition to the trustees against his appointment, signed by 400 persons. A copy of his letter
to the Bishop of Lichfield in 1830, deprecating his
presiding at a meeting of the Bible Society, was
apppended to the document. The following is the
memorial :—

To the Trustees of the Advowson of the Vicarage of Leeds.

We, the undersigned inhabitants of the parish of Leeds,
and members of the Established Church, beg leave respectfully to memorialise you upon the pending election to the
vacant vicarage. We have heard with considerable alarm
that there is every probability that the Rev. W. F. Hook
will obtain a majority of your suffrages. We beg to submit to you our decided opinion that, on account of the very
peculiar tenets maintained and published by that gentleman, such election will be attended with the most mischievous consequences to the interests of the Establishment
in this parish.

The following are some of the doctrines which Mr.
Hook avows in his published works, and which we consider
in the highest degree objectionable. He denies the right
of private judgment in matters of religion. He maintains
that Holy Scripture is an insufficient guide to salvation ;
and that no man ever did, and few ever could, form their

code of faith and morals from the Bible, and the Bible only. He virtually excludes Methodists and Dissenters of every name from the pale of Christianity. He is the avowed opponent of the British and Foreign Bible Society, and we have reason to believe that he is unfriendly to the Church Missionary Society and to the Society for Promoting Christianity amongst the Jews. He addressed an expostulatory letter to the Diocesan of his present Incumbency upon the occasion of his taking the chair at one of the meetings of the first, a copy of which we beg to subjoin.

Your memorialists observe, with unfeigned satisfaction, a growing disposition in the members of the Church of England, in this parish, to unite, as in a common cause, in the advancement of its interests. They beg respectfully, but firmly, to avow their conviction that the immediate effect of Mr. Hook's election will be to interrupt this holy harmony, by reviving those irritating discussions, the existence of which between her members has so long been the subject of regret with every true friend of the Church; thereby not only to open again that division within her own bosom which they had hoped would soon have been altogether obliterated, but ultimately to widen it into a hopeless and incurable schism. It is also observable, and your memorialists allude to the fact with the utmost pleasure, that the asperities of other classes of Christians in the parish against our Church have of late been considerably modified and softened down, and that many among them are disposed to listen to the strong arguments which may be adduced in her favour, and to attend upon her services. The effect of the election of a clergyman of Mr. Hook's avowed opinions upon such persons is sufficiently obvious. Having only been attracted thither by the prevalence of sentiments diametrically opposed to his, they will with proportionate force be repelled, and finally estranged, from her communion.

We do not wish to go too minutely into matters of objection; still less do we desire to take an offensive attitude, or do anything that may wear the appearance of dictation. We disclaim all motives save those arising from what we believe to be a christian duty. It is in this spirit that we would respectfully call upon you to consider the appointment about to be made, not merely as one of taste or expediency, not as one of personal feeling, but as one involving the everlasting welfare of souls. We would venture to add that your office was instituted for the benefit of the inhabitants ; and we earnestly hope and pray that you may so fulfil it as to promote the paramount object which we trust we all have in view.

This memorial, however, was instantly followed by a counter-declaration signed by about 300 persons.

To the Trustees of the Advowson of the Vicarage of Leeds.

March 17, 1837.

We, the undersigned frequenters of the Parish Church, and other friends of the Establishment generally, beg leave respectfully to address you on the subject of certain recent measures which have been taken to influence, if not to coerce, your choice, of a Vicar for this extensive parish. We wish to express to you that we have viewed the proceeding with considerable regret ; and that we utterly disclaim and disavow any participation in it. We sincerely trust that in the execution of your high duty you will set aside all such representations ; and we can assure you that we rest with the most perfect confidence in the rectitude of your judgment, and in your well-known and long-tried attachment to the doctrines and principles of the Church of England.

On Monday, March 20, the trustees assembled in the vestry for the purpose of election. All were present except Mr. John Hardy and Mr. Peter

Rhodes. Each wrote his own name on one side of a card, and on the other the name of the candidate for whom he voted. One of the trustees collected the cards, the sides on which the names of the electors were written being uppermost. When handed to the chairman they were reversed, so that he saw the names of the candidates only. Having examined the cards, the chairman, Mr. Henry Hall, said that the Rev. W. F. Hook was elected by sixteen trustees out of twenty-three. He then went into the choir and announced the result of the election to a large crowd of parishioners. He declared that the trustees had been influenced by the purest motives, and deprecated a hasty judgment of their choice. They had sought, and believed that they had found, a man of piety and learning, of amiable disposition and literary attainments; one who in the late scene of his labours had been indefatigable in ministering to the wants, spiritual and temporal, of all his parishioners.

The announcement and address was received by the assembly with much applause, only mingled with a few murmurs and faint cries of 'Stowell.' The church bells rang out a joyful peal, and Mr. Henry Hall started with a full heart to carry the good news to Coventry.

The feelings with which the recipient of the tidings was affected will best be gathered from the letters placed at the end of this chapter.

The sentiments of his old parishioners were well expressed in one of the principal local journals. 'It is with mingled feelings of triumph and regret,' wrote the 'Coventry Standard,' 'that we announce

that the Rev. W. F. Hook was on Monday last
elected Vicar of Leeds by a very decided majority of the trustees.   He will carry with him not
only the respect and good wishes, but the warm
gratitude, the individual personal affection, of a large
portion of the inhabitants of this city, both rich and
poor ; and although his future lot be cast far away
from those among whom he has ministered for
several years, yet he will ever live in their memories
a a most zealous and indefatigable minister, a
judicious and affectionate friend.'

This prediction has thus far been verified.   In
the brief but excellent sketch of his life which
appeared in the parish magazine of Trinity parish,
Coventry, in November 1875, one month after his
death, the writer says, ' Thirty-eight years have not
effaced from the grateful minds of his old parishioners
the remembrance of their Vicar.   A generation has
indeed grown up which knows him not, and yet his
name is so familiar to us all that we find it difficult
to realise the long lapse of time since he was living
and working in our parish.   The work he did in
Coventry has been permanent and abiding. . . . it
is almost impossible to over-estimate the manner in
which he quickened Church life.'   These are not
vain words.   How vividly he is remembered and
how deeply honoured by the aged, the writer of this
biography can testify, being under obligation to
many who have been as eager to impart information
concerning the work of their former pastor, as during
his life-time they were zealous to assist him in that
work.   The stained glass in the great west window
of their magnificent church is the visible proof of

the affection, gratitude, and respect of the parishioners of Holy Trinity for that Vicar who, in the
words of one who preached on the occasion of the
window being completed,[1] 'undertook his ministry
in days when earnestness in Church life was rare,'
and where manifested 'was frequently received with
aversion if not with contempt': who 'in much
difficulty, misapprehension, and misrepresentation
laid here the sound foundation of Church principles,
and commenced the system of parochial administration which has become more and more firmly established under his successors.'

He was instituted Vicar of Leeds on April 4,
and the next three months were occupied by the
painful and harassing process of severing his connexion with one place and forming it with another.

On Sunday, the 16th, he 'read himself in.' His
rich, powerful, melodious voice produced its full
effect upon the musical ears of the northern people,
and he had not proceeded far in the prayers before
a godly old Dissenter present was heard to say,
smiting his knee with his hand, 'He'll do; he'll do.'

On this Sunday he preached twice, enormous
crowds being present at both services. He was
labouring under a heavy cold, a very rare occurrence
with him, and had difficulty in speaking so as to
be heard, which was a great vexation to him in the
morning, as his sermon was mainly a declaration of
his principles, and of the line of conduct which his
parishioners were to expect from him. 'You see
before you,' he said, 'a firm, determined, consistent,
uncompromising, devoted, but I hope not unchari-

[1] Rev. H. W. Bellairs, June 24, 1877.

table, son, servant, and minister of the honoured Church of England. It is as a minister of the Church of England that I am placed here. I am *not* placed here to indulge in speculations of my own as to what *I* may think to be useful, or what *I* may think to be expedient—I am instituted under the Bishop to administer the discipline, the sacraments, and the doctrines of Christ as the Lord hath commanded, and as this Church and realm hath received the same. I am to labour for the salvation of souls and the edification of the Church, but *not* in ways and modes of my own devising, but according to the laws, the regulations, the spirit of the English Church. And immediately that I find that I cannot conscientiously adhere to those rules and act in that spirit, I shall tender my resignation to the Bishop, and feel myself bound, not only as a Christian but as a man of honour, to retire from a situation the duties of which I am unable to discharge. The Church is not infallible; but as we find her now existing in this country I believe her not to be in error, and my conduct shall always be regulated by her authorised decisions.' After pointing out the value of tradition as elucidating Scripture, and the supremacy of Scripture as the test of tradition, after declaring his intention not to 'select one or two doctrines, and representing these as all-sufficient, to overlook in carelessness or reject in rashness all the rest—for if this kind of preaching would suffice, why should the Bible be so thick a book, or rather such a large collection of books?'—after maintaining that through an unbroken episcopal succession the three Orders in the Church of England could satis-

factorily prove their commission to act as ambassa-
dors of Christ and stewards of the mysteries of
God, he concluded: 'And in asserting this shall I
give unnecessary offence to my Dissenting friends,
and many such I hope to have? I say, No. For
my part I think better things of the candid, honest,
conscientious Dissenter. By vindicating the doctrine and discipline of the Church of England I do
indeed by implication assert that he is in error.
But does he not do the same by us? Does not he
imply that we are in error, when he secedes from
our communion, or refuses to conform to it? This
he must do if he would justify his secession. And
if he does think us in error, he will never find in
me one who will censure him for explaining to his
hearers the ground of his dissent. However erroneous I may consider those grounds, I shall ever
contend that he is more than justified, that he is
bound to state them honestly and fairly to his
people: only let all things be done in charity,
gentleness, and courtesy. What I ask then for
myself is no more than what I am fully prepared to
concede. . . . One of the great blessings of a full
and free toleration is this: that we may now all of
us contend fully and freely for the truth, and the
whole truth. As a lover of truth then I am a friend
to toleration. When the law assumed that all men
were Churchmen, and on that account compelled all
men to attend the service of the Church, the chari-
tably disposed would, of course, be ready to sacrifice
many portions of truth to satisfy the scruples of
weaker brethren. *Now* we are not required to
make *any* such sacrifices: we may now keep our

eyes steadily fixed upon the truth, and if any man think that the truth is not with us, he suffers no hardship in withdrawing from us. And as a lover of peace, as well as of truth, I thus openly, fairly, and honourably avow my principles. Depend upon it we promote peace, not by falsifying facts, and telling men that we *do* agree when we do *not* agree, for this only leads to endless disputes, but by stating clearly and firmly what our differences are, and by then agreeing to differ thereon. Those persons who thrust themselves into a promiscuous throng are liable to inconveniences and quarrels : but draw a line decidedly between disagreeing parties, and then over that line of demarcation opposite parties may cordially shake hands. With Dissenters, therefore, in religious matters I may not act, but most readily will I number them among my private friends. Never in my almsgiving will I make any distinction of persons : in such cases Samaritan and Jew shall be both alike to me. I *will* say to them, and I will *not* take offence if they retort the saying upon me, that I think them in error : but every person who happens to oppose what we hold as the truth is not of necessity a wilful opposer of truth as such. Their love of truth may be as great as ours. Our *principle*, therefore, will be the same, though the application of that principle may be different, and for our common principle we may love and respect, while we may sometimes oppose, each other. We must indeed all of us learn to forbear one another and to forgive one another, even as Christ our blessed Redeemer, who died for our sins and rose again for our justification, hath forgiven us.'

I have quoted rather largely from this inaugural sermon, not only as being in itself instructive, but also because this bold and manly declaration of his principles, at the outset of his career, procured for him the respect of adversaries with whom he might otherwise have been brought into unpleasant collision. He adhered without wavering to the principles thus early avowed, and was consequently saved from the misery experienced by amiable but vacillating characters who seek to conciliate and please all, and too often end in exasperating all. One of the local papers, referring to the sermon, remarked : ' The Vicar has already made a strong and favourable impression upon his parishioners. He has clearly expounded his doctrines and developed his plans. With regard to the latter there will naturally be a variety of opinions : but it must be universally admitted that he commenced the duties of his office with manly candour, that his abilities are first-rate, and that his demeanour is most kind and conciliating.'

The month of June was the last of his residence at Coventry. A parting address in May, signed by thirty-three male and thirty-two female teachers of the Sunday school, concluded with these touching words : ' We cannot omit to congratulate you upon the success with which your exertions have been crowned by the great increase in the number of communicants, and the flourishing state of our schools ; and at the same time to express our warmest thanks for the spiritual instruction and consolation we have received from you as our revered pastor and affectionate friend. That the blessing of the Lord God Almighty may rest upon you and yours, that the Spirit of Truth may guide you even to the end, and that you and we likewise may be of that happy number who shall be blessed at the coming of our Lord, is the hearty desire and humble prayer of the teachers of Trinity Church Sunday School.' The Vicar ended his reply by saying : 'My parting injunction to you is, Love the Church. You live in evil days, when evil tongues are railing against all that is great and good and holy in the land. May I always hear that the teachers of these schools continue to be what they now are, loyal, dutiful, zealous children of the dear old Church. May you grow in grace as you grow in years. May you increase in faith and all the fruits of faith, and to this end I exhort you to be earnest in prayer, regular in your attendance on the duties of the sanctuary—frequent communicants. Let us all persevere in this course and then our parting will not be an eternal one : we shall all meet before the throne of God and of the Lamb, where those who meet meet to part no more. You have often received my blessing, and you have been taught to regard it as the blessing of one com-missioned by God to bless His people. With my blessing therefore I now conclude. The peace of God,' &c.

On June 12 he preached his last sermon at Coventry. There were not many dry eyes in the vast congregation when in the well-known voice, unrivalled in sweetness and pathos, to which his feelings on the occasion lent an additional tenderness, he said : 'And now I have finished my ministry in

this parish. My friends—for you are my friends,
and, thanks be to God, I know not an enemy in the
parish—my friends, who have made so much allowance for my many deficiencies, who have received
so very kindly the little good of which God in His
mercy has used me as the instrument; my young
friends whom I have trained in the way of truth;
teachers of the Sunday school, members of the
vestry (may you always continue to be as united a
body as you have been during the last nine years);
you who have assisted me in visiting the sick and
needy; you, with whom in your sorrows I have
wept and who in my sorrows have wept with me;
you whom I have been the means of reconciling
after disagreements; my poorer brethren whom I
have ever held in honour; my elderly friends with
whom I have taken sweet counsel; my Christian
friends, whose sacrifice of prayer and praise it has
been my blessed duty to offer to the throne of grace,
whom through my ministry Christ has fed with the
bread of life—friends one and all—my prayer to you
is, may God deal kindly with you, as ye have dealt
kindly with me and mine: my exhortation is, those
things which ye have learned and received and
heard of me do, and the God of peace shall be with
you, for you have heard of me, not my own con-
jectures, but the words of truth as the Church has
received them.'

Capacious as is the church of the Holy Trinity
it could not contain all the people who thronged to
it on that Sunday evening, and hundreds waited
outside to give their Vicar a parting shake of the
hand, and to exchange a few farewell words. And

so he departed, full of zeal and energy, full of high aims and aspirations, full of confidence, not in himself, but in the Master whose he was and whom he served. The Evangelical party in Leeds and throughout the country were dejected and apprehensive, but the ' Record,' writing more in sorrow than in anger, counselled quiet resignation to the inevitable : they had done all they could to prevent so calamitous an appointment, and now that it was made in spite of them, it only remained for them to pray that it might be overruled by God for the good of His Church and the spiritual welfare of the great community at Leeds. The gratitude of the Church is due to the ' Record ' for recommending a prayer to which such an abundant answer has been vouchsafed.

To his Wife—A Day of Discomfort.

Coventry : February 23, 1837.

My dearest Love,—If you were in the dumps when you wrote I shall be able to pay you in kind. I have a cold, which always depresses me. Tom Minster is out, and all those who help me in visiting the sick are ill. Sixteen sick persons demand what I have not physical strength to give, daily visiting. I have just returned, completely wet through, from trudging all over the parish, after having performed services, baptisms, and funerals. At the last the pitiless storm drenched me. I think I should have been in despair, if Russfield had not very kindly offered to visit some of the people for me. I had come home, hoping for two hours' rest before going to deliver my lecture ; but I have come to a fire nearly out, and have letters to answer, not all of them the most agreeable. Here is one from my mother, saying that Georgiana has been seriously ill.

I should certainly go over and see them, but besides my lecture to-night, I have a sermon for to-morrow, and three in prospect for Sunday, for Woodward is engaged, and Sheepshanks is unwell. . . . Here is also a letter from a Mr. Robert Hall, another of the trustees, asking whether if I were appointed, I should consider it 'a call.' I shall answer him much in the manner I answered Dr. Barnes. At my time of life, approaching forty with a constitution of fifty, and nerves shattered with those dreadful fits, it is natural to think twice before I determine to break up entirely new ground. I had never thought of going north. I had always expected to settle either in this neighbourhood or in London. But I now heartily hope that we may obtain Leeds. I foresee that if we remain here, the cares of a straitened income will be fatal to our happiness. . . . I do not expect to see you back next week, for I am morally certain that you will soon quite break up. You have undertaken more than you can get through. But I will not go on this melancholy strain. I am worried, over-worked, chilled, and, in short, as you were when you wrote. By the time you receive this I may be better. I am almost sorry I let Minster go. *I* had not a single holiday the first four years I was in orders.

To W. P. Wood, Esq.—Self-examination.

Coventry : March 10, 1837.

My dearest Friend,—The questions put by his cate-chist to Mr. Hall [1] have sent me to the duty of self exami-nation. His catechist is a right worthy man, such as my heart loves ; he has heard that I am an ungodly wretch, and he wishes to prevent my doing mischief. Surely he is justified in this. I have carefully examined myself as to the motives he attributes to me ; I will tell you the result. 'Party-spirit': now I do confess that I find myself to be a little too much influenced by that ; mine is a falling

---

[1] See above, p. 309.

party, and I feel a little complacent in adhering to it ; and
I fear that I might do as the worthy catechist has done,
occasionally attribute a wrong motive to another, in the
heat of my zeal ; of this I repent, and by God's grace will
amend.   But certainly party-zeal has not been for sixteen
years my motive, in labouring as I have laboured for Christ,
and His Church ; for if ever party-feelings are excited,
they almost immediately cool, and I feel sorry for any
excesses of which I have been guilty.   However, the impu-
tation of this motive to me, though incorrect, shall make
me very watchful for the future.

Next comes 'restlessness of temperament'; here I am
certainly not guilty, for indolence is the besetting sin of my
natural man.   You know not how very loth I am to quit
my easy chair, to go about my Father's business in my
parish : you cannot conceive the pain it frequently is to
me to act the prominent part I do in the clerical affairs of
the district.

'Ambition': when I was ambitious, it was of literary
fame, which was the only fame I cared for ; to renounce all
hopes of literary distinction as I did, when I entered into
orders was pain and grief to me, but I had grace to do it.
As to professional honours I value them not a rush ; were
I desirous of them, I should be much more likely to attain
them by staying where I am, than by seeking to go to Leeds.
I am not insensible to the advantages of station, but my sole
wish for any advancement of that kind would be, not selfish, but to extend my usefulness, by giving greater weight
to any arguments among those of my younger brethren
whom it is my great delight to lead.   You cannot imagine a
person who cares less for these things than I do.

'Vanity': on this point I have suspected myself, but
certainly my vanity would never lead me to any great exertions.   I rather pique myself on having formed a just estimate
of my own powers, and that is a very low one.   I fall so infinitely short of what I intend in all that I do, that I have
never done anything without being plunged into despond-
ence ; and therefore a little praise instead of puffing me up

encourages me. It makes me feel that while I know that I have failed, yet that I have not failed so entirely as I feared ; I dread disgrace more than I covet praise. Now in whatever degree those faults may influence me, unknown to myself, we may easily find other motives for my sixteen years of labour. You know what my temper was in boyhood, and you know what it is now ; it seems to me sometimes as if a miracle had been wrought in me, my temper has become so improved. People will not believe me sometimes when I tell them how bad my temper was ; and they see how well I am able to keep it under severe provocations. I have had other passions in my time to contend with ; I had a very bad soil to cultivate, but by the grace of God I am what I am, still a sinful, alas! my dear Wood, a very, very sinful creature, but one who has found grace, and who has grown in grace ; and when I feel and know what great things the Saviour has done for me, I have only to ask you not to consider me as a brute beast, in order to make you certain that I must be actuated by zeal for my dear Master's service. Gratitude alone would inflame my love, and love inflamed would urge an eager mind on to action. Indeed I think at times that nothing but a regular education and a keen sense of the ridiculous would keep me from fanaticism. Gratitude to my God, the Father, Son, and Holy Ghost, is sufficient to inflame my love for Him, the Holy Trinity, and His Church ; and common feelings of humanity would urge me to endeavour to procure for others the great blessings I have enjoyed and do enjoy myself. If Mr. Hall's catechist knew how much more has been done, because needed, for my poor soul than for that of most men, he would not have sought for inferior motives to account for my conduct. To me much has been forgiven, and therefore I love much. Will you pardon all this egotism ? you have always been my father confessor, and I think it right to lay the whole case before you now, because, as you have doubtless been sponsor for my piety to Mr. Hall, I wish to let you see whether you can safely stand up for me. But I am still so very conscious of the indwelling of sin in this mortal body of mine, that I would not have you say much. I know that many better persons may be obtained for Leeds than I am, but certainly there can be none more desirous of doing his duty to his God, his Saviour, and his Church.

From Robert Hall, Esq., Congratulatory on His Election to the Vicarage.

Leeds : March 20, 1837.

My dear Mr. Vicar,—My father will have informed you how the Almighty has disposed our hearts to confer upon you a station of much responsibility. May He turn it to the everlasting benefit of thousands of immortal souls and your own welfare, both here and hereafter.

My father relieves me from the necessity of writing to you at any considerable length, though I shall probably do so when my spirits have subsided into their ordinary course. I am still too much agitated to write in a business-like manner. You will be pleased to hear that, notwithstanding the attempt at agitation, the announcement of your election was very favourably received by a numerous assemblage of parishioners who were collected in the chancel awaiting the result. My father of course will consult with you as to the proper period of your making your appearance here. One of the churches is to be reopened on the 30th. I have no doubt you will be requested to officiate, but if the time now proposed be too early, I have little doubt it might be postponed for a short time. . . . Wherever we may be, I need hardly assure you that my wife and I shall have the greatest pleasure in being of every possible service to Mrs. Vicaress and yourself. That God may bless you both and make you blessings to others is, I assure you, the reiterated prayer of

Yours very faithfully,

Robert Hall.

To W. P. Wood, Esq.

Coventry : March 21, 1837.

My dearest William and not less dear Charlotte,—Mr. Hall senior, a man whom I can take to my heart, has just arrived with the presentation to Leeds. I am stupified, and therefore cannot express my feelings. I am really overwhelmed ; the thought of leaving dear Coventry is full of sadness ; the responsibility of my new position alarms me : thus I may be pardoned for not actually feeling joy. Pray for me, pray for us, my dearest friends ; and God Almighty grant that our new promotion may be attended by a corresponding growth in grace. I have, of course, many letters to write, and two services daily during this week, so no more at present from

Your devoted grateful Friend.

To Rev. E. Gibson.

Coventry : March 23, 1837.

My dear Friend,—Understanding that you were apprised of my success by my most kind and zealous friend Sheepshanks, I did not write yesterday, as I had many friends at a distance impatient to hear from me. But did you argue from this that I am ungrateful for all your judicious exertions on my behalf ? No ! or you would not be the Edward Gilson I love—and love especially because he always finds out the virtues and is rather blind to the faults of his friends. Believe me that I shall never forget your kindness.

To my wife and me this is not pleasure without alloy. The thought of leaving dear Coventry, where we have so many friends, where we have spent so many happy years, where we have so many kind parishioners, where one blessed child is buried, is a thought full of grief. But so is everything in this world ; all happiness must be of a mixed nature, or this world would be heaven.

Remember me, dear Gibson, in your prayers, and pray that I may bear in mind the verse of Gregory Nazianzen,

ὅτ᾽ εὐπλοεῖς μάλιστα μέμνησο ζάλης.

Your ever grateful Friend.

To Rev. T. H. Tragett.

Coventry : March 23, 1837.

My dear Tragett, ... Be it known to you, that out of twenty-three trustees sixteen voted for me, though there were thirty-five candidates. The 'Evangelicals' represented me to be a gambler, a drunkard, and a Papist; at last they found out that I was a Whig! They were most fierce against the Oxford Tracts, making them speak all sorts of heresies ; but then one of my supporters silenced them by saying that I was not one of the writers of those Tracts, and that therefore I was not to be judged by them : but it was urged, 'he is known to be the friend of Pusey, Keble, and Newman.' 'Yes, and this is one of his testimonials.' What higher honour can a man have on this earth? Will you thank that apostolic man Keble for writing in my favour, as I am told he did.

I am, your most affectionate Friend.

From the Bishop of Ripon.

40 Devonshire Place : March 23, 1837.

Dear Sir,—Allow me to offer you my sincere congratulations upon your election to the vacant vicarage of Leeds. From the prevalence of Dissent and from the variety of opinions in matters of religion which exist there, it may be considered as the most important cure in the diocese of Ripon ; but from what I hear of your power of conciliating those who differ from you, without surrendering your own principles, I trust that we shall before long see that influence beneficially exerted in your new sphere.

In my Archdeacon, Mr. Musgrave, you will find a person most able and most willing to render you any assistance in his power on your first entry upon your new duties, and I regret that I am not at present in the country to afford you my services also—but be assured that my prayers shall not be wanting for a blessing on your labours.

Believe me, dear Sir, your faithful friend and servant,

C. T. RIPON.

To W. P. Wood, Esq.

Coventry : March 30, 1837.

My dearest Friend, ... I cannot but think it very mean and paltry, if not something worse, on the part of your wife, to presume on her merits as being my patroness and as having got me a living for the purpose of indulging in gross personalities. The trustees who came here had indeed received such accounts of my personal appearance that one of them said, ' We expected to see a Saracen's Head get up into the pulpit, whereas we found *rather a good-looking man* than otherwise.' So to settle disputes I thought, I'll paint it, and shame the fools. The likeness is considered admirable. An ugly fellow I must confess I am. The artist came to me and asked me to sit, as he wished to publish the engravings. I said, No. He said that if he succeeded it would be a very great thing for him ; and then charity whispered, why should not he as well as I have some of the good things of Leeds ? He was to give me the painting ; but as I will not give you what costs me nothing, I shall make him a present of his ten guineas ; what is the use of having money, but to make those around us happy ? and how pleased Mrs. Rosenburg will be when Mr. Rosenburg goes home and counts out the money he did not expect to receive ; and then who knows but what they will remember their benefactor in their prayers ; and thus I shall have made a righteous use of mammon. Though

I write pleasantly, I am very much depressed with the thought of what is awaiting me. Firmness, gentleness, patience, these are the weapons with which I shall have to fight. When my firmness is displayed, then there will be fierce attacks, foes will rage, the crafty will try flattery, friends will frown and call me obstinate ; you will hear all manner of evil against your friend. Then I shall up with the shield of gentleness ; they may rage, but I shall seek for grace to remain calm, firm in principle, courteous in conduct. At last patience will have her perfect work: the good among my opponents, seeing that I will not go round to them, will come round to me. I have confidence in my success, if only I have health and strength for two or three years. My only annoyance is about that dear good man Robert Hall ; he thinks that I have only to go to Leeds and all the Evangelicals will be at my feet. I know them better ; when they find that I do not renounce my principles and embrace theirs, then their fury will be great ; by gentleness I intend to appease it, but do impress upon dear excellent Hall's mind that I must have time ; perhaps two or three years.

Yours devotedly.

To W. P. Wood, Esq.—First Sermon at Leeds.

Armley House, Leeds: April 19, 1837.

My dearest Friend,—I send a line because I know that you and your lady will wish to hear of us. Most calamitously, I was so hoarse on Sunday that, though surrounded by an immense mob, I could not do more than whisper my sermon. To my annoyance, however, there were reporters present from the three newspapers, and I was strongly urged to print my sermon by Mr. Hall, on behalf of the trustees. As I had not the remotest idea of printing it when I wrote it, this is a bore ; but as it will most likely be misrepresented in the newspapers, I thought I had better send it to the press, which I have accordingly done.

After so much success and flattery, I look upon this failure (for a complete failure it was) as a merciful Providence; it is a warning to me not to be too confident in myself; it tells me on whose strength I must wholly and solely rely. I am happy to say that I did not feel any annoyance whatever from such feelings as might arise from mortified vanity; I have regarded the failure as a mercy, and not been annoyed at it the least, except so far as I failed in my wish to let my mode of conduct be known. This will be remedied by the publication. I look upon all this with some complacency, as it proves to me that I have grown in grace. Indeed I can conscientiously say that all that has occurred of late has been as yet to my spiritual improvement; I have not so much of youthful enthusiasm and fervour as I once had, but I have more childish reliance. We like everything we see here extremely; the church has capabilities about it, and I hope to turn it inside out. The services of the church cannot now be properly performed in it; it is like a conventicle built up in a church. I have arranged to keep a third curate, and my curates will cost me 260*l.* a year, which is a large deduction from my income.

Advice to his Sister about the Spiritual State of one of her Friends.

Armley House, Leeds: April 19, 1837.

My dearest Mother, ... Georgiana's poor friend's mind is in a morbid state, and do what she will, she will be unhappy until God's good time arrive for making a change in it. The fault seems to be, both on her part and on Georgiana's, that they are looking for some display of *feeling*, which must naturally depend on temperament. Let her rather think on her *actions*; God has given her grace, through the merits of the Saviour in whom she believes, to lead a good life, and that is an earnest that He will give her, for her Saviour's sake, life everlasting. It is certainly very sinful on her part never to have communicated; and most probably it is on that account that she is now deprived of spiritual comfort. Let her amend on this point, but let her not suppose that she is to find immediately all the comfort that a regular communicant enjoys, though this does sometimes happen. Georgiana should bear in mind that this is a case for special grace, and that prayer for her friend will be of more avail than reading or talking to her ; but she may read for her comfort the account of our Saviour's agony, and show to her from thence that the withholding of spiritual comfort for a time is not a proof of God's disfavour.

LETTER FROM LORD HATHERLEY
TO THE EDITOR.

My dear Nephew,—I write in fulfilment of my promise to supply you with a brief account of the school and college life of my late dear friend, your father-in-law. Our friendship began in 1812, soon after I had become a commoner at Winchester, and continued to his death in 1875. It commenced almost at first sight ; though nothing could be imagined more improbable than that our several ages, dispositions, prejudices, and family training should have allowed such a result.

In the first place when we met each other in 1812 at Dr. Gabell's school, which was associated with the ancient foundation of William of Wykeham at Winchester by the style of 'Commoners,' 'Hook Senior' (for we knew no Christian names) was over fourteen years of age, and I was not yet eleven ; he was tall, strong, and impetuous, I was a short, small, and ordinarily quiet child. He had been imbued from childhood with High Church notions as they were then understood, and with the genuine old Tory doctrines of the political party then in power. I had been brought up in the Church of England, but my political instruction had been in what was then thought to be the radical school, and these impressions had been strengthened by very constant reading, even in childhood, of the ' Morning Chronicle' and ' Cobbett's Register.' To this it may be added, that the positions in life of our parents were wide apart. His father was a beneficed clergyman, and a Canon or Prebendary (as he was then called) of Winchester Cathedral, and his career, through the influence of his father-in-law, Sir Walter Farquhar, had been attended by the favour and personal notice of the Prince Regent ; whilst my father was engaged in business in the City of London, and was, not long after this time, honoured by the personal confidence of the Princess of Wales, the Regent's ill-used wife.

Besides these discrepancies, both ' Hook Senior' and his brother Robert had brought with them from Tiverton school but little acquaintance with Latin and Greek, and on the part of my friend I may say but little disposition to acquire it ; whilst I found from an early period perhaps too much pleasure in entering into competition with others in these studies whenever the opportunity was offered me.

Notwithstanding the improbability of our forming a friendship for life, it was by God's providence so ordered that from December 1812, or thereabouts, till October 1875, when he was taken from us, we scarcely passed a fortnight without either meeting or hearing from each other by letter.

Our friendship began in a most unsentimental manner. His backwardness in study had occasioned him to be still in a low form of the school, and therefore subject to fagging, and we first foregathered at a large fire in Commoners' Hall, being engaged, under the system of domestic slavery which then existed, in preparing the breakfasts of our respective masters. This led to our interchanging such thoughts upon the pursuits most agreeable to us as our young minds could suggest, and I soon found that, though backward in the studies of the school, he was very forward and vigorous in mind.

He was far beyond, not only myself, but most other boys nearer to his own age in the school in his acquaintance with English Literature. He was especially well acquainted with the great works of Shakspeare and Milton, and with other standard authors of English poetry, whilst he had already begun, under his father's roof, to read some of the then accepted authors in Divinity. At that time, I think, the works of Archbishop Secker, and Nelson's ' Fasts and Festivals ' were most commonly referred to by him. As a proof that I am not antedating, by defect of memory, his early acquaintance with Shakspeare, I may mention that I have since his death been allowed to possess myself of the very edition in which we often read together, and which on the fly leaf bears his name with the date 1811.

In a few months after our return to school in January 1813 we became inseparable. I was able to assist him in the ordinary course of school study, which service he more than repaid by forming my mind to an enjoyment of our English authors, and an appreciation of Shakspeare and Milton not common in early boyhood. Besides these, our favourite authors, we read together as years passed on any new works that made their mark. He was plentifully supplied with these from home. Amongst others I recollect Walter Scott's successive poems, Maturin's 'Bertram' and Milman's 'Fazio'; the latter, however, was, I think, sent to me by Hook after he had gone to Oxford. But whilst thus assisting me in the perusal of our English classics, he did me the yet greater service of forming my mind to a genuine delight in reading for its own sake, whereas the desire of excelling rather than a delight in excellence had been my motive to exertion. And even now looking back on our long course of life side by side, I own his moral superiority in this respect. He was singularly free from the low ambition of surpassing others, and though there may at one time have been some degree of self-indulgence in his avoiding the labour of acquiring knowledge through the medium of languages with which he was not familiar, yet even in his schooldays he conscientiously encountered this labour when convinced that it was his duty so to do, irrespective of any competition with others.

I will not enter into details of the progress of our friendship from year to year, but may briefly state the course of our school life. I passed him in the school owing to his comparative indifference to competition in the study of Latin and Greek; but when I had reached the sixth or highest form in the school, I strongly urged on him the desirableness of an effort to reach that form in which we should then pursue our studies together, and at the same time he would have the advantage of being solely under the direct tuition of Dr. Gabell, the Head Master. The regulation established by Dr. Gabell facilitated such an exertion. Any boy who had once attained a place in the form immediately below the sixth was offered promotion at any time to the sixth form on condition that he passed a voluntary examination in a book of Livy and one Greek play. I had myself been thus promoted over the heads of several boys otherwise before me in the school, and I succeeded in directing Hook's mind to the same course. He had no great difficulty in achieving our object. I went over with him the same book of Livy and the same play, the Medea of Euripides, as I had myself taken up for my examination, and we had the great pleasure of pursuing exactly the same studies together for the residue of his school career, that is till 1817, or more than half a year.

Meanwhile our English readings had become more and more frequent, especially during the summer evenings, when we used to build ourselves an arbour for the summer in a thick hawthorn tree, and taking our several editions of Shakspeare with us, read out by turns the various parts of each play. Besides his pocket edition, already referred to, he possessed one by Reed in twenty-one volumes, the whole of which (notes and all) we swallowed if we did not digest them. In the year 1814 (I think) he instituted an 'Order of St. Shakspeare and St. Milton;' April 23, Shakspeare's birthday and death-day, being our chief festival. Of this Order we two were styled the Founders and Knights Grand Masters, and to it were admitted a few of our common friends as Knights Grand Crosses, amongst whom was the present Sir W. Heathcote.[1] We did

---

[1] The following is the description of the Order copied from the blank page in one of the volumes of the pocket Shakspeare:—

not omit to read prose authors, and the 'Spectator' was a book in frequent use.

From what I have already stated you will readily understand that he obtained but few school distinctions. A book prize attended his successful effort to reach the sixth form *per saltum,* and he gained the silver medal for public speaking, being undoubtedly the best orator of the school. He was also at the end of his career distinguished as our champion, and was selected to fight any inhabitant of the town (including on one occasion some soldiers of a regiment in the barracks) in case of infringement by them of our privileges.

Dr. Johnson has said that a debt of gratitude is due to the memory of all schoolmasters by whom men who have distinguished themselves, as did my friend, were trained ; and I cheerfully and gratefully acknowledge the debt we both owed to Dr. Gabell as an instructor. That, indeed, was the only title (*informator*) that he enjoyed as connected with the foundation: the Warden (at that time Dr. Huntingford, Bishop of Hereford)

A List of the Knights of the Most Poetical Order of SS. Shakspeare and Milton.

W. F. HOOK, W. P. WOOD,	Founders and Knights Grand Masters.
HENRY MINCHIN, * EDWARD AUSTEN, WILLIAM HEATHCOTE, PHILIP HEWETT,	Knights Grand Crosses.

By His Majesty's Command.

W. F. HOOK,
W. P. WOOD, } Secretaries of State.

GOD SAVE KING

SHAKSPEARE.

* Better known as Austen Leigh, a nephew of Miss Austen the novelist, and author of a memoir of her.

being the chief governor of Wykeham's College. But of Commoners' Gabell was the 'master,' and I always thought him very deficient in the qualifications necessary for that post. His chief deficiency was a total distrust of the boys, which led him never to believe their statements. It was this defect which (subsequently to Hook's leaving the school) led to a rebellion. But as a teacher Dr. Gabell excelled. He possessed the happy art of thoroughly searching out every boy's ability and industry, by methods of his own, with which I ought not to encumber your pages, and further he felt, and therefore conveyed to generous and intelligent young minds, an enthusiastic love of the best classical literature. Learning by heart formed a prominent part of the teaching of the school, and this circumstance probably in a great measure kept Hook back in his progress. His memory was not accurate in details, while the amount of recitations from Latin and Greek poets of which some boys were capable was portentous. A noble lord is yet living [1] who committed to memory the whole (I think) of Virgil's Æneid and several books of Homer. Winchester has always been a hard working school. Accuracy was insisted upon ; work was not slurred over, nor was brilliancy considered to be any compensation for indolence. The school has produced hard workers through life. The Archbishopric of Canterbury and the Speakership of the House of Commons have been each held once, and the Great Seal three times, by Wykeham-ists within my memory, and I have sat in a Cabinet where three out of sixteen members had been educated at Winchester.

[1] Lord Saye and Sele.

As boys we all took much interest in politics, though I think out of 200 probably less than one-quarter were Whigs, and I was almost a solitary Radical. Hook established a Parliament which sat in the deserted Palace of the Bishop. I think that of its members only Sir Alexander Malet and myself have survived. Our debates were no doubt highly esteemed by ourselves : they were perhaps none the worse for the absence of reporters, or even a gallery.

I have not yet noticed the tie which more especially bound my dear friend and myself together from boyhood to age. It so happened that I became a prefect at the early age of fifteen. The prefects were entrusted with the discipline and management of the school. There were eight of them in Commoners presiding over 142 other boys, and two in each week were responsible for the general order of the school. It had become almost a rule that these eight boys should receive at stated times the Holy Communion. I had not been confirmed, and this led me to think very seriously about the whole subject ; and first whether I ought, as it were compulsorily, to take so serious a step at all, and secondly whether I could properly do so before confirmation. This latter point, however, was, shortly before the time for communicating, set at rest by the Warden of the College, Bishop Huntingford, holding a confirmation in the College Chapel. I submitted my anxieties on this head to my friend, as I did all my other difficulties in matters of religion. I need not dwell more on the subject. Suffice it to say that he consulted his father and some others of the clergy upon it, supplied me with books on the subject of Confirmation and Holy Communion, instructed and encouraged me in every way; and thus my first Communion was the special cement of our life-enduring friendship, and a foundation was laid on which, notwithstanding every difference of opinion in matters less grave, we could rest as on a rock.

During our holidays we used to see each other occasionally only. In the winters of 1815 and 1816 my father, having been elected Lord Mayor for two successive years, resided at the Mansion House. Hook, when in town, lived in Conduit Street at the house of Sir Walter Farquhar, his grandfather. He contrived a plan of our meeting for an hour or two each day in St. Paul's Cathedral. At that time anyone could be admitted there on payment of twopence, and was allowed to remain as long as he pleased, and many a time did we pace the aisles together for hours when the service was over. In the summer holidays my family usually resided at Little Strawberry Hill, Twickenham, and at times Hook was in that neighbourhood at Roehampton, staying with his uncle, Mr. Thomas, afterwards Sir Thomas, Farquhar.

The first letter of a series which continued without interruption for nearly sixty years was written to me by Hook on December 29, 1816. It is dated from Winchester, where his father was then residing as Prebendary, and addressed to me at the Mansion House. I copy a small part of it. He was still a school-boy, but intended (as ultimately was the case) to leave Winchester School at the end of the long half-year terminating in July.

I went on Thursday to Southampton to see Mrs. Siddons, whom I heard so much ridiculed here by two of her acquaintances that I scarcely expected to be able to tolerate her; but I found her most kind and pleasant. She said she had known me when I was a child, and was happy to renew the acquaintance. In the evening, after dinner, she gave me my choice of what she should read to me, and I chose Macbeth, which she read through, passing over a few uninteresting scenes. She acted Macbeth quite as well as Lady Macbeth, and of course surpassed Kean in every respect. Though she is sixty-two yet she looked most beautiful when she was reading, and I can very well fancy her once being ' with matchless beauty crowned.' But what I liked most to hear, was Satan's speech to the Sun, in Milton, which she read most charmingly : her voice and manner suits entirely with Milton. I took a long walk the next morning, with Miss Siddons, who is a very sensible, agreeable girl, and some people think very handsome. Mrs. Siddons was very condescending, and in talking over several of Shakspeare's plays, showed a great deal of taste, learning, and judgment. She took, however, the part of Lady Macbeth, in which I could not quite agree with her, and her daughter helped me to defend poor Macbeth, against whom Mrs. Siddons was rather spiteful. . . . By the bye, I shall have free access to John Kemble's library, which you know, according to Steeven's account, is the best in England for old books and valuable and scarce editions, not of classics, but of old English authors.

At the beginning of February 1817 I received another letter from him, of which I give a short extract in order to show the passionate enthusiasm which his affection always evinced towards me. It was poured forth in prose and verse, and from youth to age, and I will only give this specimen of what you and all he loved well know to have been his characteristic : the most unselfish, ardent devotion to his friends. He refers to his returning to school a week before I should be there, owing to his father leaving Winchester, to explain which it may be mentioned that the school was open for the reception of the foundation boys who returned a week before the commoners were obliged to do so.

. . . . I shall not be able to avoid going to Commoners on Sunday night, and thus I shall spend a whole week without you; you may well imagine how miserable I shall be, for I could better spare you in any other place than that in which every turn I take will bring you to my remembrance; but stay as long as you can, for you may be assured that I can have no greater pleasure than knowing that you enjoy yourself; and if you could, I would not wish you to hurry back into Commoners on my account as I do not reckon myself at all selfish, but I *think* and hope that I feel more pleasure in your happiness than in my own, and I only write this that you may take compassion, and whenever you have a moment to spare and *remember me*, may just send me a line of consolation, even if it is every day, and but a line. I write to you now because I am very dull, too dull to read even our dear Shakspeare, and I want to complain, and so pitch upon you to be the person to be plagued with hearing my complaints. I had an offer of going to Oriel this instant, there being a sudden vacancy, and not going back to Winchester, but I much prefer returning: indeed I should be wretched if I did not go back this half-year, for though Oxford may have some greater comforts than Winchester, yet the enjoying your company at the one and not at the other would make the one most delightful, the other most uncomfortable, and though we shall separate at the end of next half-year, the thought of not spending one more half-year with you, would have made me wretched. Gabell most *strongly* advised my staying, and I am glad to stay.

When the end of the long half-year arrived, July 1817, we underwent our first real parting, and very sad it was. We paced the long galleries at the back of the bedrooms in Commoners for an hour or two in great grief. In the holidays he met with some slight accident, and I went from Twickenham to see him in London, after which he wrote me a letter, of which I have copied a small part to show the extreme warmth of his feelings in return for a very slight service.

My most beloved Friend,—I cannot possibly wait an instant, without expressing to you my deep and heartfelt gratitude for your conduct towards me during the last two days. Had you not before this had possession of my heart, your late kindness would certainly have given you a just title to my affection. Indeed I do not repent of my foolish action, since by that means I enjoyed so very much of your society, and since owing to that, I spent two of the happiest days that I ever did spend. Again, my dearest Wood, let me express my gratitude to you for foregoing the pleasures of your holidays, and shutting yourself up in the room of a poor sick fellow.

I returned to Winchester in September 1817, and in November received a letter from him referring to a squib which he had sent to the 'Sun' newspaper. He had at all times much of the exuberant humour of his Uncle Theodore, subdued as years went on by the graver realities of his life, but always ready to break forth when he was in the company of an intimate friend. I insert the first portion only of this letter.

I have become an author already. On Sunday last I sent a squib to the 'Sun' newspaper which it has published in yesterday's edition. The name of it was, 'The Meeting of Jacobins.' I will send you the paper if I can get one. I ought not to send you a copy as there is in it 'The Lord M——r and Jacobins of the City of London. The Lord M——r returned thanks.' Tell me directly if you are sulky. I tell you honestly, I am not certain whether it was not an interpolation of the 'Sun,' because it is not in my foul copy, and because they have thought fit to insert a puff at the end of it in favour of their paper, but I plainly tell you that I should have inserted it if I had thought of it, but I rather think I did not. Not that I think your father a Jacobin *precisely* ; but as I call Lord Grey, under the title of Lord Dapple, a Jacobin, and likewise Mr. Brougham, you will not be angry. . . . I shall cut you up some time or other. God bless you. I love you with all my heart and soul.

I spent the Christmas holidays of 1817 in Paris, whither my father summoned me and my younger brother from Winchester. Whilst there I received a letter from him dated Winchester, December 30, A.N.A. 5, the latter form being an abbreviation for 'Anno nostræ amicitiæ,' which he adopted to mark the date of our friendship, begun in 1812. In this letter he affects to treat me, not very consistently, as a Jacobin and as a friend of Napoleon. The following is a short extract :

I took it most kind in you, my beloved Wood, to write to me so soon after your arrival, when you could so well have pleaded want of time and various other excuses. I do nevertheless earnestly request you not to think that I shall be offended if you do not write often, for it is my wish that you should see everything, and as your stay is but short in Paris, I will wait patiently till you leave it to hear of all the wonders to be seen there ; but you must not humbug us untravelled folk, and you must not return as the monkey that had seen the world, for let me tell you, Mr. Alderman, I will have none of your airs. Your letter was as instructive as it was amusing, as replete with good advice as it was with just observation. I was scarcely ever better pleased with a letter even from you, and all your letters must please your adoring friend. I see that you did not sleep in the diligence, but had your eyes and ears open, and from the beginning I augur well of your excursion. It will enlarge your ideas by letting you have an insight into the ways and customs of foreign nations, and make you, Mr. Jacobin, learn to respect, love, and reverence the sacred establishment of our blessed constitution in Church and State. You seem to have seen a great deal in a short time, and to have been struck, as everybody is, with the magnitude and magnificence in which Royalty lives in France, and the misery of the poorer orders. You will not, I conclude, wish for those sumptuous palaces in England. Let our Prince have his 'Thatched Cottages,' and be able to keep up the dignity of his state—we want no more. I would rather see the Louvre and Tuileries in France than in England. With the pictures perhaps you were at first dazzled, but I think your taste will soon reject the false style of French artists, for I understand since the departure of your friend at St. Helena, most of the pictures are of the French school, which, in my humble opinion, is no more to be compared to the English, than I to Hercules. We have undoubtedly more and better pictures in England, but in a free state the sovereign cannot monopolise all the good things. Every nobleman and almost every gentleman in England has at least two or three pictures by first-rate artists. Not so in France, where I believe you will find that almost every picture of worth belongs to the royal family. Were all the first-rate pictures of the English, Italian, and Dutch schools in England to be collected, I doubt not but that we should fill a room much longer than half a mile. Your English indignation is justly roused by the plan of justice in France, and your English heart naturally revolts at the idea of want of liberty of the press ; but I think if you con-sider the present character of the French, and the weak foundation of the French government, you will acknow-ledge that France is not at the present time fit for liberty of the press, which is always so much open to abuse that it is even at times dangerous to our firmly fixed government, and consequently would be replete with danger to the ill-built fabric of the French Constitution.

In the next letter, dated from Whippingham January 4, 1818, A.N.A. 6, he tells me that he is to go to Christ Church, Oxford, in about a fortnight. There are some observations I feel impelled to quote from this letter, owing to the happy direction which at this early period it gave to the subsequent correspondence of a life.

May our affection, which is already gigantic, grow every year till it reaches that heaven where it can never be made twain. Remember, my adored friend, that the first and the most essential part of friendship is to mark the faults, and *then* to love the virtues, of the object of our affection. Remember that none but a friend can tell us our faults ; that it would be presumptuous and invidious in anyone else so to do ; and, therefore, I put the marking of our faults before the admiring of our virtues. But the seeing them is not enough ; they must be told. No man can view his own errors ; they must be told to him, and pointed out to him, before he repents. Bear in mind that when Cassius says, 'a friendly eye would never see those faults,' Brutus admirably replies, ' Flatterers would not, though they be as huge as high Olympus,' thus drawing the direct line and denominating him, who, by most men, would be called a friend, to be, in many instances, nothing more than a flatterer. This I do not mean to apply to the morals, habits, and customs, but even to the lowest and least observed faults. When we were together such freedom we always exercised without reserve ; therefore, in our letters let our remarks on one another's train of thought, style of letter-writing, and action be free, open, and more inclined to blame than to praise, for I mean to tell you honestly and truly everything I do, everything I think, everything I feel. Amen. Thus ends my sermon ; and if you are not asleep, I will now be a little merrier.

My correspondence with Hook after he left school was constant. I missed him and his guidance only too much ; for a growing dissatisfaction with

Gabell's mismanagement of the school, especially his want of confidence in the boys, led to a rebellion in May 1818, in which I took part. It is enough to say that although I then thought, and still think, that grave grounds of complaint existed, I have never ceased to regret the pain I gave to our Head Master, with whom personally I was rather a favourite, and the greater pain I must have given my parents. Happily no evil consequences resulted from it to the school, nor indeed to my own subsequent career. I was deservedly sent away from the school, an opportunity being first offered me of saying that, owing to my youth, I had been over-persuaded. This notion was not true in fact, nor under any circumstances would it have been likely to meet with my assent. But besides this, all the head boys had signed a paper before the rebellion broke out, to the effect that whatever happened to one should happen to all. The Head Master and second master in conclave called up the first and third boys and expelled them, keeping me confined in a separate room till this had been done ; but from the window of this room I saw and conversed with these two boys, and then on being summoned to judgment stated all the facts, and said that my course was clear. I then went home, taking also my younger brother [1] with me, who had signed the same paper. These statements will explain my friend's next letter.

. . . . I am heartily sorry for the Rebellion. In the first moment I was so pleased with it that I scarcely considered the merits or demerits of the case ; but now,

---

[1] Mr. Western Wood, afterwards M.P. for the City of London.

when I reflect upon the great kindness and affectionate
care of Gabell for the school, I cannot but feel sorry when
I consider the injury it may do him. But all this would
not affect me in any serious manner, as your banishment
perhaps will. All my fears have been roused by Heathcote telling me that Coplestone, the Provost of his college,
says that he shall not receive Porcher if he hears that he
has been at all active in the Rebellion. Are you, my most
beloved Wood, sure of getting in at Cambridge? Is there
no doubt? Did you take an active part in the business
yourself? Austen, who saw Ward, tells me that you did. I
hope you did not, but, my most dear William, think not
that I mean to upbraid you ; I should myself have done the
selfsame thing, but I should have repented of it afterwards
most likely. I trust that by this time your father has forgiven you. Send me word if he has or has not.

My younger brother was sent back to school,
and before the end of May I was travelling alone
through France to Geneva. At Geneva I remained,
passing through the usual course of philosophy at
the 'Auditoire,' for two years. My way was made
smooth by the presence of some near relatives at
Geneva, who before my arrival had made arrangements for my living *en pension* at M. Duvillard's,
the Professor of Belles Lettres. There were, at
different times, some six or seven people, English,
German, and French, in the same pension ; one of
the Englishmen being an old Winchester schoolfellow. I alone, however, followed the course of
the Auditoire. I wrote a few lines to Hook from
Calais, and again from Geneva, where I received
my first letter from him, dated Christ Church, May
24, 1818, and during the two years of my residence
at Geneva our correspondence never flagged. I

will not, however, overload this narrative by further
extracts from his letters. Suffice it to say that they
indicate much divergence of his thoughts from the
work of the place, and contain constant expressions
of regret at his disappointing those who were interested in his distinction, and who believed (as I
ever had) in his powers of mind, if he could once be
brought to fix them earnestly upon his work. He
wrote once or twice a poem for the Newdegate
prize, which he sent to me for criticism, but with the
exception of Divinity he read little which could
avail him from a University point of view. His 'set'
of companions, though always young men of ability
and worth, were, owing to his college being Christ
Church, men of higher worldly position than himself,
and did not encourage him in study. In a letter
dated March 6, 1819, he says: 'You asked me in
your last whether I study with anybody—no, nor
ever will without I can do so with you. You asked
with whom I most associate. My acquaintance
here is not extensive, and I am not a bit more with
one person than another.' His college tutor was
Dr. Vowler Short, afterwards Bishop of St. Asaph,
to whom he was much attached, and of whom he
always spoke with gratitude.

My letters interested him because we had many
interesting persons then living at Geneva, with
whom I had such acquaintance as a boy can have
with men. Amongst our Professors were De Candolle
the botanist, De la Rive, Pictet, and Rossi, afterwards a peer of France, and finally Prime Minister
of Pius IX. in his days of zeal for reform, in whose
service he was assassinated. He came to Geneva

as a refugee from the despotic government of Pius
VII., which drove him from Bologna.   Dumont,
Sismondi, and the late Duc de Broglie were also
then residing at Geneva.

On July 1, 1819, Hook wrote me a rapturous
account of his first pilgrimage to Stratford-on-Avon.

In May 1820, just as I was about to pass an
examination for the degree of ' Bachelor of Letters '
at Geneva, Queen Caroline happened to pass through
that town on her way to England.   My father was
anxious that I should avail myself of an offer to
travel in her suite.   We were to meet him and Lady
Anne Hamilton on the road.   This I accordingly
did, meeting them at Montbard, and all of us proceeding to St. Omer, where we met Brougham,
then the Queen's Attorney General, and Lord
Hutchinson.   It was then that the offer was made
to the queen to receive a large annuity, on condition
that she should not take the title of queen, or attempt
to land in England.   Her answer was her departure
that same evening from St. Omer to sleep on board
an English packet, whence she despatched a letter
addressed to Louis XVIII., stating her desire to
free him from her unwelcome presence on French
soil, though she had thought that some of the ordinary tokens of respect might have been paid to one
whose brothers had perished on the field in supporting the monarchy of France.   I pass over, however,
this episode of my life, intensely interesting as it
was at the time to me ; believing, as I then did, and
still do, that the wicked charges against that persecuted woman were false.   I only mention the mode
of my return to England because it occasioned some

trouble, as I afterwards learned, to my dear friend, whose family were strong Tories, and had been personally favoured by George IV. Hook, however, never wavered even for a moment in his devotion to me; his mother, also, was aware of his affection for me, and she was uniformly kind in promoting it.

It so happened that I was laid up with ague, caught whilst travelling by night through the marshes of St. Omer. I could not, therefore, go to him, nor indeed did we meet till late in 1822; for as soon as I had recovered from the ague I made a journey, lasting from June to October, with persons employed in getting up the case of Queen Caroline abroad, to whom I acted as a volunteer interpreter for the Italian witnesses, until a regular interpreter could be obtained. In one letter written to me just before I left England he says : 'I forgot in my last to tell you that I called on Gabell as I passed through Winchester, and after having laughed at the likelihood of your becoming a real rebel, he said, "Remember me, when you write, most particularly and kindly to him, and tell him that he will always find a welcome in my house." He expressed the greatest regard for you. When I was there I met a young lady who asked me much about our Oxford Commemoration, and I told her how delighted I was to hear the simultaneous hurrah, the magnificent and glorious burst of enthusiasm, the moment the name of Robert Southey was mentioned : that it was also not a little pleasant to see one poet applauding another—Milman cheering his brother bard Southey, and quoth Dr. Gabell, "you have the honour of speaking to Miss Milman."'

I met Gabell myself not long afterwards, when he was most kind to me, and I felt all my penitence for the rebellion renewed. I had to cut short my Italian journey just as I was about to leave Rome for Naples and Sicily. The horses were at the door when I received a letter from my father, enclosing one from the Rev. G. Macfarlane, Fellow of Trinity, who was to be my private tutor at Cambridge, informing me that if I were not in England by October 21, I should, by the University regulations existing at that time, lose a whole year. My friend was now working hard for his degree, and I had to set to work at my Cambridge studies in Trinity. We did not, therefore, meet till late the next year.

In 1821 he came to town for the coronation of George IV.; but we did not meet then, as no doubt there was a difficulty in our doing so either at his home or mine, the minds of our relatives being so differently affected as regarded the unhappy position of the queen.

It was not till the summer of 1822, nine months after his ordination, that Hook and I again met. I was then about to make a short visit at Southampton, and met him by arrangement at Winchester, having a delightful walk with him for a few hours over all our old haunts, especially the meadows in which we used to read. I will not attempt to describe the joy of this happy meeting, at which we agreed that if it were possible we would contrive some meeting for a longer period in the next year. Unhappily for the remainder of my vacation in this year, I suffered from disordered health, chiefly in the form of a most troublesome giddiness, which was afterwards yet more aggravated, and threw me very much back in my preparation for my degree. Our scheme consequently, which included a visit from him to me at Cambridge, had to be postponed till the next year. I had numerous letters of the kindest sympathy from him during the whole of my illness. In one of these, dated September 17, 1822, he says, 'I have read lately nothing—yet I have read the novel of "Evelina," and am trudging through "Sir Charles Grandison."' I mention this because about the same time I had often talked of Richardson's novels with Macaulay (then an undergraduate), who, when I said that I had got through 'Sir C. Grandison' after seven attempts, replied, 'You will not enjoy it till you have read it seven times through.'

In a letter dated June 1822, after some remarks on Scott's last novel, the 'Fortunes of Nigel,' and upon a novel by Lockhart, called 'Adam Blair,' he proceeds : 'By the way, I must not omit to recommend to you a book which has entertained me very much, entitled "Pen Owen." It is a new novel, and what pleases me is that it is quite void of that canting and whining sentimentality and that sometimes blasphemous saintism and methodism with which so many modern novels abound.'

Several years after this I discovered that his father was the author of the book. I had often laughed at his vehement 'John Bullism,' which adhered to him through life, and in reference to this he says, writing in December 1822, 'I am not quite so national as you think, and if ever you give me a little more of your much desired society, and talk of foreigners as you did and can do, I will promise to be an apt disciple to liberality : to *your* liberality, not to Leigh Hunt's.' (Leigh Hunt was at that time the editor of ' The Liberal.')

In January 1823 he writes, after reading Moore's ' Loves of the Angels,' and the first act of Byron's ' Heaven and Earth ' in ' The Liberal' :

I think it (Moore's Poem) a complete failure, and in parts quite wicked ; although I will do him the justice to say that I believe he did not intend to be so. I am very much averse to poets coming into contact with the Almighty, or straying into the infinitely incomprehensible. He is pleased to represent the angels of God, the participators of infinite happiness, as finding heaven dull, and descending upon earth to gratify, not their love, but their lust. I am indignant and sorry. The fact is that even the sublime and heavenly Milton soared too high, and in his third book he offends me much by introducing the reader to the Almighty Himself. But if Milton did not succeed in the regions of heaven what modern poetaster can hope for success ? Lord Byron's ' Heaven and Earth ' in the ' Liberal' is in parts extremely fine, and throws Tommy Moore quite into the background. There are parts which are almost sublime. . . . But when I praise ' Heaven and Earth ' I may be influenced by having heard it most beautifully read by my uncle Theodore.

In May 1823 he wrote a letter, from which I extract the following passage. The playful ideas about our future careers which it contains were in some respects singularly in accordance, in others as singularly contrasted with the actual facts of our subsequent lives.

I am, at present, in the most melancholy mood— distressingly so. Some evil must be impending, or is it the sudden return of winter after the summer-like autumn we have spent ? I feel that loneliness of heart and mind of which I do often complain. I think after all I must get me a wife ; but where shall I find one to suit my taste and disposition, and if I do find such a one, will she not be worse than a fool if she accepts such a wretch as I am? How delightful would it be to have a small cottage in some sequestered shady valley, with a wife who could understand all the sentiments of my heart, and enter into all my feelings as you used to do : to have her there equally the friend of my friend, who would find in my house a pleasant retreat from the toils and worries of a lawyer's life. I could fancy you nursing, with almost parental fondness, my second boy, William Wood Hook, taking a delight in his improvement, and urging him by presents in the career of learning, while I should hold you up to him as the model of perfection in virtue and true religion as well as learning. Then we should laugh heartily at all your bachelor peculiarities, and fit up one room peculiarly for you, just according to your taste and ideas of comfort. N.B. When we pay a visit to London we shall always refuse your offer of a room in your house in the most delicate terms we can, dreading the damp beds, and unaired dungeony rooms of a bachelor's house— but we shall be very happy to dine with you. At length a change will take place ; and we shall feel a little awe at your approaching visit, and mount wax candles instead of muttons in our candlesticks, and talk big among our neighbours ; ' because why ? why because ' my Lord Chancellor, the Earl of Lignum, and Baron Billy-squad is coming to pay us a visit—and we shall find you just the same good, dear, affectionate, unaffected creature as before ; and your lordship will take my son, William Wood Hook, under your lordship's more immediate protection, and will give my eldest boy a living, and offer to get me a Deanery or a Bishopric, which I of course shall refuse ; and then I shall be proud of having such a friend, and I shall make a memoir of your life, and, *à la* Jimmy Boswell, take minutes of your conversation and treasure your *bon-mots*, and make selections from your letters, and leave it to my son to be published when we are both dead and gone; and then—and then will be an end of our eventful history.

He was indeed most blessed in the wife to whom six years later he was united, but he did not pass any portion of his married life amid rural or sequestered scenes. I soon followed his example as regarded marriage, and fulfilled his anticipations by presenting my godchild (not, however, bearing my name), his second son, but the eldest surviving, to the first benefice which became vacant after my appointment to the office of Lord Chancellor. Alas! after a short life of usefulness, he was but a little while since removed from this life, but reunited, as I hope, to his loving and beloved parents.

I answered his letter with some corresponding wish, common enough to those who have a laborious life before them, that we might live in 'some secluded abode, blessed with our own society and that of our wives and children;' for in a letter dated June 4, 1823, he quotes this passage and says, 'I do assure you that with the addition of health I should think this dream of yours, if fulfilled, would be happiness complete. Let us labour some twenty years hence to bring it about. But alas! twenty years! how awful is it to think of the change which may take place between this and then! To one or both of us Time will perhaps—nay, will probably be changed into eternity; or, if permitted to linger yet longer in this world of misery and turmoil, our hopes, our wishes, our ideas may suffer a dismal change: a dismal one, I say, because few persons are bettered by contact with this filthy world. Well, my dearest friend, let us pray for the blessing of the

Almighty, and may He grant what I hope and think may really be the case, that our friendship may never, never end.'

After the six years of friendship during the remainder of our unmarried life which succeeded this letter, we lived to thank God for forty-five years of uninterrupted friendship between ourselves, our wives, and his children—a union broken only by the sad removal of his wife four years before his own decease. But such retirement as I had imagined was not reserved for us : once only did I again, some years after we were both married, refer to the possibility of it, and I was struck with his reply, ' When you have no more work to do you will die.' A sense of the privilege of working for his heavenly Master was never absent from his mind. It overcame his strong bias to literary self-indulgence, the strongest temptation that can be offered to men of vigorous powers of thought.

In January 1824 I took my degree, and in October 1825 I obtained a Fellowship at Trinity ; but as I was reading for the bar in the chambers of an equity draughtsman throughout the year 1824, whilst Hook was occupied in his clerical duty as his father's curate at Whippingham, we seldom met, but our correspondence was constant. When his father was made Dean of Worcester in 1825 my friend frequently resided at the Deanery, but early in the year 1828 his father was unexpectedly seized with a fatal illness and died at Worcester, aged fifty-six. Writing in February 1828 soon after this event, Hook says : ' Our circumstances are at present not the most brilliant, but I am philosophical enough not to care about that. Much interest was used with the Lord Chancellor (Lyndhurst) to procure for me my dear father's living of Stone, worth about 800*l.*, which had been taken in exchange for Whippingham ; but his lordship merely sent me a very kind letter, promising future patronage and offering me a living (which proves not to be vacant) of 300*l.* a year. He was an old friend and schoolfellow of my father.' In fact, my friend's family was but ill provided for. His younger brother was placed in a way to be provided for in Herries and Farquhar's bank, but his mother and a sister much younger than his brother were left with himself dependent on a very slender fortune.

In the summer of 1828 his mother took for a time a small house at Leamington, whither he accompanied her and his sister for a short holiday, and here I paid them a visit. He preached a sermon at Leamington which attracted the attention of Dr. Jebb, the Bishop of Limerick, who was then staying there on account of his health. Bishop Jebb asked him at once to visit him, and they had much happy intercourse, their acquaintance speedily ripening into friendship. He was greatly pleased with this occurrence, having much revered the character of the Bishop, and being in a manner almost acquainted with him by perusal of the well-known 'Correspondence' between him and Mr. Alexander Knox. Several of the letters that passed between Hook and the Bishop have been printed in the 'Life of Bishop Jebb,' by his chaplain, the late Rev. Charles Forster.

During my stay at Leamington the benefice of

Holy Trinity at Coventry became vacant. This was a benefice in the gift of the Lord Chancellor, and on talking over his letter before referred to, we resolved to go over to Coventry to make enquiry about the nature and special character of the duties that would be required of an incumbent of that parish. The result was that Hook applied to the Lord Chancellor, and on October 3, 1828, he wrote to me, 'I have just heard from the Chancellor. He has, in the most kind and flattering manner, conferred upon me the Coventry living. I have no time at this agitating moment for more than most earnestly to request your prayers.'

We had both been somewhat misled in supposing the income of the benefice to be 500*l.* a year, but I do not think that the facts, if known, would have altered Hook's wish to undertake the work, for he could not but be conscious that he had powers of usefulness which waited but the opportunity for development.

On November 29, 1828, he wrote to me to mention the error about the income of the living; not with any great amount of disappointment, but in that easy temper with which he always took matters of mere worldly consideration. 'The living,' he writes, 'is only 360*l.*, and there is no house. This is a bore on two accounts. First, I cannot do all the good in my parish that I could wish with so small an income : and secondly, I cannot marry.'

On February 11, 1829, he slept for the first time in his parish and wrote me a letter, from which I transcribe the following passage :

I write to you at night just before I sleep for the first time in my parish. Think of the overpowering sensations

of thus entering upon a new sphere, where the good that I
may be the instrument of doing is great, but where the
mischief of which I may be the cause is incalculably
greater. I have been rash and presumptuous in seeking
this situation, for which, unless I am strengthened from
above, I am utterly unfit. Think of this, and think of poor
me when you are praying. You know not half my weakness; you know not how much I stand in need of the
renovating, the assisting grace of God. There is a communion of saints, and one Christian benefits in the prayers
of another. It is delightful to reflect on this: it is delightful
to think that we may, in some way or other to us unknown,
contribute to the welfare of our friends by our prayers—
that there is unseen fellowship among true Christians.
May the God of heaven, for His blessed Son's sake, shower
down upon you, my most dear friend, every blessing, both
temporal and spiritual; and now, while I am praying for
strength, now when I am incurring these awful responsibilities, let your prayers be united with mine. Pray for me
and my flock, that I may be able to do my duty and they
theirs.

Scarcely more than a month after this I received
a letter from him dated March 11, 1829, full of joy,
announcing his engagement to your dear mother-
in-law, the commencement of happiness which was
never interrupted save by her death; and in the
following August I was enabled to mention my
engagement to her with whom I have enjoyed up to
the present hour every blessing that a union, un-
clouded by aught but that which may at times have
overshadowed us from without, could bestow. It
pleased God that the marriages thus formed increased
our friendship, and more than doubled its brightness
by the no less warm attachment of those who had
succeeded to the first place in our affections. And
here I fitly break off the narrative of our youth,

leaving to you the exposition of his later years ; and only making, in conclusion, a few remarks upon the salient points of his character and career.

There was in him a rare combination of genius in devising, and industry in carrying into effect, schemes for the full development of the power of the Church ; first, in evangelising those large masses of our population whose hearts so few have been able to reach, and then in building up their faith upon a firm foundation. His special inspiration in this great work was, as we who knew him best believed, to be found in the unbounded sympathy of his Christian love, first, towards his Saviour, and through Him to all for whom that Saviour died. He was thus delivered from narrow exclusiveness on the one hand, and on the other from an unreal, though apparent, breadth of fellowship with any save those who were, like himself, devoted to his Master's cause. For the one great characteristic of his course was in all things reality. Hence in more than one instance he gave support to men from whom, in many serious respects, he differed, if only convinced of their Christian earnestness. I remember especially the period when Mr. Newman published his celebrated Tract XC. After having received a letter from Hook expressing his great regret at the publication, and his disapproval of its tone, I was surprised by another letter consequent on the part taken by the Oxford authorities against the author, in which he says, ' I have nailed my colours to the mast, and intend to stand by Newman.' His firm adherence, however, to his own principles became so well known after a short experience of his parochial ministrations in Coventry and Leeds, that he found ardent helpers ready to support him in any work which he undertook. Hence the extraordinary results of his ministry in increased churches and schools. I remember going with him one evening to a gathering of 600 Sunday school teachers who had 12,000 pupils under them. But this energy of feeling, if confined to sympathy only, would have done but little. His industry was unparalleled. He rose before five o'clock, and was at his literary work from six to nine, and after his breakfast at the latter hour he devoted his whole time to his parish, morning and evening, with the exception of a Saturday evening's holiday. He was bold and fearless to a degree which is rarely experienced in one who was also tender and loving as a woman. He was keen in discerning and persevering in up-holding the true interests of the great Anglican branch of the Church Catholic, now extended over the larger portion of the globe. Whatever doubts might be suggested as to the expediency of Bishop Luscombe's appointment, in which he took a leading part, it was the beginning of our largely developed colonial and foreign episcopate. For the Church in the great borough of Leeds he acquired a position which it had never before attained. On all public occasions, such as the opening of the new Town Hall by her Majesty, and the like, he and the other clergy, mainly through his influence, were to be found occupying a prominent official position. His influence was built up on a solid basis of Church principle, and was felt to extend to many of the neighbouring industrial centres of our manufacturing districts. To the present day ' T' ould Vicar and t' wife' are household words among the old inhabitants of the great parish of Leeds.

He foresaw the development that education must receive in a free country, and he was one of the earliest to secure for the Church her true position in forwarding that great work, not by the exclusion of others from the field of labour, but by her own superior activity. He was intolerant only of pretension and indolence, and in the midst of indefatigable labours he had no leisure for petty ambitions. The scanty portion of leisure that public duty permitted him to enjoy was devoted to his home, and that devotion was requited by the unbounded affection of his happy household.

CHAPTER VI.

SETTLEMENT AT LEEDS.

JULY TO DECEMBER 1837.

IN May 1837 the new Vicar took his degree of D.D. at Oxford, and preached twice on Sunday at St. Mary's, the church being thronged with an immense crowd up to the very steps of the pulpit. The beginning of July saw him and his family fairly established in the house in Park Place, Leeds, which was to be their happy home for twenty-two years. There were no buildings at that time on the opposite side of the road ; the situation was airy and pleasant ; within easy reach of the heart of the town, yet not so near as to be overwhelmed by the smoke of its multitudinous factories and mills.

And now the gigantic magnitude of the work which lay before him became day by day more clearly visible. It was enough to appal the stoutest heart, and bewilder the steadiest brain. In the character of its inhabitants, and in the condition of their religious life, Leeds was a typical specimen of a West Riding town.[1] The common people were

[1] For a very interesting account of the Church in the West Riding during the past century, see the *Quarterly Review* for April 1878.

rough, uncouth, headstrong, and independent in a degree calculated to daunt and repel a stranger, until he discovered that below this rugged surface there often glowed warm hearts, generous feelings, and strong earnestness of purpose. John Wesley owned that at first he had been startled and dismayed by the wildness and rudeness of the inhabitants of the West Riding, but he soon perceived that nowhere would a heartier response be made to his awakening appeals ; nowhere was he destined to reap a richer harvest of disciples. The temperament indeed of the people, excitable, impulsive, and emotional, supplied a peculiarly favourable soil for the reception of Wesley's doctrines. While the spirit of the Church was torpid, and her outward development was hampered by causes to which the attention of the reader has been directed in a former chapter,[1] Methodism grew and flourished ; Methodism alone kept pace with the rapid and enormous increase of population in the northern manufacturing towns, and struck its roots deeper and deeper year by year into the affections and understandings of the people. The Evangelical pastors of a former generation, such as Henry Venn of Huddersfield and William Grimshaw of Haworth, had promoted rather than impeded the growth of Dissent, and the religion of pious Churchmen was of a Methodistic type.

The Church had now just become alive to her responsibilities. The See of Ripon, after much vexatious opposition in Parliament, had been founded

---

[1] Chap. iv. page 146.

in 1836, so that Bishop Longley and Vicar Hook almost simultaneously began the labours by which they were destined under God to win back for the Church her long-lost supremacy in that part of the country.

It was indeed none too soon to begin the work; for there were enormous arrears of duty which nothing but the most persevering and energetic industry could overtake; there was ignorance on the part of Churchmen which only patient teaching could enlighten; apathy, which only burning zeal could quicken; and, on the part of political and religious opponents, there were prejudice and suspicion which only the most forbearing charity could surmount.

The conditions then which the Vicar of Leeds was called upon to face at the outset of his ministry were briefly these. First, a huge and rapidly increasing population; secondly, ignorance; and thirdly, active opposition.

The population had risen from 53,162 in 1801 to 123,393 in 1831. The provision on the part of the Church for the spiritual necessities of the place was and had long been miserably inadequate. The parish comprehended the whole of the town and a large portion of the suburbs. In 1825 there were only four churches in the town besides the parish church, and nine in the suburbs. The total number of the clergy was eighteen. Ten years later the town-churches had been increased to eight by the erection at considerable cost of three large and ugly Peel churches, which proved to be total failures. They were without endowment, the congregations were very scanty, and the stipend derived from pew rents was next to nothing. The town churches were mere chapels of ease to the parish church; no districts were assigned to them, the patronage of nearly all was vested in the Vicar, and most of the baptisms, marriages, and funerals were performed at the parish church, the fees for such offices amounting to about 600*l.* a year.

The Vicar of Leeds in 1837 was patron of the churches of St. Paul, St. James, St. Mary, Christ Church, Armley, Beeston, Bramley, Chapell Allerton, Farnley, Headingley, Holbeck, and Hunslet. He had the joint patronage of St. John's with the Mayor and the three senior Aldermen, and of Trinity Church with the minister of St. John's and the Recorder. With the exception of the districts of Woodhouse, Christ Church, and St. Mary's, he was responsible for the entire pastoral charge of the whole township. Yet the clerical staff of the parish church for a long time past had consisted only of the Vicar, one curate, and a clerk in orders. Nearly the whole of their time was occupied in discharging the more mechanical functions of the clerical office. They were at the parish church from eight to half-past eleven every morning for marriages. They baptized twice and churched twice every day, and burials were performed daily; in winter twice a day, and in summer three times. One of the curates of the late Vicar who remained in charge of the parish during the vacancy, observes in a letter to Dr. Hook that the want of districts to each church in the town and the inordinate labours consequently heaped on the Vicar and his curates, prevented the successful prosecution of any plans for bringing the Church to bear on the people : the schools were only in the proportion of one in twenty-three of the population. ' Had we ten new churches,' he writes, ' with a corresponding staff of clergy, and ten new schools, we should not have one too many.'

Weak, however, as the Church was, the Dissenters and Socialists entertained the most implacable animosity against it, and the appointment of a Vicar reputed to be bold and lofty in his aims, and indefatigable in energy, provoked them to put forth all their strength. The contest began immediately after his election and before his residence in Leeds. The opposition called loudly upon the people to muster in force at the vestry meeting in April for the election of churchwardens, and to take good care that only such men were appointed as would act on a system of rigid economy and pay deference to the wishes of the vestry. A set of High Church and extravagant churchwardens might be the means of imposing a heavy church-rate on the parishioners against their will, might sanction or introduce strange or distasteful practices, and involve the parish in most vexatious and costly proceedings in the spiritual court.

The result of this appeal was that a large mob attended the vestry meeting in the parish church. The parishioners chose the seven whom they were entitled to elect. Most of them were Dissenters, or men otherwise unfavourable or indifferent to the interests of the Church. The Vicar had the right of choosing one for Kirkgate ward; but the Vicar was not present. Mr. Taylor, the curate in charge, occupied the chair, as his representative, and nominated Mr. Garland—a good Churchman—for the office of Vicar's churchwarden. A turbulent scene ensued. It was alleged by a large section of the meeting that, in the absence of the Vicar, the right of electing his churchwarden lapsed to the vestry. The curate and a few supporters maintained, on the contrary, that it devolved on him who acted as the Vicar's delegate. The chairman acted with spirit and firmness. The opposition proposed a resolution embodying their view, but he refused to put it to the vote. He was bullied for two hours, but held his ground; and finally, amidst groans and hisses, entered the name of Mr. Garland in the minute-book as having been duly appointed by the Vicar's representative. The opposition appended a protest to this entry, and the meeting was dissolved.

The parish churchwardens proved true to the spirit in which they had been elected. The Vicar on his arrival found the surplices in rags and the service books in tatters, but the churchwardens doggedly refused to expend a farthing upon such things. When they assembled at the church for a vestry meeting, they and others like-minded piled their hats and coats upon the holy table, and sometimes even sat upon it; but the new Vicar with stern resolution quickly put a stop to such profane outrages. He told them that he should take the keys of the church, and that no meetings would be held there in future. ' Eh !' said one, ' but how will you prevent it ? We shall get in if we like.' ' You will pass over my dead body, then,' replied the Vicar. Archdeacon Musgrave also paid a visit to the church, met the churchwardens in the vestry, and told them that unless the necessary things were provided, within a given time, steps would be taken to compel them ; or if they called a vestry and a rate was refused, the vestry would be proceeded against. The churchwardens grumbled excessively at these demands, and complained more especially of the increased expenditure for sacramental wine, owing to the weekly celebration of Holy Communion. It was their custom at this time to remain in the vestry during the administration of that Sacrament, ostensibly to guard the wine, but the Vicar had reason to suspect that they themselves occasionally consumed it.

The malignant hostility to the Church and the Vicar, of which the seven churchwardens were the official instruments, displayed itself on a large scale at a church-rate meeting held on August 19. The building in which the meeting was convened could not contain the masses who thronged into it, and it was proposed that they should adjourn to a large oblong enclosure, surrounded by the buildings of the Cloth Hall, and commonly called the Old Cloth Hall Yard. Here, on being called to the chair, the Vicar found himself confronted by a mob of nearly 3,000 persons. A statement was made of the probable expenses for the coming year. They amounted to

355*l.* 11*s.* 6*d.* A halfpenny rate was proposed and
seconded. A Baptist preacher named Giles then
rose and delivered a furious harangue, directed
partly against church-rates and partly against the
Vicar. At the conclusion of his philippic the Vicar
got up and began by observing that the speech of
the gentleman who had just sat down might be
divided into two parts, one consisting of an attack
upon the system of church-rates in general, and
the other of abusive language towards himself—the
vicar. 'Into the general question of church-rates,'
he continued, ' I shall not enter upon this occasion.'
' Eh ! why won't 'ee ? ' shouted a thousand sturdy
Yorkshire voices. ' Because, my friends, you
wouldn't listen to me if I did (laughter). I will
only observe that the settlement of this particular
church-rate rests entirely between yourselves and
the churchwardens. I personally am not concerned
in it. You have elected your own churchwardens.
You know they will not do more than the law
requires, and that the law will compel them to do
what the law requires to be done. Therefore if you
do not grant the church-rate the Church itself will
sustain no injury, because the money will come
out of the churchwardens' pockets (laughter). With
regard to the second part of my friend's speech, that
which consisted of personal abuse, I would remind
you that the most brilliant eloquence without charity
may be but as sounding *brass* ' (the tone of his
voice and the twinkle in his eye as he uttered these
words are described by an eyewitness of the scene
as irresistibly comic), ' and,' he proceeded, ' I am
glad to have this early opportunity of publicly acting

upon a Church principle—a High Church principle—
a very High Church principle indeed—' (a pause,
and breathless silence amongst the expectant
throng)—' I forgive him ; ' and so saying he stepped
up to the astonished Mr. Giles and shook him
heartily by the hand, amidst roars of laughter and
thunders of applause from the multitude.

The day was gained. The rate was passed, and
a vote of thanks to the chairman was carried with loud
acclamation. None could appreciate better than a
crowd of Yorkshiremen the mixture of shrewdness,
good humour, and real Christian feeling by which
he had extricated himself from the difficulties of his
position and turned the tables against his opponents.
It was the first great public occasion, outside the walls
of the church, which enabled the people to see of
what stuff he was made, and it did much to procure
for him that sympathy and respect from the working
people which he continued to enjoy to the end of his
career at Leeds. Meanwhile, both by his ministrations in the church and by pastoral and social intercourse he was rapidly winning over large numbers in
all ranks, not only to himself, but to the principles
of the Church. Even before he had taken up his
abode in Leeds Mr. Robert Hall had discerned with
delight evident symptoms of coming success.

' So you have made up your mind,' he wrote, ' to a
three years' martyrdom. Believe me, unless like the
ranter in the play you ' love to be persecuted,' you will
either manage very ill or you will be agreeably disappointed. At present, let me tell you, you are almost more
popular than, as a politician, I could have wished. The
reason is, in part, that those who condemned you *unread*

are, most of them, compelled to absolve you *read*; in part,
it is common reaction; in part, that the Wesleyans of
Coventry have sent a high character of you to the Wesleyans here, so that the Evangelical attempt to awaken
the antipathy of that body has signally failed. You really
would admire the commendable appetite with which some
of them are eating their own words. . . . On the other hand
I cannot but look upon the late opposition as almost a
providential means of awakening the old High Church
principles, which had been slumbering in the hearts of
the congregation of the parish church, and though even
they will require gentle treatment at first, you will find
them prepared to listen to you with docility.'

The congregations at the parish church soon
became so large that scarcely standing room could
be found at the Sunday services. Much space was
wasted by the large appropriated pews and galleries
with which the church was encumbered. The poor
sometimes went an hour before the time of service,
yet were unable to get in. Some of them would go
to the afternoon service, which was less numerously
attended, and sit on to retain their places for the
evening service, when the church was most densely
thronged. The old parish church was a very large,
and in many respects a very handsome fabric, but
singularly ill adapted for public worship. It was a
great cross church of extraordinary breadth in the
nave—ninety-seven feet, owing to double aisles—and
with a chancel of extraordinary length, which for
practical purposes was completely severed from the
nave, not only by the bulky piers and arches, which
supported a massive central tower, but by a heavy
gallery built across the eastern arch. The double
rows of columns also which supported the nave and

aisles were such serious obstructions to sight and sound that most unseemly behaviour often occurred in those distant parts to which the eye and even the powerful voice of the Vicar were unable to penetrate. Early in the autumn of 1837 an address was presented to him, signed by 640 parishioners, praying for the improvement of the parish church, and a subscription list was shortly afterwards opened, headed by the Vicar, Mr. Benjamin Gott, and Mr. Christopher Beckett, with donations of 200*l.* each. According to the plans first prepared by Mr. Chantrell the architect, it was proposed to take down the tower and rebuild it on the north side, to widen the chancel and fit it for service, to remove the galleries, and great pews from the nave, and generally to repair the whole structure. The estimate for carrying these alterations into effect was 6,000*l.* In any case it was necessary to remove the tower, for on examination it was discovered that the piers, two of which were cracked from top to bottom, rested on a rotten foundation of loose stones and rubbish, a very little way below the surface of the ground; and the safety of the fabric could not be ensured from one day to another. On further consideration, also, the inconveniences arising from the great width and obstructive columns of the nave appeared so objectionable, the foundations and walls of the whole building were discovered to be so insecure, and the cost of restoration seemed likely to be so much greater than was at first expected, that the plan of remodelling was abandoned, and it was determined that a wholly new church should be erected.

There can be little or no doubt that in the present day some parts of the old structure, and the general character of the whole, would have been preserved; and the extreme dislike of the Vicar to the church, which is so strongly expressed in the letters at the close of this chapter, arose from his inability to detect the real beauties which were concealed beneath deformities of modern growth. But he was also convinced, and perhaps rightly, that the construction of the building was very ill adapted for the proper and devout celebration of the services of the Church of England. Any attempt moreover at what is now called 'restoration' would probably, at that time, when the revival of architectural knowledge and taste was in its infancy, have proved a complete failure; and the new church, although it doubtless deserves, from a purely architectural and artistic point of view, some of the severe criticisms which have been freely bestowed upon it, possesses several great merits to which attention will be drawn in the proper place.

Feeling strongly as he did that a due celebration of Divine Service was impracticable in the old church, the Vicar devoted all his energy, and all the means at his command, to promote the successive schemes of alteration and rebuilding. Trade was in a deeply depressed condition, but he knew well that there was wealth more than sufficient for the purpose, and he was determined that the rich men should do their duty. One of the most eloquent and successful speeches which he made in the first year of his appointment was at a great meeting, held November 8, to consider the best means of rendering the church

suitable for public worship. The plan for shifting
the position of the tower and remodelling the interior
of the church was at that time the only plan which
had been brought forward.

'The Parish Church of Leeds,' said the Vicar,
'has been described by Thoresby as "black but
comely." Black, I am sorry to say, it still is, but
comely it has ceased to be, because owing to various
alterations which have taken place from time to
time, not upon any fixed plan, the convenience of
individuals rather than the accommodation of the
public has been considered. As the church at present stands it is almost, nay altogether, impossible
to perform the services of the sanctuary with that
order and decency with which we ought to perform
them. Owing to the wide aisles and passages where
persons can loiter without taking any part in the
service or hearing the sermon, but wait to see where
they may get convenient places, great noise and
confusion during the early part of the service must
necessarily prevail.' After observing that the Communion Service could not be performed in the
chancel, and that the church was the most difficult
for the voice of all the churches in which he had
ever officiated, he proceeded to say, 'at present it
holds about 1,500 people : by the proposed plan we
shall get 1,200 more kneelings. I use the word in
preference to the term sittings, that persons may be
reminded that they come to church not to sit and
hear a sermon, but to kneel before their God in
prayer. And of these 1,200 fresh kneelings, 700
will be free for the use of the poor. I think I have
stated reasons sufficient to convince anyone who

may be tempted to ask the Judas question, To what purpose is this expense? I think I have used arguments sufficient to convince the utilitarian; but I must remember that I am addressing Churchmen —men accustomed to take a higher aim, to be influenced by a holier sentiment and a diviner principle. To them I say go and look at the parish church, and then tell me if that be a church befitting a parish so distinguished for opulence as this. I bid them leave their homes, decorated by every art which elegance, refinement, and taste can suggest, and I tell them to go look on the Church of God, and I think the blush of shame will mantle on their cheeks when they reflect that while they are dwelling in their ceiled houses, the tabernacle of God is dwelling behind curtains. I consider a handsome church to be a kind of standing sermon, saying to the people, See how Churchmen love and honour their God, oh come hither and worship in the beauty of holiness! I trust we shall be animated with the spirit of David, who desired to build a house for the Lord exceeding "magnifical, of fame and of glory throughout all countries." I trust we shall be animated with the spirit of Solomon, who loved the House of God, and the house which he built was great, for he said, " Great is my God above all gods." I trust we shall be animated with a desire that when the children of our people go forth to distant parts of the land, or to foreign countries, they may cast a longing lingering look upon their native town, and speak of the holy and beautiful house where their fathers worshipped. I trust we shall be influenced by the Spirit of that Blessed Being of whom when

He became incarnate and died for our sins it was said, " The zeal of Thine house hath eaten me up " : and I trust it is under the influence of His Holy Spirit that I now say to you in the words of the prophet, " Go up to the mountains and fetch wood, and build the house of the Lord, and the Lord will have pleasure in it, and I will be glorified, saith the Lord." '

The conclusion of the speech was followed by loud and prolonged cheering ; and Mr. Christopher Beckett in seconding a vote of thanks to the Vicar as chairman, observed that it was impossible to estimate the value to the town of such a man : for the good influence which he had in six months exercised on all classes of the community in Leeds was indescribable. The meeting testified its appro-bation of these remarks by passing a vote of thanks to the trustees for having elected such an excellent Vicar for the town.

The enthusiasm, kindled at this meeting, for the work of remodelling or rebuilding the parish church was never suffered to flag. A committee of sixteen, with the Vicar as chairman, was formed who carried on their labours with unabating zeal until the completion of the new church in 1841.

An unusual number of important speeches were made by the Vicar during the first two years of his ministry at Leeds ; and they were probably the most eloquent and effective which he ever delivered. It has commonly been said that he was not a good speaker. This statement, however, must be ac-cepted with great reservations. It is true, if by a good speaker is to be understood one who can be depended upon to speak with a certain degree of excellence on all occasions and on any subject, whether he understands it or not. It is not true if the designation may be extended to those who, though they may be unable to speak well always, everywhere, and on all subjects, nevertheless can at times speak powerfully, and even brilliantly, upon subjects with which they are thoroughly acquainted, and in which they feel a deep interest.

The Vicar of Leeds was one of this class. There were two conditions under which he could speak eminently well. One was when he was thoroughly roused and put upon his mettle by the presence of a multitude either warmly sympathetic or fiercely antagonistic. 'Large mobs,' he once remarked to me, 'inspired me to speak : under excitement and before a large multitude, when I got into a declamatory and rather rhetorical vein, I could go on unceasingly ; but I never could speak much or fluently at small private meetings.'

The second condition which enabled him to speak effectively was when his interest and feelings were thoroughly enlisted in a subject, and the speech itself was the outcome of much previous thought and study. The preparation of such speeches cost him much labour, but they were for the most part very telling in delivery. 'I have made three or four great speeches' he said 'in the course of my life—speeches, I mean, which took more than an hour to deliver, were much applauded at the time, and frequently quoted afterwards ; but the effort of mind was very great to me, because I am not naturally a speaker, and my memory is not good. My plan

was to have a distinct outline in my head, a peroration, a certain number of points prepared and
assigned to particular parts of the speech, and others
to be brought in as well as I could.' Speech-making
at meetings was a part of his duty which he never
relished, and would gladly ofttimes have avoided,
had it been possible or right to do so. But as it
was an unavoidable necessity, especially at the outset
of his career in Leeds, he girded himself to discharge
this, like every other duty, with all his might.

At the time that he became Vicar of Leeds and
Dr. Longley Bishop of Ripon, very great ignorance
prevailed in the West Riding concerning the true
principles, and the deep claims upon Churchmen, of
the two venerable Societies for Promoting Christian
Knowledge, and Propagating the Gospel in Foreign
Parts. One of the Leeds parish churchwardens
who had attended morning service at St. John's
observed to a friend as he came out : ' We have been
having a sermon and collection for *a* Christian
Knowledge Society : can you tell me what the
Society is for ? ' A very great increase in the
support given in Western Yorkshire to the two societies dates from the zealous and eloquent pleading
of their cause by Vicar Hook and Bishop Longley.

A large meeting on behalf of the Propagation
Society was held in the Music Hall at Leeds on
October 17, 1837, the Bishop presiding. And this
was the first occasion of the kind on which the
oratorical powers of the Vicar were manifested.
After describing at considerable length the history
and the nature of the society in clear and forcible
language, he concluded in the following words :

' If the Society in a great measure confines its exertions to the dependencies of the British Empire, it is to be remembered that on the British Empire the sun never sets, so that everyone will agree that here is " ample room and verge enough " for the most extensive operations. The Society feels that charity ought to begin at home, and it knows that he is worse than an infidel who does not provide for his own household. To her colonies and dependencies, indeed, the debt owed by England is great. For those colonies and dependencies have become ours—how ? By right of conquest. Now I can admire and glory in the valour of our army and navy. I can admire and glory in the skill and genius of our generals, our Wolfes, our Clives, our Cornwallises, our Lakes, and our immortal Wellington, who fought his country's battles on the plains of India, as well as on the fields of Spain and Waterloo. I can admire, I say, the valour of our troops and the skill of our generals, but in vain were that valour and in vain that skill unless our arms had been crowned with success by the God of battles. And who is the God of battles ? It is the Lord strong and mighty ; it is that Blessed Being who, when for our sakes He became incarnate and died upon the cross, gave us that commandment to which I have alluded before, " Go and disciple all nations." And can He have given us the victory merely to pamper our national pride—pride in all its shapes, national and individual, being condemned in His Gospel ? Did He give us the power to tread down our enemies and to laugh them to scorn, merely to increase the wealth of our merchants that

they might become, as they have become, the princes
of the earth ?   Oh no, my friends !   He crowned
our arms with victory that a way might be opened
to the most religious nation of Europe—that a way
might be opened to the piety of England to preach
the pure and unadulterated truths of the Gospel, to
administer the Christian Sacraments, and to organise
the Christian Church.   And I hope that it will be
the glory of the reign of our beloved youthful
sovereign to see this object accomplished.   We
look back to other reigns for the success of our
arms ; may posterity look back to the reign of
Victoria as the period in which Christianity was
propagated, and the Church established, throughout
the vast dominions of the British Empire—

> These be thy trophies, Queen of many isles,
> On these high Heaven shall shed benignant smiles.'

The Bishop in his speech at the close of the
meeting, after commenting on the extraordinary
ignorance respecting the nature of the Society which
had prevailed in the West Riding, and the very
slender support which in consequence had been
given to it, observed that, so far as the town of
Leeds was concerned, ignorance could no longer be
pleaded ; and even if there was a disposition on the
part of any to persist in such ignorance, he could
not but think that after the eloquent, fervent, and
stirring address of their gifted and beloved Vicar
they would be ashamed of their ignorance, and
would henceforth gladly aid in the diffusion in
foreign parts of the everlasting Gospel of the great
Captain of their Redemption.

The Vicar was equally indefatigable in explaining the principles of the Society for Promoting Christian Knowledge, and in establishing branches in connexion with it, not only in Leeds, but in many of the neighbouring towns. The local papers between 1837 and 1842 contain such very numerous reports of his speeches on these occasions, that out of so many it is difficult to select the best; but at any rate I think few better specimens could be found than the following, delivered at one of the annual meetings of the Leeds District Committee.

It illustrates also very well the manner in which fixed principles were blended in him with Christian charity and liberality of sentiment, and the distinction between principles and opinions here made was one which he was very fond of drawing. . . . 'The question may be asked with reference to this society, How do you propose to effect the object which you have in view? And, in the name of the Society, we answer, *by the Bible rightly interpreted.* The Bible contains all things necessary to salvation, and it is from the Bible that we ascertain the will and word of God; but of course the Bible *wrongly* interpreted does *not* express the mind of the Lord: the whole stress therefore of the question lies on the right interpretation of Scripture. The Society consequently in the first place circulates freely the Holy Scriptures, and then it circulates books and tracts by which men may be enabled to understand the Bible rightly. In the first place, books and tracts are supplied for the young that, as reason dawns, and before they proceed to the study of Scripture, their minds may be thoroughly imbued in Church principles: prepared, *prejudiced*, if the term is preferred, for understanding the Scriptures in the sense of the Church. And in the next place books and tracts are provided for adults—such books as will instruct them to reduce Scripture principles to practice, and will prevent them from drawing from Scripture heretical conclusions. Such is the course pursued by this Society to speed Christian knowledge by the Bible rightly interpreted. The responsibility incurred by the Society in so doing is very great, and before we can give it our support we must ascertain the principle under which the Society itself acts in thus seeking to lead men to the right understanding of Scripture. There is scarcely a doctrine of Scripture which has not been controverted by some sect or party: there must be a *right* sense to be applied to each of these controverted doctrines. The Society undertakes to lead men to the *right* sense: but how are we to know that the Society itself has acquired the right sense ? What is the guide of the Society ? To this the answer is, the Society is guided by the Church. Now here another question would arise if the claims of the Society were brought under the notice of persons who were not members of the Church. We should then have to show why the Church has authority in controversies of faith, and why the sects by which the Church is surrounded have *not* such authority. But this is not necessary in addressing Churchmen, for they will accept our twentieth Article, which declares " that the Church hath authority in controversies of faith." According to that authority we act in interpreting Scripture, and so we come to a decision on the fundamental

doctrines of Christianity which are controverted.
But although the principles of the Society are such,
when we go to the depository we take up one book
or tract and say, " This is an excellent work : I shall
circulate it," and then perhaps we take up another
and say, " I do not at all like this tract, and shall
not purchase it." How can this be ? will perhaps
be asked ; and to answer this question we must
consider the difference between a principle and an
opinion. By a principle we mean a doctrinal statement asserted and defined by the Church. If to
this we are perversely opposed, we are heretics. But
then consistently with adherence to this principle a
variety of subordinate opinions may be held. This
may be illustrated by another reference to the twentieth Article. In that Article it is said that " the
Church hath power to decree rites and ceremonies."
To deny this would be heresy. But notwithstanding
this, we may hold and express an opinion as to the
wisdom, or the contrary, of any particular rite or
ceremony so decreed. For instance, the Church
appoints that we should kneel at public worship, but
some may hold an opinion that kneeling is not the
best attitude. Few perhaps would maintain that
the usual attitude of sitting or lounging is more
reverential than kneeling ; but we know that in the
primitive ages some churches, while directing the
people to kneel at other times, directed them to stand
on Sundays in order to testify that the feast of our
Lord's Resurrection is a joyful holiday, and there
may be persons who think that it is a better ceremony
than that which is adopted by us. Or, take a more
solemn subject. The Church teaches us that in the

blessed Eucharist "the body and blood of Christ
are verily and indeed taken and received by the
faithful." To deny this would be heresy; but as
to the *manner* of His presence, "who is verily and
indeed taken and received"—this is an opinion, and
in asserting our opinions there may be considerable
difference allowed, so long as we do not adopt the
opinion transubstantiation, which is by our Church
condemned. . . . And now, my Christian friends, I
have endeavoured to point out to you the distinction
between principle and opinion, that you may see
how it is that persons belonging to the same branch
of the Catholic Church may hold the same principles,
and yet differ in many of their opinions. I wish
you to observe how, in spite of such differences,
there *may* be brotherly love, there *may* be friendly
intercourse, there *may* be union, *except* where it is
the interest of worldly-minded men to foment
differences, lest their occupation should cease ; *except*
where parties are formed and party spirit cherished
by the low ambition of individuals who seek through
faction an ephemeral distinction, conscious that the
mediocrity of their talents is insufficient to secure
for them permanent respect. With regard to those
who are not members of the Church, *union* with
them is impracticable, for between us and them
there is a difference of principle : there is no common
stock of principles to which we can appeal. But
among spiritually-minded Churchmen there may be
union, notwithstanding great differences of opinion ;
and where there is not a *worldly* object in keeping
parties separate, I am confident that by mutual
explanation it would be found that the differences

are not so great as they appear to be, and as persons interested in creating or maintaining parties would represent them. As a case in point, I know some persons who refuse to support this very Society, on behalf of which I am now pleading. If I were to say to them, Here is the Society for Promoting Christian Knowledge, and because you refuse to belong to it you are not friends to the promotion of Christian knowledge, I should act most uncharitably: they are as zealous as you or I can be for promoting Christian knowledge, but they are of opinion that this Society is not the best for effecting that object. For my part, my opinion is in favour of this Society, and I call upon you to support it with zeal. But at the same time I protest against that exuberance, that intolerance of zeal, which can induce the advocates of this or any other self-formed Society to anathematise those who are conscientiously opposed to it. Such an anathema *has* been heard, as you are aware. Anglo-Catholics, among whom there are many spiritually-minded men, whose thoughts are more in heaven than on earth, have been denounced, because they are opposed to a self-formed Society,[1] as "agents of Satan" : they have been called " serpents who pollute our churches and leave their slime about our altars—serpents who ought to be crushed," whether by bell, book, and candle, whether by the faggots of Smithfield or the racks of the Inquisition, the deponent sayeth not. These are very dreadful words, for they were intended to apply to me and

---

[1] The London City Mission which had lately sent an agent to Leeds. The Vicar had been fiercely denounced by a part of the press for declining to co-operate with him.

to the majority of this great assembly. But it is charity to believe that they were not *real* words—that the Christian brother who uttered them did not think of the awful meaning of these expressions; but that, forgetful of the solemn account which for every idle word he will one day have to render, he used them as mere rhetorical flourishes, as flowers of oratory to point a period. I only hope that such flowers of rhetoric will not be employed to-day. We are Christian people assembled for a sacred object: let us act on Christian principles, and, above all, in a Christian temper.'

But it was not only by speeches at large annual meetings of this kind that the vicar promoted the work of the Society. Before the close of the year 1837 a scheme had been devised for dividing the whole town into twelve districts, in each of which a branch of the Society was to be established. The committees of these branches were to consist of a chairman, the clergyman of the district, and two visitors for every thousand inhabitants. A depository was to be established in each district, where specimens of the publications of the Society should be kept and exhibited, and notices placed in the window directing the attention of the public to the name, nature, and design of the Society. The duty of the visitors was to call upon persons of all classes, in order to discover who were in want of Bibles and Prayer-books amongst the poor, and amongst the richer people to advocate the claims of the Society upon their support. Once a month they were to report progress to the chairman, and once a quarter the chairmen of the several districts were to meet the general committee for the transaction of business at the Central Depository. The first of these branches was opened in December 1837, in St. Mary's Bank School, which was densely crowded when the Vicar as chairman explained the nature of the work which this and the other branches would have to perform. And from this time forward, as branch after branch was formed in this district and in that, the Vicar was always at his post as president, making his addresses a vehicle of instruction in the primary principles of the Church generally, as well as of the Society, and thus casting the net of the Church's influence further and further into the broad and deep waters in which he had been called to labour.

But the most direct influence which he exercised upon the minds and hearts of his people was of course through his sermons and pastoral intercourse. Seldom did any preacher so happily blend instruction with exhortation in his sermons. Sunday by Sunday, with great weight of learning and with great force and perspicuity of language, did he unfold the true nature and principles of the Church of England ; her apostolical succession—her foundation by St. Augustine, her purification by the Reformers of the sixteenth century, her harmony in creed and practice with the Primitive Church. Sunday by Sunday did he, in his sermons and in catechising the school children in church, exhibit the meaning, the beauty, and the value of the Anglican Liturgy. But with the didactic he never forgot to mingle the hortatory and practical ; he never forgot for a moment that the supreme duty of the pastor is to win men to Christ, and to lead them to cast their sins at

the foot of His Cross ; and all his teaching about the
ordinances of the Church was intended to show that
they were, when rightly and faithfully used, means
to this great end; that they were the hem of Christ's
robe, through which men might touch Him and be
healed of whatsoever spiritual disease they had. No
Evangelical—no Methodist, ever preached 'Christ
crucified' more fully, freely, fervently, constantly
than he did ; he only differed from them in pointing
out the rich provision made by Christ in His Church
for aiding men in drawing near to Himself, and in
exhorting believers to look to a steady course of
obedience rather than feelings and frames of mind
as tests of spiritual growth.

The effects of such teaching became visible in
the course of even a few months. The whole number of communicants when he entered on his charge
at the parish church was little more than fifty, and
amongst these there were no young men, and very
few men of any age. One who had been the Vicar
of St. John's for thirty years declared he had never
seen a young man at the Lord's table. A steady
and rapid increase set in after Dr. Hook's arrival,
and in the course of two or three years we find him
speaking of 400 and 500 persons communicating on
Easter day. The more frequent confirmations which
were instituted after the establishment of the See of
Ripon were of course a great assistance in promoting
this improvement. Formerly they had taken place
once in seven years only, when a vast number of ill-
prepared young people were brought together from
great distances. The occasion was frequently the
scene of scandalous festivities and improprieties, and

many of the candidates returned to their homes ini-
tiated in vice, instead of being confirmed in goodness.
After the appointment of the Bishop of Ripon the
confirmations were at first triennial and ultimately
annual. The first confirmation at Leeds after the
election of Dr. Hook took place in October 1837,
when upwards of 1,000 candidates of various ages
were presented by him and the other clergy of the
township.

But the most remarkable result of his teaching
this year was the conversion to the Church of three
Methodist preachers, with a certain number of
their followers. The movement was purely spontaneous on their part, for it was not the custom of
the Vicar to seek or allure proselytes from the ranks
of Nonconformity. His business, he conceived, was
to proclaim truth rather than to combat error, to
build up the Church rather than to attack the sects
who had seceded from it.

The Methodist teachers came to him and informed
him that, having become convinced of the truth of
Church principles by his sermons and speeches, they
wished to be received into the fold ; but there was
one difficulty which weighed upon their minds
and the minds of their followers. They felt unwilling to abandon the practice of class-meetings : a
practice to which they had always been accustomed,
and which they considered to be salutary in its
effects. ' Do not let this be an impediment,' said the
Vicar ; ' by all means have your class-meetings, and
I shall be delighted to become one of your class-
leaders.' To this they readily assented. The first
meeting, however, at which he was present, he

attended more in the capacity of a distinguished visitor than of a leader. It was held at the house of one of the principal members of the connexion, who presided at the head of a long table in the middle of the room. The Vicar, and one of his curates who accompanied him, were invited to occupy chairs near the leader, while the members of the class sat round the walls facing the table, until the leader gave out a hymn, when they all turned their faces to the wall. The hymn being ended, the leader read and expounded a portion of Scripture, after which the members of the class were called upon to 'tell their experiences.' For some time there was no response to the invitation, although it had been made in the most encouraging tones. At length a man got up, and beginning, 'this night I set up my Ebenezer,' proceeded in a declamatory style to inform the meeting how he had formerly believed that he saw the light of truth and followed the path of righteousness, but how he had been smitten by 't' Vicar's sermon t' other night,' and now perceived that he had been all the while walking in darkness and ungodliness. This remarkable experience having been related, and no more being offered on the part of others, the Vicar was invited to 'improve the occasion.' He had discerned clearly enough that the intention of the speaker had been to gratify him by paying compliments to his persuasive preaching, and to magnify himself in the eyes of all present by getting credit for his superior discernment of the Vicar's great powers. The Vicar, therefore, began by observing that his visit to the class-meeting had been most interesting and instructive to him, for he now saw the full value of the practice of telling experiences.   Here was a man who had himself believed, and had led others to believe, that he was a pillar of truth and a pattern of godliness, but who now came forward to declare that all this had been a mistake and an imposition.   ' So now, brother,' continued the Vicar, ' we see what your fault has been—self-deceit, brother, and hypocrisy, too—yes, hypocrisy, brother. Oh ! what a hypocrite you have been, brother ; you must repent of your hypocrisy.'   The feelings and countenances of the assembly, especially of the member thus addressed, may be better imagined than described, as the unmerciful Vicar ran on in this strain.   To bring matters to a close the leader proposed that the Vicar should ' engage in prayer,' upon which he took out his Prayer Book and said the greater part of the Litany in a tone and manner described by an eyewitness as peculiarly impressive and affecting, after which he shook hands with the leader and departed with his companion, to discuss at the Vicarage the singular scene at which they had assisted.

The result of his deliberations was, a resolution that while willing to allow class-meetings, under the superintendence of himself or one of his curates, the ' telling of experiences ' should be absolutely forbidden, as likely to minister to spiritual pride and presumption.   Many of the Wesleyans, however, were not content to enter the Church on this condition, and only a few of the more sober kind actually came over.   The Church ' class-meeting,' which had its origin in this occurrence, became a weekly meeting of communicants and church workers for instruction and counsel under the Vicar, and has been carried on from that time to this.

The following is a copy of rules for the class, which I have found in the handwriting of Dr. Hook.

1. This class consists of persons who are communicants, or preparing to become so, and is to be regarded as a private meeting of my friends: as private as if we were to assemble at the Vicarage.

2. Strangers, therefore, can only attend when introduced by a member, and any person becoming a member will be considered as such for half a year at least.

3. Those members of the class who are willing to take or distribute tracts will signify their desire to do so to me, and will pay a penny a week to the treasurer of the fund. But it remains optional to any member of the class to become a tract distributor or not.

4. For those who undertake to distribute tracts I shall provide a fresh tract every week. They will lend the tract among their neighbours as they shall see fit, and then they may keep the tract to form part of a library for the use of their servants.

5. Covers are provided for those who wish to lend their tracts.

6. Many of the tracts will be of a superior description, for sending, not merely to the poor, but to better educated classes of society, who may be prejudiced at present against the principles of the Church, or who may require confirmation in the principles which they profess.

The meeting was in fact a weekly instruction by the Vicar in some book of Holy Scripture, or some portion of the Liturgy. It was one of the principal means by which he rallied round him a body of earnest and intelligent workers, so that it became a centre in which religious light and warmth were gendered, and from which they were diffused to others.

The following letters will complete the sketch which I have attempted to draw of his first half-year at Leeds, a period which, being of an eventful and exceptional character, seemed to demand a chapter for itself.

To his Sister—First Impressions of Leeds.

The Vicarage, Leeds : July 5, 1837.

My dearest Georgiana,—We this night sleep for the first time in the Vicarage, and as you have been a good girl, and written to me (for you) very well of late, I will indulge you with a letter. Things are now beginning to be very comfortable : the house is a delightful one, just the kind of house I particularly like—lofty rooms but not too large. I have a delightful study, which is the only room completely furnished, besides our bedroom. Pratt is like a brother, and seems highly pleased with everything. He manages to understand the Yorkshire lingo better than I can. To Yorkshire manners I am becoming a little reconciled. I am beginning with the greatest delicacy to hint to the people that this house is not quite public property. Hitherto everybody seems to have thought himself justified in entering it, and in criticising all that the Vicar has been doing ; while sturdy beggars, men out of work, meet me at every turn, and almost demand relief. I am now in full work ; the poor curates, sexton, clerk, &c., are surprised : they evidently thought that I should let them go on in their own slovenly way, while I should be employed in some grand undertakings, such as building new churches and schools ; whereas the learned doctor (they doctor me here, 'Yes, Doctor, No, Doctor,' at almost every second word), says, 'fair and softly,' one thing at a time. They heard nothing of me the first week. I first set my study in order, and next the parish church must be put in order; so to show how things shall and must be done, I am taking all the full curate's duty; I have this day offered the prayers three times, besides burying, baptizing, and churching. The stated services in this church are prayers three times a day; and instead of seeking for a congregation, the curates, sexton, clerk, &c., have endeavoured to prevent one being formed, and then used that as an excuse for having no service. I have ordered the sexton whenever there is no congregation, to go into the street and to give two old women sixpence a-piece to come in and form one; so that no sham excuse can be tolerated. The curates have now but little to do, though I make them attend; for when I have ordered the funerals to be properly performed, they have urged that it was impossible, so with baptisms &c.; and, therefore, in order to refute them, I have taken the duty myself, just to prove that 'what is impossible can sometimes come to pass.' The black looks with which I am regarded, notwithstanding the soft words used, are rather amusing; but the services of the Church *shall* be performed as they ought to be, before anything else is done. I am also busily employed with an architect, devising some plan to make decent my nasty, dirty, ugly old church. I am determined to get that into something like order, if possible. The difficulties are tremendous, but I am in good heart.

To the Rev. J. W. Clarke—Nature of the Work to be done at Leeds.

Vicarage, Leeds : July 7, 1837.

My dear Clarke,—I write to you again to say that now you are appointed lecturer, you may entirely suit your own convenience, and what you think to be due to your two parishes, about the time of your coming here. The curate and clerk in orders make not a little fuss about the work they have to do, which, nevertheless, is but little; and your absence does not add to their labours though your

coming will diminish them.   My system is to do one thing
at a time, and not to have too many irons in the fire; and
my business now is to get the ministerial work at the
parish church properly performed; I am therefore myself
undertaking full curate's duty.   Nothing could have been
more slovenly than the proceedings at the parish church—
baptisms, marriages, funerals, all slurred over; this I am
resolutely reforming in spite of the curates, clerk, sexton,
&c.   Their system has been, not to consult the convenience
of the public, but to save themselves trouble.   My system
is, not to care for the trouble of the clergy, but to consult
the convenience of the public, and to enamour them of
our services by having them solemnly and devoutly performed.   In this good work I shall look forward to your
kind and cordial co-operation.   If you and I show that we
attach importance to the solemn performance of even the
slightest duty connected with our dear Master's service;
that we consider even the office of a doorkeeper in His
house an office of honour; that, convinced of His presence,
we are as devout in offering the prayers when only two or
three are present, as when there are two or three hundred;
we shall find His blessing attending us, and we shall be
the means of converting others.   I confess I attach the
very greatest importance to the solemn performance of
the occasional duties.   As in this respect you will have to
act as my strict ally, I wish, if you have time, you would
read again and attentively Wheatley on the Common
Prayer, and any other similar work.   I prefer Wheatley
to Shepherd, because the ἦθος of Wheatley's teaching is
more Catholic, more in accordance with the Church spirit.
It might be well also to read over the Oxford Tracts; not
that I care whether you agree with them or not, but
because the people here are all reading them, and it would
be expedient to know something of them, and because,
however you may differ on particular points, you cannot
but be delighted with the fine, noble, and truly Christian
spirit with which they are written.

                           Your affectionate Friend.

*To the Rev. Samuel Wilberforce—Clerical meetings—
Character of Churchmanship in Leeds.*

Vicarage, Leeds : July 1837.

My dear Friend, ... My next object in writing is to
request you to give me a few hints as to the rules of your
clerical society, with a copy of the prayer you use at meeting.　There are altogether twenty-two clergymen in this
parish, who are somewhat under my jurisdiction, and I
propose giving them a breakfast once a month at my
house, where we shall form a kind of club.　There are three
' Evangelicals' of the old school, about four or five high
Establishment men, beginning to understand a little about
the Church, and the rest are 'orthodox-men' of the old
school ; all steady, quiet, but (except the four or five I
have alluded to) illiterate men.　These are my materials :
my wish is to infuse into them a Church spirit.　Any
advice will be gratefully received from you, who have
succeeded so well in the Isle of Wight. The announcement
of my intention to give these breakfasts has given much
satisfaction.　I prefer breakfasts, not only because it will
be most convenient to all parties concerned, but because in
a town great clerical dinners would give rise to evil report.
I do not find my position here an easy one.　The town you
know, and therefore I need not tell you that it is more
smoky than any town in England ; the vicarage is, I am
thankful to say, a comfortable, airy house, or I should fear
for the health of my children.　We meet with much civility
and kindness from the people ; but the lower orders are
disagreeably uncouth in their manners.　The church is
the most horrid hole you ever saw ; dirty, and so arranged
that it is impossible to perform the Communion service in
the chancel ; and moreover it is situated in the very worst
part of the town, the very sink of iniquity, the abode of
Irish papists. Part of this evil I hope to remedy by raising
a sum of money for re-edifying the church.　I could do

much for about 3,000*l.*, but trade is now so bad that I do not venture to commence the subscription list. As to Church feeling, to Catholicism, the thing is utterly unknown to clergy and laity. The *de facto* established religion is Methodism, and the best of our churchpeople, I mean the most pious, talk the language of Methodism; the traditional religion is Methodism. An Independent teacher of some celebrity remarked to me the other day, that his sect is affected by this fact just as we are, so that I have to begin and lay a new foundation. I intend, please God, to begin soon a course of sermons on the Liturgy, and I fancy some persons who think themselves good Churchmen will rather stare when I speak of the Liturgy as absolutely good, their mode of defence having hitherto been that it is not absolutely bad; that it needs great reforms, but still it is not so bad as to force them to desert the Establishment; which is here the all in all of Churchism.

You see I have no easy course before me; but I shall hope that God has called me to this post to be the instrument of a great change, and I shall expect the prayers of all true friends of Catholicism. I am proceeding by degrees. I am now labouring to effect a reform in the mode of administering the occasional services of the Church, which have been sadly neglected. Believe me to be,

Your obliged and affectionate Friend.

To W. P. Wood, Esq.—First Impressions of Leeds.

Vicarage, Leeds: July 1837.

My dearest Friend,—I am in your debt for two letters, and perhaps they will long remain unanswered if I do not avail myself of the present half-hour to write to you; not that I can answer for having so much time at my own disposal, the interruptions here being incessant. Trade is so very bad that half the population are begging; such sturdy beggars as the Yorkshire beggars it has never been my

fortune to meet; in Coventry, in the worst of times I never
saw the like.   But let me begin at the beginning, and tell
you first how I like Leeds, that parish in which you, under
Providence, have placed me.   On the whole I am well
pleased, though the labour which I anticipate is great.   The
house is airy and pleasant, and this is with me a great
point; I really think that if I had had a good airy study
at Coventry, I should never have left it.   I am disappointed
in the country round; indeed one can hardly get into the
country till a horseman, not of the first order, is prepared
to return to the town, for the suburbs are very extensive.
But oh! my dear Wood, such a church as I have!   I
really loathe it; I cannot preach comfortably in it, I can
scarcely make myself heard; and the dirt, the indecorum,
&c., &c., quite distress me.   You know my system as I
learnt it from Bishop Jebb.   I do not oppose Dissenters by
disputations and wrangling, but I seek to exhibit to the
world the Church in her beauty; let the services of the
Church be properly performed, and right-minded people
will soon learn to love her.   But here, all that is thought of
is preaching; partly, without doubt, because the church is
so arranged that to perform the services well and properly
is almost impossible; then among the curates, sexton,
clerk, &c., there has been a system of doing as little as
possible.   Here I have been obliged to act contrary to my
nature, and to be a stern reformer; though, as my wish
always is to give as little offence as possible, I think I have
not made enemies.   The morning and evening services
have been neglected on the week day, i.e. the curates
have attended, but finding no congregation, have declined
what they call 'reading prayers.'   This I have met by
ordering the sexton to make a congregation, even if he
have to pay people for attending, so that now there can be
no shuffling; and to bring the thing into repute, I have
not only attended daily, which is a blessing and comfort,
but performed the service myself.   So likewise baptisms,
funerals, have all been most slovenly performed; I have
laid it down as a rule that the convenience, not of the

clergy, but of the public, shall be considered in every instance. I am much annoyed on Sundays by persons coming to hear me preach; but they will soon find out that I am not that most detestable of all characters, a popular preacher. And then I shall get my regular flock around me, and I am longing to preach a course of sermons on the Liturgy, which will, I think, surprise the Leedites, as they imagine that there can be only two subjects for sermons, Justification and Sanctification. The real fact is, that the established religion in Leeds is Methodism, and it is Methodism that all the most pious among the Churchmen unconsciously talk. If you ask a poor person the ground of his hope, he will immediately say that he feels that he is saved, however great a sinner he may be; so that you see I have much to contend with. Last night, the teachers of the Sunday schools (Sabbath schools, as they rejoice to call them) met together to deliver to me a congratulatory address. Delicia and Mrs. Johnstone went with me, and we were all highly disgusted (the ladies more than myself, for they are more unused to it) at the presumption and spiritual pride, as well as impertinence of the leading teachers, not the whole body. Meek and gentle Mrs. Johnstone seems quite roused about it. They proposed forming themselves into a society, to meet every month; to begin every meeting with prayer and praise; upon which, being up to their tricks, I immediately said that I highly approved of their design, and that, as they were Churchmen, I would give them the greatest of all possible pleasures; they should come to church, attend evening service at seven o'clock, when I would preach to them, and they should afterwards meet in the vestry. It then came out that they had been accustomed to assemble for extempore prayer, which they wished to be continued; upon which I suggested that those who wished to be Churchmen would of course prefer the privilege of the Church prayers. When they begged me to pray, out I brought my prayerbook, and went through the Litany, which seemed deeply to impress the majority, and having

begun with one of Wesley's hymns, they ended with the
hundredth psalm, I having evidently succeeded in raising
a Church spirit among the majority.   Mrs. Johnstone was
present at the address of the Coventry teachers, and was
much struck with the difference of the spirit between the
two parties ; however, I hope by God's blessing to remedy
all this.   I shall begin to catechise in church (D.V.) the
first Sunday in August.   I have been much worked lately
with committees and public meetings ; on Monday I had
to make two eloquent speeches ; one on an address to the
Queen, when I applied to her the words of Shakspeare
(Archbishop Cranmer) to Queen Elizabeth, 'Truth shall
nurse, holy and heavenly thoughts still counsel her,' &c.;
the other on raising a subscription for the poor.   I make
a point of going everywhere and doing everything, as it is
important at first to show what one *can* do ; afterwards we
may rest on our oars.   On Wednesday I am to preside at
a floral show.   The worst of it is, that I cannot preach
here; I know that there is no one in church who can have
a thought in sympathy, that even my very expressions are
not understood, and I do not find the spirit in me ; this is
a fault, and must be remedied by prayer.   Love to your
wife, to great E. and little E. ; my lady is very busy
a-furnishing.

Your devoted Friend.

To W. P. Wood, Esq.—Cathedral Choirs—Accession of Methodists.

Leeds : August 1837.

. . . . I perfectly agree with you in your regrets at the
carelessness of our English choirs.   The fact is, that chant-
ing and all old Catholic practices have only been tolerated
in England, the majority of our people being ultra-Protestants.   I have always wished that a body of the laity
would come forward with a remonstrance to the ecclesiastical commissioners, reminding them that the interest of

the laity ought to be attended to in their arrangements; and since they *will* re-arrange the cathedrals, that the income of one stall at least should be appropriated in each cathedral to increase the efficiency of the choirs. . . . You will be delighted to hear that my success here already exceeds my most sanguine expectations. Churchmen have hitherto been accustomed to think the Church *bad enough*, but *not too* bad for them as *Tories* to belong to it. They seem quite delighted to hear me prove that the Church is *absolutely* excellent. My course of sermons on the Church and Liturgy is received enthusiastically; and—glory be to God!—my most earnest prayer, it seems, is likely to be granted, for this morning I received an intimation that some of the leading Methodists, convinced by what I have said, are desirous of leaving their society and of acting under me on Church principles. If I can but enlist their Methodism, their godly enthusiasm, in the right cause! I have offered to meet them with rapture. It is a great advantage to be so thoroughly grounded in my principles as I am, for I know exactly how far to concede and where to stop. I have thorough confidence in myself on these points.

To the Rev. T. H. Tragett—Settling at Leeds.

August 21, 1837.

My dear Tragett, ... We have here a large, airy, comfortable, delightful house. I could not wish for a better; it is situated in the best part of the town, and will reconcile us, if anything can, to a town residence. Furnishing goes on very slowly. You can easily imagine the higgling and haggling and bargaining which is constantly going on. Mrs. Hook and Mrs. Johnstone have found out all the cheap shops, and if in the morning they manage to have saved a penny, you cannot imagine what pleasant companions they are in the evening. As to religion, the traditional or established religion in Leeds is Methodism; and consequently, as is natural, since we breathe a Methodistic atmosphere, everything has a Methodistic tendency. A pious Churchman here means a person who likes an establishment, and consequently supports the Church ; but then the Church is not sufficient to supply his wants ; so that he probably institutes two or three prayer-meetings in some large house or warehouse on the week-days, where he can indulge in extemporaneous prayer and Methodistic rant. Nor do the people venture to entertain a notion that the Church is *right*; their mode of defence is to show that it is not so *very wrong* that it is sinful to belong to it ; they *do* therefore belong to it, looking forward to the day when it will be reformed, i.e. brought down to the state of some Methodistic sect. Even many of the clergy, without knowing it, shape their doctrines and style of preaching according to the Methodistic system; and those who are not humdrum, labour not to instruct, but to excite. Then I have, to meet all this, a dirty, ugly hole of a church, in which it is impossible to perform divine service properly ; the chancel for example, being formed into an almost distinct church, and the body of the church being arranged to look as near as possible like a conventicle ; which same ugly old church is located in the very St. Giles's of Leeds. I am now preparing a plan for pulling the church half down, and rebuilding it ; but this will cost between three and four thousand pounds, and I fear to start the subscription now while trade is so bad. I am stirring up the clergy by insisting upon the strictest rubrical observance in all the occasional services—baptisms, marriages, and funerals. Nobody here seems to have a notion that baptism is anything more than a form of registration ; I think it my duty therefore to have it always administered with peculiar solemnity. They do stare sometimes when I tell them that before administering the Sacrament, I require them to attend the prayers of the Church, and pray with me : they think by the Sacrament I must needs mean the Lord's Supper.

Visit to the Archbishop of York (Harcourt).

Bishopthorpe Palace : October 27, 1837.

My dearest Mother,—Although I am but a naughty boy touching our correspondence when I am, as I generally am, overwhelmed with business, yet you must do me the justice to admit that whenever I have leisure I am accustomed to bestow my tediousness upon you. I have now nothing very particular to say, further than to tell you that the kindness I experience in this house is beyond all description great. The condescension and kindness of the dear Archbishop is to me an honour and a pleasure; he talks with me every morning from breakfast to luncheon, and I sit by him on the sofa all the evening. He asked me yesterday whether I had ever a relation at Westminster, and when I told him of my father, he said that when he was Subdean of Christ Church, and went as an examiner to Westminster, he remembered seeing some funny figures painted on the wall, and they said, ' Those are some of Hook's doings.' This is a most extraordinary memory. He must mean my father, because he said afterwards, he must have been contemporary with Greville Howard. The only persons staying here besides the family have been Lord and Lady D——. Lady D—— begged to be introduced to me, and is coming here with Lord —— to-day. Miss Harcourt says Lady —— is very anxious to see something of me, and I have been asked to remain here the rest of the week; but I have declined, as I have much to do at home. The odd thing is, that whenever I come here I am always treated as the great man, and am directed to hand out the great lady, next to the Archbishop. This, as you may imagine, is very different from what I have been accustomed to, and I feel terribly shy; I can get on with the Archbishop admirably, but the ladies make me shockingly nervous. Lady Wenlock asked to be introduced to me yesterday, and Lord Ashley (whom I do not know, and

who, I should think, was much opposed to me) asked Miss
Harcourt immediately whether they had seen anything of
Bishop Hook. 'I always call him Bishop Hook,' he said,
'and I hope he will be such soon.' He left a message for
me, stating that he should have spent a day with me at
Leeds, if he could have delayed his journey. You will be
amused with this gossip, and therefore I write it; but you
must not think it will make me worldly. I never enjoy myself as I do when engaged in my parish duties; and, on the
other side, the detestation with which I am regarded by
the Peculiars, is not to be described; wherever I go they
preach to their people, and warn them, at the peril of their
souls, not to come near me.

To W. P. Wood, Esq.—Hard Work—The Oxford School.

Leeds: November 13, 1837.

My dearest Friend,—Although every moment of my
time is occupied, I must write a line to thank you for your
letter, and to thank you also for having thought of me
when you were in foreign parts. I cannot tell you how
much I miss the advantage of that correspondence with
you, which has been the blessing of my life; from which I
have perhaps derived more of benefit than from any other
thing whatever. But I now have to preach four times a
week: twice on Sundays, once on Wednesdays at Mr. R.
Hall's school, which I have had licensed, and on Friday
evenings at church. This, with constant interruptions—
everybody exhorting me not to overwork myself, but
everybody thinking that his own particular business ought
to be made an exception to the general rule he would lay
down—gives me much occupation. I have sent you an
'Intelligencer,' which will gladden your heart; but you
must not suppose that all things are going on smoothly.
As to the success which seems to have attended me
hitherto, it humbles me to the dust; it seems as if God
intended to use me as an instrument of good, while I am

horribly afraid that I may be a Balaam, that my heart is
not so completely converted as it ought to be. This feeling
has depressed me ever since the meeting, but I had much
profitable prayer yesterday, and was in tears during the
greater part of the morning service. I certainly do not
find my progress what I wish, and I am dreadfully afraid
of being myself a castaway ; and yet on one grand point—
temper—the progress of grace has been such as to make
me humbly hope that the great work is going on in me.
I agree with much that you say about my Oxford friends ;
they are certainly the most injudicious of mortal men.
Palmer, you know, has long cut the connexion with them.
I am afraid they will upset the coach, they are such very
Jehus. What you say about ceremonies meets my view,
only that I should wish to see many ceremonies gradually
and imperceptibly restored. The Oxford school system is
decidedly bad, but you have only looked on one side of
the question, and do not perceive their principle, which
must be taken into consideration when forming a judgment.
We are on the eve of a new controversy with the papists,
who are breaking up new ground ; they do not now insist
on image worship, worship of saints, &c., &c., as necessary
doctrines ; they say it is only a part of the discipline of
the Church to which individuals are at liberty to object if
they will. This system of explaining away the obnoxious
parts of Romanism was invented by Bossuet, and is carried
out by Wiseman. They then say their worship, their
mode of propounding doctrines, their ecclesiastical language, and their ceremonies are much nearer to what we
read of in the primitive times as the practice of the
Universal Church than those of the English Church. Surely
then, they argue, you had better be with us ; we will not
compel you to believe more than you now do, but you will
be nearer the primitive model. You are not aware how
great a weight this has with many people. I know it,
because I have now under my tuition two of the daughters
of my neighbour, Mr. Newton, the celebrated Methodist
preacher, who are resolute to go over to Popery ; their

feeling is what I have described, and it is the case with others. Now the Oxford school say (and I agree with them) that all this is owing to our having, ever since Cromwell's time, endeavoured to assimilate both our mode of stating our doctrines and our forms *with the conventicle*, with ultra-Protestants. Work the Church of England, they say, as she ought to be worked, attend to her real instructions as to ceremonies, state your doctrines, e.g. Regeneration, as she states them in her formularies, and you rob the papist of this argument. Where I disagree with them is in the abruptness of their proceedings, and their disregard of weaker brethren; they act really from a dread of Popery, but seeing all its strong points, against which ultra-Protestants rather declaim than argue. It is time for a committee, and I must conclude. Our love to your good wife.

Yours devotedly.

From the Rev. Hugh James Rose.

Addington Park : December 18, 1837.

My dear Friend, ... I cannot say how much your account of Leeds and your own proceedings interested me, nor how thankful I am that it has pleased God's Providence to raise up such a powerful instrument of good in so important a place. I have long maintained that if the richer manufacturing laity are taught their duty to the souls of those whose bodies they use as machines for making money, and in consequence (for I believe fully that it would be a consequence) they build churches, and the clergy then use the opportunity, the manufacturing districts may become towers of strength for the Church. Till quite lately, no attempts have been made to ascertain these its great points ; you will go far to have them ascertained, for it is not merely directly that you will operate ; the impression made at Leeds will be carried far and wide. May it please God to preserve and prosper you ! The principles on which you go will at first gain attention by their entire novelty, and then, we may believe and trust, will hold it by their truth. Within the last ten years they have revived wonderfully, and have made their way. I deeply regret that some of their most powerful and valued advocates will put weapons into their opponents' hands, and thus render the progress less sure and less rapid : for example, they, in that most learned and useful tract on the Breviary, give a *service* for Bishop Ken ; it could not be a matter of *principle* to do so, for at best it is an *illustration* of what had been said ; and of course the cry at once was, 'Oh, here is *canonisation !'* &c., &c. This is really building up walls on purpose to knock one's head against, and I am really often inclined to believe that Newman goes on Luther's principle about his marriage : 'I did not wish to marry ; I was not in love, but I wished to drive the papists mad.' Again, the handling matters of detail as to uniformity of practice just now, is another most inexpedient way of proceeding. We have certain great notions to inculcate—the Church, the Sacraments, the Apostolical Succession. Let us be content with attending to these now ; when these are generally accepted, they will bring forward their fruits in due season of humble, docile, obedient minds, anxious to be guided and directed, and then a sufficient uniformity will follow ; to dwell on it now is only to give the adversary occasion, and thereby to endanger the acceptance of those vital principles and doctrines to which I allude. This our friends will not see, but to all such representations they only answer that this is expediency, humbug, and is the natural and *necessary* result of living in London, a soil in which they hold that all principle perishes. Indeed, I have my doubts whether they do not think that all commerce with mankind (i.e. reducing principles to practice) is destructive, and that the article cannot be had genuine except in a college (? whether even a college at Cambridge would do). I grieve for this, knowing the value of the men, and their power, their zeal, their excellence.

Believe me, affectionately yours,

H. J. ROSE.

CHAPTER VII.

IT is proposed in the first part of this chapter to sketch what may be termed the public life of the Vicar during the first three years of his ministry, including under this head his speeches, published sermons, and pamphlets. The second part will contain an account of his parochial work during the same period.

In April of the year 1838 a Conservative banquet on a very large scale was held in Leeds. The short-lived administration of Sir Robert Peel in 1835 had been beaten on a resolution moved by Lord John Russell, 'That the House should resolve itself into a committee of the whole House to consider the state of the Established Church in Ireland, with the view of applying any of its surplus revenues, not required for the spiritual care of its members, to the general education of all classes of the people, without distinction of religious persuasion.' The majority, however, against Sir Robert Peel's Government on this motion had not been more than thirty-three in a very full house. The Melbourne administration was weak, and was forced to purchase stability by a closer alliance than many of its supporters relished with the Irish Roman Catholic leader O'Connell and his party—'O'Connell and his tail,' as they were

vulgarly called. Churchmen were filled with apprehension also lest the Government should be tempted
to buy the support of the Socialists in England, by
taking away some of the property of the Church for
the purposes of national education on secular
principles.

On all accounts, therefore, the Conservative
party deemed it of the utmost importance to rally
their forces with energy and promptness. On the
one hand there was a reasonable prospect of their
succeeding, by a determined and united effort, in
overthrowing the Liberal Government; on the other
the continuance of that administration in power was,
in their judgment, fraught with peculiar perils to the
Constitution both in Church and State. The hopes
of their party centred in Sir Robert Peel. They
trusted that he might succeed in uniting the more
moderate reformers with those members of the Tory
party who, like himself, were prepared, however
reluctantly, to concede changes which the spirit of
the age seemed to demand ; to soften and conciliate
adversaries by a timely surrender, short of sacrificing
principle, instead of exasperating them by a stub-
born and ineffectual resistance.

The Vicar of Leeds was one of those who considered that the best chance of averting calamity
from the Church at this crisis lay in the return of
Sir Robert Peel to power. He therefore departed
for once from his general rule of holding aloof
from all political demonstrations. He attended the
banquet in Leeds, and made one of the most
eloquent and effective speeches, lasting nearly an
hour, which he ever delivered.

Rarely has a larger festival of the kind taken place in any of the great provincial towns of England. A special pavilion, designed by Mr. Chantrell, was erected for the occasion on a plot of ground near Park Row. The dining saloon was 120 feet long, by 80 broad. Nine tables, each 99 feet long, in the body of the hall, and a cross table 65 feet long at the top, accommodated 1,200 guests, whilst 500 ladies in the gallery, and 200 servants, made up a total of nearly 2,000 persons present.

The Chairman was Mr. William Beckett; and among the principal speakers were Sir George Sinclair, Lord Wharncliffe, Lord Maidstone, and Sir Francis Burdett, who indeed was honoured as the most distinguished guest of the evening, occupying a place on the right of the Chairman, next to Lord Wharncliffe. Immediately below Sir Francis sat Sir George Sinclair, and next to him the Vicar.

The health of the Vicar and clergy of Leeds was proposed, about the middle of the evening, by the Hon. Philip Savile, and was drunk with four times four amidst tremendous cheering, which was renewed and lasted for a long time when the Vicar rose to return thanks. 'Gentlemen,' he began, 'I rejoice to hear those shouts, for they have been raised not as an idle compliment to the clergy of Leeds—they are not intended as a compliment to me individually —they are intended—are they not ?—to attest your zeal, your loyalty, your devotion to the cause of the Church. I see before me many familiar faces, many who are accustomed to attend my ministry. To them I have had other opportunities of stating the spiritual claims of the Church, the spiritual advantages, the spiritual privileges of belonging to the Church. But I stand before you this day not as your pastor, but as one of your fellow subjects come here to declare my adhesion to the Conservative cause—my determination to unite with you, by every lawful means and measure, to uphold and maintain those rights and privileges to which as an Englishman I am entitled. To the rights and privileges of an Englishman, to the blessing of living under a limited monarchy, of living under the most glorious constitution ever devised by the wisdom of man (blessed be the providence and grace of God)—to those rights and privileges I was born. And when I was ordained to the ministry by the hands of the Bishop, those rights and privileges I did not renounce ; and not having renounced them, I am justified in coming forward to state that I will defend them by every lawful means, when I think they are in danger, as I now think they are in danger. To the rights and privileges of a Roman citizen St. Paul was born, and he did not think it inconsistent with his duty as an Apostle of Christ to defend them upon fitting occasions. Therefore I am not to be daunted by that clamour which is sometimes raised against the clergy when they dare to meet their lay brethren for a political object. I have never been a busy politician because I had neither time nor inclination. Once and only once in my life before this have I attended a political dinner ; but I have abstained, not because I had no right to be present, but because I thought my attendance might interfere with my ministerial usefulness—a regard for which is my first and primary

duty.   And, gentlemen, I am present this day at
this glorious, this splendid festival, because I verily
believe that my *absence* would have interfered with
my ministerial usefulness.   I think that you would
have considered your Vicar as wanting in his duty,
if in this cause he had shown himself afraid to come
before you from any dread of the pitiless pelting of
a profligate Whig press—a press which seems to act
upon the assumption that a Popish priest can do
no wrong, and a Protestant clergyman can do no
good.'

He then proceeded to dilate upon the danger
that a Government which had depressed the
Church and favoured the Roman Catholics in
Ireland would depress the Church in England, not
indeed of deliberate purpose, but from the exigencies
of their situation, by weakly yielding to the counsels
of the Secularists and the Dissenters on the subject
of education.

'The attempt' he said 'to establish Infidelity in
this country is proceeding thus.   The patrons and
propagators of Infidelity are going throughout the
length and breadth of the land.   They are exciting,
not, observe me, the pious Dissenters, for the pious
Dissenters on this question are with the Churchmen,
but the political Dissenters—they are stirring them
up by their speeches, by their penny cyclopædias,
by their twopenny trash, by their semi-official publications, to demand the establishment of some system
of secular education to be paid for by the country,
to be conducted by commissioners appointed by the
Government.   Now, gentlemen, the education of
the people of this country is, at the present time,

conducted thus. In the first place the Church undertakes the education of the people. This in remote villages and country places is done almost entirely by the Church. Of course the system of education conducted by the Church is based upon religion—that religion being the religion of the Bible, the Prayer Book, and the Catechism. In our larger towns, however, a very respectable body of men object to the education we give, because they object to our religion. They, therefore, set up rival schools and conduct the education of a part of the people themselves. They think we are wrong, and we think they are wrong, but still we are united. The pious Churchman and the pious Dissenter are united in considering that the education of an immortal being—a being who is to be educated not merely for time but for eternity—must be based upon religion; and happy am I to know that the religious feeling of this religious community has been roused upon the subject. The advocates for the secular system of education say " No, there shall be a system of secular education, not based upon religion, and then, after that, the people may send their children for religious instruction where they please." I should like to know what time the children of the poor would have to give to this double system of education, as every person who has been at all employed in education is well aware that two-thirds of the children sent to our schools are sent there not for the sake of religious instruction but for the sake of the general information we give, the price we demand being that they shall also receive religious instruction. So that if this secular system be established, two-thirds of the children will be brought up without any religious instruction, without any knowledge of their Saviour and their God.

'I say I rejoice to find that attention has been called to this subject, and that ministers have said that they will not give their sanction to any education that is not based upon religion. But judging of their past conduct, we have a right to ask : What do you mean by religious instruction ? Do they mean scriptural education ? Yes, some of them reply. Well, but we may ask what kind of scriptural education ? Do you mean such as that which is given in Ireland ? Now the scriptural education given in Ireland is not the whole Bible, but selections from the Bible. It is very true that good selections may be made from the Bible, containing every leading doctrine of our religion, but if we go to Ireland we find that the leading doctrines are excluded from their extracts, so that their system of religious teaching is very much like an orange with the juice squeezed out of it. But let that pass; and the question may again be asked, What do you mean by religion ? Is it the religion of the Church of England ? No; because, if that were so, the present system would require no alteration, and that would exclude the Dissenters. Is it the religion based upon Protestantism ? No; because that would exclude the Papists. Well then, let us ask, do you mean Christian principles ? No; that would exclude the Deists. So then their exclusive system of education would include no religion at all.' After observing that the Government had been deterred from bringing forward a scheme of education based on the Prussian plan, on account of the large sum of money, about 300,000*l.*, for which they would have to ask Parliament, he proceeded, ' The Government, then, not finding themselves strong enough to ask for such a sum, have laid aside their project for the present, and their friends, in their writings and cheap publications, are pointing out a species of property which they think may be made available for their object; that is, the Church property. They ask for a portion of the Church's property for the purposes of their secular education. They reason thus : they say they intend the education of the people—for the education of the people, indeed, in part they do intend; but, as we all know, only in part. The Church, we know, was established for the sanctification of the people, and education is only one branch of that work. But they shirk that part of the question; and they say that the whole of the people will not be educated by the Church, and therefore they must take a part of the property of the Church, as they will compel the people to be educated in their way. And they say that the State may at any time take away the property of the Church, because it was originally given to her by the State. Now if I were to meet a man in the street to-day, and were to give him half-a-crown, am I, if I meet him to-morrow, to take it back, and say I have found some one more worthy ? But I deny their premisses altogether. When did the State give property to the Church ? Where is the Act of Parliament by which it was given ? '

He then proceeded very lucidly to demonstrate by reference to facts, well known to every student of history, the origin of ecclesiastical endowments in the gifts of individual benefactors, and also to expose the fallacy, more common then than it is now, of supposing that at the time of the Reformation this property was taken from one Church and handed over to another.

He concluded his speech as he had begun, by warning his hearers against such a system of secular education as must lead to Infidelity. ' But, gentlemen,' he said, ' I have not much fear : I had not much fear when I came into the room, and after the able speeches we have heard this evening from our senators, my fears are fewer. . . . It cannot be very long before he is called to the head of affairs—the pilot admitted by all persons to be the pilot best qualified to weather the storm—Sir Robert Peel. He is our leader : he must be our leader : and he is worthy to be our leader. Of his learning the schools of Oxford are witness; his piety is attested by his unimpeachable morality and his regular attendance on the ordinances of religion. By his wisdom, his statesman-like qualities, his grasp of mind, all Europe has been astonished. He is too wealthy to desire office for the mere coming of Quarter Day. He is too great a patriot to desire it for anything but for his country's welfare. He was great as a minister, and in my humble judgment he has been greater still in the ranks of the Opposition. When he joins the ranks of the Opposition he seems to have determined never, for any party purpose, to violate a single constitutional principle, or to forget his loyalty to his sovereign ; and from this position he has not been driven by the jeers of taunting foes or the exhortation of enthusiastic friends. He has scorned to be the leader of a faction, that he might become, as he will become, the leader of his country. Under his guidance, supported as he will be by Wellington, the hero of the age : by Stanley, second only to himself; by the manly Graham, by our own Beckett, by Lord Wharncliffe and all the Wortleys, —by Lord Maidstone and all the youthful senators; and though last, not least in our estimation, by the worthy baronet who has honoured us this day by his company—under Sir Robert Peel's guidance, I say, assisted by these, we cannot greatly fall : but the Church and State will be upheld—which may God Almighty of His mercy grant.'

All the newspapers in their comments on this festival concur in pronouncing the Vicar's speech to have been the most striking of all which were made that evening. None were comparable to it in weightiness of matter, in sustained eloquence, and in the musical voice and dignified manner of the speaker. None elicited more frequent and enthusiastic applause from the assembly. I have made rather copious extracts from it, not merely as illustrations of his powers of oratory, but as expressions of his views on the subject of national education : views from which he never departed in principle, although the scheme proposed in his celebrated pamphlet hereafter to be noticed, ' How to Render more Efficient the Education of the People,' was erroneously imagined by many to be inconsistent with them.

The eulogy on Sir Robert Peel is a remarkable expression of the admiration and respect which he entertained for that eminent statesman : an admiration and respect greater than that which he ever entertained for any politician, save for one of a yet loftier and more comprehensive genius—William Ewart Gladstone.

In June of this year (1838) he preached at the Chapel Royal, before the young Queen and her court, the memorable sermon, ' Hear the Church ! ' It deserves the epithet which I have applied to it, because it excited much commotion at the time in the political and fashionable world, and ran through twenty-eight editions, in which about one hundred thousand copies were sold. But in the present day it is difficult to comprehend the sensation which it produced (a proof how much the doctrine it set forth has gained ground) ; and even then it was astonishing to those who thoroughly understood the sermon—to no one more than the author himself. It was an old sermon, originally composed at Coventry as one of a series on the Gospel of St. Matthew, and subsequently delivered at Leeds and other places. A few alterations only were introduced to adapt it to the occasion, and the sermon itself was selected because he thought it would answer the aim which he had in view as well as if he had written a new one. That aim simply was to lay before the young sovereign the claims, the character, and the privileges of the Church of which, in the providence of God, she had been called to be the temporal Head. Surrounded as she was at that time by ministers whose ignorance of the history of the Church, and misconceptions of its true principles and constitution might, as he feared, prejudice her mind with fatal errors on the subject, he conceived it to be his duty, so far as in him lay, to prejudice her mind in favour of the truth.

He began by stating that he was going to speak of the Church not as a mere National Establishment, but in itself—as a religious community—intrinsically independent of the State: in other words, that he was about to treat of the Church *not* in its political, but purely in its religious aspect. After pointing out that the mere fact of establishment by civil government could not in itself constitute the claim of any form of religion to our obedience, since on that principle we should have to become Presbyterians in Scotland and Holland, Papists in Italy and France, and Mohammedans in Turkey; after demonstrating on the other hand that the dissolution of the tie between the Church and State, though it would be highly injurious to the State, and probably destructive of the monarchy, could not vitally impair the energies of the Church—a fact of which the Church in America was a standing witness—he proceeded to indicate the real claims of the Church to the allegiance of Englishmen, by answering the question, When and by whom was this Society which we call the Church instituted ?

It would be needless in the present day, even if the sermon were not accessible to all who may choose to refer to it, to follow the preacher over well-known ground. That the Church of England was not founded but reformed in the sixteenth century; that the Roman Catholics in England are descended from a party who, in the reign of Elizabeth, quitted the Church because they thought it was reformed too far, just as the Protestant Dissenters quitted it because they thought it was not reformed far enough ; that the Bishops of the English Church trace their origin by a continuous succession back to the Apostles, and hence claim to derive their authority from Christ Himself—these are historical facts which are now familiar to most well-educated persons, facts which no one who pretends to a moderate acquaintance with history can venture to dispute, whatever his opinion respecting their doctrinal significance may be. They were, however, startling to some who heard them for the first time as they were announced by the preacher in the Chapel Royal. They were disbelieved or misunderstood ; by many they were misrepresented as defiant assertions, by an ecclesiatical bigot, of exacting and overweening claims on the part of the Church ; claims which, if pushed to extremity, might be dangerous to the civil constitution. The consequence was that the sermon became invested with an exaggerated importance never expected, still less intended, by the preacher. The unnecessary agitation, however, respecting it had the good effect of leading thousands to read the sermon who otherwise would never have even heard of it, and thus helped to spread far and wide the truths which the writer so earnestly desired to propagate. There are many who can date from the perusal of that sermon an increase in their attachment to the Church, or the creation of an attachment never felt before. There are many who can remember how, for the first time, they perceived the bearing on personal religion of right knowledge respecting the origin of the Church,

when they read the words, ' Let us ever remember
that the primary object for which the Church was
instituted by Christ, its Author and Finisher, and
for which the Apostolical succession of its ministers
was established; that the primary object for which,
through ages of persecution and ages of prosperity,
and ages of darkness and ages of corruption, and
ages of reformation and ages of latitudinarianism,
and now in an age of rebuke and blasphemy, now
when we have fallen on evil days and evil tongues
—the primary object for which the Church has still
been preserved by a providential care, marvellous, if
not miraculous, in our eyes, was and is to convey
supernaturally the saving merits of the atoning blood
of the Lamb of God, and the sanctifying graces of
His Holy Spirit, to the believer's soul. In the
Church it is that the appointed means are to be
found by which that mysterious union with Christ is
promoted wherein our spiritual life consists : in Her
it is that the Third Person of the Blessed Trinity
abideth for ever, gradually to change the heart of
sinful man, and to make that flesh which He finds
stone; gradually to prepare us for heaven while
our ascended Saviour is preparing heaven for us.'

Many, too, can remember how a spirit of zeal
was kindled within them as they read the burning
words with which the sermon ends. 'Against the
Church the world seems at this time to be set in
array. To be a true and faithful member of the
Church requires no little moral courage. Basely to
pretend to belong to her, while designing mischief
against her in the heart—this is easy enough ; but
manfully to contend for her, because she is the

Church, a true Church, a pure Church, a holy Church, this is difficult to those who court the praise of men or fear the censure of the world. May the great God of Heaven, may Christ, the great Bishop and Shepherd of souls, who is over all things in the Church, put it, my brethren, into your hearts and minds to say and feel as I do, " As for me and my house we will live in the Church, we will die in the Church, and if need shall be, like our martyred forefathers we will die *for* the Church." '

Earnest and decided Churchmen of course rejoiced in this clear and courageous vindication in high places of the character of the Church. Letters of congratulation and gratitude poured in from all directions. Dr. Doane, the American Bishop of New Jersey, wrote that he had long been following the author with his eye and heart as the able and fearless advocate of the principles to which his life was pledged, that he secured with eagerness all his publications as they came out, and he had been so deeply impressed with this sermon that he had printed it, and presented a copy to every clergyman in his diocese, and to most of the leading laymen.'

Henry, Bishop of Exeter, said he had read it with unmixed gratification, and 'I heartily thank you,' he writes, ' for the fidelity as well as the ability with which you have placed the important subject before the mind of Her to whom of all others it is of the highest consequence that the mighty truth should be familiar.' He proceeds to say that he had at first understood that her Majesty was displeased with the sermon, but had since learned, from a quarter which could hardly be misinformed, that this was not the case, but that she expressed herself interested in the subject, and " seemed to feel it to be *new as well as momentous."* '

The following letter to his wife shows how completely unprepared the writer was for the commotion caused by his sermon.

10 Dean's Yard : June 20, 1838.

My dearest Love, ... It is quite astonishing what a noise my poor sermon at the Chapel Royal has made ; there were some thirty or forty peers unable to get in, and there were all kinds of reports about what I said. Robert heard someone say yesterday at Lady Wemyss's party, that nothing is talked about but the duel (Lord C.'s about Grisi) and the sermon. The Bishop of London, who was present, was very kind ; he told me at the levée, (from which I have just returned) that some persons about the Queen wished to make out that it was political, and he had just been sent for to give his opinion. He asserted that there was not the slightest allusion to politics, unless it were political to speak of the Church of England as a true Church. The Duke of Wellington spoke to me at the levée, and said he heard that I had preached a very fine sermon last Sunday. The Archbishop of Canterbury apologised for not having written to thank me for my Life of Hobart, the preface to which he particularly liked. Sir John Beckett is kindness itself ; he introduced me to the Duke. All this seems to me very strange, for I only preached that old Leeds sermon which you remember. They say at the Carlton, that the Queen was much affected, and on returning home retired for about an hour ; if this be true, one may hope that good has been done.

It will be seen also from this letter that the writer was led to believe that no offence had been taken, where certainly no offence was intended to be given. Nevertheless a report got about that he had been forbidden to preach in the Chapel Royal again. He wrote to the ' Times' to contradict the truth of the report, adding that he had not any reason to suppose that her Majesty was otherwise than pleased with the sermon.

In August 1838 he preached at the primary visitation of Bishop Longley, held in Leeds ; taking as his text Acts vii. 26, ' Sirs, ye are brethren : why do ye wrong one to another ?' The sermon was entitled ' A Call to Union on the Principles of the English Reformation.' [1] Some of the leading Evangelicals in Leeds and elsewhere, as well as those journals which were the organs of the Evangelical school, persisted in identifying him with the writers of the Oxford Tracts, and further accused him and them in common of being untrue to the principles of the Reformation. Taking their stand upon the celebrated, but obscure and much abused, saying of Chillingworth, ' The Bible and the Bible only—the religion of Protestants' as the cardinal principle of the Reformed Church, the assailants vehemently denounced the Tract writers and the Vicar of Leeds, on account of the deference which they paid to the voice of the Church, as expressed in the writings of the primitive Fathers, in the decrees of General Councils, and in her ancient liturgies and creeds. The aim of the Vicar in his ' Call to Union' was to demonstrate that this appeal to antiquity was the very principle upon which the English Reformation was conducted, and that consequently a departure from that principle was chargeable, not upon himself or upon the Tract writers, but upon their opponents

[1] Printed in vol. i. of ' The Church and her Ordinances,' p. 90.

He supported this argument by a great mass of historical evidence, partly woven into the body of the discourse, partly introduced into notes appended to it, proving point by point how careful our Reformers were, alike in doctrine, ritual, and formularies, to base every part upon primitive models; how earnestly they deprecated on all occasions the supposition that they were devising, or wished to devise, novelties—or that they trusted to their private judgment. He contended, therefore, that, however much members of the Church might differ in opinions about details, they ought to find a principle of union in the Ritual, Liturgy, and Articles of the Church, because in deferring to them respect would be paid, not to the judgment merely of individuals such as Cranmer, Ridley, or Parker, but to the traditional doctrine of the Universal Church as it existed in those days when the Church was substantially one, and a strict correspondence on all vital matters was maintained between the several branches of it. He earnestly exhorted all to bear in mind that nothing could excuse the introduction of faction and discord into the Church. The duty of every clergyman at least was plain; if he could not conscientiously conform to the teaching and practice of the Church, he was free to withdraw; and, as an honest and honourable man, he was bound to withdraw from her communion. 'Every conscientious English clergyman,' he said, 'acts on the principle that while Scripture, and Scripture only, is his rule of faith, he is, in the interpretation of Scripture, to defer to the Ritual, Liturgy, Articles, and formularies of the Church of England; he is to promote the glory of God, peace upon earth, and goodwill among men; but to do so, *not* in the way which he may imagine to be the wisest, but according to the regulations, canons, rubrics, customs of his Church. To these he is bound by vows the most solemn to conform'—if he could not conform, let him depart. 'And where are we to look,' he continued, 'for unity, if we find it not here? And what terms of reprobation can be sufficiently strong to designate the conduct of those who, by causing discord among brethren, in principle united, would thereby make music for our enemies?' The concluding part of the sermon is pitched in the same strain. 'Remember that if the propagation of evangelical truth be one portion of our duty, it is no less our duty, by the sacrifice of all personal considerations. . . . to preserve "the unity of the Spirit in the bond of peace." Remember that our enemies are many and mighty; the two extremes of Romanism and ultra-Protestantism are banded together with infidelity against us; and if, like Samson's foxes, they are pulling different ways, the brands which are attached have one and the selfsame object—our destruction. And is this a time to divide our house, and to form parties and factions?'

An extract from one of the notes to this sermon will present to the reader a clear view of his attitude at that time towards the Tract writers. Having pointed out that when Mr. Wilberforce, in his later years, and some of the more moderate leaders of the Evangelicals, encouraged a spirit of deference to the authoritative decisions of the Church of England, the question then arose, What are Church principles?

Is any party consistently acting upon them ? 'At such a time,' he proceeds, 'the celebrated Oxford Tracts made their appearance. The reputed writers of the Tracts were men of ardent piety, who had been attached to the Evangelical school, and it was among the younger men who had been educated in that school that they created a strong sensation. Hence, perhaps, the bitterness with which they are assailed by some of the older partisans of that section of the Church. To those who, like the present writer, had been educated strictly on the principles of the English Reformation, and belonged to the old orthodox school, they brought forward nothing new ; and though we may have demurred to some of their opinions, and have thought that in some things they were in an extreme, we rejoiced to see right principles advocated in a manner so decided, and in a spirit so truly Christian. Against some of the pious opinions supported in these Tracts objections may occasionally be raised, for perfect coincidence of *opinion* is not to be expected. I do not myself accord with all the opinions expressed in them, or always admit the deduction attempted to be drawn from the principles on which we are agreed. I think, too, that while manfully vindicating the principles of the English Reformation, in their fear lest they should appear to respect *persons* too highly, they did not appreciate highly enough the character of some of our leading Reformers, or make due allowance for the difficulties in which they were placed.' At the same time he expressed his conviction that the object of the writers was 'to imbue the public mind with those Catholic principles by the maintenance of which the

English Reformation was gloriously distinguished. This cannot be done unless on those principles opinions are formed, and from them conclusions drawn; and at the very time that we may combat a particular opinion, if we admit the truth of the principle on which it is based we only confirm the principle, and impress it more deeply on men's minds. I am not one of those who would say, " Read the Oxford Tracts, and take for granted every opinion there expressed ; " but I am one of those who would say, " Read and digest these Tracts well, and you will have imbibed principles which will enable you to judge of opinions." Their popularity will increase, since their arguments are not answered or their statements confuted : they are opposed simply by railing.   And those who judge of such things only by second-hand reports and garbled quotations, and anonymous misrepresentations in newspapers, will of course rail on.   May the day come when they may be awakened to a sense of the danger of thus violating the golden rule of charity.   In the meantime the wise, the candid, those who are not the mere partisans of religion, but really religious, will themselves read the Tracts ; and if they do read they will commend.   They may censure particular opinions, but they will commend the whole.'

These remarks may have been partly due to a long letter received from Dr. Pusey a short time before, in which, after showing how seriously the intentions of the Tract writers were misunderstood and maligned, he entreated the Vicar to befriend them, as opportunities of so doing might occur.   He had pointed out in this letter that the Tracts did not profess to be *tests* of Catholicity, but only *guides* to it; and as such he hoped that the Vicar would be able to give them a general support. 'As for your being a disciple of us,' he continued, 'the thing is absurd. Newman said that you had formed your views long before many of the writers—long before myself, upon many points.'

But what more especially provoked him to make this defence of the Tract writers was the indignation which he felt at the violent denunciation which had been lately flung at their productions (more especially the Remains of Mr. Hurrell Froude) from the university pulpit by Dr. Faussett, Margaret Professor of Divinity, Oxford. He himself also was suffering from similar treatment at the hands of Evangelical preachers in Leeds and other parts of the country. He pointed out in his sermon that such conduct was a violation of the fifty-third Canon, which directs ' that if any preacher shall in the pulpit purposely impugn or confute any doctrine delivered by any other preacher, in the same church or in any church near adjoining, without permission from the Bishop, a complaint shall be made to the Bishop by the aggrieved party, and the said preacher shall not be allowed any more to occupy that place which he hath once abused except he faithfully promise to forbear all such matter of contention in the Church, until the Bishop hath taken further order therein.' And in a note he remarks: ' Of all the glaring violations of this Canon none is of course so conspicuous as that which has been lately exhibited by Dr. Faussett. . . . The present discourse is sufficient to show that I am not any more than Dr. Faussett inclined to approve of Mr.

Froude's Remains. I deeply, indeed, regret the publication of that work without a protest on the part of the editor against the author's many paradoxical positions. With a kind heart, and glowing sensibilities, Mr. Froude united a mind saturated with learning, but from its very luxuriance productive of weeds together with many flowers. Though he always took an original, he sometimes took a morbid, view of things, and while from his writings all must derive much food for thought, from many of his opinions the majority of his readers will, like myself, dissent. But if, in contemplating the evils inseparable from a great movement, he does not sufficiently appreciate (and I think he does not) the wisdom of our Reformation or the virtues of many of our Reformers; if, while condemning the Romish, he censures the English, Church, we may think him to be in error in these particulars without condemning him wholesale. Still less ought those persons to condemn him for not fully appreciating our Reformation who consider the work of the Reformers in retaining our present Baptismal Service "a burthen hard to bear," and the service "an absurdity which they do not believe in their hearts." Had Dr. Faussett contented himself with writing a pamphlet or a review, while we might have considered him incompetent to sit in judgment on such a mind as Mr. Froude's, we should have had no cause of complaint. But cause of complaint the Church has when he makes one work a pretext for attacking certain of his clerical brethren whose learning he may be unable to appreciate, but whose piety and zeal he would do well to imitate. . . . If

Dr. Faussett has a right on one Sunday to attack his brethren in the ministry, than whom he is not himself one whit more infallible, the brethren thus attacked might Sunday after Sunday ascend the pulpit and assail Dr. Faussett and his projected new Oxford school of Divinity. If, with equal indiscretion and no greater regard for the regulations of the Church, they had done so—if, deducing their own conclusions from Dr. Faussett's manifest opposition to fastings and mortifications of the flesh, they had headed their discourses with the taking title " Revival of Sensualism " just as he has charged them with "The Revival of Popery,"[1] Dr. Faussett, indeed, would have had no ground for complaint, but the Church would have had to deplore an exhibition the most disgraceful, though the natural consequence of Dr. Faussett's conduct.'

After this note had gone to the press the charge of the Bishop of Oxford (Dr. Bagot) was published ; and the Vicar added some remarks upon it, contrasting its sober judgments, wise counsels, and affectionate fatherly tone with the coarse, indiscriminating invectives of Dr. Faussett. ' The Bishop,' he observed, ' had a right to do what Dr. Faussett had no right to do ; his lordship had a right to pronounce sentence *ex cathedrâ*, after examination, on the conduct and doctrines of his clergy, among whom are the writers of the Oxford Tracts.' And he then gives some extracts from the charge, in which the Bishop declares that, after diligent inquiry, he had been unable to find anything in the conduct or writings of the persons alluded to which could

---

[1] The title of Dr. Faussett's sermon.

fairly be interpreted as breaches of the doctrine or discipline of the Church of England. 'Generally speaking,' said the Bishop, 'I may say that in these days of lax and spurious liberality anything which tends to recall forgotten truth is valuable ; and when these publications have directed men's minds to such important subjects as the union, the discipline, and the authority of the Church, I think they have done good service ; but there may be some points in which, from ambiguity of expression or similar causes, it is not impossible but that evil, rather than the intended good, may be produced on minds of a peculiar temperament. I have more fear of the disciples than of the teachers.' At the same time the Bishop continued, 'I would implore them by the purity of their intentions to be cautious, both in their writings and actions, to take heed lest "their good be evil spoken of ;" lest, in their exertions to re-establish unity, they unhappily create fresh schism ; lest, in their admiration of antiquity, they revert to practices which heretofore have ended in superstition.'

The Bishop, in the difficult and delicate situation which he then occupied in relation to the Tract writers, was particularly grateful to the Vicar of Leeds for the line adopted in his sermon, and more particularly for the support given to the Charge, which, notwithstanding the gentleness of its tone, some of the Tract writers were disposed to think implied so much disapproval of the Tracts, that the publication of them ought to be discontinued.

'I have read your sermon,' wrote the Bishop, 'with the greatest pleasure and satisfaction, agreeing entirely with all you say throughout, and I feel much indebted to you for the note respecting my late Charge. It will do more than anything else could have done to quiet and satisfy the minds of those excellent men (some I may call friends) whose high principles of obedience to authority, but whose over-sensitiveness made them apprehensive that my Charge might be construed (but surely only by perversion) into a *censure* upon the Tracts, and make them liable to a charge of inconsistency if they did not discontinue the publication.

By a private correspondence with Dr. Pusey and Mr. Newman I sufficiently satisfied their minds to induce them not to adopt such a course, and that nothing could be further from my wish than to cast a general censure upon the work. I merely state this to prove to you how very valuable to them such a note as you have kindly added with reference to my Charge was, and how peculiarly well-timed.

The sermon gave great satisfaction not only to the Bishop of Oxford and the Tract writers but also to a large body of moderate Churchmen.

On the other hand the ultra-Protestant section of the Church could not forgive him for having demonstrated that they, and not the high Churchmen, were unfaithful to the spirit of the Reformation; and their journals and reviews discharged a volley of attacks upon the sermon, more distinguished for acrimony of tone and vehemence of language than for weight of learning or strength of argument. 'Fraser's Magazine,' among others, took up the cudgels, and produced an article in January 1839 which was exceedingly applauded by a large portion of the press, but of which it may suffice to observe here that the flippancy and vulgarity of the style in which it is written are only equalled by the strange misconceptions displayed of the main positions of the writer whom it attacks.

From those storms of controversy which are the products of human infirmity and passion, it is rather a relief to turn for a moment to an account of one of those convulsions of nature for which man is not responsible. One night in the month of January 1839, a tempest of extraordinary fury raged over the North of England. The Rev. H. W. Bellairs was on a visit to the Vicar of Leeds, and has kindly supplied me with his reminiscences of the storm. Early in the morning, above the roaring and raving of the wind, he heard a terrific crash, and on opening his bedroom door discovered that a part of the roof was blown away; and the strange creaking and cracking sounds throughout the house led him at first to imagine that the hurricane was accompanied by an earthquake. ' I went downstairs,' he writes, 'and, hearing voices, followed them to a room on the basement where I found the Vicar with a child on either knee, his servants, and a captain of artillery, who was staying in the house, standing round him. The Vicar was perfectly unmoved; calming, comforting, and reassuring all with those words of faith, hope, and love which none knew better than himself how to use. Whilst we were there another fearful crash came, breaking through the roaring of the wind, which even in the house was overpowering. In a few minutes some one came in, I think from the next house, saying that a chimney there had fallen through the roof, burying two female servants in its ruins, and that the master of the house was in the street utterly beside himself. The Vicar put down the children, went to the window, and saw the poor fellow cling-

ing to some iron railings opposite the Vicarage.
The storm was raging with such violence that it
was almost impossible for anyone to stand unaided.
The Vicar, however, struggled across the road, got
hold of the man and brought him into the Vicarage,
and calmed him until he was able to return to his
house. The quiet courage, strong faith, and affectionate bearing of the Vicar in that hour of fear and
peril, no one who witnessed it can ever forget.'

The following letter from him to Mr. Wood is a
vivid description of the hurricane.

January 17, 1839.

My dearest Friend,—You have not I hope been visited
with that dreadful hurricane which alarmed us here in these
northern regions. Never did I hear wind blow as the
wind blew on the morning of last Monday se'nnight. The
beds rocked under us, and a tremendous crash was heard;
when Delicia begged me to go upstairs, and bring the
children down to our own room. Imagine my horror,
when, as I approached the stairs I heard screams; and
imagine my joy when I counted my children and found
none wanting, at the time when the wind pierced me to
the very bones, blowing upon me from the open sky, for
the roof of the day-nursery had fallen in with a terrific
crash. No one in that room could have escaped with life.
In the very next room our dear little Jemmy was asleep;
and the darling girls in the room adjoining that. Two
hours later, for the downfall happened at six o'clock, they
would have been dressing in the day-nursery, and must
have perished. Three stacks of chimneys were blown
down in our house. We have been obliged to send the
children away, and Delicia and I have been confined to
two rooms, the only two in which fires could be lighted,
and have been driven from one to another. In the midst
of all this, a cold from which Delicia had long suffered

became worse. Inflammation and fever have ensued, and
she has been confined to her bed. God be praised she is
much better now . . . . These things come to tell us what
ungrateful wretches we are. How little we value the
blessings which appear to be common blessings—health
and peace—till we lose them. How applicable to the
circumstances of the storm is the twenty-ninth Psalm. I
read it afterwards at my family prayers, and preached on it
last Sunday. It was indeed merciful that in all Leeds only
one life was lost.

The year 1839 was a critical one for the Church
in respect to the question of National Education.
The ' Central Society of Education ' was pressing its
demands for a secular system, under which religious
instruction of any kind should be absolutely forbidden, while the Government in February proposed its
scheme for the establishment of a Board of Education, and of a model or normal school, with teachers
of divers religious persuasions, and a Rector of no
religion in particular. The Board, which was to
consist of the President of the Council and five other
privy councillors, did not need any Act to call it
into being ; and thus that remarkable dynasty known
by the title of ' my lords,' whose wonderful and inscrutable decrees are a source of annual amusement,
or vexation, to school managers, came into existence
at once—fully armed, like Athene from the head of
Zeus. The remainder of the measure passed the
House of Commons by a majority of two in the
month of June, but in the House of Lords a series
of resolutions, to be embodied in an address to the
Crown against the Bill, was moved by Archbishop
Howley, supported by Bishop Blomfield in one of

the ablest speeches he ever delivered, and carried by
a large majority.

The interval between the first proposal of the
scheme in February and the debates in June, was
occupied by Churchmen in great efforts, both to
convince the public mind of the work which the
Church had already accomplished in the cause of
national education, and to devise plans for enabling
her to strengthen and extend her operations. The
Vicar threw himself into this work with immense
energy. He foresaw indeed that the day was not
far distant when the State would be compelled to
undertake the education of the people, and he also
perceived that in a country where the forms of
religious belief were so manifold as in England, the
only education which the State could provide, consistently with discharging its duty towards the *whole*
population, must be of a purely secular kind. But
at present he did not very frequently or publicly
enlarge upon this topic. Meanwhile there were
two calamities which he exceedingly dreaded, and
laboured most sedulously, as far as in him lay, to
avert. One was the appropriation by the State of
ecclesiastical property, at the instigation of Socialists,
to the purposes of secular education. This, as has
been seen, was the topic on which he more especially
dilated in his speech at the Conservative banquet in
1838. The other was the acceptance by the Church
of any specious offer from the State of some diluted
form of religious education, which he was convinced
would be a mere counterfeit—a system under which
children would receive only vague and indistinct
ideas about religious truths, and consequently grow

up into 'nothingarians.' The honesty and thorough-
ness of his nature, and his firm persuasion that clear
dogmatic teaching was the only guarantee for sound
morality, the only solid platform upon which it could
be built up, revolted against the notion of any com-
promises and cheats in connexion with this matter.
As an escape from such evils he had already conceived in his mind the germ of that bold and original
scheme, which, eight years afterwards, he formally
propounded in his celebrated letter to the Bishop of
St. David's. The outlines of it are sketched in the
following letters, written at the close of 1838, to Mr.
Wood. Let the State undertake the secular part of
education, which is all that it *can* honestly and consistently undertake, and let the Church and the sects
undertake the religious part, the State taking care
that all have a fair field. Such were the ideas
already working in his mind, which were afterwards
developed in the pamphlet to which allusion has just
been made.

Education Scheme.

I am still sadly in want of some one to manage the
educational affairs of this parish; if you hear of any enthusiast, pray tell me of him. All I should require would
be, his having Church principles. On the subject of education, I have been thinking more of late, and am in correspondence on the subject with some influential people. My
advice is, to find from all parties what concessions can be
made without sacrifice of principle. I propose a measure,
which is this; that a board of education be formed in every
parish; the Incumbent chairman, his curates *ex-officio*
members, and a certain number of ratepayers to complete
the board. If pressed, I would concede that Dissenting
ministers, resident in the parish three years, should also be

members.   The board to have power to lay a rate, and to decide on the books to be used; no direct religious instruction to be given; but no child to be admitted who cannot bring a certificate of being a member of some Sunday-school, where religious instruction is given.   Absence for three Sundays from Sunday-school without leave, to be punished by three months' expulsion from National school. Each clergyman, or Dissenting minister, to be permitted to attend on Fridays to instruct his own children; a separate room to be provided for the purpose.   A normal school to be established in London for training masters by Government, under directors; the two Archbishops, and Bishops of London, Durham, and Winton, directors always; the rest to be appointed by Government, provided that they appoint five Dissenting ministers.   You see we here provide for general education, and yet assert the necessity of religious education.   Probably we shall have to define religious education to be Biblical, or the Socialists may so denominate their system.   I should like to know your opinion of this scheme.   It is rather liberal, but while it concedes much to Dissenters, it gives the Church the lead; and this point Dissenters ought to concede.   I shall feel extremely obliged to you not to mention this plan till you hear from me again.   I have particular reasons for particularly wishing this.   I am so accustomed to tell you all things, that I cannot help mentioning my plan to you, but it is for the present a secret.

Education Scheme—A New Magazine—Parochial Reading Rooms.

Vicarage, Leeds: November 28, 1838.

My dearest Friend, ... Anything like a semi-religious education, I deprecate, but I have no objection to let the State train children to receive the religious education we are prepared to give; the State at the same time insisting on their coming to us for the purpose.   But of course, on consideration, I shall not propound my plan to anyone;

being not a little surprised to find that I am more liberal than that odious Whig fellow, William Wood. I cannot help suspecting that evil communications with you corrupted my good manners. I am, however, delighted to find that our sentiments so entirely accord with respect to education : our principle is, I see, precisely the same ; only I, in despair, was prepared to make a larger sacrifice than you think quite necessary. I rejoice to know this. Only let us have anything rather than a mutilated Bible, a semi-religion, which is worse than an avowedly Infidel education ; *worse* because it leads to the same end without causing that alarm which the avowal of Infidelity would excite. As to my plans here, I have heard of a man from Sam. Wood, who, he thinks would suit us ; perhaps, if you could call on Mr. Wood, your knowledge of the Leeds localities might assist him further in forming his judgment. He seems to me to be just the kind of person ; but then he cannot afford to come, I suspect, under 100*l.*, or 150*l.*, a year, but this sum I cannot (so says my woman of business) at present spare ; I have, however, written to my good lord Bishop, and asked him to form a board of education in this town ; if he will do this in the course of two or three months, as a paid secretary will be wanted, I think I shall send for this gentleman and run the risk of his being appointed, engaging him at the lowest salary at which he will come. I have never found Providence to fail me, and I think that this is a kind of thing in which I may be a little bold.

At present, his School Board scheme was only whispered to intimate and confidential friends as a kind of esoteric doctrine. The disclosure of it would have been too rude a shock to the feelings of those who still clung to the belief that the Church, being called the National Church, was not only bound to educate the whole people but was competent to discharge the task. The immediate duty of Church-

men he considered at that time was obvious : namely,
to make the most of their opportunities, to show
that they could at least take the lead in the work of
national education, and so to deepen the claim of the
Church upon the gratitude of the nation.   The establishment of local boards of education in populous
places would, he thought, assist in the consolidation
and extension of the Church's educational work, and
he was therefore anxious, as mentioned in the letter
transcribed above, to form one with as little delay
as possible for the parish of Leeds.

Accordingly on March 14, 1839, a large meeting
was held in the Music Hall, the Bishop of Ripon
being in the chair, to take steps for the purpose.
The Vicar made a long and elaborate speech on the
occasion, and as it contains some very interesting
information respecting the state of national education
at that time, I shall not hesitate to present to the
reader some rather full transcripts and paraphrases
of his remarks.

He began by observing that, as he was addressing an assembly of Churchmen, he should assume as
a fact indisputable among themselves that no education could deserve the name which was not based
upon religion.   If education consisted in training up
a child in the way he ought to go, no Christian man
could venture to suppose that this end would be accomplished unless religious principles were brought,
indirectly at least, to bear upon all the instruction
given.   If this were acknowledged, it clearly behoved
Churchmen at that crisis to bestir themselves.   ‘We
must offer to the country the best possible education,
or the State will take the duty of education upon

itself, and if the State does this it must eventually adopt a purely secular education—an education not based upon religion. The only country in which a State education is consistently conducted is Holland, and there religion is avowedly excluded. In Prussia religion is assumed as the basis, but there the Government cannot act consistently on the principles it asserts. It must be obvious that when a State undertakes the education of the people it cannot make religion its basis. It may pretend to do so at first, but the State religion will be found on investigation to be no religion. Let us suppose the State were at the present time to undertake the education of the people—let us suppose it to concede the principle that education must be based on religion—the question immediately occurs on what religion is it to be based ? Shall it be the religion of the Church of England ? If so, no change is necessary. But a change is demanded to meet the views of those who dissent from the Church. The State, it will be said, is to provide for the education of *all* the people. Well, then, let us now ask, is the education to be exclusively Protestant ? No, not if the principle is adhered to, for that would exclude the Romanists. Carry on the principle, and we may ask, again, is the education to be Christian ? If Infidelity prevails (and, alas ! it does prevail to a fearful extent), Jews, Turks, and Infidels will all demand that the education of the country shall be so conducted as not to exclude them. And *then* what is the religion on which the State education is based ? It certainly looks as much like *no* religion as possible. I do not say that this will be the immediate consequence of a State education, but it is its direct tendency. The objection to Church education is its exclusiveness. If the State forms a new system of religion less exclusive, still, since it *must* exclude *some* parties, the argument against exclusiveness may be brought to bear against that State sect also, and so on until at length it is found that every religion must be exclusive, and that nothing is really liberal but Atheism. As soon as the State undertakes to control religion, religion must be corrupted, for it will then cease to be busied with God's truth and will be dabbling with expediency. The question will be, not what does the all pure and all perfect God command, but what will man—fallen, corrupted, wicked man—consent to receive.'

After showing that one of the purposes for which the Church was endowed was to educate the people, except such as dissented from her teaching; that this work had been much neglected during the middle ages, revived during the sixteenth century by the establishment of Grammar Schools, but in abeyance during the depression of the Church in the days of the Commonwealth, he proceeded to sketch the work accomplished by the Church on behalf of national education, from the foundation of the Society for Promoting Christian Knowledge in the reign of William III. 'One of the first objects,' he said, 'of that Society was to found and endow public charity schools'; and such was the success of its labours that in the year 1741 we find it had established more than 2,000 schools in different parts of the country. After observing that this was the first Society which had advocated and supported the general education of the people, and that it was essentially and entirely an offspring of the Church, he continued : ' Nor may it be forgotten that in thus advocating the cause of education the Church was, for a long time, rowing *against* the stream. It is easy now to call meetings and urge upon society the duty of educating the poor, because the topic is a popular one. But the Church during the last century had to fight against a prejudice, many great and good men of all parties being prejudiced against the education of the people. I myself remember twenty years ago that in our charity sermons all we attempted to prove was that there could be no *harm* in educating the people— that there was no probability of that injury resulting from it to society which some persons seemed to fear ; that the danger was not from over-educating, but from under-educating the poor. And is the Church now to be upbraided, as if her increased zeal for the education of the people was the result of a pressure from without ? By whom is the accusation made ? By the representatives of those who, during the past century, did *nothing* for education. Is not the doing something better than the doing nothing, and has not the Church done much if she has preached down the prejudice which for a time existed against the education of the poor ? Until that prejudice was annihilated it was impossible to do great things. The Government was unwilling to aid because the Government was unwilling to do an act which might be unpopular among those classes of society to which it looked for support. Thanks be to God that prejudice has been overcome, and

Christians are now prepared to admit that our Creator would not have given to man a reasonable mind to distinguish him from the brute unless He had intended the intellect to be cultivated, and that it is the duty of the rich to assist the poor in the cultivation of their minds.   The better educated the poor man is, the more ready will he be to listen to the dictates of his reason and his conscience—the less likely to be led astray by the inflammatory sophistry of the demagogue, the more likely will he be to become loyal to his Queen and true to his Church.'

He then entered into some statistics to prove the extent to which, at that time, the Church was discharging her duty in respect of national education, especially as compared with the various nonconforming communities.

Of daily scholars above the age of seven
    there were in Dissenting Schools   .   47,287
Of Sunday scholars in the same .   .   550,107
        Total of all ranks and descrip-
        tions in Dissenting Schools .   597,394

In schools connected with the Church there were :—
Of daily scholars in Grammar Schools
    and Colleges   603,428
In elementary schools connected with
    the National Society, which was esta-
    blished by Churchmen in 1811 .   .   514,450
        Total of daily scholars   .   .1,117,878

Sunday scholars only, in Church Schools   435,550
Total of all ranks and descriptions in
    Church Schools 1,553,428

'We may, then,' he said, 'fairly assert that we

have the education of the people in our hands; and
why should it be taken away from us? We have
received no favour from Government; whatever
money has been voted by Parliament for educational
purposes has been offered to the Dissenters equally
with ourselves. But the people flock to our schools.
. . . Five years ago it was proposed by Lord Althorp that 20,000*l.* should be voted for the purposes
of education, and this sum has been annually voted
ever since. And the two Societies, the National
Society on the part of the Church, the British and
Foreign Society on the part of the Dissenters, were
selected as the administrators of the fund. The
grant was to be distributed to these two societies,
on a principle of perfect fairness, each Society taking
a share proportionate to the sum which it raised by
voluntary contributions. This was hailed as a boon
by the British and Foreign School Society, and
seemed likely to operate in favour of Dissent;
yet it has turned out that the National Society has
been able to avail itself of the grant to nearly double
the amount of the British and Foreign School Society.
The returns are as follow of the applications made
by the two Societies :—

	1834	1835	1836	1837	1838	Total
National Society .	11,081	13,002	17,130	11,456	17,041	69,710
British and Foreign .	9,796	7,168	5,281	5,810	6,090	35,285

He then advocated the adoption of some plan of
compulsory education. 'It is said that there are
112,035 children above the age of seven utterly
destitute of any kind of education whatever. How

can the Church help that? We open schools in all
places, but we cannot *compel* the parents to send
their children to them. There is no lack of means of
education; the misfortune is that there are 100,000
wicked parents who will not avail themselves of the
means provided. How is this to be remedied? It
is said, by schools supported by Government. But
why should those schools be more likely to be attended than the existing schools? Is the attendance
to be compulsory? There is no need to establish
Government Schools on that account, for the children may be as well compelled to attend existing
schools as any other newly devised schools. I do
not mean that they should be compelled to attend
Church Schools. Let the parents have the choice
of the schools, but let there be some law which will
empower the magistrates to insist on all children
being sent to *some* school. If a parent neglects to
educate his child, he is doing an injury not only to
the child but to the community itself, which suffers
from that child's ignorance and vice. If the State
may interfere for the *punishment* of crime it may
surely interfere for the *prevention* of crime; it may
surely take the part of the poor neglected child
when it exclaims, "Save me from my wicked
parents. Compel them to give me that which I
have a right to demand at their hands—the means
of becoming a good man and a good Christian."
This is virtually the utterance of every neglected
child who is crying in our streets.' He advocated
some such plan as that suggested by Mr. Horner,
that 'the enjoyment of certain privileges and civil
rights, the admission to certain offices and employ-

ments, should depend upon the possession of a certain amount of education; and I believe,' he added in conclusion, 'that it will be found that what the people are opposed to is, not the act of compelling men to educate their children, but that of compelling them to educate in those particular schools which the Civil Government may appoint.'

The point in which he considered the work of education at that time to be most deficient, and to which he earnestly exhorted in his speech that more attention should be paid, especially by the National Society, was the training of masters. 'The fault,' he said, 'of the National Society has been, not in adhering to Dr. Bell's system, but in making the observance of that system the primary object of attention. The Society recognises the duty of training masters, but it does not see that this is the first and grand object. We want not systems but masters;' and here he cited the opinion of men who had studied the subject in Prussia, that it was the master and not the system which made the school, and that attention should be chiefly directed to the formation of training schools, in which good masters might be prepared for their important and responsible duty.

The last needs upon which he touched were Infant Schools, and good Middle Class Schools in connexion with the Church. It had been calculated, he said, that the infant population between three and seven years of age amounted at that time to a million and a half. And although many Infant Schools had been established the number compared with what was required was next to nothing. With regard to commercial or middle class schools he thought it would be highly advantageous if the Board, at the request of the masters, were to conduct periodical examinations, and award prizes to the best scholars, publishing their names. The terms of connexion with the Board for such schools should be that the respective schools should be conducted on truly religious principles, in accordance with the doctrine and discipline of the Church of England, and that no religious instruction inconsistent with the same should be given or be permitted to be given in the schools.

The resolution which he moved at the conclusion of his speech was that a Local Board of Education, embracing all the townships of the parish of Leeds, should be established. The other resolutions passed at the meeting were—

That the Board consist of all the clergy officiating in the parish of Leeds ; of a committee of laymen to be appointed by the Bishop ; and of a secretary.

That the Board be requested to take immediate steps :

1. To raise fresh subscriptions for the purpose of education.

2. To promote the building of new National, Sunday, and Infant Schools.

3. To unite with the Board existing Schools or Academies conducted by members of the Church.

4. To ascertain the educational statistics of the parish.

5. To adopt measures for the formation of a Training School for Masters.

6. To institute a commercial school which may serve as a model school.

The Board of Education thus founded was the germ of the Diocesan Board, which has been for nearly forty years the principal instrument of elementary and middle class education throughout the Diocese of Ripon.

The following letter to the secretary of the National Society, about a year after the formation of the Leeds Educational Board, shows how apprehensive he was lest the Society should be tempted to surrender the least particle of its principles for the sake of some supposed advantage. The Factory Act alluded to in this letter was passed in the year 1833, under the guidance of Lord Althorp : it limited the hours for the employment of children in factories, and provided that part of the time when they were not engaged in labour should be spent in school.

Letter to the Secretary of the National Society.

Reverend Sir,—I have the honour to acknowledge the receipt of your letter, dated the 11th instant, in which you desire me to give my opinion with regard to the working of the Factory Act, so far as those provisions are concerned which respect the education of the poor.

You inform me that 'it has been urgently represented to you from various quarters that a special provision should be made by the National Society for the case of the factory children, whose education is made compulsory; and that some measure should, if possible, be taken to remove the difficulties which, under present circumstances, prevent them from attending schools which are either now in union with the Society, or might hereafter be united.' Now here I may be permitted to remark that although the factory children are compelled to attend *some* school, they are not compelled to attend *any particular* school ; and that there exists at present no difficulty whatever to prevent their attending schools in union with the National Society, except in places where the school hours are not made to correspond with the arrangements of the factory. In a large school in my own parish we order the business of the school so as to meet the factory hours, and the majority of the children come to us for instruction. It does not seem to me necessary, under existing circumstances, for the National Society to do more than recommend a similar arrangement in all manufacturing districts. To the instruction we are prepared to give, some parents or guardians will object; but they suffer no hardship, because schools will be always open for their children, which, conducted by Dissenters, are many of them equal, some of them superior, to the schools in union with the National Society, with the single important exception that in them the Church Catechism is not made the basis of education.

You inform me further that it has been recommended, in order to remove a difficulty, which does not at present exist, that 'so far as concerns any child whose parents or guardians specially request that it should not be taught the Church Catechism, the managers of schools should not be required to enforce instruction in that formulary.'

I presume that no circumstances can arise which will justify the National Society in acting upon this recommendation. If I understand rightly the object of the National Society, it is *not* to provide for the general education of the people, but to provide a *particular kind of education.* If the National Society, ambitious to conduct the education of the people generally, is willing to renounce the peculiar features of a Church education, and to adopt some undefined principles of religion as the basis of the instruction to be given in the Society's schools, it seems to me that the committee of the National Society ought to coalesce with the committee of the Privy Council; or if it refuse to do this, I apprehend that a vast number of the clergy will prefer to receive their directions from the Privy Council. The question of inspection is, in the minds of many, one of very minor importance; and, indeed, under the proposed alteration, the inspection of persons appointed by Government will be preferable to that of persons appointed by the Society, as *cæteris paribus* the superintendence of a committee of Her Majesty's Privy Council is preferable to that of a voluntary association, which, notwithstanding its charter, the National Society to a certain extent still is.

But if, on the other hand, the National Society professes to be a Church Society, and to conduct the education of the people on the principles of the Church, it is utterly impossible for it to accede to the measure proposed without ceasing to be what it professes to be. We might just as well entertain a proposition for filling our churches by suspending the use of the forms of morning and evening prayer, as accede to a proposal that we should abandon the Catechism when instructing the young. The same Church which has imposed upon us a formulary for morning and evening prayer, has appointed a formulary to be used by us when instructing the youth of our flock; we are as much bound by that formulary as we are bound to observe the Liturgy when conducting the morning sacrifice of prayer and praise. It ought to be clearly understood that the Society is recommended to give up a fundamental principle, for if the use of the Catechism may under any circumstances be suspended, we have only to make out a strong case of expediency, and it may be suspended under *all* circumstances. And if the Society thus concedes a principle, it will not only offend the conscience of many pious Churchmen, but convert into its most decided opponents some persons who are now its warm supporters.

You observe in conclusion that 'the chief question to be considered is, whether the Society, by refusing the concession called for, would, as is confidently asserted, forego the opportunity to give full instruction on Church principles to many thousand children whose parents and guardians are willing they should receive it.'

On this passage I remark that it is not to the *words* but to the *doctrine* of the Catechism, that is, to the doctrine of the Church, as briefly stated in the Catechism, that the parents and guardians are supposed to be hostile.

If, then, the concession be made, the Society will be

virtually pledged, and in honour bound to abstain from
giving to the children of such parents or guardians *any*
instruction in Church principles ; the Society will therefore
be pledged to educate them in the principles of Dissent,
(for you teach error, if you abstain from teaching truth) or
else in principles disconnected with religion of any kind.
And in the West Riding of Yorkshire, where the Dissenters
are very numerous, and where a vast number of professing
Churchmen, who are willing for political purposes to uphold an Establishment, are vehemently opposed to the use
of the Catechism, especially to that part of it which asserts
with such peculiar force the doctrine of the Sacraments, I
have no hesitation in giving it as my opinion that more
than three-fourths of the parents and guardians will apply
for the exemption, so that the Society will be doing, in fact,
what in theory it condemns :—it will be giving a non-
religious education.

It is, I am well aware, stated that an attempt is to be
made to compel the masters of factories to provide schools,
as well as to afford time for the education of the children
employed in their factories. Until this be the law of the
land, there can be no reason why the National Society
should legislate on the subject. But even if it *were* the law
of the land, I would rather propose to the manufacturer
to erect his schoolrooms so as to admit of two departments,
one for the education of Churchmen, in which a master
might be provided by the National Society ; another for
the education of Dissenters, than recommend the Society
to give up one of its fundamental principles.

On these grounds I hope that before you make the
concession, you will very seriously consider the whole
subject. The facts of the case are not precisely as they
have been represented to you. If you give up the important principle which you are recommended to concede,
you actually gain nothing while you lose much. You may,
it is true, have a greater number of names on the books of
the Society, but you will educate fewer than you now do
on sound religious principles, for many will *now* send their

children to our schools, *in spite of* the obnoxious Catechism, who (professing Churchmen as well as conscientious Dissenters) will reject it if they have the option. And if you conciliate for a time those political Churchmen who uphold the Church merely or chiefly because it is Established, and forms part of the Constitution of the country, but whose views may change with the changing circumstances of political warfare, you will at the same time alienate from the society that large and increasing body of persons who, caring little or nothing for the political importance or dignity of the Establishment, belong to the Church of England because they believe it to be the Holy Catholic and Apostolic Church in this country, and support the National Society because it is regarded by them as an institution through the instrumentality of which they can carry out the principles of the Church in the education of the people.—I have the honour to be, Reverend Sir,

Your faithful and obedient servant.

In the autumn of this year (1839) he published a pamphlet entitled ' Presbyterian Rights Asserted.' It is a vindication of the claims of the second order in the hierarchy to their due share in the administration of the Church, against a too prevalent tendency, as he conceived, to the assumption of arbitrary power on the part of many of the Bishops. Even his own diocesan, mild and amiable as he was, seemed to him occasionally to err in this respect. The pamphlet was, I believe, the only production which he ever published anonymously; the reasons for withholding his name in such a case being weighty and obvious. In concentration of evidence, in force of reasoning, and in touches of humour, it has been surpassed by few, if any, of his writings. The subject was one on which he had thought much and felt deeply, and it is remarkable what a clear view he had of some points in connexion with it which are only just beginning to be generally acknowledged in the Church.

'The present circumstances,' he began, 'of the Church of England, and her future prospects, render it highly important for the clergy of the second order in the ministry to understand their real position in the Church : their duties and obligations to the first order on the one hand, and their own rights and privileges on the other.'

That a very general ignorance prevails on this subject it is impossible for anyone to doubt. By the generality of our legislators it is unknown that we possess *any* peculiar rights and privileges ; they regard us as mere servants of the State, and they look upon the Bishops as magistrates to keep us in order. This, too, is perhaps the view generally taken by those of the clergy who are designated Low Churchmen. . . . Some of those who are styled High Churchmen are apt to err in the opposite extreme. Being deeply impressed with the divine right of Episcopacy, they forget that the right of the Presbytery is equally divine, and draw the hasty conclusion that Episcopacy is a despotism, and that to the caprice of their diocesan all the clergy of a diocese are bound without questioning to submit. . . . I believe that, with very few exceptions, there has never existed a body of men more desirous of doing their duty than the existing Bishops of the Church of England. But their notion of Episcopal duty varies considerably. Some appear among us as spiritual peers, associating with the other clergy as the Lord-Lieutenant of the county with the inferior magistrates. These are generally the best, though not apparently the most active, Bishops in the Church. They never needlessly interfere with the parochial clergy, but are always willing to assist them ; they are great patrons of learning and piety. Other prelates seem to regard themselves as schoolmasters ; indeed, I have heard it said of a high Establishment prelate that his notion of a Bishop is, that he is an *examining master* plus a *proctor.* Others, again, consider the whole diocese as one parish, and every parish priest as their curate ; thus reducing the clergy in point of fact to two orders, bishop and deacon. These are the most busy prelates ; but their activity, as we shall see, is not always advantageous to the Church. They seem most of them to have forgotten the authority, rights, and privileges of the second order of the ministry, which possesses authority, rights, and privileges scarcely inferior to their own. . . .

‘ Now the present writer was a zealous supporter of Episcopacy at a period when to speak of the Apostolical succession was looked upon as a sign of dementation by many who are now the most able advocates of the doctrine . . . But he did this not from any exclusive regard to the honours of Episcopacy. He was influenced only by his love for the Church of Christ. “ Pro ecclesiâ Dei—pro ecclesiâ Dei ” was his motto then as it is now—the motto which he hopes will cling to his parched lips as he breathes his last breath. The well-being of the Church requires that *due* honour should be paid to the Episcopate ; but the well-being of the Church requires that *more* honour than is due to it should *not* be rendered.'

He then proceeds to show that most evils arose in the body ecclesiastical as in the body physical, or in the moral system, from a disproportion between the parts. Lay influence had undoubtedly of late been too great in the Church. Laymen had thrust themselves into the places of the clergy—sent forth missionaries, done ministerial acts, and in turns were securing to themselves by means of the five-trustee churches the powers exercised by the lay Dissenters, of whose tyranny the most vehement advocates of schism among Dissenting preachers loudly complained. To counteract this usurpation the clergy had been zealous in pointing out the rights of Episcopacy, until there was a risk of violating proportion in that direction. It should be remembered that all members of the Church of Christ, lay as well as clerical, were consecrated; the laity at baptism to preach the Gospel by a holy example. As heads of families they inherited patriarchal rights; they were to instruct their households in the Gospel and minister at the domestic altar. The Presbyter was ordained to preside over an assembly of families, the Bishop over an assembly of parishes, the Metropolitan over an assembly of dioceses. If the Presbyter unduly interfered with the family arrangements, confusion ensued:—a confusion also ensued if the Bishop unduly interfered with the parochial arrangements.

The Bishop was a πατὴρ πατέρων, an episcopus episcoporum (a father of fathers, an overseer of overseers). These were their titles in the early ages of the Church: high titles, but titles which recognised the authority of the Presbytery. 'If the Bishop be spiritual overseer to us let him not forget that we are spiritual overseers to the laity : if he be a spiritual father to us we are spiritual fathers to our people.' Did the Bishop in the existing Church thus respect the authority of presbyters ? The question was more easily asked than satisfactorily answered. Straws showed which way the wind blew. At most visitations the Bishop was to be seen sitting within the chancel while the presbyters humbly stood outside. Yet by the fourth council of Carthage it was decreed that, whenever the Bishop took his seat, the presbyters should not be allowed to stand ; and one of their titles in the primitive Church was 'the clergy of the second throne,' because they were accustomed to sit with the Bishop, though on less elevated seats, within the rails of the sanctuary, the deacons standing round.

So again the episcopal charges of the day, though courteous and kind in style, were rather the addresses of a magistrate to his subjects than of a supreme ruler to his *co*-rulers. And he proceeds to prove, by reference to a great number of authorities, that in the ancient Church the presbyters were regarded, not as the servants, but as the councillors and coadjutors, of the Bishop. 'If we are to do nothing without the Bishop, the Bishop is to do nothing without us.'

Yet in recent times this principle had been strangely forgotten alike by Bishops, presbyters, and laity. Take, for instance, the composition of the Ecclesiastical Commission appointed under Sir Robert Peel. How was it constituted ? The laity of the Church were represented ; the first order of the clergy were represented ; but of the second order not one was called to the council : they were utterly disregarded. If the laity and the Bishops agreed, the second order—the presbyters—were to be compelled to submit.

So again with the Church Discipline Bill. 'Facilities were introduced for correcting delinquent clerks of the second order, but not a word is said of facilitating actions against delinquent clerks of the first order. Let it not startle the high Churchman that I thus speak : he is not really a high Churchman who maintains the divine right of the Episcopate, and forgets the divine right of the Presbyterate. In the primitive ages Bishops were (not frequently, but as occasion required) deposed.'

So again it was said that the Dean and Chapter of a diocese formed the ecclesiastical senate which the Bishop ought to consult.[1] Yet 'we never hear a Bishop stating in his charge that, having consulted with his Dean and Chapter, he has decided on this or that line of conduct in the government of his diocese.' But, granting this to be a point which might require further consideration, one thing at least was certain, that if a Bishop ever consulted his presbyters he was bound to do so when he entered their parishes for the discharge of Episcopal offices. Yet there were some prelates who did not hesitate to head a faction against the incumbent of the parish. 'Let us suppose a hard-working painful parish priest to have matured all his plans for the management of the parish over which the Holy Ghost has made him overseer ; let us suppose him

---

[1] Blackstone, bk. i. c. 11.

to have united the Churchmen, always excepting a factious few; to have shown from Scripture and the teaching of the Church the principle upon which he gives his support to some and withholds it from other religious societies; to have been proceeding cautiously, introducing first one institution then another—we can easily understand his feelings if all of a sudden he shall hear that the Dissenters, having united with the factious few of the Church who happen to be opposed to him, have determined to hold a meeting of the Bible Society, or the Religious Tract Society, or the Lancasterian School Society, or some similar institution, and that the Bishop, without deigning to consult him or even to apprise him of his intentions, will preside at it. The spiritual peer attends, accompanied perhaps by one or two temporal peers and other great men desirous to conciliate the Dissenters before the next election; and thus he who ought to be the centre of unity becomes the rallying point of schism. The liberal sentiments of the spiritual peer are applauded the more loudly because they are contrasted with the exclusive Church principles of the pastor of the parish; and, as his lordship passes through the street, his condescension on the platform to his reverend brethren of the Baptist, Independent, and Unitarian "Churches" is compared with the cold distant bow with which, in the embarrassment occasioned by some undeveloped consciousness of having done wrong, he meets the minister of the Established Church, that is, of the Church which, in common with his Independent and Unitarian brethren, he does not regard as *the* Church of the

parish, but only as that one Church out of many
which happens to be established by law.   And so
all parties separate: the Dissenters to laugh at
"the humbug of the Bishop's apron;" the factious
Churchmen to eulogise the spirituality of the Episcopal leader of their schism; the spiritual peer to
declaim to the temporal peers on the extreme want
of judgment in the incumbent of the parish, who
ought to concede something to the Dissenters, while
his lordship is in turn congratulated on the popularity he is by his liberality securing for "the Establishment;" the profane to laugh at the flooring of
their pastor; the worldly-minded to express their
indignation at the idea of an incumbent with only
150*l.* a year thinking that the Church and her principles are dearer to him than they are to a Bishop
with 4,000*l.* a year; the poor to lament the insult
offered to their best friend; the presbyter himself
to weep in private and to pray; and of prayer he
will have ample need lest he should be disgusted
into inactivity.   The true Churchmen also will
grieve in private and ask what ought to be done?
. . . . Now, it is one of the objects of this pamphlet to let people see what ought to be done.
They ought to remonstrate.   The presbyter should
protest against the invasion of his rights.   He may
even appeal to the Metropolitan.   I contend that he
may do, that he *ought* to do, this on high Church
principles. . . . It becomes us to assert the principle
that the Bishop has no right to enter into our parish,
or to hold a meeting there, without having first consulted the incumbent and the other clergy of the
parish.   If he do so he commits an act of schism.

Let no fear of being deemed unfilial deter us. If the Bishop be our father the Church is our mother; and if our father injure our mother we must protect her even against him. I once heard of a man of rank who was about to strike his wife. His son interposed, bound his arms, and carried him out of the room, and then he immediately loosed him and let him go. The father instantly raised his hand to strike his son. The pious son put his hands behind him and said, " You may strike *me* if you will, I will bear it all; but you shall *not* strike my mother." And so we must deal by our Bishop, when he would damage the Church by violating her principles. I do not say that the Bishop may not support the Bible Society, or any similar institution, if he will. He may be able to explain away all the texts which command us to keep the unity of the body—that is, the visible Church—as well as of the spirit. . . . All I contend for is that in the principles shown to be those of the Church in this pamphlet, he has no right to enter a parish to support the Society where the presbyters are opposed to it.'

Having illustrated a similar contempt for the rights of presbyters by a reference to the Church Building Acts, armed with which a faction opposed to an incumbent frequently planted a church in his parish without his consent and to his great annoyance, the Bishop abetting them in his ignorance of the locality and the circumstances, he concludes the pamphlet by affirming that in all which he had said he had not the least intention or desire to depress the Episcopate. He would ever value a Bishop's blessing, ever maintain the honour of the order; but when Bishops were tempted to assume authority which did not pertain to them, and to apply to Parliament for the power of the sword, he would not hesitate to apply to them the words of St. Jerome, ' Contenti sint honore suo ; patres se sciant esse, non dominos, amari debent, non timeri.'

In November of this year (1839) he attended a great meeting at Manchester on behalf of the Society for the Propagation of the Gospel. The local papers state that such a large gathering for a religious purpose had seldom if ever been witnessed in Manchester. The principal speakers were the Rev. Richard Durnford, now Bishop of Chichester, the Rev. Hugh Stowell, and the Vicar of Leeds.

The Vicar's speech occupied more than an hour, and the glowing eulogies upon it with which the newspapers abounded for more than a week afterwards seem to prove that it was regarded as the speech of the evening. The most powerful and telling part of the speech was that in which he justified the Society's principle of attending first to the colonies and dependencies of the English Empire. ' The Crown of England,' he said, ' has seventy-five millions of heathen and Mohammedan subjects : until we have converted them we have certainly enough to do. If our objectors will enable us to convert the seventy-five millions of our heathen and Mohammedan fellow-subjects, we shall be happy to go elsewhere. The colonies indeed have a very solemn claim upon us. We have heard allusion made to the condition of the pious colonist who goes out, we will suppose, to the backwoods of America, and sometimes an appeal is made to our feelings, and we are told to think what his feelings must be as the Lord's day dawns upon him, when he hears no chime of the village church bell calling him to the sanctuary of the Lord. This is indeed a subject which may move our hearts, but we are to remember that, of those who go out of our country, the majority, I greatly fear—No! I dare not judge, for our Lord says "Judge not"—have very little regard for religion. They go to a place where there is no pastor to remind them of their duty, to attend them in adversity and sickness, to preach to them the doctrines of repentance, and to lay before them the glories of redemption. Their little stock of religion soon diminishes, their children are unbaptized, they never hear their Saviour's name, unless perhaps it lingers in some traditionary curse. And so England— Christian England—is engaged in establishing the empire of Infidelity. We have heard allusions made to Australia : let us come to a few facts. To Australia we have transported one hundred thousand of our fellow-subjects for the selfish purpose of protecting our property and our lives. We have made no provision of any kind, till very lately, for preaching to them the doctrine of repentance and of the cross. There were 900 persons last year transported from London, and between 2,000 and 3,000 from England and Wales, and you may judge of the condition of that colony when I tell you that in Sydney with a population of 16,300 there are 219 beershops. The police magistrate could not reckon the number of spirit shops, but he knew that the average consumption of spirits was four gallons per man per annum, and that every kind of vice was there prevalent.

'However, I will pass from the colonies, because it is in India that we already begin to see how the application of our principle works. We find that ever since the Church has presented in India an imposing front, ever since we have had Bishops there, and a regularly organised clergy, the natives are beginning to think that the English are a people who have some religion. They know that we are a wise and understanding people, and they are beginning to enquire what is the religion that we profess. What more do we want? We know that we have God's truth, and we know that if the spirit of enquiry be excited, God's truth will ultimately prevail.'

He then glanced at some of the most cruel and revolting superstitions of India as constituting an appeal to common humanity, and ended with an appeal to the feelings of those who knew and valued the blessings of Christian faith. 'In His name, whose you are and whom you are bound to serve; in His name who has bought you with a price, even the price of His own most precious blood, that He might make you a peculiar people, zealous of this very thing, zealous of good works; in His name whom, if you really believe in Him, you must love and adore; in His name for whom, if you really believe in Him, you must be prepared to spend and be spent, to labour, to suffer and to die; in His name, His sacred name (in humble reverence I pronounce it), the name of our Lord Jesus Christ, we call upon men to listen to that voice which sounds from the East and from the West, saying, "Come over and help us!"' This conclusion of the speech was greeted with a loud burst of cheering which lasted for several minutes.

The propagation of Christianity in India, boldly and honestly, was a duty on which he most earnestly insisted, maintaining also that the matter was one in which duty and interest coincided : for he had the sagacity to foresee that the false and timid policy adopted by the Indian Government, of endeavouring to conciliate the goodwill of the people by patronising their heathenism, and dissembling if not repudiating our own Christianity, was fraught with peril to the stability of our tenure; a presentiment which was indeed fearfully verified by the outbreak of the Indian mutiny. He spoke with eloquent indignation on the subject at a meeting for the Society for Promoting Christian Knowledge held in Leeds in the spring of 1840. 'Till very lately,' he said, 'no native convert could be employed by the British Government, though the native idolater could. Is this the way to support religion ? Look to the island of Ceylon. When the Dutch were in possession they built churches and schools ; but when England came into possession we thought that bad policy. The churches were neglected, the schools were suffered to decline, the former system of idolatry was re-established, and its priests had increased salaries awarded. Those who would condemn a religious establishment in England, who would diminish the income of the Christian clergy, were found to advocate an idolatrous establishment in Ceylon. And this was considered good policy. It is well indeed that we no longer profit by the pilgrim tax, but we still pay 6,000*l.* a year to support the old idol of Juggernaut. Look at what was done last year. Nineteen of our soldiers refused to take part in some Hindoo idolatrous ceremony : of these nineteen one was a Mohammedan, the rest were Christians. They were all put under arrest. The Mohammedan pleaded conscience, and *he* was suffered to go free. The Englishmen pleaded conscience, too, but they were put in prison : that is to say, those who were in authority feared the Mohammedan population, but they did not fear the Christians' God, who though unseen will surely punish. And His punishment seems even now impending. Already our enemies are intriguing, and the Burmese are in a state of insubordination. Let the Church in England implore a merciful God to avert the impending calamity. Let us bestir ourselves to make the Church in India more efficient, so that, if our nation shall be cast out, the Church of Christ may still exist there—I trust under native bishops.'

END OF THE FIRST VOLUME.

D.

LONDON : PRINTED BY
SPOTTISWOODE AND CO., NEW-STREET SQUARE
AND PARLIAMENT STREET

www.ingramcontent.com/pod-product-compliance
Lightning Source LLC
Chambersburg PA
CBHW052335110726
47901CB00005B/1232